RAVES FOR REGINALD HILL,
WINNER OF THE
CARTIER DIAMOND DAGGER AWARD
FROM THE CRIME WRITERS' ASSOCIATION,
AND HIS LATEST DALZIEL/PASCOE MYSTERY,
THE WOOD BEYOND

"An outstanding procedural series. Reginald Hill has
raised the classical British mystery to new heights."
—*The New York Times Book Review*

"A BRILLIANT TALE THAT POSES QUESTIONS
ABOUT HUMANKIND FOR WHICH THERE ARE
NO ANSWERS—ONLY BEMUSEMENT."
—*The Orlando Sentinel*

"Hill's polished, sophisticated novels are intelligently
written and permeated with his sly and delightful
sense of humor. More than most other mystery
novels, Hill's Dalziel/Pascoe novels are enjoyable as
much for their characters as for their complicated,
suspenseful mystery plots."
—*The Christian Science Monitor*

"SO THOUGHTFUL . . . GRACEFULLY WRITTEN . . .
A SENSITIVE PROBING OF COMPLEX NOTIONS
OF HEROISM AND CONSCIENCE."
—*Publishers Weekly*

"SUPERB . . . Mr. Hill refines his own talent to the
highest levels of mystery fiction."
—*Dallas Morning News*

"A POWERFULLY AFFECTING SUBPLOT . . .
THE BEST DIALOGUE FOUND IN THE MYSTERY
GENRE OR ANYWHERE ELSE . . . THE VERY
TOP OF THE CLASS."
—*Morning Star-Telegram* (Ft. Worth, Tex.)

Books by Reginald Hill

THE WOOD BEYOND

A Dalziel/Pascoe Mystery

REGINALD HILL

A DELL BOOK

Published by
Dell Publishing
a division of
Bantam Doubleday Dell Publishing Group, Inc.
1540 Broadway
New York, New York 10036

ISBN: 0-440-21803-9

Reprinted by arrangement with Delacorte Press

Printed in the United States of America

Published simultaneously in Canada

April 1997

10   9   8   7   6   5   4   3

RAD

And what may I deem now, but that this is a land of mere lies, & that there is nought real and alive therein save me. Yea, belike even these trees & the green grass will presently depart from me, & leave me falling down through the clouds.

William Morris, *The Wood Beyond the World*

No evidence was found to lead us . . . to think that the convictions were unsound or that the accused were treated unfairly . . . we cannot re-write history by substituting our latter-day judgement for that of contemporaries. . . .

John Major, *Response (Feb. 1993) to request to reconsider cases of British soldiers executed during World War I*

Si canimus silvas, silvae sint consule dignae.
(If we must sing of woods, let them be woods that are worthy of a prime minister.)

Virgil, *Eclogue IV*

Author's Note

The epigraphs to the four parts of the novel are taken from Andrew Marvell's poem *The Nymph Complaining for the Death of her Faun.*

PROLOGUE

MONDAY MORNING, start of a new week, air bright as ice in a crystal glass, brandy-gold sun pouring from delft-blue sky, the old bracken glowing on the rolling moors, the trees still pied with their unblasted leaves, the pastures still green with their unmuddied grass, as October runs into November and thinks it's September still.

Edgar Wield drove slowly out of Enscombe, slowly because on mornings like this what you were driving through was far more important than where you were driving to, and also because during the short time he'd been living in the village he'd learned that only a fool assumed that the narrow roads ran clear farther than the next bend.

His caution was rewarded when he eased round a corner and found George Creed shepherding the stragglers of a flock of sheep through a gate into a field set up with holding pens. The sight made him smile at the echo of his first sighting of Creed doing much the same task on this very road. Since then they'd become both neighbors and friends.

"Morning, George, fine-looking beasts," he called through his open window.

Domicile entitled him to this pretension of expertise, though he wasn't altogether sure whether the term *beasts* could legitimately be applied to sheep as well as cattle.

"Morning, Edgar," said Creed. "Happen they'll do. Sounds daft, but I'll be sorry to see them go."

"They're off then?" said Wield, now taking in the significance of the pens.

"Aye, folk have got to eat, that's what farming's all about. But the older I get, the more it bothers me, selling off what I've bred up. Don't be saying owt of this down in the Morris else they'll be thinking I'm going soft in the head!"

"Which market are you taking them to?"

"No market. I've always dealt man and boy with Haig's of Wharfedale. They give me top price 'cos they know my stock, and I sell them my stock 'cos I know they'll see them right. So watch out for their wagon on your way into town. Take up most of the road them things."

"I'll be careful," said Wield. "No hurry on a morning like this. I'd as lief be staying here to give you a hand if you'd have me."

"I'm always willing to set on a likely lad," laughed Creed. "But I think you'd be wanting your cards afore the end of the day."

He glanced upward as he spoke and Wield followed his gaze into the unflawed bowl of blue sky.

"You're never saying it's on the turn, are you?" he asked skeptically. "Looks set for another month to me."

"Nay, it'll spoil itself by teatime, and make a right job of it too."

"You reckon? Well, even if it does, you're better off here than where I'm going. Wet, dry, hail, or shine, there's no place like Enscombe. See you, George."

He engaged the clutch and continued his leisurely progess down the valley road which aped the twists and turns of the River Een as though it were of the same ancient natural birth. A couple of miles farther on he saw the juggernaut of the livestock transporter coming toward him and pulled off the road into a small piece of woodland to let it past. The driver blew his horn in appreciation and Wield waved as the huge truck with its legend D. HAIG & CO LIVESTOCK WHOLESALERS rumbled by.

When it was past and out of sight, he continued to sit for a while, enjoying the cool breeze through the open window and the way the amber sunlight scintilla'd through the trembling branches. He had the feeling that if he got out of his car and strolled off into the wood, he could keep going forever with nothing changing, no aging, no hunger, no cold, no crime, no war . . .

And certainly no rain!

Yes, that was one thing he was certain of. He was a great respecter of the rustic eye, but towns had weather too and Detective Sergeant Wield of Mid-Yorkshire CID wasn't often caught without his umbrella. No, this time George had got it wrong. This Indian summer had a lot of wear in it yet. He couldn't see any end to it himself. And what you couldn't see the end of, surely that must be forever?

PART ONE

SANCTUARY

*The wanton Troopers riding by
Have shot my Faun and it will dye.*

I

Dear Mrs. Pascoe,

I do not know if Peter ever mentioned to you that I was his superior officer for some time. Indeed one of my last acts before I was invalided out was to confirm his promotion to sergeant. You may therefore understand with what dismay I received the tragic news of his death, and I wanted to write to you at once to say that in my opinion he was one of the finest men I had the privilege to command, and in no way does the manner of his death divert me from that judgment.

I realize that at a time like this you will scarcely feel able to look ahead, but with a young daughter to bring up, the future and its problems will all too soon demand attention. Recognizing that you may have needs which are pressing and immediate, I beg you to accept the accompanying small initial contribution and my assurance that as soon as the opportunity arises I shall

*take steps to ensure you and your child are cared for as
Peter would have wished.*

Meanwhile I remain yours in deepest sympathy.

Herbert Antony Grindal

II

IS THIS THING WORKING? Right. Here we go. Here we go
here we go . . . sorry. Just testing. Okay, from the
start. Getting into the wood were easy. Out of the
ditch, over the top, and there we were. Mind you, it
were like jumping into a raging sea. Wind howling, everything shaking and creaking and groaning like the
whole bloody issue was alive, and so much stuff flying
around you were in danger of getting your head took
off. But we pressed on regardless, taking our direction
from the glow up ahead. Even when you can't see your
hand before your face, there's always that glow.

Then at the edge of the trees we hit wire, and we
paused here to get our breath and count heads.

We were all present and correct, the whole eight of
us, and Cap started in on the wire. You'll have met the
Captain? Useless with the cutters but won't let anyone
else have them. Sort of badge of office. Eventually
there was a hole of sorts and we started through. Jacksy
—that's Jacklin, the well-made one—got snagged and
swore. Cap said, "Keep it down," like someone might
hear in all that din, and Jacksy said, "If I could keep it
down, I wouldn't have got it stuck," and a couple of us
got the giggles. It's easy done when you're shit scared.

Not that it mattered or Jacksy swearing either. Like I said, it were pissing with rain and blowing a gale, and you would have needed a lot more than a giggle to get noticed.

Then we were all through and the laughing stopped. There's nowt to laugh at out there. It's a wasteland. Used to be trees but after the big raid last summer, they blew them all to hell, roots and all, and when it rains for a week, like it's been doing, the holes all fill with water and the ground gets so clarty, you can feel it sucking you down. Smells too. Don't know why it should. It were once good mixed woodland like what's still there. But now it stinks like a plowed-up boneyard.

Someone—don't know who—said, "This is bloody stupid. We should head back." Seconded, I thought. But I kept my trap shut 'cos if there's one thing guaranteed to make Cap head east, it's hearing me speak up for west. I should've known better than to try diplomacy. It never works. Might as well start scrapping right off and get it over with. Cap just glowered at me as if it had been me mouthing off, and said, "Follow me. Keep close." And we were off, no pretense of a discussion. Whatever happened to universal suffrage?

God, it were hard going. Two steps forward, one back, and as for keeping close, with that rain coming down and the mist coming up, it was all you could do to see where your next step were going to land, let alone keep an eye on anybody else. So it came as no surprise when somewhere over to the left I heard a splash and yell and a voice crying "Oh shit!" all spluttery. Someone had gone into a crater. My money was on Jacksy, but I didn't waste time speculating. Even someone a lot better coordinated could drown in one of them holes as easy as the middle of the Atlantic. So I headed for the noise like everybody else. Only I must've been a bit more headstrong than the rest 'cos when I got there, I didn't stop but slid right over the edge, and next thing, I were down the bleeding hole too!

For a while I thought I were going to drown, but once I got the right way up and persuaded Jacksy—I'd been right about that—to stop grabbing my hair, I realized there were only two or three feet of water down there, which was fine so long as you didn't lose your footing. The real problem was how to get out, 'cos the walls started sloshing and crumbling every time you tried to get a hold of them.

Cap and the others had arrived by now and were reaching down to grab us. They got Jacksy first and I pushed like mad and got nowt but a faceful of boot for my pains. But eventually the useless bugger got hauled out and it were my turn. I reached up and felt someone get a hold of my right hand, I couldn't see who, my eyes were so full of mud and water, and I thrashed around with my left till finally I found another hand to get hold of. Then, kicking my toes into the side, I started to haul myself out.

I soon caught on I were getting a lot of help with my right hand—turned out to be Cap who were doing the pulling—but nowt at all with my left. But before I could start wondering why, my feet slipped out of the hole I'd kicked in the side of the crater and my hand slipped out of Cap's, and I started to slide back in, putting all my weight on whoever had got a hold of my left hand.

And it just came away, the hand I was holding on to I mean. And I slid right back down into that filthy water with my fingers still grasped tight around that thing, or like it seemed then, with that thing's fingers still grasped tight round mine, and I started to scream, and some on the others started to scream too, and eventually even them buggers in the green uniforms started taking notice, and next thing there was a whole platoon of them all around us shouting and shoving and that's how we ended up getting captured. Me ciggies are all sodden. You've not got a dry one, have you?

III

FAMILIES ARE a fuck-up, thought Peter Pascoe.

Otherwise, how come he was standing here in a crematorium chapel with all the inspirational ambience of a McDonald's though without, thank God, the attendant grilled burger odors, being glared at by his sister, Myra, and squinted at by a bunch of geriatric myopes, as he attempted an extempore exordium of a grandmother he hadn't seen for nearly two years?

"Hello. I'm Peter Pascoe and Ada was my grandmother and I'm doing this because . . ."

Because when he'd arrived and discovered Myra had ordered a full fig C of E service right down to "Abide with Me," his guilt had vaulted him onto a high horse and he'd gone through the arrangements like Jesus through the money changers, till at his moment of triumph Myra had brought him crashing to earth with the question, "Okay, smart-ass, just what *are* you going to do?"

". . . because as you probably know, Ada didn't reckon much to organized religion. She always said that when she died the last thing she wanted was a funeral-chasing parson droning on about her unlikely virtues. So I'm doing it instead . . . not droning on, I hope . . . and not unlikely . . . anyway, I'm doing it."

And a right cock-up you're making of it too. He could see Myra's fury moderating into malicious pleasure. If only there'd been time to make a few notes. Only a fool relied on divine inspiration when he'd just dumped God!

"Well, I'm not going to make a lot of notes . . . I mean fuss, because Ada hated fuss. But equally I'm not going to let the passing of this remarkable old lady pass un . . . er . . . remarked."

This got worse! Pull yourself together. If you can brief a bunch of CID cynics and pissed-off plods, no need to be fazed by a pewful of wrinkles. What was Myra rolling her eyeballs at? Doesn't she know a dramatic pause when she hears one?

"Ada was born in Yorkshire though she didn't stay there long. The event which changed her life, changed all our lives, come to think of it, was the Great War. So many died . . . millions . . . numbers too large to register. One of them was Ada's father, my great-grandfather. After she got the news, my great-grandmother took her three-year-old daughter and headed down here to Warwickshire. I've no details of how they lived. I only discovered the Yorkshire connection because I was a nosy kid. Ada wasn't one to go on about the past, maybe because there was too much pain in it for her. But I can guess that one-parent families had it even tougher in those days than they do now. Anyway, here they came and here they stayed. This was where Ada grew up and in her turn got married. And in her turn she had a child. And in her turn she saw her husband, my grandfather Colin Pascoe, go off to the wars.

"Did she know as she said goodbye that in her turn she too was never going to see him again? Who knows? But I think she knew. Oh yes. I'm sure she knew."

That had them. Even Myra was looking rapt.

"The child they had was, of course, Peter, my father. Naturally he wishes he could be here today. But as you probably know, when he took early retirement a few years back, he decided to follow my eldest sister, Susan, and her family out to Australia, and unfortunately urgent commitments have prevented any of them from making the long journey. But I'm sure we will be very much in their thoughts at this sad time."

He caught Myra's eye and looked away, but not before they'd shared their awareness that any thoughts turning their way in that antipodean night would probably need the attention of an oneiromantist.

"So in 1942 Ada got the same news from North Africa that in 1917 her mother had got from Flanders. Another young widow. Another fatherless child. No wonder she hated uniforms and wars and anything which seemed to be celebrating them. She could never look at an Armistice Day poppy without feeling physically sick, and one of her last cogent acts was to rebuke a British Legion volunteer who came round the ward selling them."

Rebuke? What she'd actually said according to Myra was "Sod off, ghoul." Which message it might appear he was passing on to this well-poppied congregation. Ah well. You can't please all of the people all of the time.

"But Ada did not let the past destroy her present. She joined one of the accelerated teacher-training courses after the war, and despite her late start, she climbed high, finishing as Head of Redstones Junior, which I myself had the privilege of attending. As you can imagine, having your gran as head teacher was a mixed blessing. Certainly in school I got no favors, just a first-class education. But outside, I got all the love and indulgence a growing boy is entitled to expect from his gran."

He caught Myra's eye again and read the message clearly. *Favorite!* So what? Boy with two bossy elder sisters needed an edge somewhere. Another eye was catching his, the crem super's, reminding him of his warning that despite the nanny State, dank Novembers still meant frequent hearses and any overrun could quickly blacken up the bypass. Time to wrap it up. Pity. He felt he was just getting into his stride.

"Even after retirement, she remained at the center of things, as a school governor, a member of innumerable committees, and a tireless campaigner in the corridors of power and on the pavements of protest."

Now he was really motoring! Great phrase, that was. Even though getting the rhythm right meant a solecistic drift from the nounal trochee to the verbal iamb. How old Ada would have rapped his knuckles. The crem super too looked close to physical violence. Big finish!

"I doubt if she went gentle into her good night, but gone she has, and the world is a sadder place for her going. But she left it a better place than she found it, and that would have been the only epitaph she wished."

Big finish nothing. Big cop-out was more like it. Ada had had no illusions about progress. Watching the telly peepshow of famine and disaster and war, she used to rage, "They've learned nothing. Absolutely nothing!" Oh well. At least he'd taken his poppy out.

Time for the final music. Myra had gone for Elgar's *Enigma*, which to Ada's tin ear probably sounded like bovine eructation. The crem's alternatives were all just as classically solemn. Then Pascoe had recalled the one time Ada ever talked about her father, the day he found the photo in the secretaire, and he'd rummaged through the tapes in his car and come up with Scott Joplin. He saw the shock on Myra's face as "The Strenuous Life" came floating out of the speakers. He'd explain later, sharing his secret knowledge that Ada's sole recollection of her father—indeed her first recollection of anything—had been of a shadowy figure sitting at an upright piano picking out a ragtime melody.

So the circle closes . . . so the circle closes.

IV

"AT HIS GRANDMOTHER'S FUNERAL?" said Detective Superintendent Andy Dalziel. "You'd think a bugger wi' letters after his name could come up with a better excuse than that."

"He did tell you about it, sir," said Sergeant Wield, shouting to make himself heard above the lashing rain.

Dalziel viewed him gloomily through the bespattered car window which he'd lowered by half an inch in the interest of more efficient communication. He was not a man totally insensitive to the comforts of his inferiors, but the sergeant was swathed in oilskins and the Fat Man could see no reason why the torrents Niagaraing around their folds should be diverted to his vehicle's upholstery.

"Aye, and my gran told me not to mess around wi' mucky women and I paid no heed to her either," he said. "Still, last time he were here, he wasn't much use, was he? Okay, lad. Let's have it. What've we got?"

"Remains, sir."

"Man? Woman? Child? Dog? Politician?"

"Remains to be seen," said Wield.

Dalziel groaned and said, "I hope you're not letting happiness turn you humorous, Wieldy. You've not got the face for it and I'm not in the mood. I were driving home to a warm bed when I were silly enough to switch me radio on and pick up the tail end of this shout. All Control could tell me was there was a body and there was a bunch of animal libbers and it was out at Wanwood. So is this another Redcar or what?"

Five months earlier in May there'd been an animal rights raid on the laboratories of FraserGreenleaf, the

international pharmaceutical conglomerate, near Redcar on the North Yorkshire coast. As well as releasing
the experimental animals, the raiders had vandalized
the premises and, most seriously of all, left security officer Mark Shufflebottom, father of two, lying dead
with severe wounds to the head. Several weeks later
there'd been another raid, bearing all the hallmarks of
the same group, on the research labs of ALBA Pharmaceuticals located on Mid-Yorks territory in a converted
mansion called Wanwood House. Happily this time no
one had been injured. Unhappily neither the Teeside
CID in whose jurisdiction Redcar fell, nor the Mid-
Yorkshire team led by Peter Pascoe, had met with any
success in tracking down the culprits.

"No, sir. This body's been here long enough to turn
into bones. That's not to say this couldn't be the same
lot as were here in the summer, though of course it was
never established for certain they were the same bunch
that raided FG."

Wield was a stickler for accuracy, a natural bent refined paradoxically by years of deception. Concealing
you were gay in the police force meant weighing with
scrupulous care everything you said or did, and this
habit of precise scrutiny had turned him into one of the
most reliable colleagues Dalziel had.

But sometimes his nit-picking could get on your
wick.

"Just tell us what happened, Wieldy," sighed the Fat
Man long-sufferingly.

"Right, sir. This group—I gather they call themselves ANIMA by the way—the name's known to us
but not the personnel—sorry—they entered the
grounds with the clear intention of breaking into the
labs and releasing any animals they found there. But if
they were the same lot who were here in the summer,
they must have got a bit of a shock, as ALBA's taken
some extra precautions since then."

"Precautions?"

"You'll see, sir," said Wield, not without a certain well-concealed glee. "And on their way through the grounds they sort of stumbled across these bones."

"Couldn't have brought them with them just to get a bit of publicity?" said Dalziel hopefully.

"Doesn't look like it, sir," said Wield. "They kicked up such a hullabaloo that the security guards finally took heed and came out. When they realized what was going off, they took the demonstrators inside. Gather there was a bit of trouble then. They got loose and ran riot for a bit before they were brought under control."

"Violent, eh? So there could be a link with Redcar?"

"Can't really comment, sir. Mr. Headingley's up at the house interviewing them. He told me to sort things out down here."

"Good old George," said Dalziel. "Perk of being a D.I., Wieldy. Start taking an interest in your promotion exams and you could be up there in the dry and warm."

Wield shrugged indifferently, his features showing as little reaction to horizontal sleet as the crags of Scafell.

He knew you didn't learn things from books, you learned them from people. Like that other George, Creed. He'd pay a lot more attention to his weather forecasts from now on in! Also he knew for a fact that not all the elevated rank in the world was going to keep the Fat Man dry and warm.

He said, "Yes, sir. I expect you'll be wanting to view the scene before you head up there yourself."

It was a simple statement of fact, not a challenging question.

Dalziel groaned and said, "If that's what you expect, Wieldy, I expect I'd better do it. Teach me not to turn my bloody radio on when I'm driving home to a warm bed. Get me waterproofs out of the boot, will you, else I'll be sodden afore I start."

Watching Dalziel getting into oilskins and Wellies through the streaming glass, Wield was reminded of a film he'd seen of Houdini wriggling out of his bonds while submerged in a huge glass jar.

The car gave one last convulsive shake and the Fat Man was free.

"Right," he said. "Where's it at?"

"This way," said Wield.

At this moment Nature, with the perfect timing due to the entry of a major figure on her stage, shut off the wind machine for a moment and let the curtain of sleet shimmer to transparency.

"Bloody hell," said Dalziel with the incredulous amazement of a Great War general happening on a battlefield. "They had Dutch elm disease or what?"

On either side of the driveway a broad swath of woodland had been ripped out, and this fillet of desolation which presumably ran all the way round the house was bounded by two fences, the outer a simple hedge of barbed wire, the inner much more sophisticated, a twelve-feet-high security screen with floodlamps and closed-circuit TV cameras every twenty yards.

Neither light nor presumably cameras were much use when the wind, as it now did once more, drove a rolling barrage of sleet and dendral debris across this wilderness.

Wield said, "These are the precautions I mentioned, sir. We've got duckboards down. Try and stay on them else you could need a block and tackle."

Was he taking the piss? The Fat Man trod gingerly on the first duckboard, felt it sink into the glutinous mud, and decided the sergeant was just being typically precise.

The wooden pathway zigzagged through the mire to avoid the craters left by uprooted trees, finally coming to a halt at the edge of one of the largest and deepest. Here there was some protection from a canvas awning, which every blast of the wind threatened to carry away along with the two constables whose manful efforts were necessary to keep its metal poles anchored in the yielding clay.

At the bottom of the crater a man was taking photographs, whose flash revealed on the edge above him, crouched low to get maximum protection from the billowing canvas, another figure studying something in a plastic bag.

"Good God," said Dalziel. "That's never Troll Longbottom?"

"Mr. Longbottom, yes, sir," said Wield. "Seems he was dining with Dr. Batty, that's ALBA's research director, when the security staff rang him to say what had happened. Dr. Batty's up at the house."

"And Troll came too? Must've been losing at cards or summat."

Thomas Roland Longbottom, consultant pathologist at the City General, was notoriously unenthusiastic about on-site examinations. "You want a call-out service, join the RAC," he'd once told Dalziel.

His forenames had been compressed to Troll in early childhood, and whether the sobriquet in any way predicated his professional enthusiasm for dead flesh and loose bones was a question for psycholinguistics. Dalziel doubted it. They'd played in the same school rugby team and the Fat Man claimed to have seen Longbottom at the age of thirteen devour an opponent's ear.

He gingerly edged his way round the rim of the crater and drew the consultant's attention by tugging at the collar of the mohair topcoat he was wearing over a dinner jacket.

"How do, Troll. Good of you to come. Needn't have got dressed up, but. You'll get mud on your dicky."

Longbottom squinted up at him. Time, which had basted Dalziel, had wasted him to an appropriate cadaverousness.

"Would you mind staying on your own piece of board, please, Dalziel? *Facilis est descensus,* but I'm choosy about the company I make it in."

Education and high society had long eroded his native accent, but he had lost none of the skill of abusive exchange which forms the basis of playground intercourse in Mid-Yorkshire.

"Sorry you got dragged away from your dinner, but I see you brought your snap," said Dalziel, peering at the plastic bag which contained a cluster of small bones.

"Which I shall need to feast on at my leisure."

"Looks like slim pickings to me," said Dalziel. "So what can you give me off the top of your head? Owt'll do. Sex. Age. Time of death. Mother's maiden name."

"It's a hand, and it's human, and that's all I'm prepared to say till I've seen a great deal more, which may be some time. This one, I fear, like Nicholas Nickleby, is coming out in installments."

"Can't recall him," said Dalziel. "What did he die of?"

Longbottom arose with a groan which comprehended everything from the joke to the stiffness of his muscles and the state of the weather.

"Just look at my coat," he said. "Do you know how much these things cost? I shall of course be making a claim."

"I'd send it to ALBA then. Your mate, Batty. Do you reckon he keeps anything to drink up there?"

"I should imagine there's a single methanol in the labs."

"That'll do nicely," said Andy Dalziel.

V

PETER PASCOE COULD HAVE done without the funeral meats but felt he'd gone as far as he dared in disrupting his sister's arrangements. In fact it worked out rather well, as under the influence of cups of tea and salmon sandwiches the wrinklie clones turned into amiable, intelligent individuals, several of them well below retirement age. Some even went out of their way to compliment him on his address, saying how pleased Ada would have been with the service and how much they'd like something like that when their turn came.

Myra clearly took all this in because when they'd waved the stragglers goodbye, she said, "Okay, so as usual you were right."

He smiled at her but she wasn't ready for that yet, and turned back into the old cottage which had been Ada's home for fifty years.

"Only room for one in that kitchen," she said. "I'll do the washing up. You can carry on with your inventory."

When she came back into the living room, he was maneuvering an old mahogany secretaire through the doorway.

"You're taking that old thing then?"

"Yes. I thought I'd get it on the roof rack now so I can make a quick getaway in the morning. Don't worry. It's on the inventory. I'll get it valued and make sure it goes into the estate."

"I didn't mean that . . . oh think what you will, you always did."

She turned away angry and hurt.

Oh shit, thought Pascoe. Whatever happened to old silver tongue?

He reached out and caught her arm and said, "Sorry. I was talking like an executor. Maybe a bit like a cop too. Listen, you don't have to say anything, but anything you do say will be taken down."

She stared at him blankly and for a second he thought she'd forgotten the grubby little schoolboy joke he'd tried to embarrass her with all those years ago.

Then she smiled and said, "Knickers," and through the eggshell makeup he glimpsed the girl who'd been his closest ally in the long war of adolescence. Okay, so her motivation had a lot to do with resentment that Sue, the eldest, could get away with shorter skirts, thicker lipstick, and later hours than herself. Whatever the reason, their closest moments within the family had been together.

"What about you?" he said. "Isn't there anything you'd like?"

"Far too old-fashioned for our house," she said firmly.

"Something small, as a memento," Pascoe urged.

"No need for that. I'll remember," she said.

There was something in her tone, not acerbic exactly, but certainly acetic. She'd never been anyone's favorite, Pascoe realized. Susan had been the apple of their parents' eye, would perhaps have been their only fruit if their chosen method of contraception had been more efficient. He himself had been Ada's favorite—or, as he sometimes felt, target. Driven by the loss of two men in her life (three if you counted the disappointment of her own son) she'd focused all her shaping care on her male grandchild, leaving poor Myra to find her own way.

It had led to marriage with Trevor, the kind of financial advisor who bores clients into submission; an ultramodern executive villa in Coventry, a pair of ultra-

Neanderthal teenage sons in private education; and a resolve to show the world that what she'd got was exactly what she wanted.

So, no appetite-spoiling bitterness this, just a condiment sharpness.

Pascoe said, "About the music . . ."

"It doesn't matter, Pete. I've said you were right."

"No, I'd like to explain. Here, let me show you something."

He opened the drawer of the secretaire, reached inside, pressed a knob of wood, and a second tiny drawer concealed by the inlay pattern came sliding out of the first.

"Neat, eh?" he said. "I found it when I was ten. No gold sovereigns or anything. Just this."

From the drawer he took a dog-eared sepia photograph of a soldier, seated rather stiffly with his body turned to display the single stripe on his sleeve. His face, looking directly into the camera, wore the solemn, set expression demanded by old technique and convention, but there was the hint of a smile around the eyes as if he was feeling rather pleased with himself.

"Know who this is?"

"Well, he looks so like you when you're feeling cocky, it must be our great-grandfather."

Pascoe couldn't see the resemblance but felt he'd probably earned the crack. He turned the picture over so she could see what was written on the back in black ink faded to gray.

First lance corporal from our draft! December 1914.

Then Pascoe tipped the photo so that it caught the light. There was more writing, this time in pencil long since erased. But the writer had pressed so hard, the indented words were still legible. *Killed Wipers 1917.*

"All those years and she couldn't bear to have it on display," mused Pascoe.

"All those years and you never mentioned it," accused Myra.

"I promised Gran," he said. "She caught me looking at it. She was furious at first, then she calmed down and made me promise not to say anything."

"Another of your little secrets," she said. "The Pascoes must have more of them than MI5."

"You're right," he said, trying to keep things light. "Anyway, that was when she told me her only recollection of her father was of him playing on their old piano. Her mother must've told her it was ragtime, I doubt if Ada could tell Scott Joplin from Janis Joplin. And that's what made me think of that tape."

Myra took the photo from him and said, "Poor sod. Can't have been more than twenty-two or -three. What was he in?"

"West York Fusiliers. That's how I found out about the Yorkshire connection."

"She really hated uniforms, didn't she?" said Myra, dropping the picture back in the drawer. "I still remember how sarkie she got when I joined the Brownies."

"Think of how she must have felt with Dad playing soldiers in the TA once a week. Not to mention him turning out a Hang 'em and Flog 'em Tory."

"Still voting for the revolution, are you, Peter? Funny that, you being a cop. Now, that was really the last straw for poor old Ada, wasn't it?"

She sounded as if the memory didn't altogether displease her.

"At least it got her and Dad on the same side for once," said Pascoe, determined not to be lured back into a squabble. "He told me he hadn't subsidized me through a university education to pound a beat. He wanted me to be a bank manager or something in the City. Gran saw me as a reforming MP. She was even more incredulous than Dad. She came to my graduation thinking she could change my mind. Dad had given up on me by then. He wouldn't even let Mum come."

Despite his effort at lightness he could feel bitterness creeping in.

"Well, you got your own back, getting yourself posted up north and finding fifty-seven varieties of excuse why you could never make it home at Christmas," said Myra. "Still, it's all water under the bridge. Gran's gone, and I bet Dad bores the corks off their hats down under boasting about my son the chief inspector."

"You reckon? Maybe I'll resign. Hey, remember how you used to beat me at tennis when I was a weedy kid and you had forearms like Rod Laver? Got any of those muscles left?"

Between them they maneuvered the secretaire out of the cottage and up onto his roof rack. He strapped it down, with a waterproof sheet on top of it.

"Right," said Myra. "Now what?"

"Now you push off. I'll finish the inventory and start sorting her papers. You've got to be back here tomorrow morning to meet the house clearance man, remember?"

Pascoe had been delighted when Myra volunteered for this task, being justly derided by his wife as probably the only man in Yorkshire who could haggle a price upward.

Myra, a terrier in a bargain, bared her teeth in an anticipatory smile.

"Don't expect a fortune," she said. "But I'll see we're not cheated. You're not expecting me to sell *that*, are you?"

That was a plastic urn in taupe. Were Warwickshire's funerary suppliers capable of a bilingual pun? wondered Pascoe.

"No, that goes with me."

"You're going to do what she asked with the ashes then?"

"If I can."

"Funny, with her hating the army so much."

"It's a symbolic gesture, I assume. I won't try to work out what it means, as I'd prefer to be thinking holy thoughts as I scatter them."

"It's still weird. Then, so was Gran a lot of the time. I shouldn't care to spend the night in this old place with her ashes on the mantelpiece. You sure you won't change your mind and come over to us? Trevor would be delighted to see you."

Pascoe, who had only once set foot in Myra's executive villa and found it as aesthetically and atmospherically appealing as a multi-gym, said, "No, thanks. I've got a lot to do and I'd like to be off at the crack."

They stood regarding each other rather awkwardly. Myra looked untypically vulnerable. Me too maybe, thought Pascoe. On impulse he stepped forward, took her in his arms and kissed her. He could feel her surprise. They'd never been a hugging and kissing family. Then she pressed him close and said, "Bye, Peter. Safe journey. Give my love to Ellie. Sorry she couldn't make it. But I know about kids' colds when they're that age."

And I know about urgent business appointments with important clients, thought Pascoe. At least Rosie really had been snuffling in bed when he left.

And perhaps Trevor really did have an urgent deal to close, he reproved himself.

He gave Myra another hug and let her go.

"Let's not make it so long next time," he said.

"And let's try not to make it a funeral," she replied.

But neither of them tried to put any flesh on these bones of a promise.

He stood in the porch and watched her drive away. He felt glad and sad, full of relief that they'd parted on good terms and full of guilt that they hadn't been better.

He went inside and addressed the urn.

"Ada," he said, "we really are a fucked-up family, us Pascoes. I wonder whose fault that is?"

He worked hard on the inventory till midevening, then made a neat copy of it to leave for Myra. He'd need another copy to send to Susan in Australia.

One thing he felt certain of. His eldest sister might not be able to fly halfway round the world for her grandmother's funeral, but she would expect any money making the journey in the opposite direction to be accounted for down to the last halfpenny. The will, of which Pascoe was executor, left various legacies to Ada's favorite causes and the residue to be divided equally among her three grandchildren. Whether this evenhandedness had postdated his fall from grace, Pascoe wasn't sure, but he was glad that in this at least the old accusation of favoritism was clearly given the lie. Not that there was much—Ada had lived up to her income and the cottage was rented. But Pascoe had seen blood shed over far smaller amounts than were likely to be realized from Ada's estate and he'd already arranged to have all the paperwork double-checked by Ada's solicitor, a no-nonsense woman called Barbara Lomax, whose probity was beyond aspersion.

He boxed up some books that interested him or might interest Ellie and scrupulously made a note on the inventory. Next he started sorting out Ada's papers, starting with a rough division into personal/business. He was touched to find every letter he had ever written to her carefully preserved, an emotion slightly diluted when he realized that this urge to conservation also included fifty-year-old grocery receipts.

His stomach rumbled like distant gunfire. It seemed

a long time since the salmon sandwiches. Also he felt
like stretching his legs.

Taking a torch from the car he strolled the half mile
to the village pub, where he enjoyed a pint and a pie
and a reminiscent conversation about Ada with the
landlord. As he walked back he found he was knee-
deep in mist drifting from the fields, but the night sky
was so bright it felt like his head was brushing the
stars. The pub telly had spoken of severe weather with
gales and sleet in the North. Dalziel was right, he
thought with a smile. The soft South really did begin
after Sheffield.

He resumed his work on the papers but found that
his starry stroll had unsettled him. Also after a while he
realized he was more aware than a rational man ought
to be of the screw-top urn squatting on the mantel
shelf. In the end, slightly ashamed, he took it out to the
car and locked it in the boot. As for the papers, home,
where he had a computer, a calculator, and a copier,
plus a wife who knew how to work them, was the place
to get Ada's affairs sorted. It was time for bed.

Getting his clothes off was an effort. His limbs felt
dull and heavy and the air in the tiny bedroom, though
hardly less sharp than the frosty night outside, seemed
viscous and clinging. The cold sheets on the narrow
bed received him like a shroud.

Sleep was a long time coming . . .

    . . . *a long time coming—maybe because I wouldnt
take any rum—no shortage here—how the lads ud
lap it up!*

    *And when it did come darkdream came too terri-
ble as ever—only this time there was more—this
time when the muzzles flashed and the hot metal
burnt I didnt scream and try to wake but went right
through it and came out on the other side and kept
on going—heart pounding—muscles aching—lungs*

bursting—like a man running from summat so vile he wont stop till he falls or knows he has left it far behind.

In the end I had to stop—knowing somehow it werent just miles Id run over but years—seventy or eighty of them maybe—near clean on out of this terrible century—and Id run home.

Where else would a frightened man run to?

O it were so good Alice! Fields so fresh and green —woods all bursting with leaf—river running pure and clean with fat trout shadowing all the pools. Away yonder I could see mucky old Leeds—only now there werent no smoke hanging over it—and all that grimy granite were washed to a pearly grey— and shooting up above the old quiet chimneys were towers and turrets of gleaming white marble like a picture in a fairy tale.

As for Kirkton it were just the same as I long to be back in only so much better—with all them tumbledown cottages alongside Grindals turned into gardens—and the mill itself had big airy windows and I could see lasses and lads laughing and talking inside—and that old bog meadow out towards Haggs Farm that used to stink so much was all drained and the river banks built up so thered be no more flooding—and High Street seemed wider too with all them slimy cobbles that broke old Tom Steddings head when his horse slipped covered over with level tarmac—and the Maisterhouse away through the trees with its red brick glowing and it pointing gleaming like it were just built yesterday.

Even St Marks looked a lot more welcoming cos the parson had ripped out them gloomy windows that used to terrify us kids with their blood and flames—and in their stead hed put clear new glass which let sun come streaming through like springwater. Even the old tombstones had been cleaned up

*and I took this fancy to see my own—only I thought
on that Id not be buried here with tothers of my
name but far away across the sea where none would
ever find me—and soon as I thought that I felt myself being hauled back to this awful place.*

*But I werent going easy and I fought against it
and hung on still and peered over the wall into the
schoolyard to see the kiddies playing there all so
happy and strong and free—and I wondered whether
any on them was descended from me—and I
thought I saw a familiar face—then came the sound
of a distant crump like they was blasting out at
Abels Quarry—only I knew they werent—and a
voice a long way off saying some poor sods catching
it—and I didn't want to blink though the sun was
shining straight in my eyes—but I had to blink—and
though it was only a second or even less when I
opened my eyes again sun were gone and kiddies
were gone and all I could see were the night sky
through the window red and terrible as that old
stained glass—and all I could hear were the rumble
of the guns—and all I could feel was the straw from
my paillasse pricking into my back . . .*

Pascoe awoke. Had he been dreaming? He thought he
had but his dream had gone. Or had it? Did dreams
ever go? Our present was someone else's future. We
live in other men's dreams . . .

He closed his eyes and drifted back to that other
place.

*. . . but Ill try to keep them dream children bright
in my mind my love—you too—and tell little Ada
about them—I still cant credit a bible heaven spite
of old padre preaching at me every other day—so
unless this lots going to teach us summat about the*

way we live here on earth wheres the point of it all eh?

Wheres the bloody point?

VI

WANWOOD HOUSE HAD HAD pieces added to it in the modern Portaloo style, but basically it was a square solid Victorian building, its proportions not palatial but just far enough outside the human scale to put a peasant in his place. Thus did the nineteenth-century Yorkshireman underline the natural order of things.

His twentieth-century successors were more self-effacing, it seemed.

"Don't advertise much," observed Dalziel, looking at a discreet plaque which read ALBA PHARMACEUTICALS *Research Division.* "And there's nowt on the gate."

"Might as well have put a neon sign on the roof for all the good it's done them," said Longbottom, ringing the bell.

The door was opened by a man in a dark green uniform with the name PATTEN and a logo consisting of an orange sunburst and the letters *TecSec* at his breast. He was leanly muscular with close-cropped hair and a long scar down the right cheek which, helped by a slightly askew nose, suggested that at some time the whole face had been removed and rather badly stitched back on. Dalziel viewed him with the distaste of a professional soldier for private armies. But at least the man sized them up at a glance and didn't do anything silly like asking for identification.

He ushered them through the nineteenth into the twentieth century in the form of a modern reception area with a stainless steel desk, pink fitted carpet, and hessian-hung walls from which depended what might have been a selection of Prince Charles's watercolors left standing in the rain.

One of three doors almost invisible in their hessian camouflage opened and a slim fair-haired man in his thirties and a dinner jacket, who reminded Dalziel of someone but he couldn't quite say who, came toward them saying, "My dear chap, you're soaked. No need, I'm sure. The fuzz must have plenty of pensioned-off sawbones all too keen to earn a bob doing the basics."

Assuming none of this solicitude was aimed at him, Dalziel said, "Aye, and we sometimes make do with a barber and a leech. You'll be Batty, I daresay."

"Indeed," said the man, regarding Dalziel with the air of one nostalgic for the days of tradesmen's entrances. "And you . . . ?"

"Superintendent Andrew Dalziel," offered Longbottom.

"Ah, the great white chief. Took your time getting here, Superintendent."

"Got the call on my way back from a meeting in Nottingham," said Dalziel. He saw Longbottom smile his awareness that the meeting in question had taken place under floodlights on a rugby pitch.

"Well, at least now you're here, perhaps you can tell the bunch of incompetents who've preceded you to get their fingers out and start imposing some sort of order on this mess."

"I'll do my best," said the Fat Man mildly. "Talking of messes, sir, that's a right one you've got out there. Looks like a health hazard to me."

"On the contrary, it's a cordon sanitaire," said Batty. "After the damage those lunatics did last summer, it was quite clearly beyond the police force's competency to protect us, so we took steps of our own to thwart these criminals."

"Criminals," echoed Dalziel as if the word were new to him. "You'll be prosecuting then, sir?"

Batty said, "If it's left up to me, we will! Normally we don't care to give these lunatics the oxygen of publicity, but I suspect in this case some exposure is already unavoidable?"

"Aye," said Dalziel. "Having a body dug up in your backyard usually gives off a lot worse stink than oxygen."

"As I feared, though I suppose the exact nature of the publicity depends on how diplomatically things are handled. Troll, what can you tell us?"

Dalziel gave the pathologist a look which dared him to speculate an inch further than he'd done on the edge of the crater.

"Early days, David, early days," murmured Longbottom.

"And getting close to early hours," said Dalziel, looking at his watch. "Mebbe I could see the witnesses now . . . ?"

"Yes, I suppose so. Patten will take you along. Troll, let's try to get your outside dry and your inside suitably wetted."

With an apologetic mop and mow at Dalziel, the pathologist let himself be led away. Dalziel, who kept his slates as carefully as any shopkeeper, chalked up another small debt against Batty's name and followed the security man through one of the hessian doors and down a long corridor.

"We've got them locked up down here," he said.

"Locked up?"

"They are trespassers, and once they got into the building, they ran amok. One of my men got hit in the stomach, I was threatened . . ."

"Oh aye?" said Dalziel, interested. Mebbe this could have some connection with Redcar after all. "Anyone get really hurt?"

"More dignity than owt else," said Patten enigmatically. "That's where they are."

They'd turned left at a T-junction in the corridor. Ahead, Dalziel had already observed another TecSec man slouching against a door, his head wreathed in smoke. As soon as he became aware of their approach, he straightened his uniform and snapped to attention. There was no sign of a cigarette. Dalziel admired the legerdemain and bet on the big front pocket of the dark green trousers.

"At ease, Jimmy," said Patten. "This is Superintendent Dalziel."

"I know," said the man. "How do you do, sir."

Dalziel was used to being recognized but liked to know why.

"Do I know you?" he said.

"Not exactly, sir. But I know you. I was at Dartleby nick till I took the pension. Uniformed. PC Howard, sir."

"Jumped ship, did you? All right, lad. You can piss off now."

The man looked unhappily at Patten, who said, "We do have our orders . . ."

"That's what Eichmann said, and they hanged him. So bugger off. And by the way, Howard . . ."

"Yes, sir?"

"Your cock's on fire."

Leaving the ex-policeman beating at his pocket, Dalziel stepped into the room and halted dead in his tracks.

"Bloody hell," he said.

Gently steaming against a big radiator were eight women, each mucky enough to have set Dalziel's granny spinning in her grave.

That Wield, he swore to himself. He kept quiet on purpose. I'll punch the bugger handsome!

One woman detached herself from the huddle and

came toward him, saying, "Thank God here's t'organ grinder. Now mebbe we can get shut of the monkeys."

She glared toward Patten as she spoke. He returned the glare indifferently. Dalziel on the other hand studied the woman with the intense interest of a gourmet served a new dish. Not that there was much to whet the appetite. She had less meat on her than a picked-over chicken wing and her cheeks were pale and hollow as wind-carved limestone.

Memory stirred. That business down the mine when Pascoe got hurt . . .

He said, "You're one of them Women Against Pit Closures lot from Burrthorpe. Walker, isn't it? Wendy Walker?"

She stepped by him and slammed the door in Patten's face. Then she said, "That's right. Got a fag?"

He pulled out a packet. He rarely smoked now, not because of health fears, still less because of social pressures, but because he'd found it was blunting his ability to distinguish single malts with a single sniff. But he still carried fags, finding them professionally useful both as icebreakers and cage rattlers.

"You're a long way off the coal face, luv," he said, flicking his old petrol lighter.

"Coal?"

She drew the word into herself with a long breath that reduced the cigarette by an inch of ash.

"What's that?" she said on the outgoing puff. "They shut Burrthorpe last year like they've shut most on t'others. Them bastards made a lot of promises they didn't keep, but when they said they'd pay us back for the strike, by God they kept that one!"

"It's still a long way from home."

"Home is where the hate is, and there's nowt left to hate in Burrthorpe, just an empty hole in the ground where there used to be a community."

"I'm sorry to interrupt this reunion and the Channel

Four documentary, but you, whoever you are, how long are we to be restrained by these thugs in these disgusting conditions?''

The voice, as up-to-Oxford county as Walker's was down-to-earth Yorkshire, belonged to a small sturdy woman, her short-cropped black hair accentuating the determined cast of her handsome features. This one too brought a memory popping up in Dalziel's mind, hot as a piece of fresh toast, of a woman he'd known and liked—more than liked—down in Lincolnshire after Pascoe's wedding. . . . He hadn't thought about her for years. What could have pressed that button? he wondered as he stared with undisguised pleasure at the way this woman's wet sweater clung to her melopeponic breasts.

"Nay, lass," he said. "No one's restraining you, whoever *you* are. You can bugger off any time you like, once you've made your statement. You have been asked to make a statement, Miss er . . . ?''

"Marvell. Amanda Marvell. Yes, we've been asked, but most of us are refusing till such time as we have proper representation.''

She glared accusingly, and in Dalziel's eyes, most becomingly, at Wendy Walker, who snapped, "Yeah, I've made my statement. In fact, when it comes down to it, I'm the only one who's really got owt to state. Mebbe more than you'll care to hear, Cap. All I want is to get out of here.''

"You surprise me, Wendy," said Marvell, all cool control. "What happened to all the big talk about going for the jugular and taking no prisoners? First sign of trouble, and you're all for breaking ranks.''

"Yeah? Mebbe I should have been more choosy who I formed ranks with in the first place," snarled Walker.

"Really? You mean we don't match up to the standards of your mining chums? Well, I can see that. Once

they encountered real opposition, they pretty soon
crumbled too, didn't they?"

There was a time when a provocation like this to a
Burrthorpe lass would have started World War III, and
indeed a small red spot at the heart of those pallid
cheeks seemed to indicate some incipient nuclear activity. But before she could explode, a round-faced blonde
who looked even wetter and more miserable than the
rest said, "Wendy's right, Cap. This is serious stuff. It
was bones we found out there, a *body*. Let's just make
our statements and go home. *Please.*"

Marvell's *et tu Brute* look was even more devastating
than her *j'accuse* glare, and Dalziel was experiencing a
definite wringing of the withers when the door opened
and George Headingley's broad anxious face appeared.

"Hello, sir. Heard you were here. Can we have a
word?"

"If we must," said Dalziel reluctantly, and with a
last mnemonic look at Cap Marvell's gently steaming
bosom, he went out into the corridor.

"All right, George," he said. "Fill me in."

Headingley, a pink-faced middle-aged man with a
sad moustache and a cream tea paunch, said, "That lot
in there belong to ANIMA, the animal rights group,
and they were . . ."

Dalziel said, "I don't give a toss if they belong to the
Dagenham Girl Pipers and they've come here to re-
hearse, they're witnesses is all that matters. So what
did they witness?"

"Well, I've got one statement on tape so far. The
others aren't being very cooperative but this lass . . ."

"Aye. Wendy Walker. First time in her life she's
been cooperative with the police, I bet. Let's hear this
tape then."

Headingley led him to a small office where the recorder was set up. Dalziel listened intently, then said,
"This Cap, the one with the chest . . ."

"Marvell. Captain Marvell, get it? She's the boss, except that she and Walker don't see eye to eye."

"I noticed. She sounds a bit of a hard case."

"Yes, sir. Patten, that's the TecSec chief, reckons she had serious thought about taking a swing at him."

"Could pack quite a punch with that weight behind it," said Dalziel, smiling reminiscently.

"It were a set of wire cutters she was swinging. We've got them here, sir. Give you a real headache if these connected."

Dalziel looked at the heavy implement and said, "Bag it and have it checked for blood."

"But no one got hurt," protested Headingley.

"Not here they didn't."

"You don't mean you think maybe Redcar . . . but they're women, sir!"

"World's changing, George," said Dalziel. "So what else have you been doing, apart from collecting one statement."

"Well, I had a talk with Dr. Batty when I got here . . ."

"He was here when you arrived?"

"Yes, sir. Expect that Patten rang him first. Then I got things organized outside, and I thought I'd better see if we could organize some sort of refreshment for the ladies. I asked that fellow Howard—he used to be one of ours—but he said he couldn't leave the door, so I went to look for myself. Found the staff canteen, got a tea urn brewing . . ."

"You must be the highest paid teaboy since Geoffrey Howe left the cabinet," said Dalziel. Still, at least old George knew his limitations. Why get wet and in the way outside when you had someone like Wieldy, who could organize a piss-up on a Welsh Sunday, fifty miles from the nearest brewery.

"So what now, sir?" said Headingley. "Statements?"

Dalziel thought, then said, "Walker's the only one with owt to state and we've got hers. Give them all their cup of tea, take details, name, address, the usual, keep it all low-key and chatty, but see if you can get any of them to let on they've been here before."

Headingley was looking puzzled and the Fat Man said with didactic clarity, "Tie 'em in with last summer's raid here and we're well on the way to tying 'em in with Redcar."

"Oh yes. I see. You really think then . . ."

"Not paid to think, George. I employ someone to think for me, and the bugger's at a funeral so we'll have to get by on our lonesome. Patten!"

Closed doors and thick walls were no sound barrier and a moment later the TecSec man appeared.

Dalziel said, "The ladies are going along to the staff canteen for refreshments, then they'll be going home. I presume you've got all your animals locked away?"

"Don't worry. They won't get anywhere near the labs," said Patten confidently.

"Nay, lad, it's your men I'm talking about. No more strong-arm stuff, you with me?"

"Because they're female, you mean? Listen, that chunky cow, the one they call Cap, she nearly took my head off with a bloody great pair of wire cutters."

"Is that right. Your head looks okay to me," said Dalziel, examining it critically.

"No thanks to her," said Patten. "All I'm saying is, if my men get assaulted . . ."

"They should count their blessings," said Dalziel. "There's a place in Harrogate where it costs good money to get beaten up by a handsome young woman. Like the address? All right, George? Everything under control?"

"Yes, sir. What about you, sir?" said George Headingley. "Where are you going to be?"

"Me?" said Dalziel, smacking his lips in anticipation. "I'm going to be wherever Dr. Batty keeps his single methanol."

VII

AS PASCOE DROVE north the following morning, the weather got worse but his mood got better. By the time he got within tuning distance of Radio Mid-Yorkshire, his car was being machine-gunned by horizontal hail, but the familiar mix of dated pops and parish pump gossip sounded in his ears like the first cuckoo of spring.

I must be turning into a Yorkshireman, he thought as he sang along with Boney M.

A newscast followed, a mixture of local and national. One item caught his attention.

"Police have confirmed the discovery last night of human remains in the grounds of Wanwood House, research headquarters of ALBA Pharmaceuticals. Tests to ascertain the cause of death are not yet complete and the police spokesman was unwilling to comment on reports that the discovery was made by a group of animal rights protesters."

It sounded to Pascoe's experienced ear that Andy Dalziel was sitting tight on this one, and with one of those mighty buttocks in your face, even the voice of nation speaking unto nation got a bit muffled.

It also confirmed him in his half-formed resolution that it was worth diverting to dispose of Ada's ashes. Dalziel believed that time off on any pretext meant you owed him a week of twenty-five-hour days. With a possible murder on his hands, he'd probably raise that to thirty, particularly as Pascoe had been in sole charge of the investigation into the ALBA raid last summer. It had only merited a DCI's involvement because of the possible connection with the killing at FG's labs up at Redcar. There's always a certain pleasure in solving another mob's case, but Dalziel, who was a good delegator, had neither interfered nor complained when Pascoe had reported that the investigation was going nowhere. On the other hand Pascoe did not doubt he would be held personally responsible for not having noticed the presence of human remains out at Wanwood even if they turned out to have been buried six feet under!

So, dispose of Ada, else the urn could end up sitting on his mantelpiece for some time, and his guess was that even someone as conscientiously house-humble as Ellie would draw the line at such a hydriotaphic ornament.

Leeds was only a little out of his way. With luck he could be in and out in half an hour.

This pious hope died in a one-way system as unforgiving as a posting to the Western Front. Even when he arrived where he wanted to be, where he wanted to be didn't seem to be there anymore. At least the hail had stopped and the blustery wind was tearing holes in the cloud big enough for the occasional ray of sun to penetrate.

He pulled into the car park of a pile-'em-high-sell-'em-cheap supermarket and addressed an apparently shell-shocked old man in charge of a convoy of errant trolleys.

"Is this Kirkton Road?"

"Aye," said the man.

"I'm looking for the West Yorkshire Fusilier's barracks."

"You've missed it," said the man.

"Oh God. You mean it's back along there," said

Pascoe, unhappily regarding the one-way street he had just with such pain negotiated.

"Nay, you've missed it by more 'n ten years. Wyfies amalgamated wi' South Yorks Rifles way back. Shifted to their barracks in Sheffield. Call themselves the Yorkshire Fusiliers now. War Office sold this site for development."

"Bugger," said Pascoe.

Ada's wishes were precise if curious. *My ashes should be taken by the executor of my will and scattered around the Headquarters of the West Yorkshire Fusiliers in Kirkton Road, Leeds.*

Knowing her feelings about the army, Pascoe did not doubt that her motive was derisory. She would probably have liked to leave instructions that the urn was to be hurled through a window but knew she would need to moderate her gesture if she hoped to have it carried out. But moderation must surely stop a long way short of being scattered in a car park!

"Museum's still here but," said the man, happy to extend this interruption of his tedious task.

"Where?" said Pascoe hopefully.

"Yon place."

The man pointed to a tall, narrow granite building standing at the far end of the car park, glaring with military scorn at the Scandinavian ski-lodge frivolity of the supermarket.

"Thanks," said Pascoe.

He drove toward the museum and parked before it. Close up the building looked even more as if it had been bulled, boxed, and blanco'd ready for inspection. Pascoe collected the urn from the boot, scuffed his feet on the tarmac to make sure he wasn't tracking any dirt, and went up the steps.

The lintel bore a mahogany board on which was painted a badge consisting of a white rose under a fleur-de-lis, with beneath it WEST YORKSHIRE FUSILIERS –

REGIMENTAL MUSEUM. The paint was fresh and bright, the brass doorknob gleamed like a sergeant major's eye, and even the letter box had a military sharpness which probably terrified any pacifist postmen.

Pascoe turned the knob, checked to be sure he hadn't left fingerprints, and entered.

He found himself in a large high-ceilinged room, lined with display cabinets and hung with tattered flags. It was brightly lit and impeccably clean, but that didn't stop the air from being musty with the smell of old unhappy far-off things and battles long ago.

Pascoe moved swiftly through a series of smaller rooms without finding any survivors. He even tried calling aloud but there was no response.

Sod it! he thought. The absence of witnesses should be making things a lot easier. All he had to do was scatter and scarper! But somehow, even without a witness, the thought of sullying these immaculate surfaces with powdered Ada was hard for an obsessively tidy man. Ashes to ashes, dust to dust . . . but there had to be some old dust for the new dust to go to!

He tried a pinch in the darkest corner he could find but it stood out like a smear of coke on a nun's moustache. Finally he settled on a fireplace. Even this looked to have been untroubled by coal for a hundred years, and the Victorian fire irons which flanked it stood as neat and shiny as weapons in an armory. But it must have known ash in its time. And what after all was this philopolemic building but a mausoleum in need of a body?

His conscience thus quietened, Pascoe unscrewed the top of the urn, took out a handful of dust, examined it for fear, found it, and with an atavistic prayer, threw it into the grate.

"What the hell do you think you're playing at?" demanded an outraged voice.

He turned his head and looked up at a tall gray-haired man wearing an indignant expression, a piratical eye patch, and a hairy tweed jacket with the right sleeve pinned emptily across the breast.

Time, thought Pascoe, for the disarming smile, particularly as the man's present hand was pointing what looked like a flintlock pistol very steadily at his head.

"You may find this a trifle hard to believe," said Pascoe. "But I do hope you are going to try."

VIII

IT WAS CLEAR that Troll Longbottom's forecast was right. These bones were going to be a long time coming.

The drenching dark which had finally made them abandon the hunt the previous night had been replaced by fitful sunlight, but visibility did little to make the job more attractive.

"Could lose a man down there," said Wield, looking into the water-filled crater.

"I can think of a couple we'd not miss," said Dalziel. "Even if we pump it out, the mud's going to be a problem."

"The lads last night reported a lot of big granite slabs," said Wield. "They should give us something to work from. But you're right. We could spend more time digging each other out than old bones."

"Same thing in my case," said Dalziel. "Good God, have you got a twin or what?"

This last was to Troll Longbottom, who was edging his way toward them along the duckboards.

"Just thought I'd check to see if you had anything

more for me yet," he said with a smile which wouldn't have looked out of place at a pirate masthead.

"Oh aye?" said Dalziel. "If they'd asked you to take a look at Julius sodding Caesar, you'd have told 'em to wait till they invented the video camera. So how come twice in twelve hours I've found you up to your fetlocks in clart, breathing fresh air?"

"Friendship, Andy. Friendship."

"Well, thanks a lot, Troll. I didn't realize you cared."

"Not for you," said the pathologist with a grimace not so different from his smile. "For David Batty."

"What's that mean? You shagging his missus or something?"

"Or something, Andy. So, anything more for me to look at?"

"Give us a chance! And did you not get plenty last night? Thought all you needed for a life history was a fingernail and a pinch of belly button fluff."

"You flatter me," said Longbottom. "But I do need just a little more in order to confirm my preliminary dating."

"You've got a dating? Why'd you not say so? Come on, let's hear it."

"I should say from what I've seen so far that the remains were certainly more than five years old."

"More than five?" echoed Dalziel in disgust. "Is that the best you can manage? I've got lads just out of training could have come up with that!"

"Well, it *was* mainly monosyllabic, wasn't it? What I really need is a jawbone. You can tell a lot from dental work. And a bit of flesh would be a real godsend."

He spoke with such enthusiasm that Dalziel laughed.

"Tell you what, Troll," he said. "If I were you, I'd turn vegetarian."

"And I you," said the pathologist elliptically, prodding the Fat Man's gut. "Now I must be off. Some of us have work to do."

"I'll be in touch," bellowed Dalziel after him, then turning to Wield he asked, "So, what do you think?"

"Bit of mutual back-scratching?" suggested Wield. "This Batty's not just research director, he's the son and heir of Thomas Batty who owns the whole company. Useful contact for Mr. Longbottom."

"Don't use a lot of drugs when your specialty's dead 'uns," objected Dalziel.

"I think you'll find Mr. Longbottom's an influential man on his NHS Trust's governing body, sir. Also I hear he's got a twenty percent share in that new private hospital on the Scarborough Road."

"By God, Wieldy, I thought mebbe life out among the turnip tops were turning you soft, but now I see it's turning you cynical!"

"I just state the facts, sir," said Wield. "And here's another. ALBA, as Mr. Longbottom likely knows, have been here just four years."

"Meaning Troll's saying the bones are at least five years old just to stress that Batty and his staff can't be in the frame? You don't reckon he's fixed the figures as a favor, do you?"

"No, sir. I'd mebbe not care to do business with him, but when it comes to his job, as we've all found out, he doesn't give an inch. You've known him longer than anyone, but, so you must know that."

"I'm afraid so, Wieldy," sighed Dalziel. "Pity though. If I thought he'd stretched it to five for Batty, I'd have made bloody sure he stretched it to fifty for me. Still, it's early days. Mebbe it'll still turn out to be archaeology. I'm off to have another word with Batty, tell him the good news."

"I bet you'll find Mr. Longbottom's told him already," said Wield.

"Very like, but one thing you're forgetting, Wieldy."

"Yes, sir?"

"The wanker keeps a nice drop of malt. See about getting this water shifted, will you?"

"My pleasure," said Sergeant Wield.

This morning there was a receptionist on duty in the hessian-hung hall. She informed Dalziel that the director was in the labs but would no doubt make himself available as soon as was convenient. Meanwhile if the superintendent cared to take a seat . . .

Ex-constable Howard was hovering behind her. He'd changed his burnt trousers but looked pretty bleary-eyed.

"Working you hard, aren't they?" said Dalziel sympathetically.

"Bit short-staffed, sir. Also Dr. Batty wanted extra men on duty."

"Someone should tell him about stable doors. Someone like me. Take me to the labs, lad."

Without hesitation, Howard opened one of the doors and led the way through, pursued by the receptionist's indignant twitter.

To Dalziel's inexpert eye, the lab he entered looked like a cross between a small menagerie and a high-class bog. Batty's features crinkled in a frown when he saw Dalziel but cleared almost immediately. He'd learned quickly—probably coached by Longbottom—that you didn't trade blows with the Fat Man, not unless you'd got a horseshoe up your boxing glove. Last night he'd poured the Scotch with a generous hand and they'd parted on excellent terms, which didn't prevent either from heartily despising the other.

"Andy," he said. "Good morning. Any news?"

Nowt the Troll won't have told you already, thought Dalziel. And nowt that a drop of the Caledonian cream wouldn't improve.

"Just thought I'd let you know we'll be working out

there most of the day I'm afraid. Good news is them bones were likely here when your company took the place over, so I shouldn't have to bother your staff."

"Excellent. We're very busy at the moment so could ill afford an interruption. And, Andy, I must compliment you on the way you've handled the media. Hardly a mention this morning. Our PR department are very impressed. Many thanks both personally and on behalf of ALBA."

Dalziel smiled with false modesty. False, not because he hadn't called in a lot of favors and up a lot of threats to minimize response to all the phone calls Marvell had made as soon as she got home, but because he permitted this twat to go on thinking it had anything to do with him or his sodding company.

"When we've got a closer dating we'll need to look back at the history of the house," he said.

"Anything we can do to help, you've just got to ask," said Batty. "As I explained last night, all the records will be stored at Kirkton of course."

Kirkton, an industrial suburb of Leeds, was ALBA's home base. Here the company had begun and grown, developing into a large rambling complex which Batty (once the truce had been struck the previous night) had described as a security nightmare. "As I explained to your chap who came out when we had that first lot of bother in the summer, Pascoe his name was I think, seemed a very decent kind of fellow . . ." (His faintly surprised tone had not passed unremarked.) ". . . The reason we decided to move our research labs was because they were far too vulnerable at HQ. Chap from some animal mag just strolled right in and started taking pictures. Bloody cheek! So we decided to move out here, lock, stock, and barrel. It had been used as a hospital or clinic or something for years, so that was a step in the right direction and it meant we could give the impression that all the refurbishment and extension work had something to do with resuming its old function."

"Oh aye," Dalziel had interrupted. "With no one knowing what was going off but a few lawyers, and all the contractors, and your own staff members and every bugger living in a radius of ten miles, I can see how you might've hoped to keep it quiet."

"Put like that it does sound a touch optimistic," laughed Batty. "But we left a token presence in the Kirkton labs to fool the activists' spies, and for nearly four years it seemed to work. Must have lulled us, I suppose. Then bang! Suddenly last summer the loonies got in and really made a mess of things. That's when I realized that being remote and isolated was an advantage only till they winkled you out. Moving again clearly wasn't a solution. So we got a new security company in and gave them the brief to make us secure. The results you have seen."

He had spoken complacently. Dalziel had kept his own thoughts about those results to himself. No point in rowing with a fellow who had a half-full bottle of Glenmorangie at his elbow.

It had been empty by the time he left, but he'd noticed an unopened one in the cabinet Batty had taken his glass from. The memory rose before him now like a vision of the Holy Grail. He coughed, he hoped thirstily, and said, "Now you've had a chance to clear up, did that lot last night do much damage when they ran loose inside?"

"Not a lot and mainly superficial," said Batty. "But it's good of you to be concerned."

All this gratitude undiluted by a dram was beginning to grate a bit. Wield had entered the lab. He caught Dalziel's eye and gave a minute shake of his head to indicate he wanted a word but it wasn't desperate.

Dalziel said, "What I'm really concerned about is

making sure these aren't the same lot who were running riot in the summer."

"Oh, that's all behind us now," said Batty dismissively. "We learnt our lesson. Let's stick with the present, shall we?"

"Might be behind you," said Dalziel magisterially. "Not behind the family of that poor sod who got himself killed up at Redcar. FraserGreenleaf. Same line of business as you only a lot bigger. I'd have thought you'd have heard of them."

For a second Batty allowed himself to look irritated, then his face assumed a solemn air and he said, "Of course. I wasn't thinking. But do you really believe there might be a connection with these people?"

"Can't ignore the possibility, sir."

"Of course not. Good lord. Women. What's the world coming to?"

"We're a long way from proving a connection," said Dalziel. "What about you? Made up your mind about prosecuting yet?"

Batty smiled and shrugged.

"Like I said, not up to me. Head office decision. I know what I'd do, but I'm just a poor scientist."

Who also, if Wield was right, happened to be a member of ALBA's ruling family. Which probably meant they weren't going to prosecute, but Batty wanted to distance himself from a decision he'd opposed.

Sharp bugger this, thought Dalziel. But not sharp enough to see there was a man dying of thirst in front of him!

Wield meanwhile was taking a tour round the lab, looking at the caged animals with a distaste not even his rugose features could disguise.

He watched as a radiantly beautiful young woman in a radiantly white lab coat picked up a tiny monkey which threw its arms round her neck in a baby-like need for reassurance. Expertly she disengaged it, turned it over, and plunged a hypodermic into the base of its spine.

"Ouch," said Wield. "Doesn't that hurt?"

"Done properly, the animal hardly feels it," she reassured him.

He glanced at her security badge, which told him he was speaking to Jane Ambler. Research Assistant.

"No, Jane," he said amiably, "it was you I meant."

She regarded him dispassionately and said, "Oh dear. Perhaps before you come on so judgmental, you should talk to someone with rheumatoid arthritis."

"Okay," said Wield.

He stooped to the cage, pushed his finger through the mesh, and made soothing guttural noises to the tiny beast. Then he straightened up.

"He's against it," he said.

He found he was talking to Dalziel.

"When you're done feeding the animals, Sergeant, mebbe we can have a word."

The Fat Man led the way through the reception area where the receptionist was still sulking. He gave her a big smile and nodded at Howard, who'd snapped to attention.

Outside Wield said, "That TecSec man, don't I know him?"

Dalziel, used to being upstaged by his sergeant's encylopedic knowledge of the dustiest corners of Mid-Yorkshire, was not displeased to be able to reply negligently, "Oh aye. But not the way you're thinking. He were one of ours, uniformed out at Dartleby till he took early retirement and got himself privatized. Thinking of following suit, lad?"

"Not more than once a day, sir. Howard. Oh yes. Jimmy Howard. Didn't so much take retirement as had it force-fed, if I remember right."

Dalziel, who took too much pride in Wield's internet

mind to be a bad loser said, "You usually do. So fill me in."

"There was talk he was on the take, but before it got anywhere, he were picked up driving over the limit. Got himself a soft quack who gave him a note saying job stress, and no one stood in his way when he went for medical retirement with pension afore the case came up and he got kicked out without."

"And the other? Being on the take?"

"Well, nowt was proved. But he's a hard-betting man and those who saw him at the races reckoned he couldn't be losing that much on a constable's take-home. Makes you wonder, don't it?"

"Wonder what, Wieldy?"

"Did TecSec not know about him? Or did they know and take him on *despite*? Or did they know and take him on *because*?"

Dalziel shook his head admiringly.

"That's a really nasty mind you've got there, Wieldy. Any reason other than natural prejudice?"

"It was you who said private security companies are guilty till proven innocent, sir," said Wield reproachfully. "I've not seen much of this lot, but there's something about them doesn't sit right."

Dalziel regarded him thoughtfully. A Wield uneasiness was not something to be dismissed lightly.

"All right," he said. "Take a closer look. Let on it's these animal libbers we're interested in, how they acted when they got into the building last night. Which we are."

"Right, sir. But it doesn't sound to me like ALBA will be prosecuting."

"Big ears you've got. Listen, lad. No one tells me when to stop looking. And I'll keep this ANIMA bunch in view till I'm completely satisfied there's no link with Redcar."

"You don't really think there could be a connection,

sir?" said Wield dubiously. "I mean, from what's known about this lot, they're at the soft end of the movement."

"First rule of this job is, take nowt on trust," said the Fat Man sternly. "Keep your eye on the ball and you'll not buy any dummies."

This struck Wield as a bit rich when he recalled from Dalziel's complaint last night at not having being warned of the gender of the protesters that the main thing he seemed to have kept his eye on, and which he mentioned at least three times in the sergeant's mitigation, was Amanda Marvell's knockers.

He said, "I'll make a note of that," not bothering to muffle the sarcasm.

Dalziel snorted in exasperation and said, "All right, so what's going off? Toad-licking season started early in Brigadoon, has it?"

This was Dalziel's name for Enscombe.

"Sorry, sir?"

"Jokes last night, and back there you were coming over like the press agent for disadvantaged chimps. So what's it all mean?"

"I don't much like what they're doing there," admitted Wield. "Sorry. I know I should keep my neb out."

"Bloody right you should. Public needs protecting from a neb like yours. Any road, what was it you came in to tell me? You realize I've come out of there as thirsty as I went in, so it had better be important."

"Not really, sir. Control came through on the radio. Said that woman in charge of the ANIMA lot, what's her name, Marbles . . . ? Movables . . . ?"

Wield forgetting a name was as likely as the Godfather forgetting a grudge, but Dalziel found himself saying "Marvell" before he could stop himself.

"That's right. Seems she called in at the station, wanted to see you to make a statement. Could be you're right, sir, and she's come to confess."

"Oh aye? Well, she had her chance to confess last night," said Dalziel. "Let her wait. She can sit around till she gets piles."

"Oh, she's not sitting around, sir. When she found you weren't there, she took off. Said for you to call at her flat, it 'ud be more comfortable there anyway. Says not to worry about turning up at lunchtime as she can easily rustle up a snack. You want the address, sir?"

All this was said absolutely deadpan, and pans didn't come any deader than Wield's. But Dalziel was not fooled.

"No, I don't want the bloody address," he snarled. "And just because you look like the Man in the Iron Mask, don't imagine I can't see you're smirking!"

He strode away. And Wield, his smirk now externalized, watched him go, thinking, And just because you look like a rhino in retreat, don't imagine I can't see you're horny!

IX

IN A LONG NARROW OFFICE as chaotic as the museum was neat, Pascoe drank strong tea with Major Hilary Studholme.

The major had listened to Pascoe's story with an attention as undiverted as his pistol. With a mental moue of apology in the direction of Ada, Pascoe had felt it better in the circumstances not to explicate her probable motives, and though stopping well short of any direct assertion of regimental pride, it was as nothing to the distance he stayed from even a hint of paranoiac loathing.

The production of his police ID finally convinced the

major he was neither a dangerous lunatic nor a bomb-planting terrorist.

As Pascoe sipped his tea, the major riffled through a couple of leather-bound volumes with a dexterity remarkable in a man with only a left hand.

"Odd," he said. "Pascoe rings a definite bell, but there's no record of an NCO of that name buying it at Ypres in 1917. Could have lost his stripe, of course. There's a Private Stephen Pascoe got wounded . . . could that be a connection, do you think?"

"I doubt it," said Pascoe. "Point is, it won't be Pascoe, will it?"

The single eye regarded him blankly, then the upper lip spasmed in a silly-ass grimace which laid the hairs of his moustache horizontal and he said, "Sorry. Mind seeping out through my eye socket. Of course, Pascoe would be your grandmother's married name. So, what was her maiden name?"

Pascoe thought then said, "Clark, I think."

Studholme grimaced. "Got a hatful of Clarks in here," he said, patting the leather-bound books. "With an *E* or without? Got an initial?"

"Sorry," said Pascoe. "All I know about him is there's a photo with him showing off a lance corporal's stripe with the date 1914, then a scrawl, presumably my great-grandmother's, saying *Killed Wipers 1917.* That puzzles me a bit. I thought the big battle at Ypres was earlier in the war."

"Oh yes? If that's the limit of an educated man's knowledge, Mr. Pascoe, just imagine the ignorance of most of your fellow cits!"

Pascoe found himself ready to bridle. Studholme with his bristly moustache, clipped accent, and sturdy tweeds looked a prototypical member of the British officer class, which liberal tradition characterized as snobbish, philistine, and intellectually challenged, not at all the kind of person a young(ish) *Guardian*-reading graduate, who could get Radio 3 and sometimes did, ought to let himself be lectured by.

On the other hand, as a public servant in a police force threatened with radical restructuring, it would be impolitic as well as impolite to get up the nose of a war hero.

"I know what most educated people know about the Great War, Major," he said carefully. "That even by strict military standards, it was an exercise in futility unprecedented and unsurpassed."

Shit, that had come out a bit stronger than intended.

"Bravo," said Studholme surprisingly. "That's a start. Let me fill in a bit of detail. The first battle of Ypres took place in October and November 1914. British losses about fifty thousand, including the greater part of the prewar regular army. First Ypres marked the end of anything that could be called open warfare. During the winter both sides concentrated on fortifying their defenses and after that it was trench warfare from the North Sea to the Swiss border till 1918."

"So why was Ypres so important?"

"It was the center of a salient, a considerable bulge in the line. A breakthrough there would have enabled the Allies to roll up the Boche in both directions. Disadvantage of course was that a salient means the enemy can lob shells at you from three sides. Service in the Salient was not something our lads looked forward to even before Passchendaele. My father managed to be in both Ypres Two and Ypres Three. He used to say there was always a special feel about the Salient even at relatively quiet times. Its landscape was more depressing, the stink of its mud more nauseating, its skies more lowering. You felt as you left Ypres by the Menin Gate that it should have borne a sign reading All Hope Abandon Ye Who Enter Here."

"Sounds like the entrance to CID on a Monday morning," said Pascoe with a forced lightness.

"No, I don't think so," said Studholme, regarding him gravely. "My father said that service there changed human nature. You reverted to a kind of subhumanity, the missing link between the apes and Homo sapiens. He called it Homo Saliens, Salient Man. I don't think he was joking."

Pascoe drank his tea. He felt the need for warmth. It was very quiet in here. The supermarket car park seemed a thousand miles away.

He said, "So what happened at Ypres Two?"

"Spring of '15. Jerry made a determined effort to get things straight. Used chlorine gas for the first time. Gained a bit of ground but the Salient remained. Our casualties about sixty thousand including one general, Horace Smith-Dorrien."

"That must have really got them worried back home," said Pascoe, drifting despite himself toward a sneer. "I mean, what's a few thousand men here or there, but a dead general . . ."

"Not dead," said Studholme. "Stellenbosched. That is, sacked. Terrible offense. Competence."

"Sorry?" said Pascoe, thinking he'd misheard.

"He was actually in the thick of things and made judgments based on realities. Also he was foolish enough to suggest to French, the C-in-C, that they were losing too many men in pointless frontal attacks. There aren't many other recorded expressions of doubt by top brass, I tell you."

"No wonder, if you got sacked for it."

"Indeed. Now, jump forward two years to 1917. Third Ypres, your great-grandfather's battle. You probably know it as Passchendaele."

"Good God, yes. The mud."

"That's right. Everyone remembers the mud. One of man's worse nightmares, a slow drowning in glutinous filth. Practically a metaphor for the whole conduct of the war."

Pascoe was now regarding Studholme with wide-eyed interest.

"You don't sound like a member of Douglas Haig's fan club, Major."

Studholme gave a snort like a rifle shot.

He said, "When they finally got rid of Sir John French at the end of '15, it was as if his main fault was not killing off his own men quickly enough. So what they looked for was a general who'd get the job done quicker. French had slain his ten thousands, but Haig was soon slaying his hundred thousands, nearly half a million on the Somme and now another quarter million at Passchendaele. Of course Third Wipers went down as a victory. They gained six or seven miles of mud. Imagine a column of men, twenty-five abreast, stretching out over those six or seven miles, and you're looking at the British dead. Bit different from Agincourt, eh?"

"Tell me, Major," said Pascoe curiously. "Feeling like this, how come you took the job of looking after a military museum. In fact, how come you got started on a military career at all?"

For a moment he thought he'd gone too far. The major was regarding him once more with the flintlock gleam in his eye. Then he sipped his tea, brushed his moustache, smiled faintly, and said, "How come a bright young fellow like you went into the police? Was it the bribes or the chance to beat up suspects that attracted you?"

"Touché," said Pascoe. "And apologies for my youthful impudence."

"Accepted. Now I'll answer you. I joined the army 'cos way back about the time of Waterloo, someone decided that the only way to make anything out of my line of Studholmes was to get 'em into uniform and send 'em out for foreigners to shoot at. No one's come up with a viable alternative since, so on we go, genera-

tion after generation, providing moving targets. Rarely
get beyond my rank, though my father made colonel.
Shot from being a subaltern in '15 to major, acting
lieutenant colonel in '18. That was one plus for that
show—lots of scope for accelerated promotion. If you
survived."

"Nice to know someone did," said Pascoe.

"Oh yes, he had a talent for it. Lived to be ninety.
Still working on his memoirs, when he died. I told him
he'd left it a bit late, but he said no point in starting till
you were pretty sure you were past doing anything
worth remembering."

"Sounds as if they'd make interesting reading," said
Pascoe. "Talking of which, is there anything you'd rec-
ommend to start remedying my immense ignorance
about the Great War?"

The major looked at him with one-eyed keenness to
see if he was taking the piss. Then selecting a volume
from the bookshelf behind him, he said, "This is about
as good a general introduction as you'll get. After that,
if you develop a taste for horror, you can specialize."

"Thank you," said Pascoe, taking the book. "I'll return it, of course."

"Damn right you will," said the major. "Chaps who
borrow your kit and don't return it always come to a
sticky end. Now let's see if we can't find somewhere a
bit more suitable for your gran than a fireplace, shall
we?"

He rose abruptly. As Pascoe followed him out of the
office, he said, "You run a very tidy museum, sir."

"What? Oh, thank you. Or do I detect an irony?
Perhaps you find tidiness incompatible with a place
dedicated to the glorification of war?"

"All I meant was . . ."

"Don't lie out of politeness, please. Policeman
should always speak the truth. So should museums.
That's what I hope this one does. If it glorifies anything

it is courage and service. But when the truth is that men were sacrificed needlessly, even wantonly, in the kind of battle your great-grandfather died in, a place like this mustn't flinch from saying so. We owe it to the men who died. We owe it to ourselves as professional soldiers too."

They had entered a room at the back of the house, formerly the kitchen but now given over to an exhibition of catering equipment. Studholme pointed through the window into a small paved yard with a single circular flower bed at its center. It contained three brutally pruned rosebushes.

"Looks better in the summer," he said. "White roses surrounded by lilies. The regimental badge. Used to be an old joke. You always get a good cup of tea from the Wyfies, they even advertise in their badge. Roses, fleur-de-lis; Rosy Lee, you follow? Not a very good joke. Also new recruits are called lilies; passing out, you get your rose. Sorry. Regimental folklore. Set me off, I go on forever. What started this?"

"My grandmother's ashes," prompted Pascoe.

"Indeed. The rose bed. Good scattering of bonemeal wouldn't go amiss there. Or . . ." He hesitated then went on. "Just say if you think it a touch crass but down in the cellar . . . well, let me show you."

He opened a door onto a steep flight of stone steps.

"Cold, damp, and miserable down there," said Studholme. "Couldn't think what to do with it. Cost a fortune to cheer it up. Then I thought, why bother? Go with the flow, isn't that what they say? Not original, of course. Imperial War Museum does something similar, but I reckon for atmosphere, we've got the edge."

"I'm sorry . . . ?" said Pascoe.

"My fault. Rattling on again. Bad habit. Here, take a look."

He pressed a switch on the wall. Below lights came on, not bright modern electric lights, but the kind of dull yellow flicker that might emanate from old oil lamps. And sound too, a dull basso continuo of distant artillery overlaid from time to time by the soprano shriek of passing shells or the snare drum stutter of machine-gun fire.

"Go down," urged Studholme.

Pascoe descended, and with each step felt his stomach clench as his old claustrophobia began to take its paralyzing grip.

At the foot of the steps he had to duck under a rough curtain of hempen sacking and when he straightened up, he found he was standing in a First World War dugout.

There were figures here, old shopwindow dummies, he guessed, now clad in khaki, but their smooth white faces weren't at all ludicrous. They were death masks, equally terrifying whether belonging to the corporal crouched over a field telephone on a makeshift table or the officer sprawled on a canvas camp bed with an open book neglected on his breast.

In the darkest corner, face turned to the wall, lay another figure with one leg completely swathed in a bloodstained bandage. Close by his foot two large rats, eyes glinting in the yellow light, seemed about to pounce.

"Jesus!" exclaimed Pascoe, uncertain in that second if they were real or stuffed.

"Convincing, ain't they?" said Studholme with modest pride. "Could have had the real thing down here with very little effort, but didn't want the local health snoops down on me. Everything you see is authentic. Kit, weapons, uniforms. All saw service on the Western Front."

"Even this?" said Pascoe, indicating the sleeping officer's book.

"Oh yes. My father's. Not a great reader, but he told

me that at that time in that place, it was a lifeline to home."

Pascoe picked up the book.

"Good God," he said.

It was a copy of the original Kelmscott Press edition of William Morris's *The Wood Beyond the World*.

"What?" said Studholme.

"This book, it's worth, I don't know, thousands maybe. You really shouldn't leave it lying around down here."

"Spoken like a policeman," said Studholme. "Didn't realize it was valuable to anyone except me. Still, kind of johnny who comes down here isn't likely to be a sneak thief, eh?"

"Spoken like a soldier," said Pascoe, opening the book and reading the inscription *To Hillie with love from Mummy, Christmas 1903*. It was clearly a well-thumbed and well-traveled volume. Lifeline to home, Christmas, mother, childhood . . .

"Take your time," said Studholme. "Bit more dust round here won't be noticed, richer dust concealed, eh? But if you feel it's too macabre, there's always the rosebush. I'll leave you to have a think."

He turned and vanished up the steps. Carefully Pascoe replaced the book on the dummy's chest, taking care not to touch the pale plastic hand.

"So, Gran, what's it to be?" he said to the urn, which he'd placed by the telephone. "Up there with the flowers or down here with the roots?"

He'd already made up his mind, but some pathetically macho pride prevented him from going in immediate pursuit of the major. Next moment he wished he had as one of the passing shells on the sound tape failed to pass, its scream climaxing to huge explosion with a power of suggestion so strong that the whole cellar seemed to shake and, simultaneously, the lights went out.

Coincidence, or part of Studholme's special effects? wondered Pascoe, desperately trying to stem the panic rising in his gut.

The telephone rang, a single long rasping burr.

His hand shot out to grab it, hit something, then found the receiver.

"Hello!" came a voice, tinny and distant. "Who's that?"

"This is Pascoe."

"Pascoe? What the hell are you doing there?"

"Is that you, Studholme?" he demanded.

"Don't be an ass, man. This is Lieutenant . . ."

And a voice behind him at the same time said, "Someone wanting me? Damn these lamps!"

For a moment it seemed to his disorientated and panicking mind that the voice came from the camp bed. Then a torch beam shone in his eyes and the major went on, "Sorry about this. Often happens when one of those supermarket juggernauts goes up the service road behind us. Sometimes feels like the whole damn place is coming down. Lights should be back on in a tick . . . ah, there we are."

The pseudo oil lamps flickered back on. Pascoe blinked, then looked at the dummy on the bed. It lay there with the book where he'd replaced it.

Studholme said mildly, "Ringing for help?"

"What?" He realized he was still holding the telephone. "I thought it rang . . ."

"Does sometimes," said the major. "Little battery-operated random ringing device I knocked up. Helps with the atmosphere. Makes people jump, I tell you. Oh dear. Your decision or has your grandmother chosen for herself?"

Pascoe followed his gaze and saw that when he'd grabbed for the phone he must have knocked the urn off the table. It had cracked open when it hit the floor and a spoor of ash marked where it had rolled a few inches.

Pascoe replaced the telephone.

"Can't argue with fate," he said, trying to establish control.

He picked up the urn and scattered the ashes into the corners of the dugout where, as Studholme had forecast, they blended in imperceptibly.

He felt he ought to say something. But what? It would come out flip, or pseudo-religious, which was worse. In the end he contented himself with thinking, There you go, Ada. This world was a bit of a disappointment to you. I hope the next comes up to scratch.

It was a relief to get back to the ground floor.

Studholme said, "Got a number? I'll check through our records, see if I can get any details on your great-grandfather's time in the regiment if you like. Or would you rather put all that behind you?"

"No, I'd be interested," said Pascoe, producing a card. "And thanks for being so helpful."

"My pleasure. Goodbye, Mr. Pascoe."

He held out his left hand. There was a moment's awkwardness as Pascoe instinctively reached for it with his right. To cover it he said, "By they way, that pistol. It wasn't really loaded, was it?"

Studholme said, "One thing my father taught me was, never point a loaded weapon at anyone you're not willing to shoot."

It wasn't till Pascoe was driving away that it dawned on him that he still didn't know if his question had been answered or not.

X

NINETEEN EIGHTY-TWO was a key year for the Tory Party both nationally and in Mid-Yorkshire.

At its start, Margaret Thatcher's grasp of the premiership seemed rather less secure than Richard Nixon's of the principles of democracy, while Amanda Pitt-Evenlode, née Marvell, seemed set to be vice-president (Functions) of the Mid-Yorks Conservative Association for at least the next forty years.

Then came the Falklands War. Never (or at least not since Troy) in the field of human daftness had so many gone so far to sacrifice so much for the sake of one silly woman.

Its effect on the fortunes of the UK government is a matter of public record.

Its effect on the life of Amanda Pitt-Evenlode is less widely known.

What it came down to was this: On June 12, 1982, she was radicalized.

Curiously it was not the news that her only son, Second Lieutenant Piers Pitt-Evenlode of the Yorkshire Fusiliers, was missing in action, believed dead, that did that trick. That came on June 7 and left her prostrate with shock and unable to register, let alone reject, the canonical comforts of her parish priest, the patriotic platitudes of her committee colleagues, or the phylogenic fortitude of her spouse, the Hon. Rupert Pitt-Evenlode, JP.

No, it was the news that Piers had been discovered alive and, apart from a few inconsequential bullet holes, well, that pricked her into life. While all around the air was full of joyful congratulation, and talk of a possible gong, and plans for the welcome home party, all she could think of was her recent certainty that this war—any war—was a crime against humanity, and its attendant conclusion that those responsible for it, or supportive of it, or even indifferent to it, must therefore be war criminals.

She tried to pretend that such a certainty should crumble in face of her son's survival, but found she couldn't keep it up.

Other women's sons had fallen without being raised from the grave. How then could she be so arrogant as to assert the health of her own boy as the sole yardstick?

She tried to talk about her feelings with those she felt closest to, and found herself once again prayed over and patronized, and finally pushed toward a very fashionable psychiatrist who'd done wonders for Binky Bullmain's nervous flatulence.

Piers himself, far from being the hoped-for confidant, took to the role of bemedaled hero like a blowfly to dead meat and clearly regarded any hint of her new anxieties as a personal slur.

But still she looked for ways to adapt her newfound self to her family, her social circle, and her political party, and still she found herself rejected like a new heart in an old body.

So she resigned from all of them.

The old Amanda Pitt-Evenlode felt a slight pang that the sighs which marked her passing contained as much relief as sorrow.

The new Mandy Marvell didn't give a toss.

She had married at seventeen, borne Piers at eighteen, and spent the next two decades performing all the duties proper to a woman of her husband's status in society. This meant that while tennis, golf, and swimming kept her body in pretty good shape, her mind had fewer demands made upon it than would have stretched the ratiocinative powers of a footballer's parrot.

Now she found that one thought led to another in a most delightful way. Happily her father had died before succeeding in his avowed intent of dissipating all the wealth *his* father had so assiduously accrued, leaving Mandy with a sufficient private income to be able to live comfortably while at the same time paying the divorce settlement from Pitt-Evenlode straight into the coffers of various excellent charities. Her time and energy she gave generously too, but she did not miss any chance of proving all the pleasures which the hills and valleys, dales and fields, of her quiet country existence had failed to yield. She popped and snorted, drank and smoked; she read, wrote, painted, and performed; she traveled widely and tried most alternatives from the religious to the medicinal.

For ten years she overwhelmed herself in experience and at this crowded decade's end she found that all she retained any real enthusiasm for was Mexican beer, the songs of Gustav Mahler, and straight sex. She even found she'd gone off the poor a bit, not in particular, but as an insoluble symptom of humanity's shittiness. Fifty was approaching fast. She wanted to do something she could see getting done. But what?

It had occurred to her from time to time as interesting though hardly significant that her strongest memories of life with the Hon. Rupert involved animals rather than people. They had started even, but as the humans faded, the beasts came into ever clearer focus. Now ten years on, with the Hon. reduced to little more than a long nose under a silly hat, she could still recall the exact disposition of the dark spots on a pair of Dalmatians called Aggers and Staggers she'd been given on her twentieth birthday. An upwardly mobile farm cat trying to ingratiate itself into smoked salmon circles with gifts of moles and shrews was clearer to her than the infant Piers; and while she couldn't have sworn to the Hon's private parts in a lineup, the splendid equipment of Balzac, the estate's prize Charolais, was as detailed in her mind as if etched there by Stubbs.

She explained this to her current lover, an American evangelist, on their last night together before he bore his burden of souls and shekels home.

"This is your heart bleeping you, Cap. Pick up that phone and get in touch with base."

His phraseology made her wince, but against that she set the pleasure she derived from his habit of crying HALLEYLUJAH! at the moment of climax. And when he had gone she spoke to her heart.

Animals, her heart answered, were the unacknowledged legislators of mankind. They showed fortitude in adversity and temperance in prosperity. They had no need of prisons, nor did they prey on their own kind. Therefore the way humans treated them was the touchstone of their humanity.

To conclude was to act. Six months later her vigorous sampling of local loose coalitions of hunt saboteurs, cetaphiles, donkey sanctuarians, et cetera, had drawn to her several similarly minded women who agreed to form a more tightly knitted group which came to be known as ANIMA. That it was all female was not a conscious choice but a dynamic inevitability. Men fear more than they admire a powerful woman, and for her to rule over them she must normally usurp the masculine leadership of an already existing group. If instead she forms a new one, she will rarely attract male recruits till she is so successful, she doesn't want them.

The day after the abortive raid on Wanwood House, Cap Marvell laid the table in the kitchen of her flat for two.

It was simple fare: a large pie, a bowl of crisps, a green salad, a wedge of cheese, a jar of onions, and a couple of baguettes. By one place setting she put a tankard and three cans of draft bitter, by the other a tumbler and a bottle of Mexican beer.

At one o'clock precisely the doorbell rang.

Smiling, she drew open the door.

The smile faded as she saw Wendy Walker standing in the corridor.

"Wendy," she said. "What do you want?"

"I'm not selling bloody brushes, that's for sure," snapped the other.

"I'm sorry," said Cap. "I didn't mean to be rude, only I'm expecting someone for lunch . . ."

"And I'll be in the way? Well, that shouldn't bother you, Cap. You lot get trained to roll over folk who get in your way, don't you?"

Cap gritted her teeth. Why was it that every time Wendy treated her like she was still the Hon. Mrs. Rupert she found herself wanting to act like she was still the Hon. Mrs. Rupert?

She said, "Wendy, please, unless it's a matter of life or death, I wonder if—"

"Life or death!" Wendy interrupted her. "Why'd that bother you? 'Less it was some sodding animal's life or death, and even then I daresay you've slaughtered more birds and beasts than you've ever bloody well saved!"

"What is it you want to talk about, Wendy?" said Cap, dangerously calm.

"Last night, what the fuck do you think? The price of tea? You're our group leader, aren't you? Right, I want to talk to my leader about what happened on the raid last night."

"Look, I can see how it must have upset you, finding that body . . ."

"That's not what's upsetting me, no, it's not a few old bones that's upsetting me . . . look, you gonna let me in or not?"

Cap leaned forward and sniffed.

"You've been drinking," she said.

"Well, pardon me for breathing," said Wendy. "Pardon me for eating and drinking and sleeping and waking and pissing and crapping and doing all the other things that real human beings do. Yes, I've been drinking, not much, just enough for me to get the crazy idea it might be worthwhile coming round here to sort things out. . . ."

"Very impressive," said Cap. "But it will have to keep till you're a little more sober and I'm a little less busy. I'll see you later, Wendy."

"Later? Yeah sure, only it might be a bit too fucking late for you, Cap, a bit too fucking late!"

Cap Marvell stepped back and closed the door. Wendy Walker turned away and headed for the lift, but before she could reach it, Andy Dalziel, who'd been standing in it, listening, for the last few minutes, withdrew the foot which was holding the doors open, and pressed the button for the next floor up.

"Shit," said Wendy, and headed for the stairs.

Five minutes later the flat bell rang again.

Cap checked through the peephole this time to be sure, then opened the door, smiling widely.

"Hello there," she said. "No need to apologize for being late. It's permissible on a first date."

"Oh aye?" said Dalziel. "Told me down the station you wanted to make a statement. Didn't say owt about dates."

"I believe I did mention lunch. But whether you've come with that in mind or your timing is merely a happy coincidence matters little. You're here. There is food. Please take a seat."

"What if I'm not hungry?"

"You don't look to me, Mr. Dalziel, like a man in whom appetite has much to do with hunger. Do sit down."

Dalziel considered this. The woman were rig... he did sit and eat.

She watched in silence, admiring the simple almost poetic efficiency of his technique.

There was no impression of gluttony, no overfilling of or overspilling from the mouth which would indeed have been difficult given the cetacean dimension of that maw, just a simple procession of food through the marble portals of his teeth, a short, rhythmic manducation, and a quick swallow which hardly registered on the massy column of his esophagus.

The pie vanished save for the small wedge she had taken.

He said, "You going to eat or just watch?"

She began to nibble at the pastry crust, still observing with awe as he split one of the baguettes in half, expertly lined it with cheese, crisps, salad, and pickled onions, replaced the lid, and holding the esculent torpedo in both hands, raised it to his lips.

"Remember that scene in the film of *Tom Jones* where they turn each other on just by eating?" she said. "I never really understood how it worked before."

"Eh?" said Dalziel.

She said, "You'll never get it in."

Dalziel didn't reply. His mother had brought him up not to speak with his mouth full.

When the baguette had vanished like a waking dream, he poured himself the third can of bitter and said, "Right, Mrs. Marvell, what's all this about?"

"Call me Cap," she said.

"Why?"

"It was a nickname my ingenious fellow pupils at my boarding school gave me. Captain Marvell. I tried to live up to it during my adolescence. In fact it was trying to live up to it that lost me it. It seemed a Captain Marvelish thing to do to get married to an Hon at seventeen, but I soon discovered you cannot be called Cap if you're Mrs. Rupert Pitt-Evenlode. In fact with that chain of words to trail around behind you, it's difficult to be anything at all except the Hon. Mrs. et cetera. But back in '82 I got myself rechristened. I was a born-again pagan. . . . But I see I'm boring you. Why should that be? I know. None of this is news to you, is it? You've been checking up on me!"

"Aye," said Dalziel, completing his yawn. "Since they cut back on my taster, I'm careful who I eat with. *Why* didn't mean I wanted the story of your life. It meant, why should I call you anything but Mrs. or Miss or Ms. Marvell?"

"It would be friendly."

"Ah well, I try not to get too friendly wi' folk I might have to bang up."

"I take it your idiom is penal rather than penile, Superintendent? Does this mean ALBA are going to prosecute? Excellent."

"Fancy your day in court, do you? Slap on the wrist? Tuppenny fine? Headlines in the *Guardian* and flash your kneecaps on breakfast TV?"

"That would suit me nicely. But, despite your intimidatory threats, I doubt if it would suit ALBA. Such people are usually more concerned with damping publicity than provoking it."

"Could be you're right about ALBA, missus. But it's not them you should be worried about."

"I'm sorry . . . oh, you mean, you. But what charges could the police bring against me if ALBA won't press for trespass?"

Dalziel smiled like a crocodile being asked if he'd got teeth.

"Going equipped for burglary. Criminal damage. Assault. Obstructing the police."

She considered this then said, "Assault?"

"You threatened the TecSec boss with them wire cutters."

"Threatened? He must be a man of very nervous disposition. The cutters are a tool not a weapon."

And a very clean tool too. Forensic had found no trace of blood. *Surprisingly clean?* Dalziel had asked hopefully. *That would depend on the mind-cast of their owner,* Dr. Gentry, head of the Forensic Lab, who disliked the Fat Man heartily, had replied.

"Weapon's a tool for killing," said Dalziel. "And you could have taken his head off if you'd made contact. Courts don't like that sort of thing, especially not since Redcar."

At least she didn't pretend not to take the allusion.

"That was terrible, and a great disservice to the movement. It wasn't even good protest. Simply turning the poor animals loose achieves very little in terms of their well-being and nothing at all in terms of public support."

"You mean it's the tactics you object to, not killing the odd security guard?" said Dalziel.

"Of course I deplore the man's death," she said with some irritation. "It was tragic. But I cannot believe you seriously suspect my group had anything to do with it."

"Why not?" said Dalziel. "By all accounts once you got inside the building last night, you all ran wild like a bunch of lagered-up Leeds supporters. What was that all about? Premenstrual tension?"

She was unprovoked. Very cool this one. But beneath it all there was plenty of heat. The notion had him crossing his legs.

"A release of tension, certainly," she said. "We'd had a shock. Then suddenly I realized that we'd got where we wanted to be, inside the building. It seemed foolish not to make a gesture."

"A gesture?" He articulated the word as if some passing bird had crapped in his mouth.

"That's right. An act which resounds with significance far beyond its mere physical limitations. You should try one someday, Superintendent."

"At my age it happens all the time," he said. "So you took off. And headed straight for the labs. Just a bit of luck that, was it?"

"What else could it be?"

"Prior knowledge. Like, from being there before."

"Being there when?"

"In the summer, maybe, when there was a break-in at Wanwood."

"Yes, I recall . . . ah, I see your game, Mr. Dalziel. Or may I call you Andy? If I remember right, the raid on Wanwood had many of the characteristics of the raid on Redcar. Lots of mindless vandalism and the animals merely released into the countryside. And you think they could have been done by the same people. Therefore link ANIMA with the second, you link us with the first. Right?"

"Right as a confession," said Dalziel.

"Which it isn't. Do you have dates for both these raids?"

"Can't remember? I get like that," said Dalziel. "June twenty-eighth. May nineteenth."

She rose and went through into the living room, returning with a leather-bound diary.

"Here we are," she said. "On June the twenty-eighth, I had dinner with my son, Piers."

"He'll vouch for you, will he? What's his line? Urban terrorism?"

"In a manner of speaking. He's Lieutenant Colonel Pitt-Evenlode MC of the Yorkshire Fusiliers. Like his number?"

"Just tell me which bishops you were with on May nineteenth," growled Dalziel.

"Sorry. No clergy. I went to a wedding at Scarborough, but it was a civil rather than a religious ceremony. I stayed the night there. In fact, I stayed up most of the night. There was a postnuptial party which went on until dawn. I think you'll find I made my presence felt sufficiently to be recalled through the alcoholic haze."

Dalziel belched. She took it as an expression of doubt.

"Don't you believe me? Please, feel free to check."

"I may just do that. And it's nowt to do with not believing you. It's just that I never believe my luck when folk start volunteering alibis before I've even asked for them."

"That is perhaps because most of your customers are of a lower order of intelligence in which such pre-emptive thought would indeed be suspicious. If our acquaintance is to mature, you'll have to get used to dealing with someone whose brain is quite as good as yours. And also with someone who, unlike most of those others, is unworried by your ultimate threat of locking them away. For me to get a prison sentence would be a real publicity coup, so you must see that your threats, even if you meant to carry them through, which I doubt, have little weight with me."

She gave him a smile of great sunniness which was well worth basking in on a drab October day. He returned it gladly. She did after all have a point, and he never minded letting opponents build up a point's lead. The more confident they got, the more likely they were to drop their guards and reveal a fatal weakness. Like here. Anyone who seriously doubted his willingness to carry through any threat he cared to make was wide open to a sucker punch anytime he cared to throw it. But no need to rush, not with beer and crisps and pickles still on the table, and them lovely sugarloaves to leer at.

He drank and nibbled and leered, and waited to see where she would lead the conversation.

She said, "I cannot of course provide alibis for all of

my colleagues, though two of them, Meg and Donna, were in fact at the Scarborough wedding also.''

"That 'ud be Jenkins and Linsey? The dykes?''

His reaction when he'd come across this surmise in George Headingley's notes had been, "What the fuck's that got to do with anything?" But now he was happy to use the term as a possible irritant.

"That's right," she said, unirritated. "The dykes. As for the others, all I can do is vouch for their commitment to peaceful protest. Except perhaps Wendy.''

"Walker? But she acted as peacekeeper, didn't she?''·

"Rather out of character, I feel. What about you? I got the impression you were already acquainted.''

"Aye. We've met.''

"And did I get the impression you were surprised to find her in such company?''

"What're we talking here?" he said. "Class or causes?''

"Are the two really distinguishable in some people's eyes? But what I meant was, at the peaceful protest end of the activist scene.''

Dalziel laughed and said, "You call what you got up to peaceful protest? I'd not like to see you if you went to war.''

"I'll try not to invite you then. But you've not answered my question.''

She was very insistent, he thought. That little exchange he'd overheard between her and Wendy Walker must have really got her going for some reason.

He said, "What surprised me weren't so much Walker joining you lot as you lot taking her on board. How'd that happen?''

If he'd hoped to throw her off balance by reversing the question, he had failed. She was smiling rather slyly, an expression he found strangely exciting.

He crossed his legs the other way and waited for the answer.

"Oddly enough," she said, "it was through a colleague of yours in a manner of speaking, man and wife being one flesh. A mutual acquaintance introduced us. I expect you know her well. Mrs. Ellie Pascoe."

"You're not saying she's one of your lot?" he groaned.

"Not really. Sympathetic but too concerned with suffering humanity to have much energy left for the animal kingdom, so no need to be embarrassed."

Another weakness, imagining embarrassment was one of his.

"Still, a bit of a handful, isn't she? Wendy, I mean."

"She's certainly got her own ideas, and I'm not sure she'll stay with us forever. Too much energy and resentment, not perhaps enough self-knowledge. Like me, her marriage broke up, but she thinks it was because her husband was a scab, while the truth I suspect is that she so enjoyed the role she found in the strike that there was no way she was ever going to go back to the life servitude of being a pitman's wife. *Pitman.* I had my own Pitt man too, so I can sympathize. But the difference is, I changed sides, while she lost; not only a battle but a whole bloody war. So perhaps it was no wonder she was looking for a new role where the issues were clear-cut, even if it meant she has to work for a while at least alongside an old class enemy like me."

She laughed and Dalziel grinned too. Weakness three. Believing she'd got Wendy Walker and her kind sussed. Couple of weeks on the dole could root out the centuries-deep deference of the British worker, but it took major surgery to eradicate the built-in smugness of the middle class.

He sucked the last drops out of the last can. Every plate was empty. Time for business.

He said, "All right, missus . . ."

"Cap," she urged.

"All right, Cap. So why did you want to see me?"

"To make a statement, of course. You were very keen for us to make statements last night."

"Was I? Funny how you take these fancies, then go off them. Like being pregnant, they tell me."

"So you don't want a statement?" she said, disconcerted.

"Depends what you've got to state."

"I thought we could negotiate," she said, recovering. "I mean, you've got a body in the grounds of Wanwood House. I bet you've got some ideas about that already. So if it would help for me to say I saw that plonker Batty start like a guilty thing surprised when he got the news, just say the word. Or that TecSec Nazi, Patten, if it's him you fancy and you need an excuse to search his pad, maybe I could help there."

Dalziel scratched his bubaline neck and said, "What makes you think I'd take kindly to the idea of fitting someone up?"

"Oh, I know you wouldn't do it maliciously," she reassured him, her candid brown eyes gazing deep into his. "Only if you were sure it was in the best interests of justice. I mean, when I contacted the local media this morning to ask why ANIMA was hardly getting a mention, and got told that in matters sub judice it was editorial policy to afford the police full cooperation, I didn't immediately think, that bastard Andy Dalziel's put the frighteners on. No, I thought, that nice superintendent's imposed a temporary media blackout in the best interests of all concerned. No need for me to go running hysterically to my cousin who does features for Channel Four or my old school chum who's a junior minister in the Home Office, is there? Why have confrontation when you can have consultation instead?"

Not bad, approved Dalziel. Just because he'd identified three weaknesses didn't mean she couldn't still kick him in the balls. But he was still intrigued as to why she should think he was susceptible to consultation. She didn't give the impression of being thick.

He said, "Let's get things straight. I take the frighteners off the local media and you'll sign any statement I care to dictate to you?"

"More or less," she said.

"Talking about fitting folk up always makes me thirsty," he said, crushing the last empty can in his huge fist.

"Have to be Mexican," she said, going to the fridge. "It's good. So good, some of the American companies started spreading rumors the Mexican workers piss in it."

"So what? Yon reservoir up Dendale, the one supplies most of our tap water, we fished five bodies out of there last year. Cheers. Don't have another bit of pork pie in there too, do you?"

"*Another* bit?" she said.

It took him a second to work this out.

"You mean it weren't pork?"

"I don't eat dead animals, Andy, nor encourage my friends to do so. It was basically tofu."

"Bloody hell," said Dalziel, taking a long cleansing suck at his beer. "Two things I don't do, missus. One is feed folk stuff they don't know what it is. T'other is fit people up. Understand that and we might get on a bit better."

"Oh dear," she said, concerned. "I've offended you. I'm not very good on moral codes. I suppose that means goodbye to Plan Two as well."

"What's that when it's at home?" he asked suspiciously.

"Well, after our first encounter last night I had the feeling that my boobs hadn't been so closely scanned since my last radiography checkup. I thought if all else failed . . . let me rephrase that . . . I rather hoped all else might fail and I'd have to fall back on the flesh, so to speak. But naturally I'd never come between a man and his moral code."

Dalziel considered. Another man might have played for time by pretending to suck on the empty bottle or making reference to the weather, but Dalziel did his considering in plain view. Offers of trade-offs of sexual for constabulary favors weren't uncommon. He rarely bothered himself. A bang was only a bang but a good result was a collar.

On the other hand, if he was honest with himself (and with himself what was the point of being other?) he really fancied this lass. Not just the boobs. These days even Mid-Yorkshire was bulging with highly visible boobs. See two, you've seen 'em all. And not the way she spoke, which still carried too many overtones of the Pitt-Overload era, or whatever the prat's name was. And certainly not all this dotty animal rights stuff. And she wasn't young. And she wasn't beautiful. Any other strikes against her? Yes, of course, the big one. Okay, so ALBA would almost certainly decide not to proceed against her. And the possible charges he'd just listed weren't worth wasting his time on. But if he thought there was any chance at all that she'd been mixed up in this Redcar thing . . .

Very long odds against. One in a million. Less. She'd offered alibis and from what he'd seen he reckoned that she'd sussed out he wasn't the kind of cop who'd let a bit of nooky stop him from checking. So why was he looking for an excuse to reject what his whole being was urging him to grab with both hands?

Mebbe he was a bit scared of his own desire. Mebbe it was because there was something about her that hit the spot, like the bouquet of an untried single malt when you opened the bottle, telling you that this was one to be savored.

She was regarding him oddly. Calculatingly?

"What're you thinking of?" he asked abruptly.

"Old friend of mine, same name as the novelist. Balzac," she said, smiling.

Bloody incomprehensible. But which on 'em wasn't? Condition of service! And at least he now understood her motive for getting him alone. Just as he'd been identifying her weaknesses over the past hour, so she'd identified his last night, and taken a bloody sight less time about it.

Question his sodding vanity wanted answering was this. Was Plan Two a Last Resort, or really a Principle Object disguised as a Last Resort?

She read a question in his eyes, but misread it also.

She said, "I had nothing to do with the Redcar raid, Andy. And I deplore what they did, both personally and as an activist."

Well, she would say that, wouldn't she? Clever thing for a cop to reply was, I believe you.

"I believe you," he replied. "Them bones you lot found last night, looks like they could be pretty old."

"So?"

"I mean too old to have owt to do with ALBA. With a bit of luck they might even turn out too old to have owt to do with the CID!"

"That's interesting."

"Aye. Means there might be nothing at all to investigate. Certainly means you and the folk up there aren't mixed up in any investigation. I rang my media contacts on the way here, told 'em they could go to town."

There. Now let's see if the chicken still crossed the road.

The phone started ringing.

"Could be for me," said Dalziel. "I left 'em your number. Or it could be *News at Ten*."

"Shall I answer it?"

"Up to you. You're a free agent."

"Yes, I am," she said seriously. "How about you, Andy? How's the moral code?"

Dalziel didn't mind a bit of obliquity but this was beginning to sound . . . what was that word Pascoe sometimes came out with? . . . sphincteresque? Summat like that. Any road, enough was enough.

He stood up and started taking his tie off.

"Moral code?" he said. "You've just cracked it."

XI

"THAT, I HOPE, is the secretaire you mentioned. Or have you gone into the funeral business?" said Ellie Pascoe.

Pascoe, reluctantly acknowledging that the passionate welcome home embrace was over, followed her gaze to the sheet-shrouded cargo on his roof rack.

"Have no fear," he said. "Ada is safely scattered as per wishes, more or less. It was quite entertaining in a macabre way. Give me a hand with this, will you? How's Rosie?"

"At school. Memory that it was her friend Sarah's birthday today coincided with a miracle recovery."

"Ah," said Pascoe.

"Ah what? She really wasn't fit to go yesterday."

"I know she wasn't," said Pascoe mildly, thinking that such a hint of defensiveness in a suspect would have had him chiseling at the weakness till it gave. "Here we go. You've got that end? Right . . . just let it slide. Great. *Et voilà!*"

Dramatically he whipped the sheet off the secretaire. Ellie regarded it in silence.

"You are dumbfounded with admiration?" he said hopefully.

"You said it was Sheraton."

"*After* Sheraton," said Pascoe.

"About eighty long hard years after."

Pascoe couldn't argue. Out of the friendly shadows of Ada's living room, the secretaire had lost much of its antique charm and stood forlorn and rather shabby in the cruel October sunlight.

"It's got a secret drawer," he pleaded.

He opened it and showed her the photo. She studied it with interest.

"Poor devil," she said. "Gosh, doesn't he look like you?"

Pascoe took the picture from her and looked at it again. He still couldn't see it but something in those eyes spoke to him.

"It'll look better inside," he said, dropping the photo back into the drawer. "Unless this is the day you've got the *Beautiful Homes* photographers coming round?"

It was a low shot but she had it coming. Ellie was savage in her mockery of the Good Taste Theme Parks which gleamed at you out of the glossies, but this didn't stop her from being pretty finical about what stood on her floors and hung on her walls.

They carried the secretaire into the house and set it down in the hallway.

"Leave it there for the time being," said Ellie. "Hopefully it'll find its own place. Let's have a coffee and you can tell me all about everything."

She listened alertly to his narrative, laughing aloud from time to time and asking the occasional pertinent question.

"So," she said. "Ada ended up as part of a military tableau. Not her intention, I presume."

"No. I think on the whole she'd have been happier messing up one of the tidier exhibits," Pascoe admitted. "She was a lot like you, wanting people to be quite clear what she thought, I mean."

Ellie considered this. She rarely talked about Peter's family, not because she disliked them (which on the whole she did) but because Peter himself had made them a no-go area. On the surface Ada was the one she had most in common with, but when strong wills clash, common ground can often be a battlefield. Neither was happy about Peter's career in the police force but Ada's objections were the deeper. Ellie had married him because she loved him despite the fact he was a policeman, while Ada felt that all her love and care and hopes for her grandson were betrayed by his choice of career. Ellie, she implied, being the new responsible woman in his life, must bear some of the blame. Such an accusation was an irony which amusement might have rendered barbless had not Ellie surprised in herself a strong resentment which boiled down to simple jealousy that anyone else should dare to imagine they shared her right to criticize her husband! Self-knowledge, she now realized, may bring about changes in the head, but the heart doesn't give a toss for psychology.

The two women had settled into a polite neutrality easy to maintain, as contact between them was minimal. Nevertheless Ellie had encouraged Peter in his attempts to reestablish his old closeness with his grandmother, sensing that Ada was the source of most of the family warmth in his upbringing, but hope of any real rapprochement had died with the old lady's reaction to Rosie's birth.

"A girl," she said. "You planning any more?"

"We'll have to see," said Pascoe.

"Doesn't matter. Maybe it's best you should be the last of the Pascoes. I sometimes wonder if Mother didn't have the right of it after all."

Slightly enigmatic this last comment might have been, but the general tenor of her indifference to the birth of her great-granddaughter was unmistakable and, in Pascoe's proudly paternal eyes, unforgivable. Hereafter contact was intermittent and formal, which didn't stop him from feeling a tremendous upsurge of guilt at the news of her death and the realization that he hadn't seen her for almost two years.

Ellie had felt neither the indignation nor the guilt. And she would definitely have gone to the funeral, she assured herself, if Rosie's cold hadn't interfered.

Or maybe, she added with that instinctive honesty which kept her certainties this side of fanaticism, maybe I'd have found some other reason, like cleaning an old tennis shoe.

"It really got to her, didn't it?" she said. "Losing her dad like that in the war. It dominated her life. I hope I'm not that obsessive?"

"We'd better ask Rosie in twenty years or so," said Pascoe lightly. "Any calls by the way?"

"From on high, you mean? Yes, naturally. His Fatship rang first thing this morning, asked if you were back yet. Implied that you were an overeducated rat swimming away from an overloaded ship. Something about animal rights and finding bones in a wood?"

"Wanwood House, ALBA Pharmaceuticals, I was there in the summer, remember? I heard on the news some activists had got in the grounds and discovered human remains. So he's missing me? Good! What did you tell him?"

"I said that your family and fiduciary duties were such as would probably detain you in Warwickshire until late this evening at the earliest."

"Excellent," said Pascoe. "Many thanks."

"For what?"

"For lying for me."

"Isn't that a wife's duty, lying for her husband, vertically and horizontally?"

"Well, yes, of course," said Pascoe. "Tell me, how dutiful are you feeling?"

Before Ellie could reply the doorbell rang.

"Shit," said Pascoe. "If it's *him*, tell him I'm still fiducing."

"And your car came back by itself? Good trick."

Through the frosted panel of the front door, Ellie could see at once it wasn't Dalziel. Even through a glass darkly that bulk was unmistakable. With a bit of luck it would just be a Jehovah's Witness who could be told to sod off with utmost dispatch. She was feeling pleasantly randy and there was a good hour or more before she needed to think about picking up Rosie from school.

It wasn't a Witness, it was Wendy Walker, looking like a good advert for the afterlife.

"Hi, Ellie," she said. "Spare a mo for a chat?"

"Yes, of course," said Ellie brightly. "Come in."

Wendy moved past her and stopped by the secretaire.

"Nice," she said.

"Make me an offer," said Ellie. "Come into the kitchen."

They sat opposite each other at the stripped-pine table.

"Coffee?" said Ellie.

"No, thanks. Okay if I smoke, but?"

There were several reasons why it wasn't, each of them absolute.

On the other hand, to be asked permission by someone who would have lit up in Buck House without reference to the Queen was a flattery it seemed churlish to deny.

She said weakly, "All right but I'll open a window."

It was a counterproductive move, merely adding the risk of primary pneumonia to that of secondary cancer.

Drawing a curtain to cut down the draft, she said, "Sure you wouldn't like a coffee?"

"To sober me up you mean?" said Wendy aggressively.

"No, I didn't, actually. But do you need sobering up?"

"No. Sorry I snapped. Did have a couple at lunchtime but that doesn't make me a drunk."

"No, of course it doesn't. Was there something particular . . ."

"We went on a raid last night."

"Wanwood House? Was that you?"

"You know about it?"

"Only what I heard on the news and that wasn't much."

"Yeah, I think that fat bastard's put the muzzle on."

"That won't please Cap."

"Goosefeather up the arse wouldn't please her."

"I'm not sure it would do much for me either," said Ellie. "There was something about a body . . ."

Wendy told the story quickly, dismissively, scattering more ash than Etna.

Ellie said, "Good God, Wendy, no wonder you're shook up."

"Who says I'm shook up?" demanded the smaller woman.

"Well, if you're not, you ought to change your makeup," said Ellie spiritedly.

"What? Oh yeah." She managed a faint smile, then went on, "No, it wasn't that, something else . . . when they took us inside and Cap ran riot . . . look, Ellie, I need an ear . . . someone to tell me if I'm being stupid or what . . . and you said, anything came up, I should let you know, right? Or was that just one of the things you lot say to keep us lot happy?"

"Wendy," said Ellie dangerously. "That *you lot* crap only works when you're up in the fighting line and I'm with a bunch of noncombatants shouting encouragement from the back. This is about friendship or it's about nothing."

"Yeah, sorry," said Wendy. "It's just with your man being a bobby . . . he's not at home, is he? I'm not ready . . ."

As if in answer the door opened and Pascoe appeared.

"Peter," said Ellie brightly. "You remember Wendy, don't you? Wendy Walker, from Burrthorpe?"

Burrthorpe. Where he'd almost lost his life down a mine. And almost lost his wife to a young miner.

"Yes, of course. Hi. Keeping well, I hope?"

"Fine," said Wendy Walker. "Hey, look at the time. I'd better get going."

She stubbed her fag in a saucer and stood up.

Pascoe said guiltily, "Don't rush off on my account."

She said, "No, my timing's bad today. Ellie, are you going to the party tonight? Thought I might cadge a lift home afterwards if you were. Buses stop at ten and the bike's a menace when you're pissed."

"Party?" said Pascoe.

"You know, the Extra-Mural Department's do."

"But I thought . . ." He changed his mind about uttering the thought.

Wendy flashed a bright smile and said, "Cheers then," and went past him into the entrance hall. Ellie caught up with her on the doorstep.

"You haven't said what you want to talk about," she said.

"Probably all in my imagination," said Wendy unconvincingly. "Look, we'll have a chat at the party, okay? You will be there, won't you?"

She fixed Ellie with those bright unblinking eyes, like a hungry whippet that doesn't know how to beg.

"Yes," said Ellie reluctantly. "I'll definitely be there."

She watched as Walker mounted the dilapidated mountain bike which was her urban transport and stood on the pedals to accelerate away.

"Shit," said Ellie.

The party in question was basically a celebration of the university Extra-Mural Department's twenty-fifth year of running day-release courses for the National Union of Miners. Ellie had taught on the course briefly, and it was here that had begun the relationship which had caused so much pain. She'd backed off any further involvement in the course after that. Peter had urged her to go to the party, particularly as it wasn't just a celebration but a wake. The present course was the last. After Christmas the NUM wouldn't have enough miners left to make day-release viable. Samson had been brought low. The triumph of Dagon was complete.

But despite her husband's urgings, or perhaps because of them, Ellie had resolved not to go, a decision confirmed by the coincidence of his return from Ada's funeral this same day.

Now the case was altered but not in any way she could explain.

It would be nice, she thought, just now and then, to be like one of those bright-eyed brain-deads in the telly ads who never had a problem more pressing than which pack of chemical crap washed whiter.

But that wasn't an option she had been programmed for.

She turned back into the entrance hall and banged her shin against Ada's secretaire.

"And up you too!" said Ellie Pascoe.

XII

BY EARLY AFTERNOON, even with the help of a small pump to keep the water level down, Wield's team hadn't recovered as many bones from the crater as would make a good stock. These were dispatched to Longbottom, who reacted like a ravenous panther offered a harvest mouse.

His complaints were heard elsewhere because about one-thirty, Wield had a rendezvous with Death.

This was the sobriquet of Arnold Gentry, head of the Police Forensic Laboratory. Rumor had it that he had been excavated along with the Dead Sea Scrolls, and he was certainly one of the few men to make Troll Longbottom look healthy.

He acknowledged Wield's greeting with a minuscule nod, brooded on the edge of the pit for a while, then said, "Sluice it."

"Eh?" said Wield.

"From what Mr. Longbottom says, I gather there has been considerable dispersion of the remains, probably both through natural causes and as a result of the use of mechanical and explosive devices in the clearance of the area earlier this year. This means the precise disposition of the bones is unlikely to be central to your investigation. Therefore it makes sense to load say fifty or sixty cubic meters of earth onto a truck and deliver them to my lab where I will arrange to have them sluiced, thus isolating any bones or other evidential material. This will save you a great deal of time and the State a great deal of money."

"You'd best talk to Mr. Headingley, sir," said Wield,

seeing the DI approaching. "Okay if I go off to lunch now, sir?"

"Aye, why not," said Headingley with postprandial expansiveness.

Wield moved quickly away. Dr. Death's suggestion seemed a good one, but he wasn't going to let George Headingley get his feelings on record. Over the years he'd shown a growing reluctance to take responsibility though none to taking credit. That was what had kept him a superior, unlike Peter Pascoe who'd become a mate.

As Wield reached the drive, a strangulated cry made him glance back.

Gentry had been supporting his proposition by pointing to the fluid condition of the sides of the crater which made any search by manual means both slow and perilous. Headingley, in his efforts to show an alert interest while postponing decision, had ventured too near the edge and suddenly found himself proving Dr. Death's thesis. As Wield watched, the ungainly inspector slid slowly like a ship down a launch ramp into the water-filled crater.

For a moment Wield was tempted to return and supervise the rescue operation. But only for a moment. God's gifts should be savored in tranquillity, and besides there were plenty of strong young constables in thigh-length waders to pluck old George from the depths. He turned and continued up the drive.

At the top, he headed down the side of the house and into the old tradesmen's entrance, now leading directly into the TecSec quarters, which consisted of an office, a sitting room with a couple of folding cots, a washroom, and a kitchen.

Wield peered through the office door. Patten was sitting at his desk, typing on a computer. On one wall a range of TV screens showed scenes from various parts of the grounds and building. Very hi-tech, thought Wield. Must be costing ALBA a bomb.

"Okay if I clean up?" he said.

"Surprised you bother to ask. Don't get all your manners from that fat fucker, then?"

"No. Get mine from Sainsbury's. Where do you get yours from?"

The security man looked abashed.

"Sorry. Of course you can. Should be a clean towel in the cupboard."

When he came back, he found Patten on the phone. He said, "That's right. Roll 'em up, all three. You got it."

Then replacing the receiver he said to Wield, "I've just made a brew. Fancy a cup?"

"That 'ud be nice. No sugar."

"Keep healthy, eh? I've seen you down the Leisure, haven't I? Kung fu, wasn't it?"

"I try to keep in shape."

"Working with yon tub of lard must give you a real incentive."

"Nowt wrong with being a big so long as you can punch your weight," said Wield mildly.

"And he can?" said Patten skeptically.

"He's wired a few jawbones in his time," said Wield. "You army?"

"That's right. You been checking up?" said Patten with a return to his earlier aggression.

"No. Private security folk are usually ex-cops or ex-forces, and you're not ex-cop."

"How do you know that?"

Wield shrugged and said, "Way you don't stick your pinkie out when you drink your tea."

"What? Oh, I see. A joke." He sounded surprised.

Here's another thinks I shouldn't make jokes, and he doesn't even know me! thought Wield.

He said, "What mob?"

"York Fusiliers. I busted my leg on an exercise, mended fine but they were rationalizing, that means dumping bodies. Offered me a medical discharge. I offered them a fifty-mile yomp across the moors, my pension against their jobs. No takers."

It was clearly a bitter memory.

"So you've ended up desk-bound," said Wield with provocative sympathy.

"Yeah. Well, not all the time, and at least I'm doing something useful."

"Guarding this place is useful?"

"It's important work they do and they've a right to do it in peace."

"You reckon? Bit of overkill that mess out there, isn't it?"

"You reckon?" mimicked Patten. "Listen, back last summer they had one watchman and locks you could fart open. Those mad buggers just walked in, smashed the place up and helped themselves to everything, including the watchman's so-called guard dog. So we got called in. I took one look and said, first thing you want here is a fire zone. That's a piece of ground in clear view where if anything moves, you shoot it. No need to go too far. Nearer the house the better, as that keeps the circle nice and small and cuts down cost. Also it leaves enough of the outer woodland untouched to keep things from the road looking much the same as they've always done. Now if they come, they've got to cross the open. We've got lights and cameras, and there's an alarmed security fence it'll take more than a pair of ordinary wire cutters to get through. Installation's expensive, I agree. But once it's done they're secure forever, and that's worth more than money to a firm like ALBA."

"I can see that," said Wield pleasantly. "When they were clearing the wood, did the contractors say anything about hitting an old wall or something like that?

Seem to be a lot of granite slabs lying around out there."

"Not to me."

"What about Dr. Batty?"

"Couldn't say. But if they did, I'm pretty damn sure he'd have said carry on regardless. Old stones can mean a lot of bearded wonders slapping a preservation order on you if you're not careful."

He gave Wield a conspiratorial all-mates-together grin which sat uneasily on his scarred and watchful face.

Wield said, "I'll need to talk with your men who were on duty when they brought those women in last night, especially those as chased them round the offices."

"Why's that?" said Patten, matiness gone.

"In case ALBA fancy bringing charges. Trespass is no good as far as the house goes, as technically they were invited in, so they'd need to go for criminal damage, assault even. So we'll need statements."

"Save you the bother," said Patten, delving into his desk. "We got our system too. Full reports on any incident. Here, take a look, all signed and sealed."

He handed a thin file across. Wield looked inside. The reports were all there, full of necessary detail of time, place, duration.

"Everything in order?" said Patten. "Jimmy Howard keeps us straight on rules of evidence. Useful having an ex-cop around."

"Must be," said Wield. "From a quick glance, doesn't seem to have been any real damage either to person or property."

"More by luck than judgment," growled Patten. "That fat cow, the one called Cap, she belted one of my lads in the belly with them cutters and looked like she was going to have a swing at my head with them till that skinny lass caught a hold of her."

"Walker?"

"Aye. The one who found the bones in the first place. Got the impression your fat boss knew her. She been in trouble for this kind of thing before?"

"No. Not animal rights. She was one of them Women Against Pit Closures lot that got going during the strike."

"Is that right?" Patten pulled at his lip and said, "Didn't think you lot, CID I mean, got mixed up with that. Thought it was all uniformed out there beating up the pickets."

"Preserving the peace," corrected Wield gently. "No, we got involved because there was a murder, out at Burrthorpe, you might have read about it."

"No, I don't recall . . . 1984 it'd be? I was nobbut a lad, not long in the army, still pretty much a lily."

"A what?"

"Lily. What we called a sprog in our mob. So, this Walker woman, she had a change of heart, has she? Moved from miners to monkeys?"

"Some folk need a cause," said Wield. "And we like to keep a close eye on all of them. Perhaps I'd better have a word with Jimmy Howard just to make sure I've got the full picture."

"Sorry, he's gone off duty," said Patten.

"When's he back on?"

Patten swiveled round to examine a wall chart which wouldn't have disgraced the Pentagon. Next to it hung a photo of three men smiling into the camera. On the left was Patten, wearing a TecSec uniform. The man on the right—small with a round smiling face beneath tightly packed blond curls—was similarly dressed. His name tag was too small to read except for the initial R. In the center, elegant in a well-cut dark gray pinstripe suit, was a lean handsome man who looked as if he might have a very good opinion of himself, not altogether unjustified.

"Should have gone off at six this morning in fact," added Patten, "but did an extra stag 'cos of all the excitement, so I shouldn't bother him at home till he's had time to catch up on his beauty sleep."

"Oh, shan't need to do that," said Wield negligently. "Likely these reports you've given me will do. Seems a well-organized firm, TecSec. Good mob to work for, are they?"

"I don't work for 'em," said Patten, "I'm a partner."

"Sorry. I thought seeing you out here in the uniform . . ."

"Like the army, guys who really run the show are out there in the field getting shot at. My partner's out most of the time drumming up business while I'm out making sure the business we've got gets done properly. There's a girl back in the office knows where to get hold of us."

"Sounds good," said Wield, rising. "If ever I need security I'll know where to come. Thanks for the tea."

"My pleasure."

At the door Wield paused and said, "Your security fence, the inner one, you say they'd not have got through that with a pair of wire cutters. Why not use the same stuff for the first lot of wire?"

"Expense," said Patten. "Costs a fortune that stuff, and you'd need a lot more 'cos it's a bigger circle. Also . . ."

"Yes?" prompted Wield.

"No use fighting people unless you let 'em close enough to get shot," said Patten, this time with no attempt at a grin.

XIII

THE ATMOSPHERE in the Pascoe household had remained definitely overcast with poor air quality till Rosie on her return from school burst in on it like the wild west wind. She flung herself on her father as if he'd been away for a decade not a day and gripped him in a stranglehold which would have won style points from a thug, the whiles rattling off a stream-of-consciousness account of all that had happened to her during their long separation.

Also in there somewhere were expressions of gratitude for her prezzie which at first he took to be creatively predictive, and he was seeking a form of words which would explain why fathers after such a short absence on such a sad mission should be allowed to come home empty-handed, when it dawned on him that the thanks were for a present received, not a gift anticipated.

He glanced at Ellie, who mouthed, "The secretaire . . ."

"Eh?"

"Rosie saw the secretaire in the hall and she asked me if you'd brought it for her to keep her things in and I said you may very well have."

After a recent and ideologically very dubious spat between Ellie and her daughter about the state of her room, Pascoe had asserted his paterfamilial authority with the promise of a large gin and tonic for his wife and a large storage chest for his Rosie. He had in mind something in puce plastic, but the little girl's refined taste could sometimes be as surprising as her occasionally fluorescent language.

"You like it, do you?" said Pascoe.

"Oh yes. I think it's bloody marvelous," she answered very seriously.

He caught Ellie's eye again and she gave him an I-don't-know-where-she-gets-it-from look. Since going to school Rosie had moved up a linguistic gear and like Caliban, her profit on it was she now knew how to curse. The problem was to stop her from cursing without letting her know that she had been.

Pascoe said, "It belonged to Granny Pascoe and she wanted you to have it."

"Granny who's dead?"

"That's right."

"Is she a ghost?" asked Rosie uneasily.

"You know there's no such thing as ghosts, so she can't be, can she?" said Ellie briskly.

"No," said Rosie without conviction.

Pascoe put his mouth to her ear and said, "And if she is, she'll be a ghost down in Warwickshire, because everyone knows ghosts have got to do their haunting round the place where they died."

The little girl looked greatly relieved though he saw Ellie grimace at this betrayal of rational principles. But she was as pleased as he was at this solution to the problem of Ada's writing desk.

"Told you it would find its place," she gasped as they collapsed on Rosie's bed after lugging the secretaire upstairs.

"Clever old you," he said, grinning, and the truce might have been sealed with more than a loving kiss if Rosie hadn't demanded their help in tidying away all her dolls, toys, and other impedimenta into her new storage cupboard.

At seven o'clock with Rosie safely stowed in bed and Ellie making ready for her party, Pascoe was in the kitchen pouring himself a lager when the doorbell rang.

He heard Ellie's footsteps on the stairs and her voice calling, "I'll get it."

Wendy Walker again? he wondered. No. She'd just said she wanted a lift back. Or this time, perhaps it *was* the Fat Man, come to see for himself that he'd got safely home. Bastard!

But when Ellie came into the kitchen she wasn't wearing her *Apocalypse Now* face, though she was wearing a silk dress which struck him as being a touch showy for such a proletarian celebration.

"Chap called Hilary Studholme to see you," she said.

"Eye patch, one arm, and a limp?" he asked.

"Or gray hair, his own teeth, and a nice smile," said Ellie. "Could it be the same guy?"

"Not in court it couldn't," said Pascoe. "Let's see."

The major was standing by the fireplace looking rather ill at ease.

"Nice to see you again," said Pascoe, remembering to offer his left hand. "Do sit down. I was just pouring myself a drink. Can I get you anything?"

"Orange juice, anything non-alc. There are those of your colleagues who feel I shouldn't have a license. Mustn't always help the police, must we?"

He smiled his nice smile. From the doorway Ellie said, "I'll get the drinks."

Seating himself opposite his visitor, Pascoe said, "So what brings you into my neck of the woods, Major?"

"Dining out this way with friends. Was going to ring you in the morning, but thought face-to-face better. Especially as I wanted to show you something."

He picked up a large envelope which he had set down on a coffee table, flicked the flap open with his thumb and shook some photographs out.

They were all of soldiers in Great War uniform. Two were formal groups, the other was informal, showing four men resting against a gun limber. Their clothes were mud-stained and their efforts to look cheerful sat on their fatigued faces like prostitutes' smiles.

"Anyone you recognize?" said Studholme.

"Good lord," said Ellie, who'd returned with the drinks which she was setting down on the table. "There you are again, Peter."

This time, even Pascoe couldn't deny the resemblance between himself and one of the exhausted soldiers. It was less clear in the group pictures, but Ellie went with unerring accuracy to a face which had Studholme nodding his agreement.

"So what's your point?" said Pascoe. "You think this is my great-grandfather, is that it?"

It didn't seem to him a particularly exciting discovery, certainly not one to bring Studholme even a short distance out of his way.

The major said, "You mentioned a photograph you had?"

With the perfect timing she had inherited from her mother, Rosie pushed open the door and came in, barefooted and nightgowned, carrying the photograph from Ada's secretaire.

"Look what I found, Daddy," she said.

"Good God," said Pascoe, taking the photo. "I was twice your age before I learned how to open the drawer."

"Girls mature quicker," observed Ellie. "But that doesn't mean they don't need their sleep. Come on. Back to bed with you, Lady Macbeth."

"But why is Daddy wearing those funny clothes?" asked Rosie, who had learned early on that the way to delay her mother from any undesirable course of action was to ask as many questions as possible.

"It's not me, darling," interposed Pascoe. "It's your great-great-granddad, and he just happened to look a tiny little bit like me."

"He looks the spitting image of you," said Ellie. "Doesn't he, dear?"

"Fucking right he does," agreed Rosie.

Pascoe winced and glanced an apology at the major, whose one visible eyebrow arched quizzically. Ellie caught the girl up in her arms and said, "Off we go. Say goodnight."

There was a moment's pause which had Pascoe wondering if his daughter was rifling her word hoard for one of the less conventional valedictory forms such as "Don't let the bastards grind you down" or "Up yours, asshole," but she contented herself with a long-suffering "Goodnight then" over her mother's shoulder.

"She is making surprising progress at school," said Pascoe when the door had closed.

"Indeed," said Studholme dryly.

He took the photograph from Pascoe's hand and studied it, then set it alongside the ones he'd brought.

"Might be doubles," he said. "Such things happen. Anything can. But chances are they're the same. Wouldn't you agree?"

"Well, yes. But so what? Do you have a name for the chap in your pics?" asked Pascoe.

"Yes. Names for nearly all of them. One of my predecessors was very thorough back in the twenties. Double-checked with survivors. That's why I came."

"Because this is definitely Corporal Clark?"

"Sergeant at the end. And not Clark. Here. Look."

He produced a sheet of paper on which someone had patiently traced one of the groups in outline with numbers instead of faces. Below was a key.

Pascoe checked the number of his lookalike. Twenty-two. Then he dropped his gaze to the key.

He was glad he wasn't standing. Even sitting he felt the chair lurch beneath his behind and saw the air shimmer like the onset of migraine. He blinked it clear and reread the entry.

No. 22. Pascoe Peter (Corporal).

"Is this your idea of a joke?" he said steadily.

"No joke," said Studholme, regarding him closely and with concern.

"Then what? Can't be right. My grandmother was Ada Clark who became a Pascoe by marriage, so how could this be her father? Hang on, though? Didn't you say there was a Pascoe in the Wyfies at Third Wipers? Surely this is just a mixup of names?"

"That was Private Stephen Pascoe. He got wounded, not killed. This Corporal Peter, later sergeant, is some-one else."

Ellie came back in.

"I think she'll go to sleep now but don't let her play you up. I'd better be on my way. Peter, you okay?"

He forced a smile.

"Yes. Fine. I'll check in a little while. Enjoy your-self."

"I'll try. Major Studholme, nice to meet you. Sorry I've got to dash. Bye."

She was gone. She was good at exits, thought Pascoe with the envy of one who usually made an awkward bow.

Studholme was standing up.

"I'd better be on my way too," he said. "Bad form, being late."

Pascoe didn't rise but studied the other from his chair. With Dalziel breathing down your neck for all those years, one thing you practiced till it became in-stinctive was the art of detailed observation. He let his gaze drift down to Studholme's clothing from his collar to his toe caps. He was beginning to feel something which, if not anger, had a deal of anger in it.

"Late for what?" he asked. "If I had to make a guess, Major, I'd say you weren't going anywhere. All that about having dinner with friends in this neck of the woods is a load of baloney, isn't it?"

Studholme brushed his forefinger across his moustache and said in a voice which had more of interest than indignation in it, "And on what would you base such an unmannerly speculation?"

"You haven't changed from when I saw you this morning. Same shirt, same tie, same jacket, same trousers. You haven't even given your shoes a rub. Oh, you look tidy enough, don't misunderstand me, but I'm certain a man like you wouldn't go to dine with friends without changing your shirt at least."

"Man like me? Little presumptuous on such short acquaintance, isn't it?"

Again mildly curious rather than outraged.

"You've known me exactly the same length of time," said Pascoe, who could play this game till the cows came home and went out again. "Yet you feel you know me well enough to decide that whatever it really was that you came here to say might be best left unsaid. How's that for presumption?"

"Pretty extreme," the major admitted with a hint of the smile. "All right. May have been wrong. Still can't be sure."

"There's only one way to find out," said Pascoe. "Like another drink?"

Studholme shook his head.

"Thanks, but I'll wait till I get home and can treat myself to a real nightcap. No offense, excellent orange juice."

He sat down again, easing his right leg straight out in front of him. Did he have a prosthesis or just some muscle damage? wondered Pascoe. He felt a sympathetic twinge in his own leg, damaged when he'd been trapped down Burrthorpe Main. Theoretically he'd made a complete recovery from that traumatic experience. His mind had other ideas.

He said, "So what's the big mystery, Major?"

Studholme said, "Tell me first of all. Your grandmother, why do you think she wanted her ashes scattered at regimental HQ?"

It was honesty time.

"Not as a mark of respect, that's for certain," said Pascoe. "She hated all things military, and the Wyfies in particular. If I had to guess, I'd say it was the nearest she could get to spitting in somebody's face."

"Any idea why she felt so strongly?"

"She lost her father in the war."

"Millions did."

"We all find our own way of dealing with things."

"Indeed," said the major, frowning. "Though this was extreme."

"But you think you know why."

"Not absolutely certain . . ."

"I think you are," interrupted Pascoe. "Perhaps not when you arrived, but now . . . yet you were going to go without saying anything. Why?"

"Because of your face when you saw the name on that list. You looked like a man looking at his own tomb. I felt, perhaps it would be better . . ."

"Better, worse, we're past that now," said Pascoe brusquely. "Spit it out."

"All right. Like I said, the name rang a bell. Your name, Pascoe. I checked through the regimental records, found those photographs. Saw your face. Coincidence—the name, the resemblance? Possibly. I had to see the picture you had. That clinched it, though it didn't explain it."

"Clinched what, for God's sake?"

"This man with your face, and your name, got killed at Ypres in 1917."

"But you said his name wasn't on the casualty list?"

"No. He didn't die in battle."

Studholme took a deep breath and fixed Pascoe with his one unblinking eye.

He said, "Sergeant Peter Pascoe was court-martialed

for cowardice in face of the enemy. He was found guilty and in November 1917 he was executed in the Ypres Salient by firing squad. Mr. Pascoe, are you all right?"

XIV

THE FIRST PERSON Ellie saw as she entered the party was Andy Dalziel, clutching a glass in one hand and a professor of divinity in the other, to whom he seemed to be explaining some point of canon law.

When he saw Ellie he relaxed his grip and called, "Hey up! Young Woodley back then?"

"Safe and sound. What are you doing here?"

Hurt crinkled the Fat Man's face like interference on a twenty-five-inch screen and he turned in search of support, but the professor, who knew the workings of divine providence when he saw them, was speeding toward the bar.

Robbed of its audience, Dalziel's face resumed normal service as he said, "I were invited. So where's he at?"

"Baby-sitting. Who invited you?"

It was none of her business, but Dalziel as usual had pressed her armed response button.

"Friend," he said vaguely. "He'll be in tomorrow, but?"

"Depends what time I get home, I suppose."

"That kind of do, is it? Let me know when they dish out the marijuana cookies so's I can leave."

"For the sake of diplomacy?" ventured Ellie.

"To fetch reinforcements," said Dalziel. Then his

face lit up and he said, "There you are, luv. Thought you'd run out on me. You know Ellie Pascoe."

Ellie turned to see Mandy Marvell approaching. She looked back to Dalziel, trying to control her surprise. Then she thought, I'm trying not to hurt *his* feelings? and let it show.

Amanda said, "Yes. Hello, Ellie."

Dalziel said, "Nice when you've got mutual friends. Thought there might be another one here. Wendy Walker."

Jesus, thought Ellie, who'd just been looking around to see if she could spot Wendy, how the hell does he always give the impression he's got me bugged?

Dalziel, who'd tossed in the name simply because he still found Walker's transition from pits to pets puzzling, noted her reaction with interest.

"As a matter of fact we did arrange to meet here," said Ellie, recovering.

"Arrange? You keep in touch then?"

"She called today. For a chat. We didn't have as much time as we'd have liked and she said she'd probably see me tonight."

"Oh aye? Didn't think she'd approve of do's like this," prodded Dalziel.

"With her background she's a damn sight more entitled to be here than most of these freeloaders," said Ellie spiritedly.

Dalziel's grin acknowledged the shaft even as it bounced off him. He emptied his glass and said, "Aye, you're right, lass. They don't ring fire alarms to get folk moving in these places, they just open a bottle."

It wasn't a completely accurate analysis, thought Ellie as she took stock of the other guests. One or two, like the Divvy prof, were notorious for turning up anywhere at the clink of a glass. But it was the moral as much as the alcoholic freeloaders who were swelling the numbers. This was obviously the politically correct place to be.

Which didn't explain what Dalziel was doing here in the company of Cap Marvell. Like Jane Austen, Ellie had a very good eye at an adulteress, and her finely tuned sensors were detecting, though not believing, a strong physical bond between the two.

She said, "I gather you had an exciting time last night."

Cap, who'd been observing the exchange between Ellie and Dalziel with close attention, said rather sharply, "Wendy told you what happened then?"

"Not really. We got interrupted. She did seem a bit shook up, though."

"That surprises me. She doesn't really come across as the up-shakable type. It was after all just a few bones."

"That's one way of looking at it. In fact she didn't say much about the bones. I heard more about them on the news before I came out."

"Oh good. You hear that, Andy? One wave of the magic truncheon and the walls come tumbling down. With luck this means they'll show my interview on the local roundup after the main news. Andy, if you don't mind, I won't hang around too long. I'd like to get back to see how it came out."

"Please yourself, lass," said Dalziel. "I just tell the buggers what they can show, I don't have to watch it."

Curiouser and curiouser. Did this mean he was expecting, or expected, to go home with her? And was there an implication that he was in some way responsible for Cap's media exposure?

"I didn't mean you should leave early too," said Cap equably.

Funny how you can say no-strings and twitch one at the same time, thought Ellie, grinning so that Dalziel caught it.

"Just as well, luv," he said negligently. " 'Cos there's a lot of folk here I've not spoken to yet. Can't have them going home feeling offended. Bog-eye, is that you? What fettle? You paid that fine yet? By gum, that brief you brought up from the Smoke should sing for Wales. You ever kill your missus, hire him, and I bet you'd get off with probation."

Bog-eye, that is to say, Charles Burgoyne, vice-chancellor of Mid-Yorkshire University, who had just survived a drunk-driving charge with a fine but no suspension, lowered his aquiline nose to get the Fat Man in his sights, and said, "Probation, Andy? With his fees, I'd expect approbation. Don't just stand there clutching an unfilled can. Come and fill it."

And Dalziel, who never minded being bested by a worthy foe so long as he didn't let it go to his head, laughed and followed the elegantly patrician figure to the bar.

The two women watched him go.

"Incredible, isn't he?" said Cap.

"Beyond belief," agreed Ellie. "Known him long?"

"Long enough," said the other almost slyly, quickly adding as though to relocate the exchange conventionally, "but not as long as you, of course. Through your husband, I mean."

"I assumed that was what you meant," said Ellie. "Yes, man, boy, and mad beast, it's been a long long time."

There was definitely something happening here, but she was more concerned with what she felt was happening to herself. She and Cap Marvell had never been friends, merely people who covered enough common territory for their paths to cross. Ellie's belief in universal sisterhood was political, not religious, and she felt no compulsion to love all her sisters equally. Also she had suspicions that the new Cap Marvell was still the old Hon. Mrs. Rupert Pitt-Evenlode writ small, dragging her private income behind her like Marley's chain, and forever barred from full admission to the real world where people actually worked for a living. Her undoubted energies had proved useful in all kinds of worthy causes but still Ellie had reserved judgment. And she'd been right, she now found herself thinking. What did all this concern with animal rights prove but that the woman was still a middle-class dilettante who would feed her dogs fillet steak while her peasants starved in their hovels?

The vehemence of her imagery startled her. This wasn't reserving judgment, this wasn't even black-cap condemnation—this was a full-blooded lynch mob howl!

And why? I'm jealous, Ellie thought. Oh God, the horror of it! I feel possessive about Fat Andy! I don't mind others seeing him as a yob, a slob—a living negation of all civilized values—but let them start appreciating the contradictions in him, let them come within hailing distance of the steadfastness at the heart of that monstrous bulk, let them (sod *them;* I mean *a woman,* I mean *her!*), let her slip inside that joky love–hate familiarity which has developed between us over the years, and I resent it like hell. This is old Ada in reverse. Her I resented for telling Peter he was worth more than a copper's lot, which is exactly what I spend a good deal of our married life telling him anyway. And I suppose if anyone ever has the effrontery to comment on Rosie's new ripe vocabulary, I'll give them such a mouthful they'll have no doubt where she gets it from. Oh shit. Why do I understand myself so well? Why can't I be like a messiah, or a politician, or a journalist, and honestly believe I know it all!

"Are you all right?" said Cap.

"Yes, fine. Why?"

"Your lips were moving, but no words were coming out."

"It's a ventriloquist act I'm working on," said Ellie. "I think you may have spotted where I'm going wrong. Andy was telling me he's here because you invited him. How come *you're* here, if you don't mind me asking?"

"My grandfather, imagining he was rich enough for his money to last forever, decided to use some of it to give his name a similar life span. He was wrong about his money, as my father, inflation, and a lot of lethargic horses proved. As for his name, you'll have noticed it, but I bet you didn't think of me."

"Hang on. You don't mean the Marvell Collection in the library? I thought it had something to do with the poet."

"The family claim a distant relationship," said Cap. "But no, it was grandfather's bid for immortality. And in the hope that some of his descendants might have similar funds and a similar fancy, the family name remains on the university's permanent invitation list. I wasn't going to come, then I thought it might be amusing to test the depth of their desire to see me by bringing Andy along. In fact he seems more at home than I am."

"A man with roots knows where all the bodies are buried," said Ellie broadly. "I am of course quoting. Talking of buried bodies, whatever you say, it must have been a bit of a shock to you last night."

"Less than you'd imagine. You expect bodies on a battlefield and that's what it felt like out there. You've got me worried about Wendy though."

This was a change of tack. Perhaps she was all heart after all.

"I'm sure she'll be okay. She just wants a heart-to-heart. You know. Girl talk. We go back a long way."

Which was laying it on a little thick.

Cap smiled and said, "Yes, of course. Burrthorpe. And you were her sponsor, weren't you? And her guru too, it seems. Excuse me. There's Galway from Biology trying to avoid my eye. We need to talk about his rats. Catch you later, Ellie."

She moved away in pursuit of a furtive-looking man in a hispid tweed suit. Ellie felt a pang of sympathy for him. Cap's energies might be misdirected, but she was nonetheless formidable. With a bit of luck, Dalziel might for once have overfaced himself.

She looked around for Wendy once more. Still no sign. Damn her, she'd better show. Already she was feeling that she'd done her duty by the NUM and the one drink she allowed herself when driving wasn't going to last much longer. Someone tapped her on the shoulder and she turned, saying, "There you are," only to find, instead of Wendy, she was being smiled at by Arthur Halfdane, historian and former colleague, whose career had prospered at the expense of his fresh young face and curly hair.

"Ellie," he said. "You're looking great. Someone I'd like you to meet. Melbourne University prof here on a sabbatical. Fascinating character."

Bitter experience had taught her that while linguists were usually little snakes with silver tongues, and Eng. Littites frequently had both the tears and the teeth of the crocodile, your most dangerous academic fauna was a smiling historian with a burden to share.

Behind Halfdane she could see a desiccated man with irregular yellow teeth and a red line running round his brow suggesting either recent brain surgery or the habitual wearing of a tight-fitting cork-hung hat.

Ducking into the lee of a merry-faced woman in her late thirties and a flowered jumpsuit which strained to constrain her exuberant flesh, Ellie hissed, "Thanks but no thanks. I've done my Ozzie quota for the year."

"That's okay, girl. I hate you fucking Poms too," said the Rubenesque woman, her smile even wider.

"Ellie," said Halfdane with that smug historian's expression evolved through centuries of being right about everything fifty years after it happened. "Let me introduce you to Professor Pollinger."

XV

PETER PASCOE LAY in the dark and felt its weight press upon him.

Peine forte et dure . . . Who was it said "more weight"? . . . and had it been in defiance or merely a plea to hasten a certain end?

Idiot! he told himself. Over the top as usual. What cause have I for despair? There are those out there with nothing but darkness between them and the sky . . . soldiers and poor unable to rejoice . . . the lost, the dispossessed . . . while I lie here with a wife and daughter I love . . .

—with a wife and daughter who love me—o Alice Ada the thought of you should give me strength to fight—why is it the thought of you brings me to the brink of hopelessness?

Because I cant believe this is for you—not any of it—how can this filth this foulness this blood these broken bones and scattered limbs these lice these rats this helpless hopeless heedless hell have anything to do with you? What is it these horrors protect you from?—some baby-butchering Hun on a poster?—Ive seen him this monster—Ive seen him dead and Ive seen him alive—and dead he lies there like my own mates—same gore oozing from same mangled limbs—same disbelief in same uncomprehending eyes.

> *And alive he looks like a lost boy terrified the
> hand I offer with a fag will turn into a fist—and
> when he starts to believe my kindness he reaches in
> his tunic and shows me pictures of his Alice his Ada.*
>
> *Is this the monster Im protecting you from? Am I
> the monster he's protecting his family from? I dont
> know—there must be a reason and if not this then
> what?*

Peter Pascoe rolled out of bed and tiptoed from the room.

Sleep wasn't going to come tonight. He'd known it from the moment Studholme had told him the truth. The major, so reluctant at first to reveal what he knew, once that barrier was over, seemed ready to sit and talk forever. Pascoe's instinct, fine-honed on years of interrogation, knew there was more to come, a lot of questions still to answer. But not now, not now. All he wanted was to be alone in the after-rack of this bombshell. He'd almost pushed Studholme out of the house, then poured himself a Dalzielesque Scotch and roamed restless, ending up in the garden, feeling the need for space and distance and the cloudy indifference of the sky.

Cold had driven him back in, where he found his wanderings had disturbed Rosie. With a huge effort he had put a lid on his emotional turmoil so that it wouldn't overflow and be detectable by the child. A favorite story had soothed her fret and when sleep had finally relaxed those already unflawed lineaments to the breath-catching freshness of the very first spring, he had looked down on her, then closed his own eyes and imagined never seeing her again.

He opened his eyes. She was still there. He had sat by her bedside till he heard the car in the drive and knew that Ellie had returned.

They drank coffee together while she told him with

delight of Dalziel's presence at the party and the speculations it aroused. Pascoe had responded dully to both
gossip and news and finally headed for bed, pleading
his early start and long drive. He wanted to talk to Ellie, but not till he felt he had something rational, something coherent to say. There were dark places inside his
mind that he didn't feel able to share, not yet, not perhaps ever. Once when he was younger he'd have said
that love was about openness, about the utter naked-
ness each to each of two bodies and minds and souls.
But not now . . . not now . . . not now . . .

   . . . I had thought to tell Alice all of this when I
was home on leave but I found I couldnt—theres
been something called the Battle of Arras which all
the papers had written up as a famous victory—and
thats what Id been fighting in I discovered—thats
where Duggie Granger and Kit Bagley and Micky
Sidebottom and God knows how many more tens of
thousands made the supreme sacrifice which is how
they talk about having your guts blown out or your
brains sieved through your tin hat back in Blighty.
So how could I tell Alice or anyone about that?—Or
when I read about our glorious allies how could I
tell them what an officers servant on the leave boat
told me hed heard—that the Frogs to our east had
had it even worse than us and had chucked away
their guns and said they wouldnt fight any more—
and that whole troops were being marched out and
shot by their fellow countrymen as mutineers.
   What we could talk about because all the papers
were still talking about it was the revolution in Russia. When I called on Mr Cartwright at the Institute
he told me he reckoned it ud mean Russia would be
out of the war in no time and this was the chance
for workers all over Europe to unite and force their
governments to follow suit. There was a big national

Convention that week at the Coliseum Cinema in Leeds and he invited me to go along—which I did even though Alice told me to take care as I knew how Mr Grindal hated such meetings. I said—whats Mr Grindal to me now?—and went anyway. It was very exciting with Mr Snowden making a fine speech and I even said something myself—when this woman who was what they call a suffragette said that of course she wanted peace but we must make sure all the noble sacrifices made by our brave boys had not been in vain—and I jumped up and shouted that if shed seen what Id seen—the bodies of my friends blown to pieces for a hundred yards of wasted ground shed know it had all been in vain already. Some people cheered but a lot didnt and there was one little bunch of fellows in uniform who set up a chant of traitor which knocked me back till I got a closer look and realized they were all new recruits just out of training camp. One of them I recognized—Archie Doyle—my old enemy from Grindals—wearing the lily and the rose—so I worked my way round to him and said—nice to see you Archie—when are you joining the battalion— and he gave a sick grin and said he were off in two days—and I said—I look forward to that Archie.

Next day when I called at mill I asked about Archie—and got told that spite of all his hard talk hed hidden behind his wifes skirts till theyd brought in full conscription last year—and even after that by pleading his wife being sick and by running around after Mr Grindal whos on our local Board hed put it off till now. I dont like him much but I thought— poor bastard—youd have been better off sticking your hand in a loom!

Not that theres many looms left to stick anything in! Its all changed—not just that its all old men and lasses now—Id expected that—but its mainly hospi-

tal stuff theyre making—dressings and slings and all sorts of medical things—and Uncle George told me that once the gaffer had got it in his head there was more profit in Mr Sams line of business over the river hed not hesitated but started ripping out the old looms and fetching in new machinery as fast as he could manage it. Naturally we talked about Stephen too and I told him we were fit and well—but when I mentioned Mary his face went hard and he said hed have kicked her out long since if it hadnt been for the little lad—then he begged me not to say owt of this to Steve—it must be bad enough having to go through what we went through without worrying about what your wife were up to. I said naturally I wouldnt say a word then Mr Grindal who mustve heard I was there sent down for me to call in at his office.

He met me at the door looking hard and thrawn as ever—and said right off—I hear thas been making a fool of theyself in Leeds last night. I said—I told the truth if thats what tha means. Truth? he sneers. What truth?—The same truth as is keeping all them down there on your mill floor busy—I said. That took him back and he said—well I dont suppose one more fool ud be noticed in that crowd at the Coliseum. Step inside—someone here for you to meet.

I went through the door and found myself looking at an officer—so straight off I snapped to attention and threw a salute. Back it came but with a big grin—then he said—there father didnt I tell you that Peter would make a fine soldier—and then I recognized him—young Gertie Grindal looking like he were dressed for COs parade in the uniform of a Wyfie subaltern. What a lily he looked with his boots glistening like piston oil, his gloves as yellow as butter, and the pips on his shoulders standing out

*like Johnny Cadgers boils. Id not seen him since that
last summer afore the war when hed been fifteen
and his dad had set him on at the mill in his school
holiday—partly to learn job—partly as punishment
for bad reports from his posh school. Id taken care
of him—and soon learned he were still as nesh as
when a nipper and hed dragged after me round the
woods—always coming on like Jack the Lad when
the sun were on his back but running for cover at
first sign of rain. In the house with his mam—or
mine—around he knew he was master. But things
were different out in the woods. There I was in
charge and I could get my own back any time I liked
—like the time I showed him the old ice house and
told him it were where the Great White Worm lived
—then I yelled—look out its coming!—and ran off
leaving him alone. He cried so much he couldnt eat
his tea and though mam skelped my ears for it I
thought it were well worth the pain.*

*Now he said—remember the fun we used to have
when we were young together—the scrapes Id lead
us into? I said—I recall the summer you worked at
the mill—thinking mebbe that would pull him up
short—he mustve remembered how everyone called
him Gertie—but he just smiled and said—yes indeed
—more great days—remember that fifty I made
against Uncle Sams Eleven? And you were a very
steady bowler if I recall—do you manage to get any
cricket out there?*

*His fifty had been nearer ten and my seven wick-
ets had won us the match. I said—not much opportunity for cricket over there sir. Grounds not really
up to it.*

*Nonsense—he said. All you need is twenty-two
yards of flat field—Im sure even the French can
manage that. I thought of the shell shattered earth
which awaited us as we came out of our trenches*

*and set out up the ridge in front of Wancourt—and I
was going to say something a bit sarcastic when I
caught old Grindals eye—and I kept quiet—not because anything I saw there made me afraid but because I saw how afraid he was. And he had cause.*

*Gertie went on—never fear—Im sure well be able
to get some kind of game going when I get across.
Get across?—I echoed. Yes Ive got my orders. Off
tomorrow—possibly well be travelling together.*

*I didnt point out the difference between first and
third class but said—sorry sir—Ive still got three
days leave.*

*He looked as if he thought that was a small price
to pay for the pleasure of his company then he said
—one thing you can help me with Pascoe—I was
thinking about shipping my hunters across—what
do you reckon? When the breakthrough comes Id
like to be properly mounted.*

*Id seen men properly mounted galloping forward
near Monchy where some idiot brasshat had imagined a break in the line. Pennants fluttering—sabres
flashing—oh it were a sight to remember—but what
really stuck in the mind and would do till memory
died was the sound of the horses screaming as they
were hosed down with bullets from the Huns machine guns.*

*I looked sadly at the poor smiling child and
thought—three weeks—I give you three weeks. That
was about the average for a subaltern in hard fighting. Mr Hurley our present platoon commander had
managed nearly three months which was quite remarkable considering he couldnt tell left from right
without checking his Sam Browne. We all thought
he were a bit of a liability—but compared to the
poor bastards who were going to get Gertie we were
sitting pretty.*

Anyway I gave him another big salute which de-

lighted him and left. As I walked away Mr Grindal came after me and took my arm.

He said—Peter youve been out there long enough to know your way around—look out for him will you?

I knew it must have cost his pride a lot to ask my help and I knew that in his own way hes been right good to me—better than I would have expected once I took up with the Union. But I knew also this was a promise Id no right to give. This werent like stopping a kid from falling in the beck or patching him up when hed scratched himself in a bramble patch. It werent even like pulling him back when he looked like he were going to get tangled in one of the big looms which Id had to do on more than one occasion.

It takes God Almighty to pull you out of the way of bombs or bullets or flying shrapnel and theres neither rhyme nor reason to the way He does it.

But while I was seeking words to say this old Grindal nodded his head—them keen black eyes which see all for once deceiving him into seeing what he wanted to see in my face—and he squeezed my arm and said—thanks lad—thisll not be forgotten.

I know I shouldve said something but I didnt— and I cant feel guilty.

I mean—why the hell should I feel bothered that I didnt try to tell someone like old Grindal what its really like out there when Ive not yet been able to find words to tell my own dear wife what I feel about it?

"Okay, Peter, enough's enough. If I'm going to share my life with Hamlet's ghost, I'm entitled to eavesdrop on the soliloquies."

He hadn't heard her come down the stairs. Now she

padded barefoot into the kitchen, flopped down on a chair at the other side of the table and tested the warmth of the teapot with her left hand.

"I'll make some more," he offered.

"No, this'll do."

She pulled his mug toward her, refilled it and sipped the lukewarm liquid.

"It was Hamlet's father whose ghost walked," Pascoe pointed out.

"Also called Hamlet. So, who do you want revenge on?"

He considered. Was this the right note, very English, light and rational? What was the alternative? Latin emotional? Slav confessional? Scand suicidal?

He said, "The British military and political establishment might do for a start."

Then he told her succinctly and unemotionally what Studholme had told him.

He could see she found the information puzzling rather than devastating.

"But how can Ada's father be called Peter Pascoe? It doesn't make sense. It must be a mistake, compounded by the coincidence of names."

"And the coincidence of faces? No, he's the one, I'm sure of it. And I'm going to find out how it happened."

"How your maternal great-grandfather happened to have your name, you mean?"

"No. How my great-grandfather happened to end up being tied to a post and pumped full of bullets by his own countrymen."

"Peter, it's terrible, but it was all a long time ago," she said gently. "I know revenge is a dish best eaten cold, all that crap, but this has been lying around so long, even the salmonella's got salmonella! Is it really worth calling up the Furies over something like this?"

He said, still trying to keep it light, "Maybe they're up and out already."

She considered this, then said, "You mean after you, don't you?"

"Do I? Yes, perhaps I do," he said, managing, with difficulty, a smile.

"But why? I mean, what have you done? What is there in your great-grandfather's death to make you feel guilty? Think about it. How many millions got killed in the Great War? Seven? Eight? More? I doubt if there's a person alive in Britain, France, or Germany who didn't lose some relative at that time. So how come you get elected to bear the guilt?"

He felt on the edge of dangerous country which he needed to explore himself before he invited those he loved in. But she deserved something more than silence. A lot more.

He said carefully, "Look, I'm not clear myself, but it's about my family . . . as you've frequently observed yourself, we are on the whole a pretty mixed-up bunch of no-hopers . . ."

"Come on, Pete!" she protested. "Bad-mouthing your spouse's nearest and dearest is an old and socially accepted convention of marital dispute."

"So it is. Except that in this case none of my nearest come anywhere close to being my dearest. There were times long ago . . . not so long ago . . . when I used to fantasize about discovering I was a changeling and I really had this other completely different family I could make a fresh start with, only this time with me calling the shots as well as them."

"Everyone does that," she said dismissively.

"In their thirties?" he replied, only half mocking. "Look, I'm not sure I've really got this worked out, but it's something to do with justice, yes, but it's also something to do with me, what I am, what I'm not, what I would like to be. I know it's a simplification, but it's as if everything that's wrong with the Pascoes, wrong with me, stems from what happened to my great-grandfather back in 1917."

"Now, that *would* be convenient," she said. "But what if what happened to him happened because whatever you imagine's wrong with the Pascoes was there already? Please leave it, Peter."

"I can't," he said, helplessly. "When those Furies have got you in their sights, you've got to keep going till you set the record straight. That's the only sanctuary they allow."

She looked at him steadily and lovingly over her mug of cold tea. She knew what many close friends still failed to grasp, that dominant though her own personality must often seem in their relationship, his was by far the stronger will.

She said, "Okay. Go get the truth if you must. Any idea how to start?"

"God knows," he said. "But as He seems intent on chucking great lumps of my family history at me in a provocative fashion, I presume that He'll come up with some help on the research front too."

"Could be He's started," said Ellie. "I met this Australian history prof tonight. Poll Pollinger."

"A female Australian history professor called Poll?" said Pascoe as if he could believe no single element.

"That's right. She invited me up to her flat for a coffee else I'd have been home a lot earlier. . . ."

"What happened to Wendy Walker? I thought you were giving her a lift."

"Never saw her. Changed her mind or was having such a good time in another part of the party, she forgot all about me. Wendy always did think good manners were a form of social elitism," said Ellie dismissively. "Anyway, Poll's here on sabbatical to write a book about, yes, you've got it, Passchendaele. What she doesn't know about the First World War isn't worth a footnote. Best of all, she has a direct line right to the heart of M.O.D. records. I asked her how she managed that. She said, it's all a matter of reputation. I said, sorry, I didn't realize I was talking to someone really famous, and she said, not my reputation, dingo-head! It seems she knows something utterly unspeakable about some senior brass hat at whose command all doors fly open. She's really great!"

"She sounds . . . interesting. What line is she taking?"

"In conversation at least she seems to think *dickhead* and *Haig* form one word. There's a piece by her in the current *Review*. She gave me a copy. It's titled 'Lest We Forget,' not so much an historical essay as a *j'accuse* for Remembrance Day. Read it. But not now."

"Why not now?"

"Because you've got me wide-awake. Because if I remember right, Wendy Walker interrupted a very interesting conversation earlier today. Because if it's really sanctuary you're after, I can do a much better job than a whole barrow-load of Furies."

"Sanctuary?" he echoed. "I really can't imagine what you're talking about."

She reached her hand under the table and smiled.

"You always were a lousy liar," she said.

XVI

. . . *and the earth moved. Jesus Christ!—said Jammy—What the hell was that?*

It took a lot to startle Sergeant Jameson—hes got the kind of face that looks like its carved out of rock —and when he shouts on the parade ground he can

*set a whole intake of recruits pissing their pants. I
know—he did it to me—I used to think he was the
most terrible man on earth—I hated him worse than
the Kaiser—till one night in Leeds a redcap corporal
was putting me through the hoop when Jammys big
hand descended on his shoulder and he said—one
of mine—and I dont need no help to keep him
straight. The redcap remembered urgent business
elsewhere. I said—thanks sarge. For what?—he asks
like he didnt need gratitude from shit like me. For
stopping me kicking that sod in the balls—I said.
Wonder of wonders that made him laugh—and after
that I began to change my mind about him—and
him about me I reckon—cos I got my first stripe and
you didnt do that without Sergeant Jamesons say so.
But it werent till we got to France that we became
really friendly. Theres nowt like picking up bits of
your old platoon for bringing people together.*

*The battalion was still in the reserve area outside
Arras when I got back from leave but we knew from
the bombardment up to the north that something big
was coming off—so we didnt expect to stay there
much longer. And now this—about three this morning—the ground shaking like egg custard and the
sky to the north all burning red as if the devils had
tunnelled their way out of hell.*

*We were eating breakfast before we found out
that our sappers had set off this huge mine under the
Germans on the ridge near Messines. There was a
hole in the ground as big as Bradford—one signaller
said—and the Jerries were surrendering in their
thousands—most on em stark naked cos the blast
had blown their clothes off. Our boys were just
walking through the gap in the German line not
even having to bother about guns because the blast
had jammed all them as it hadnt destroyed.*

Some of our new lads were keen to get orders to

get on up there—among them Archie Doyle. I hadnt
been best pleased when I found him in our platoon
when I got back off leave—but hes not daft and hed
soon worked out it were better to act like an old
mate of your corporals than an old enemy. So he
was huffing and puffing about how we were missing
our chance for a bit of easy glory—till Jammy said—
thas not been here long enough to get chatty Doyle
—theres some of us have heard it all before. Aye
sarge—pipes Chuffy Chandler—but weve not heard
a bang like that before—which Jammy had to admit
was true.

Then Lieutenant Hurley—old Hurly-Burly we
called him—came along and said we were moving.
We all thought it would be up to Messines but gradually we realized that we were going too far north
for that—and finally Hurley confirmed it—we were
heading for the Salient.

That soon shut up all those whod ever been in the
Salient before. In all that stinking festering front line
the Salients like a bloody great boil sticking out towards the enemy. Hurley said wed be all right—the
Messines mine had taken the southern corner off the
Salient and it was only to be expected thered be a
follow up attack mounted there within a matter of
days if not hours. By the time we got there the Hun
would likely be in full retreat. And Ill be Queen of
the May—said Jammy right out loud. The lieutenant
laughed—hes a decent sort and weve all got used to
his little daftnesses like always wanting to look on
the bright side of things.

We camped near Pop to start with which were
fine—egg and chips in the cafe des Allies with a
good sing song to follow whenever you could duck
off duties—red hot weather—lots of football
matches—and would you believe it young Gertie
whod landed a job helping Captain Evenlode the ad-

jutant actually got his cricket team going till Jammy hit the only ball we had into a river—and that was the end of that. Pity the Frogs dont play—said Gertie. Nor Jerry either—I said—Could have asked them for a game. True—he said—though perhaps if Jerry did play we wouldnt be fighting this war.

Mebbe he was making a joke but I dont think so.

It had to happen. Orders to move up into the Salient came yesterday. First by train to Ypres then we marched to Zillebeke where we waited for dark before moving up into the line. We were sitting by the lake enjoying the sunshine when Jammy suddenly yells—Minnie left! Where the hell it had come from Christ knows. We should have been well out of their range—mebbe it had a following wind or Fritz was trying a new gun—but there it was—a little black spot in the air tumbling slowly towards us. Most didnt risk looking—when Jammy yelled Minnie left! you headed right and dived into the first hole you could find. Thats what we did all except Hurly-Burly. Hed loosened his Sam Browne so perhaps thats what did it. Someone said they saw him shooting off like a scalded cat—only he didnt head right but left—and all that was left of him wasnt worth collecting in a bucket.

It didnt feel like a good omen and we were more down than usual as we prepared to follow Jammy through the dark into our front line position. Then he was called up by the adjutant and a bit later he came back with someone behind him.

Corporal Pascoe—he said—This heres our new platoon commander.

I knew who it was before I saw his face and heard his voice.

Hello Pascoe—said Gertie Grindal—Isnt this jolly?

Yes sir—I said looking at Jammy whose huge face showed nowt—Where exactly is it were heading sir?

South east corner of some wood—what do you call it sergeant?

Sanctuary sir—said Jammy.

Id heard some misleading names for some terrible places but this sounded to me like it could be the worst fitting of them all.

Especially with Gertie in charge.

Thats it—he said—Lovely name isnt it—Get the men moving then sergeant—and if they need jollying along just tell them were heading to Sanctuary and that should speed them up eh? Sanctuary!

PART TWO

GLENCORSE

And nothing may we use in vain.
Ev'n Beasts must be with justice slain;
Else men are made their Deodands.

I

LEST WE FORGET:
A MEDITATION FOR REMEMBRANCE SUNDAY
by Andrea Pollinger

Passchendaele was not so much an exercise in modern warfare as an experiment in mass suicide.

The contemporary equivalent would be to devastate an area of several thousand acres with a tactical nuclear weapon, then send in a force of unprotected men to occupy it. This, I am assured by men who did National Service in the fifties, was a tactic actually rehearsed by the British Army at that time, suggesting that little had changed, and the men at the top always want to fight today's wars according to yesterday's technology. Central to the tactical thinking of World War I, such as it was, stood the proposition that if you could punch a hole in the enemy line and send cavalry galloping through, then everyone would be home for Christmas . . . or New Year . . . or Easter . . . or . . .

In fairness to Haig it should be said that his strategic plan for Third Ypres was more modest. His intention was to drive the enemy back to a line beyond Bruges and thus cut the U-boat supply line from Bruges to Ostend.

Initially there was supposed to be a simultaneous naval assault on the coast, but when the Admiralty decided this did not suit their convenience, Haig decided to go ahead, perhaps believing that the missing marine element would be supplied by his choice of battleground, basically an area of marshland which not even a complex system of drainage ditches and dikes had been able to reclaim for anything other than bog pasturage. No sensible farmer was going to sow seed on this land. But donkey Haig, having learned nothing from the ineffectiveness of the huge preliminary bombardment on the Somme a year earlier, sowed it with shells for ten long days.

This time not only did the long bombardment give the Germans plenty of warning of the attack, it also breached many of the dikes and dammed most of the ditches. And it started raining. Even a general might have been expected to notice that. And the general of any army that had been bogged down, literally and figuratively, in Flanders for nearly three years might have been expected to have gathered a little bit of intelligence about the terrain. But, standing aloof in giant ignorance, Haig ordered the attack to be pressed, and kept on pressing it for three long months, across marshland, in heavy rain, with ditches blocked and dikes destroyed, and the whole devastated landscape pitted with shell holes like the surface of the moon, except that here was no dry volcanic dust but mud; thick, cloying, drowning, sucking mud . . .

II

PETER PASCOE STOOD and looked at the mud.

Where the water hit, it seethed and surged and wrinkled and writhed as if alive. He imagined being caught in its glutinous embrace, wrapped round, caressed, held fast, and finally drawn down into dark slow-stifling depths. . . .

He turned away and found himself facing Death.

"Ingenious, though I say it myself," said Arnold Gentry with a rare flush of enthusiasm. "Three tanks with gradated filters. This first one is wide mesh. It will catch anything bigger than a half brick. The second smaller, pebble size. The third superfine, textile fragments, fingernails, hair even."

"Great," said Pascoe, whose genuine interest in and admiration for Death's work had established a relationship particularly useful in view of Dalziel's ill-concealed abhorrence of the man. "There's quite a lot of material to get through though, isn't there?"

He turned his gaze on the great mound of earth brought from Wanwood House and deposited alongside Dr. Death's patent sluice.

"We will get through it much more quickly than half a dozen constables crawling around with garden hoes," said Gentry, bridling. "And infinitely more thoroughly."

"Yes, yes, of course," soothed Pascoe. "My point exactly. I wanted you to know how much we appreciate you taking it on and releasing our men for other inquiries."

It was his emollient skills that had got him here. He'd turned up at the station that morning in good

time, in fact a few minutes early, but any hope he might
have nurtured of gaining a few Brownie points vanished when he read the scrawled note on his desk.

*Nice of you to show up, especially as we're short-
handed. George Headingley fell in a puddle and got
himself on the panel with a cold in the head which
must be pretty small to get in there beside the bone. If
you can spare a moment from your mourning, you
might take yourself down to the lab and see what yon
mate of yours is doing with the muck from Wanwood.
I'm off to see Troll down the knackers.*

Dalziel assumed his subordinates knew everything
about all current cases.

Like many of his assumptions, it was self-fulfilling.
Pascoe had managed to catch Sergeant Wield on his
way out and get a quick update. Wield's resumés were
famously more informative than other people's disqui-
sitions. "Let that bugger run Parliament," Dalziel had
once remarked, "and they could all go home on a Tues-
day, which most on 'em probably do anyway."

In exchange Pascoe had offered the, to him, still incredible news that Dalziel might have found himself a
lady love. "You mean yon animal woman?" Wield had
interrupted. "Aye, I thought he fancied her. Mebbe she
reckons he's an endangered species. Gotta dash. See
you."

So, reflected Pascoe, might Pheidippides have felt as
he staggered through the gates of Athens to see a news
placard reading GOTCHA! PERSIANS STUFFED AT MARA-
THON.

He and Gentry stood in companionable silence for a
while, watching the water jets wash the first load of
earth through the first filter. The level was getting low
and various large stones and pieces of wood were becoming visible in the now almost liquid mud. Then

something a bit whiter . . . in fact as the water hit it, very much whiter . . . smooth . . . bowl-shaped . . .

"Hold on," said Dr. Death excitedly. "There's something, let me see. . . ."

He picked up a long bamboo pole with a metal circle and a net on the end and with the expertise of a gillie slipped it beneath the object and lifted it out.

"There we are," he said with pale delight. "That should please Mr. Longbottom and even Superintendent Dalziel too."

"Yes," said Pascoe, looking down with a marked lack of pleasure at the human cranium in the plastic mesh. "I suppose it should."

III

"DEM BONES DEM BONES GONNA WALK AROUND, dem bones dem bones gonna walk around, dem bones dem bones gonna walk around, now hear de Word of de Lord."

Dalziel, recognizing his cue, said, "You've missed a bit."

Troll Longbottom turned sharply and said, "My God, for a tub of lard, you roll soft, Andy."

"Aye, and you start early. What happened? Flint up your jacksie kept you awake and you started thinking of breakfast?"

"I have been in my lab by eight o'clock every working day for more years than I care to remember," said Longbottom reproachfully. "What do you think?"

He stood aside so that Dalziel got a complete view of the bones laid out on the table. The Fat Man had

been right about missing a bit. Wield's team had
dredged up several more fragments before it was decided to accept Gentry's solution and use the sluice
technique, but the remains were still more than fifty
percent short of a full set.

"Good-looking fellow," said Dalziel. "How'd he
die?"

"Not, I would hazard, by physical violence directed
at any of the parts covered by, or indeed covering, the
bones you see here."

"There's some of 'em broken," objected Dalziel.
"Or did you not notice?"

"Good lord, what it is to have a trained eye," said
Longbottom. "Which one is it? The left? If you
brought the other up to scratch, together they might
have made the further observation that all these frac-
tures are recent, caused I would guess when the contractors blasted, gouged, and bulldozed that strip of
woodland in the summer."

"So when will you be able to tell us owt useful?"

"Anything positive, you mean? Negatives too are
useful, and I can give you some of them. Nothing has
been detected yet in the organic matter recovered to
indicate toxicity or disease . . ."

"Hang on. Organic matter?"

"Yes. Very little, but enough to work on in various
little nooks and crannies."

"This mean it's not been so long buried then?" said
Dalziel gloomily.

"Still hoping for prehistory, Andy? Sorry, that's definitely out. But dating is proving something of a problem for reasons too technical to puzzle your steam-age
mind with. There are a surprising number of contradictions . . . but as usual, I see you want positive information only. All right. Male, five eight, five nine in
height, fairly slight of build. And that's it as far as positive goes."

"They should pay you by the word," growled Dalziel. "Any sign of clothing?"

"Curiously, no."

"Why curiously?"

"I'd have expected some fibers at least in association with remains such as these appear to be. Of course once dispersion started, bones are heavy, fabric's light. I understand you are following Gentry's recommendation of pursuing your search via his sluice?"

"Aye. It made sense."

"You think so? When speed is of the essence, perhaps. But in this case . . . nevertheless, if there is any fabric which might be associated with the remains—though how you are going to tell when it has been flushed out under the good doctor's water jets, I don't know—Gentry will be your man. At the least, I hope he may come up with the missing pieces of my jigsaw. Particularly the skull. I long for the skull."

"May be able to help you there, sir," said Peter Pascoe.

This time both men started. Lightness of step was one of many things Pascoe had learned from his great master.

He placed a cardboard box carefully on the table.

"Where the hell have you popped up from?" said Dalziel sourly.

"As instructed, I went down to the lab to check on Mr. Gentry's progress. This is the first fruit of his labors."

He reached into the box and produced the gleaming white cranium.

The pathologist took it and observed satirically, "I'm going to wash that hair right out of this man. . . ."

"Dr. Death say owt about hair?" asked Dalziel.

"He seemed confident that with his system of progressively finer filters, he would retrieve anything retrievable," said Pascoe.

"Can't say fairer than that," said Dalziel. "You'll keep me posted, Troll?"

The pathologist wasn't listening but examining the cranium closely with the aid of a magnifier.

"Now we're getting somewhere," he said. "Look there, Andy. That long crack running from this compression here. I'd say that wasn't done by the summer's clearance."

"Someone bashed him, you mean? Cause of death?" said Dalziel.

"Could be. I'll let you know as soon as I'm certain, which is likely to be sooner if I'm given a bit of room to work in."

"You hear that, Chief Inspector?" said Dalziel. "Let the dog see the bone. We'll be off then, Troll. No need to see us out."

The pathologist had shown no inclination to. In fact he now seemed oblivious to their existence let alone their presence.

"Fair loves his work, old Troll," said Dalziel on the way to the car park. "Could do with a few like him under me. Enjoy your little jaunt, did you? Nowt like a good family get-together."

"It was a funeral I went to, sir, not a wedding," said Pascoe reproachfully.

"All the better. I hate bloody weddings. All them speeches and you've got to buy a present. Funerals now, no one expects you to laugh, and wi' a bit of luck, you come away better off than when you went. You cop for owt?"

"Not really," said Pascoe. "My grandmother didn't have much to leave."

"No? Hope you checked under the carpets and down the chair cushions."

He hadn't, but he had no doubt Myra had.

He said, "This body, sir. How are we playing it?

From what Wieldy said, sounds like they could be pretty old bones."

"Aye, the worst kind. I were hoping Longbottom couldn't get at cause of death. Open verdict, closed case. Champion."

"But it's not looking that way?"

"You heard what he said about the cranium. Best hope now is he can date it so far back that everyone concerned's likely to have snuffed it too. I'll mebbe lean on him a bit."

"Lean on him . . . ?"

"Few old bones of his own he'd not like resurrected," said Dalziel, smiling nostalgically. "Meanwhile, but, we'd best go on like we've got a real live murder case. First thing is to start tracing the history of yon house. That sounds like your kind of thing, lad. Lots of chat, not much mud on your shoes."

"How kind," said Pascoe. "Any suggestions as to where I might start enjoying this sinecure?"

"ALBA bought it. Happen they'll know who they bought it from."

"So, I should start at Wanwood. Talk to David Batty?"

"David, is it? Oh aye. You were out there getting nowhere in the summer. Got right friendly with this Batty, did you?"

"Not so's you'd notice. I gather his father, Thomas Batty, runs the company and most of his subordinates seem to refer to him as Mr. David or Dr. David in order I presume to avoid confusion."

"What did you reckon to him?"

Pascoe shrugged.

"We got on okay, no more than that."

"Wouldn't buy a used syringe from him then?"

"I saw no reason to doubt his honesty," said Pascoe, surprised. "It was a Dr. Fell thing really. Something about him made me feel uneasy. Probably just the way he made certain rather outmoded assumptions about our relationship."

"Aye. Tried the same with me to start out," said Dalziel. "But we ended up big muckers. Any road, don't bother wi' him. Give their head office a ring. That'll be where the records are kept."

"All right. It's in Leeds, isn't it?"

"That's right. Kirkton, just on the edge."

"Kirkton?" echoed Pascoe. Into his mind jumped Ada's passport with her place of birth given as Kirkton, Yorkshire. No mention of Leeds.

"That's right. Mean something to you?" said Dalziel, observing him shrewdly.

"No, sir. I was just thinking, it's not all that far and these things are often better done in person than on the phone. Less chance of being choked off . . ."

"You mean you want to waste time driving out there? What the fuck for? It's not your English Heritage sort of place, tha knows. Eat their young out at Kirkton, so they say."

"Nonetheless," said Pascoe.

"That's it then," said Dalziel. "No arguing with you once you start nonethelessing me. But think on, let the locals know you're treading on their patch. Very thin skins they've got in Leeds. Can't scratch their own arseholes without bleeding."

As if to demonstrate his own freedom from this grievous failing, he settled back on the bonnet of Longbottom's old Jag and rubbed his buttocks sensuously against the gleaming silver mascot.

"I'll be careful," promised Pascoe, opening the door of his car. "Where can I get hold of you in case, just in case, there is a diplomatic incident?"

The Fat Man slid off the Jaguar and started walking away.

"I'll be around," he tossed negligently over his shoulder. "Witnesses, interrogation, whatever comes along. You know me, lad, always there where I'm most needed."

Such uncharacteristic evasiveness aroused the deepest suspicion.

Pascoe applied the ultimate test. Winding down his window, he called after the Fat Man. "Time for a quick pint in the Bull, sir?"

Dalziel turned his head like a bishop's wife being propositioned by a curb crawler.

"At this time in the morning? You want to take care, Peter, else you'll be getting a reputation as a drinker."

To which there was no possible or at least no passable reply.

IV

AS FATE NUDGED PETER PASCOE ever deeper into his familial past, Edgar Wield was giving the myopic old goddess a hearty shove back.

"Sorry, mate," he said to the man he'd just contrived to collide with outside a William Hill's betting shop. "Hey, it's Jimmy Howard, isn't it? Hardly recognized you out of uniform. Mind you, I didn't recognize you in your new uniform yesterday, not till Mr. Dalziel said who you were."

He accompanied his words with an effort to rearrange his features into an expression of pleased surprise, though conscious that the effect was probably as disconcerting as one of the heads on Mount Rushmore sneezing.

"What do you want?" responded Howard, making no reciprocal effort to feign pleasure. He had after all been a policeman as well as a gambler and knew all the odds against such chance encounters.

Wield was quite pleased to drop the pretense, moving readily from old-mate to ancient-mariner mode as he fixed the other with a glittering eye and said, "I were just thinking, Jimmy. Bit out of the way, Wanwood House. Awkward to get to on nights, unless you've got a car."

He saw at once he'd hit the mark. Howard had got out of the Force ahead of his conviction for over-the-limit driving, but that hadn't stopped him getting a year's suspension which would be up at the end of the month. According to the roster in Patten's office, Howard had been doing a week-on, week-off night duty since August. Last bus to get anywhere near Wanwood ran at seven o'clock. First of the day wasn't till nine-thirty. Was Howard the kind of twit who, faced with this problem, would think, sod it! and risk driving himself there? Everything Wield could dig up about him suggested he was, and now the man's expression gave confirmation.

"Give you a lift anywhere, Jimmy?" said Wield. "You'll be pleased when you get your license back, I bet. Lose it again, and it could be forever."

"No, thanks, Sarge," said Howard. "I'm just popping in here."

He tried to push by into the betting shop but Wield's arm was in the way.

"Always give the first race a miss," he said confidently. "If you win, you just plow it back, and if you lose, well, it wasn't worth it anyway. I'll buy you a cuppa instead."

He steered the man irresistibly round the corner into a small cafe which time and the Public Health inspectorate had passed by. Wield, looking at the verdigrised spoon with which he was expected to stir his tea, wished he'd followed their example.

He said, "There is something you could help me with, Jimmy."

The man looked simultaneously uneasy and relieved that they were getting down to the nub of this "accidental" meeting at last.

"It's that report you did about what happened when those animal rights women got loose in Wanwood," said Wield, and noted with interest that relief now dominated.

"I wrote everything down," said Howard.

"Yeah, and very good it looks. Whatever else you've forgotten about being a cop, Jimmy, you've not forgotten how to write a report."

"So what's the problem?"

"If Dr. Batty goes for a prosecution, he's going to need more than trespass. You know how difficult that one is, even with the new laws. He'll need damage, and a bit of assault wouldn't come amiss either. So a bit more detail, just to make things look good . . ."

He waited with interest to see how this invitation to embroider would be taken. Howard visibly relaxed, as if feeling more at home, and said, "You mean you'd like a bit more verbals, Sarge? No problem. We'd got 'em all inside and really, they looked so wet and miserable, and a bit scared too, we didn't anticipate any problem, when suddenly that boss woman, the one with the chest, she yells, 'Okay, ladies, let's go for it!' something like that, punches Nev, who's holding her, with them wire cutters she had, and takes off like a scalded cat. Next minute they're all lashing out like rugby internationals and taking off in all directions. I went after the skinny one . . ."

"Wendy Walker," said Wield. "What about Marvell, the one who started it?"

"Long gone, but Walker followed after her, don't know if it were accidental or what, and she'd got close to the lab area when we caught her up."

"So what slowed her down?"

"Des Patten, that's what. He'd stayed back in the control room when we fetched them in. But hearing all the commotion, he'd come out to take a look, and he found Marvell. Might have wished he hadn't if we hadn't arrived. That Marvell woman looked all set to take a swing at him with them cutters, and by God, with her build I'd rather she hit me once than twice!"

"But you came to the rescue."

"Sort of. In fact it were that skinny lass who grabbed her first, then I pitched in."

"And Patten?"

"Just stood there looking. Takes a lot to faze Des. And when the big lass quietened down, he reached out and took the cutters. Then we went off to that room we locked them up in. No more trouble after that, but if you'd like a bit more color, just show me where."

"Need to square it with Des though," said Wield. "I mean, I don't want the two of you saying different."

"No problem with Des," said Howard confidently. "He knows how things work."

"I'd have guessed that. Known him long?"

"I'd seen him around. At the track. He likes a bet too."

"Was it him who got you the job then?"

"Not really. It were Rosso who said they were expanding and looking for experienced men . . ."

"Rosso?"

"Les Rosthwaite, Captain Sanderson's batman who came out with him."

"Out of the army? Same mob as Patten?"

It was beginning to fall into place. Wield had checked the TecSec company registration and found the names of the directors given as Simon Sanderson and Desmond Patten. He recalled the photo in Patten's office. The smartly suited chap in the middle he guessed was Sanderson, which meant the small chap with the baby curls was Rosthwaite.

"That's right. Yorkshire Fusiliers."

"And this Rosso is a friend of yours?"

"Well, we knew each other way back," said Howard hedgily.

"Is he a partner too?"

Howard was looking at him in surprise.

"Sorry, thought you'd know, Sarge. He's dead."

"No," said Wield. "I didn't know. What happened?"

"Car smash. He were stupid. Bit of a piss artist. Yes, I know I got done for being over the limit, but Rosso were different. He'd drive when he couldn't stand! Ran off the road into a tree a month back."

"But it was him that got you the job?"

"That's right. At least he told me they were needing more bodies 'cos they'd got this new contract with ALBA. I reckon with my record and experience I'd have walked into the job anyway."

"Lot of sympathy for guys with drunk-driving sheets, have they?" said Wield. "So when you joined they'd started the work at Wanwood clearing the woods."

"All finished," said Howard with some emphasis. "It were August when I started."

"And you've not heard anything?"

"What about?" said Howard, looking agitated.

"Well, about finding owt when they cleared the woods, for instance."

"No," said Howard. Did he sound relieved? "Like I say, it were August when I joined. I took a right good rest, I mean convalescence, after leaving the Force."

"And you look really good, Jimmy," said Wield. "They'll be glad to hear it down at Dartleby. You've still got a lot of friends out there. Once a cop, eh?"

A lie. Coppers carved their names on sand. Once

out, for whatever reason, the door closed behind you, consigning you forever to the "them" with no claims whatever on the "us." Even the mighty Dalziel when his turn came would fade like the after-grumble of a summer storm. Not that he'd look back. Which was just as well, else they'd all likely turn into pillars of the community!

"Yeah, maybe," said Howard. "Anything more I can do for you, Sarge?"

Wield regarded him thoughtfully, at the same time doing his bit for world health by bending the flimsy spoon in half and tying a knot in it.

His problem was, he didn't really have any idea what Howard might be able to do for him. He had a feeling about TecSec, but he was willing to admit to that prejudice against private security firms which Dalziel embodied and most professional coppers shared. Wanting to find something iffy was a bad starting place for looking. It made it easy to elevate a certain wariness he'd detected in both Patten and his subordinate to the status of suspicious behavior. Nothing to do but, like in a fight, keep prodding till finally if the defenses weren't sound, you saw the skin split and the claret start flowing, and then you found what kind of opponent you were really up against.

He said, "Don't think so, Jimmy. Might be able to do something for you, but."

"What's that?"

"Keep you straight," said Wield.

"Now hang about . . ."

"You hang about and I'll tell you what I mean. Mr. Dalziel's got this thing going . . ."

That had his attention. Like at nursery school, if you want to get their little darlings really listening, skip Red Riding Hood and get straight through to the Big Bad Wolf.

". . . he's been told off to vet all private security companies on our patch, dig out any stinkweed."

"Are you saying that TecSec's iffy?" demanded Howard.

"Are you saying it's not?" asked Wield.

"Yes, I mean, no . . . I mean, I've only been there since August, Sarge, and I can put my hand on my heart and say that since I joined, I've not noticed anything dodgy."

"Probably because there's nothing to notice," said Wield. "But if anything did come up, well, think on, Jimmy. You know the score from your time in the Force. With information, there's *before* and *after*. Before, and you're on the side of the angels. After, and you're just another lowlife trying to cut a deal."

Wield was glad Pascoe wasn't here to hear him talking like something out of an American cop movie.

"Well, I know nowt," said Howard, firmly. "There's been nowt, not since August when I joined. And if there was, I'd get in touch, Sarge, you can rely on it. Once a cop, eh?"

"Right," said Wield. "Hurry and you'll make the second race, Jimmy."

He sat a little longer, staring into the murky depths of his untouched tea. The cafe prop came over and looked angrily at the twisted spoon.

"What the hell happened to that?" he demanded.

Wield looked at him coldly, still not out of his tough guy role.

"It got knotted," he said. "Why don't you do the same?"

V

PETER PASCOE WAS a conscientious man, but there were several factors which made him able to head for Kirkton via the unlikely route of the University Staff Club without too bruising a moral struggle.

Firstly, as Ellie could testify with some bitterness, the job owed him for uncountable hours, days, even weeks of unpaid overtime.

Secondly, he had a strong suspicion based on a certain evasiveness of speech that Dalziel's alleged "interrogation" was taking place between consenting adults without reference to the rules of PACE.

Thirdly, though his criminological acquaintance with patterns of obsessional behavior kept nagging at his mind, he couldn't escape the feeling of being guided, or perhaps pushed, if not by an external divinity, then at least by personal intuitions whose roots lay too deep for rational excavation.

So when he'd rung the history department to leave a message for Professor Pollinger and the antipodally twanged respondent had announced she *was* Andrea Pollinger and if he wanted to talk to her it had better be in the next couple of hours as she'd be away from campus for a week or so starting that afternoon, he hadn't hesitated to make a date.

As he entered the Staff Club, a small man with a heavily nicotined moustache said, "Peter, hello, not looking for me, are you?"

This was Dr. Pottle, head of the psychiatry unit at the Central Hospital and occasional lecturer at the university. Pascoe had a double-pronged relationship with him—first as a professional consultant to the police, and second as a personal consultant to himself. Some weeks had passed since contact in either mode had been necessary.

"No," said Pascoe. "Should I be?"

"That's for you to say and me to confirm," said Pottle. He smiled as he spoke but his shrewd eyes were quartering Pascoe's face.

"I'm just meeting someone here. Sorry, don't have time to talk."

"Me neither, not now," said Pottle. "But if you did fancy a chat, I think I've got a window between say four and five. Take care."

He was gone. Damn the man, thought Pascoe. It's really come to something when the psychiatrists are drumming up business on the street!

He went in search of Pollinger.

Ellie had prepared him to some extent but the professor still surprised. Clad as though for a safari in a bosom-billowed khaki shirt and floppy shorts out of which erupted a positive torrent of leg, she invited him to join her in a glass of lager in terms which suggested refusal would be injury and any alternative drink insult. She should have been a parody, but how could anyone be a parody who was so exuberantly herself?

"Ellie, my wife, whom you met last night . . ." began Pascoe.

"Great girl. No bullshit. You got yourself a gem there, Pete."

She'd already instructed him to call her Poll. He tried it now.

"Yes, er, Poll, I know it. Ellie tells me you're writing a book about the Passchendaele campaign, Third Ypres?"

"That's right. You interested in that particular cock-up?"

"In a way. More specifically in World War One military executions. I wondered if you might have any specialized knowledge in that area?"

She wasn't looking quite so friendly now.

"Well, I know what everyone knows, that you bastard Poms shot an average of one of your own men every week of the war. Maybe if they'd shot a fucking staff officer a week too, the war would have been over a lot sooner, but I doubt it. Seems to be an inexhaustible supply of dickheads from your officer classes."

"Indeed," said Pascoe, glancing round the Staff Club to see how this academic analysis was going down. Fortunately the few other inmates seemed to be in that state of intellectual contemplation which a noninitiate might have mistaken for sleep.

"So spit it out, Pete. Why exactly do you want to talk to me?" she asked.

"Well, it's in reference to a sort of private investigation I'm engaged in—is something the matter?"

She definitely had the look of a sunbather who has noticed a crocodile in the swimming pool.

"This is the way I always look when I find some jackaroo sniffing around to pick the tidbits out of my hard-sweated research," she said. "By a peculiar coincidence, I'm thinking about doing my next book on Great War court-martials. Did I maybe let this slip to Ellie last night? And this private investigation of yours, is that maybe cop-speak for writing a book? Ellie said you were a jack, but I don't suppose you've still got a case open eighty years on."

Pascoe had forgotten how neurotic academics could be about their research. They made the world of industrial espionage seem like shoplifting from Woolies.

He said, "This really is private and personal. I've just discovered that my great-grandfather was one of the poor bastards you mentioned. I'd like to find out the details, but if this is going to cause you some professional difficulty . . ."

"Don't get your Y-fronts in a twist," she said. "This is sensitive stuff we're talking about here. I just about had to sell my body to get sight of it, and a nice sensational story in the tabloids traceable to me would slam all kinds of doors on my tits."

"Isn't it in the public domain then?"

"Sure. Like Prince Charley's dong's in the open air when he goes for a slash, but that doesn't mean we're all going to get a look at it. So why exactly do you want to get hold of these details, Pete?"

"Oh, you know . . . family interest . . ."

"Yeah, yeah, I know that one. Look up the family tree and see who's hanging there. You'll need to do better than that."

Pascoe sipped his lager, then said, "I'm sorry. I'm not sure I really know why . . . or what I want to do. . . . Like I said, I've only just found out, but since I found out, I've hardly been able to think about anything else. I suppose I want to understand how . . . why . . . and if there was a miscarriage of justice . . ."

"You for capital punishment, Pete?" she interrupted.

He looked at her in surprise, then tried to answer.

"No, it's barbarity. But it's a barbarity that has been written into our legal system from time to time and while I'm glad it's behind us, I wouldn't use its existence to argue that men should get away with murder."

"Nicely fielded, Pete. And if that's the way you think, your worries are over. Your own beloved PM has said as much in Parliament. No grounds for issuing retrospective free pardons to any of those poor bastards 'cos whatever we may think about the punishment, that's what they had coming to them under the laws and conditions of service prevailing at the time. Go down that road, he implied, and you end up pardoning a hell of a lot of sheep stealers. You go along with that, Pete?"

"The Law is sometimes an ass," said Pascoe carefully. "At certain times and in certain places, the Law is more than an ass, it is a hyena and feeds on human flesh. But when a man is hung for a sheep he did not in fact steal, then the Law, whether ass or hyena, has been abused. That is a miscarriage of justice which may not be shrugged off even if it happened a thousand years ago."

She regarded him with comic book amazement.

"You sure you're a cop, Pete? And your bosses let you roam the streets by yourself? There may be hope for this benighted country yet. Okay. You've almost got me persuaded. Give me the full pitch."

So Pascoe told her the story. She made notes as he spoke and when he'd finished, she said, "So there's still some doubt this Sergeant Pascoe really was your great-granddad?"

"There's a mystery, certainly, but not much doubt. My little girl took one look at the photo and asked what I was doing in fancy dress. I can't see the resemblance as clearly as that, I'm afraid, but then I've always thought I'm a dead ringer for Rudolph Valentino."

She looked at his thin mobile English face with its untidy mop of fair brown hair and smiled.

He smiled back and said, "So if Sergeant Pascoe rings a bell . . ."

"Hey, this isn't the servants' hall in here. I don't have three hundred plus bells all nicely labeled. Also my interest, which is still at the preliminary stage, is in *all* FGCM death sentences, not just the ones confirmed . . ."

"Sorry?" said Pascoe. "FGCM?"

"Field General Court-Martial. Different from a General Court-Martial which needed at least five officers and a legally qualified judge advocate to advise them.

In battlefield conditions this wasn't always convenient, unless it was an officer being tried. Your common or garden squaddie got an FGCM, only three officers needed with hardly a judge advocate in sight. You can see the thinking. Made life—or death—a lot easier when you were up the Front."

"And what do you mean, confirmed?"

"After sentence the verdict was passed up the line of command so's everyone could put in their two cents' worth till it landed in the C-in-C's lap. If he confirmed the sentence, that was it. Army's line of defense is that only ten percent of the death sentences were actually confirmed. Makes them sound like a bunch of crypto-conchies, doesn't it? Then you work out that three hundred plus executions from 1914 to 1918 means three thousand plus death sentences . . . makes you wonder about the old military gray matter, doesn't it?"

"But surely not all are necessarily in dispute," said Pascoe, reluctant to abandon totally his ur-faith in the protective power of the Law.

"You mean like if a crime was capital under civvy law, the same penalty should apply under military? Fair enough. If my memory serves me right, there were about thirty done for murder, and even then they didn't get the access to legal defense that a civilian court would have given. And that leaves about three hundred guys who got theirs for terrible crimes like being shell-shocked, or scared, or completely knackered, or losing their rags and punching some pompous brass hat up the hooter. That's no Law. That's fucking License!"

Pascoe smiled and murmured, "Well, I'm glad to see you're approaching your subject in a proper spirit of pure academic objectivity."

"Don't go all Anglo-superior on me, Pascoe," she snapped. "You Poms should never forget we've got the moral high ground here. Despite all pressure from your High Command, the Oz government refused to apply your primitive military legal system. For an Australian soldier, if it wasn't a capital crime in civvy street, it wasn't a capital crime in the army. Just as well, or maybe I wouldn't be here."

"Why's that?"

"My great-grandfather was at Gallipoli, they used to call him Jolly Polly when he got back. During some mix-up he came under command of one of you lot, who ordered him and some other guys to advance in broad daylight over bare rocky terrain which the Turks had covered by half a dozen machine guns. He said, 'You set off, mate, and I'll catch you up when I've finished plucking my nose hairs.' The Pom officer wanted him court-martialed for cowardice, refusing to obey an order, all kinds of things that were topping offenses in your mob. His own CO put him on shit-shoveling duties for two days, which no one minded as it kept you out of the line."

Pascoe laughed and said, "Nice. I'm glad he made it home to sow his seed."

"Jesus. The way you guys talk! But because I'm a sentimental cow and we both had great-granddads who helped make a world fit for heroes like us, I'll ignore the fact that you're a stuck-up Pom and a fascist jack to boot. Do you have an address or do you just roam the streets looking for crime?"

Pascoe pulled out a card with his home address number.

"I'll get back to you, but don't hold your breath. Jesus, is that the time? I've got a train to catch."

"Going somewhere nice?"

"London. And yes, I'll be getting my fingers dirty on M.O.D. records, but that doesn't mean I'll have the opportunity or even the inclination to dig your particular bit of dirt."

She glowered at him to make her point, then relaxed her features into a grin.

"But I'll do my best," she said.

"Not even a stuck-up Pom could ask more," he said, grinning back.

She downed the last inch of her lager and left. It seemed to Pascoe that the whole Staff Club heaved a collective sigh and settled into a deeper sleep.

He was tempted to follow its example. His chair was lovely, soft and deep. But he had promises to keep.

He rose and went to keep them.

VI

PASCOE WAS BOTH RIGHT AND WRONG about Dalziel's state of mind when they parted that morning.

It was true he had an invitation to drop in on Cap Marvell for lunch again, and the prospect filled him with a light-headed anticipation he hadn't experienced since he was a likely lad.

But nowadays such light-headedness was ballasted by a bellyful of solid experience and cynical observation, and he was far from sure he ought to go.

Last night he'd held out, but he couldn't really put it down to virtue. She had left the party not all that long after their conversation with Ellie Pascoe. When she told him she was going he'd looked at his watch and said, "Woman who lets the telly interfere with her drinking ought to buy a video."

"Didn't you know? Women aren't allowed to understand such arcane matters. If you get hungry about midday tomorrow, how about another spot of lunch?"

"That sounds good," he'd said. "But I can't say definite. My job, you never know what's going to come up."

"I understand," she'd said sympathetically. "But if you can . . . Goodnight now."

And with a kiss on the cheek, delicious because of its ease, but dangerous because of its wifeliness, she had gone.

Sometime later he'd heard himself saying to the vice-chancellor, "You got a telly round here, Bog-eye? Case I'm working on might get a mention."

"Of course. Always happy to help the police with their inquiries," said Burgoyne, and five minutes later Dalziel found himself sitting in the audiovisual department watching Cap sort out some poofy interviewer with practiced ease, even managing to weave her critique of ALBA into such a seamless web with her account of the discovery of the bones that they hadn't been able to edit it out. Somehow the sight of her electronic image affected him even more powerfully than her physical presence, and when the item finished, instead of returning to the party, he headed for his car and drove round to Cap's apartment block.

If there'd been a light in her window he'd have gone straight up, but the flat was in darkness, not even the white flicker of a TV set showing.

Then as he sat indecisive, cursing himself contradictorily for both a vacillating adolescent and a randy old fool, to his surprise he saw her emerge from the alley which led to the garages behind the flats. Now was the time to intercept her and tell her, whatever she'd been doing, she'd missed a great show on the telly and why didn't he describe it to her over a nightcap.

Nightcap. He mouthed the word greedily like a gob-stopper as he watched her move toward the entrance with a purposeful grace, a self-contained woman who knew what she wanted—and who had a life of her own he knew nothing about.

For some reason the thought was detumescent and he sat in his car till she had entered the building, then drove away. But by the time he got home he was cursing himself for a fool. There was no doubt about it, he really fancied another helping of what they'd had for pudding that lunchtime. And yet . . . and yet . . . Simple lust didn't bother him. Man who didn't get the odd twinge might as well sign up as security guard at a harem. But with Cap there was something else which did worry him. Not just his natural constabular concern that she might yet prove a professional embarrassment, but a feeling as yet too vague to stand up in an identification parade that there might be something after "afters" . . .

The phone had started ringing again as they'd uncoupled the previous afternoon, nicely cutting out that danger zone when a man could verbal himself into a lot of trouble.

As forecast, it had been the media, released from his shackles and eager for a story. Leaving her to fix up her telly interview, he'd wandered into the kitchen for another Mexican beer and almost automatically found himself checking out the notes, postcards, invitations, etc. she'd got stuck on her pinboard.

"Looking for clues, Andy," she'd said from the doorway.

She was still naked, but entirely unself-consciously so, not even attempting to suck in the middle-aged sag of her belly.

"Just being impressed by the company you keep," he'd replied, holding up the university invitation.

"I probably shan't go," she said. "Unless maybe you fancy coming along? See how our intellectual betters live, and making a hole in their booze?"

It was such a casual nonthreatening suggestion that it seemed quite clever to accept it, and once there, he'd consciously not stuck by her side and equally consciously (and childishly?) made it clear that he was as at home here as he was anywhere else he cared to go.

But he'd really enjoyed the evening, and perhaps it was this sense of more than sexual enjoyment which was making him back off from her invitations.

This kind of self-analysis was foreign to him and he didn't like it. What he did like was situations where he knew instinctively how to react, i.e., ninety-nine percent of his adult life up till now. Cap Marvell was trouble. Even if she didn't step over the bounds of the law, she was always going to be skirting its edge and he wasn't certain whether he wanted his own anarchy to be constantly tested by someone else's equal but other disregard for convention.

"I could end up like Peter Pascoe!" he told himself aghast. He had a great deal of admiration for Ellie, but there were no two ways about it, having her hand on his tiller got poor Pete sailing through some pretty perilous seas! But at least Ellie had no objection to sinking her teeth into a nice juicy steak.

The memory of the tofu pie did it. Lunch was definitely off. Pleased with having arrived at his decision, he drove out to Wanwood House. He had nothing particular in mind, but Wield's preoccupation with TecSec chimed so closely with his own general distrust of private armies that a closer look wouldn't come amiss.

When he entered the TecSec office, it wasn't Patten who looked up at him from behind the desk but a darkly handsome, athletic-looking man in a pricey pinstripe suit.

"Who the hell are you?" the stranger demanded. "Don't you know about knocking?"

"It's my life's study," said Dalziel. "I'm Dalziel. And who the hell are you?"

"Ah yes," said the man. "I should have recognized you from Des's description. Simon Sanderson, founder and senior partner of TecSec. How can I help you, Superintendent?"

Putting aside the question of how Patten had described him, Dalziel sank into a chair and said, "Thought you spent your time going around, charming jobs out of people who can't afford it."

Best way of getting to know anyone is hit 'em hard and watch how they react. Thoughts of Chairman Dalziel 244.

Sanderson smiled like he'd taken lessons off Jack Nicholson and opened a desk drawer from which he produced a bottle and two glasses, both of which he filled, one of which he passed to the Fat Man.

"Here's to our better acquaintance," he said.

"Up yours," said Dalziel.

They drank. It was Tomintoul.

Thought of Chairman Dalziel 244(a). If hitting 'em hard gets you Tomintoul, what would kicking 'em in the goolies produce?

He said, "So what did you get chucked out of the army for, Captain?"

"Embezzling the mess funds and screwing the colonel's lady," said Sanderson promptly. "That's what I always tell people. The truth, you see, is less credible and makes them think I've got something to hide."

He refilled the glasses. I could get to like this prancer, thought Dalziel.

"Every bugger's got something to hide," he asserted confidently. "Usually it *is* the truth. So try me."

"I was enjoying a little vacation in Bosnia when my driver steered my armored personnel carrier over a mine. A few days later as I opened the flood of get-well cards from my many admirers, I found among them a note from the Ministry of Defence which proved to be a get-out card instead, what is known among Other Ranks, I believe, as a redundancy notice. Here, have another snort. I can see it's been a shock to you."

"I can thole it," said Dalziel. "So you were out on your neck, money in your pocket, and nowt on your C.V. but ten years or so of giving orders and shooting people dead. That's when you started a security company."

"What else? The only kind of job I was really qualified for, one requiring nerves of steel, balls of brass, and a general indifference to the sensitivities of those who got in my way, would have been yours, Superintendent, but I couldn't face all those years of wearing a pointed hat. Now we've got me safely catalogued, how may I be of service to you today?"

This was a real smooth piece of work, thought Dalziel. Calculating, confident, cocky. But not condescending, you had to give him that. There'd been no implication of superiority in his armed response to Dalziel's assault, and this was, in a way, disarming. In fact the bugger's got me feeling flattered he thinks I'm as good as he is! concluded the Fat Man. And anyone who can manage that really needs watching.

He said, "How come a potty little outfit like thine with next to no track record landed a contract with a company like ALBA?"

"Ah, it's guilty secret time," said Sanderson. "It's all down to a homosexual relationship, I'm afraid."

"You wha'?"

"Me and David Batty. Went to the same public school, pulled each other's plonkers behind the fives court. Everyone did. I mean, lock up a couple of hundred growing boys out of reach of all female company for months at a time, what do they expect? Mere marking time in most cases, of course, but such close encounters do cement adult relationships. This is what the Old Boy network is really all about. It's not Masonic handshakes that get you favors, it's knowing where those hands have been."

"You're saying Dr. Batty set you on here 'cos you're old schoolmates?"

"More or less, though I had to give him a prompt. I read in the local rag about the raid they had last summer and I thought, security problem, there could be an opening here for a young, thrusting state-of-the-art company. So I picked up the phone and invited myself round for a drink. He liked the sound of my ideas, and here we are."

"Your ideas being to dig up half the wood and fence the place off like Colditz?"

"Not a pretty solution but it worked," said Sanderson. "No one gets in who shouldn't."

"They did the other night."

"Yes, they did, didn't they?" admitted Sanderson ruefully. "Trojan horse. Well, Trojan skeleton anyway. It won't happen again. By the way, I suppose you have considered the possibility that they brought the bones along themselves? Sorry. That was crass. Teaching my grandmother."

"Aye," agreed Dalziel. "Another possibility we're still considering is that when the remains were disturbed during the clearance last summer, either the contractors or mebbe you yourself noticed them and decided it were simpler just to pile a bit of muck on top of 'em rather than have the whole operation held up by an investigation."

"I suppose that would be what you might call a grave offense?" said Sanderson.

Dalziel didn't return his smile.

"Worse than that," he said.

"Then I'm glad that for once I can plead complete innocence."

To his surprise, Dalziel found he was inclined to believe him.

Sanderson was looking at his watch.

He said, "Time marches on. I sometimes pop along to the Green Tree in the village. Reasonable pint. Care to join me?"

Dalziel hesitated. At least he thought he was hesitating. But if he was, someone in a pretty good imitation of his voice was saying, "No thanks. I've got a lunch appointment."

Interestingly, having once said it aloud, he had no more thoughts of not turning up. Indeed he couldn't even imagine why he should have had them in the first place.

"Hello," she said in the doorway. "Glad you could make it."

He didn't reply but took her in his arms and kissed her.

"Before lunch?" she said breathlessly when she finally got unstuck.

"If it's yon toffee again, I'll need to work up an appetite," he said.

Afterward he paid her the ultimate Yorkshire compliment.

"Ee, that were grand," he said.

"Yes, it was rather. Pour us a drink. There's some whisky on the sideboard."

He wouldn't have quite put it like that. It was a bottle of the same enamel unfriendly brew he'd sampled yesterday. She'd probably got an offer at the supermarket. He might have to speak to her about that, but not yet. It was possible to have a good fuck and a vegetarian lunch on a casual just-happened-to-be-passing basis, but asking a woman to change her whisky implied a long-term commitment.

She'd pressed a button on her CD player and a man and a woman started singing. They didn't sound happy, which to Dalziel's ears was not surprising as the words were foreign, probably Kraut, which must be like singing and chewing celery at the same time.

"Is this going to be Our Tune?" he asked. "Me, I think I'd rather go for the Grimethorpe Band playing 'Blaze Away!' "

She smiled and said, "I might have known you

wouldn't go in for postcoital tristesse. I'll find something livelier."

"Nay, leave it. What's it all about, any road?"

"It's a boy off to the wars saying goodbye to his girl and telling her if she wants to find him, he'll be in a house of green turf where the beautiful trumpets are playing."

"Jesus," said Dalziel. "Your lad's in the army, you said? That him there?"

He nodded at a photo on the mantelpiece. A young officer, smart and bemedaled, smiled out at him.

"That's right. I was once told he was missing, believed killed."

"Oh aye? And did you hear beautiful trumpets?"

"Not that I noticed."

She spoke quietly, undramatically, but he felt there was stuff here he wasn't quite ready to hear yet. Telling him would be her equivalent of his complaining about the Scotch.

They listened to the end of the song in silence. He admitted its melancholy force, but even in that line he still preferred something a bit more catchy, like "Oh Where Tell Me Where Has My Highland Laddie Gone?" which his old Scots gran used to sing when she'd taken a wee drappie against the cold.

"Do you see a lot of your lad? You said you had dinner with him."

"Did I? Oh yes, the alibi." She smiled. "Yes, we meet from time to time."

In fact more often latterly than in the days immediately after her defection. Perhaps she had come to a more generously balanced assessment of the world according to the Pitt-Evenlodes. Also she suspected that Piers the Hero had come to understand, though he would never be able to admit, that his father was a bit of a prat.

"In the Wyfies, isn't he? Or whatever they are now."

"The Yorkshire Rifles. Yes. How did you know?"

"The cap badge," he said, nodding at the photo. "Kept the old rose and lily. Ever mention a Captain Sanderson? Or Sergeant Patten?"

"Patten? Wasn't that the name of that awful security man?"

"That's right. Sanderson's his partner. Both ex your lad's mob. It'd be helpful to get a bit of background."

"What on earth for?"

"My sergeant's got a notion there's something not right with their outfit," he said.

"Your sergeant? A notion?" she said with the faint scorn of one whose democratization had not reached quite as far as NCOs.

"That's right," said Dalziel. "My sergeant. And if he told me he'd got a notion Jesse Owens had a wooden leg, I'd take a closer look."

"And you want me to talk to my son to see if there's any gossip about these two, is that it? I presume you'd want me to do this without revealing that I am a police, what-do-you-call it? a snout!"

She had a nice line in indignation. He finished his drink, grimaced, and said plaintively, "I had a mam too, tha knows."

"Indeed? I thought you probably leapt out of Robert Peel's head, fully armed."

"Him with the hounds in the morning? Didn't think you lot 'ud be into that sort of thing. No, what I were going to say is, my mam had this picture on her parlor wall. This lass sitting on a bench in the garden wi' her head bent forward, looking right miserable, and this skinny lad wi' a droopy 'tash sort of skulking in the shrubbery behind her. It were called *Their First Quarrel.*"

She stared at him hard, then said, "Apart from the absence of a bench, a garden shrubbery, and a moustache, not to mention misery or skulk, I can see precisely how such a picture might have forced itself into your consciousness. As it happens I'm meeting Piers this very evening. So tell me, Andy, if I were doing you this service on a professional basis, how much would you pay?"

"Depends which service you had in mind, luv," said Dalziel, grinning.

She flung a punch at his ribs which he absorbed with scarcely a grunt and countered by grabbing her arm and locking it behind her back in the classic arrest mode. Lunch might have been postponed once more but the telephone started ringing and she grabbed it with her free hand.

"Hello," she said. "Yes. All right, calm down . . . yes . . . yes . . . I'll come at once."

She put down the receiver. She had gone pale and he felt her sway slightly. He released her arm and took her shoulders to steady her.

"Trouble?" he said.

"Yes," she said in a voice barely under control. "It's awful. That was Jacksy, Annabel Jacklin, you remember her, the nice-looking blond girl? She works at the infirmary. And she says they've just brought Wendy Walker in. She's been knocked off her bike, and they think she'll probably die."

VII

ONCE KIRKTON MUST HAVE BEEN a separate entity, a small Yorkshire village with its own life and a big enough span of open country between it and Leeds to make the premotorized journey a matter of some moment.

The nineteenth century had brought the city closer

and the twentieth had completed the job, with tentacles of urban sprawl running out like rivulets of Vesuvian lava, threatening, touching, consuming, and finally passing on, leaving a dead and dusty landscape in their wake.

Residential development had been mainly at the lower end of the market, long dark terraces rising steeply from narrow pavements still running like scars between later more enlightened attempts at council housing in redbrick blocks of four, with some pebble dashing and three almost distinguishably different designs. In the middle of this, traces of the original village remained—a church and a crowded graveyard, an old village cross and several whitewashed cottages flanking a cobbled street. This probably owed its preservation to its descent from the importance signaled by the nameplate at its opening, High Street, to the status of a mere cul-de-sac, formed by dropping a huge factory wall across the far end.

This Pascoe observed in passing. He was following a series of signs reading ALBA ALL VEHICLES, and when he glimpsed the wall dwarfing the little cottages, he guessed he was getting near.

The ALBA complex was huge, spanning a small river which may once have dimpled brightly between fields of hay, providing fresh water and fresh trout for those happy enough to live on its banks. But now, though Pascoe did not doubt that the water authorities would not let considerations of profit to their shareholders or pelf to their executives inhibit them in their priestlike task of enforcing all the innumerable regulations regarding pollution of waterways, the turgid stream looked black and lifeless.

He'd taken the precaution of telephoning in advance and his passage through the security gate was swift and painless.

"Follow the Maisterhouse sign," said the gateman.

It was a fair drive, taking him, he guessed, back toward the old center of the village, but the walls were too high for him to get confirmation from a glimpse of the church spire.

What the Maisterhouse might look like puzzled him, but when it finally hove into view behind a long low modern laboratory, he had no problem recognizing it.

It was a fine three-story Georgian House, austere but elegantly proportioned, standing amidst its industrial surrounds like a bishop in a barnyard.

As he got out of his car, a young man in a gray business suit opened the front door and said, "Mr. Pascoe? Come this way. Mr. Batty is expecting you."

"Mr. Batty?" said Pascoe. "You don't mean Dr. David from your research division?"

"Oh no," said the man. "This is Mr. Thomas Batty, our chairman."

This surprised Pascoe. When he'd rung up he'd asked if he could have access to the Wanwood House conveyance documents, which presumably would include a list of previous owners. Also he would like to have a chat with anyone who might have worked on the transfer. Why the company chairman should feel it necessary or useful to involve himself, Pascoe could not guess.

They went up a broad flight of stairs, then the man in the gray suit tapped lightly on a door and pushed it open without waiting to hear a reply.

In obedience to his gesture, Pascoe stepped through.

He found himself in a spacious drawing room, which his amateur antiquarian eye told him was furnished more to the taste of the nineteenth than the eighteenth century. A man was standing in front of the tall marble fireplace in which a tepee of pine logs gave off a comfortable heat and a pleasant aroma of resiny smoke. Through the tall sash windows a view of the top of the church spire told him his sense of direction had been good.

The man, who was of medium build, in his late sixties, with corn-colored hair now laced with gray, came forward with a welcoming smile and outstretched hand.

"Mr. Pascoe, how do you do? Come and sit down. I've got some tea here but if you'd prefer something stronger . . . ?"

His voice was strong, his accent educated but unmistakably northern.

"Tea's fine," said Pascoe. "Mr. Batty, I hope you haven't mistaken the purpose of my visit. It's really something which someone in your records office could have dealt with. Forgive me for being so forthright, but I should hate you to feel your probably very valuable time is being wasted."

That forced the issue nicely, he thought. He didn't believe for a moment that Batty was here by accident and the sooner they got on a level, the better.

"Nothing to do with ALBA can be a waste of my time, Mr. Pascoe," said Batty, firmly. "We went public many years ago, but we've still stayed basically a family firm. The minute I heard from my son about that grisly discovery out at Wanwood I gave orders that all further developments should be referred directly to me."

"I see. Your son . . . that would be Dr. David Batty?"

"That's right. My son the doctor," said Batty with a smile. "He got the scientific brain which comes from the Batty side of the family, plus, I'm glad to say, enough of the entrepreneurial spirit from the distaff side to bode well for when he takes over. Meanwhile he's where he can be most useful. Research is a young man's game. They're like professional footballers, these chaps, pretty well played out sometime in their thirties and ready to slip into management. So nature has pro-grammed David perfectly."

"That must be very satisfying to you, sir," said Pas-coe. "Having such a perfect heir. Were you a scientist too?"

"Not really. Got the basics, of course, but my grand-father's genes seem to have skipped me. I was always more interested in running the business side of things, so you can imagine how it suited everyone, especially old Arthur, when Janet and I fell for each other."

Pascoe had often noted in certain Yorkshiremen who'd achieved a measure of local prominence what he categorized as a sort of inverted braggadocio. While not feeling it necessary to blow their own trumpets, their social intercourse was based on two tenets: Not to know me argues yourself unknown; and, not to be fas-cinated by me argues yourself dull as ditchwater. This was probably the explanation of Batty's friendly volu-bility, except that as head of a national, indeed interna-tional, and highly successful business, he might have been expected to subscribe to that other more funda-mental Yorkshire precept, *see all and say nowt.* Maybe he just wanted to be loved. Pascoe decided to go with the flow.

He said apologetically, as if the name of the Queen had inexplicably slipped his memory, "Now *Arthur,* that would be . . . ?"

"Arthur Grindal, my wife's grandfather, my grand-dad's cousin, him who started Grindal's Mill here in Kirkton, remember?"

"Of course. The business brains. And the Battys provided the scientific know-how."

"That's it. Without old Arthur, my grandfather would have spilled the beans about all his ideas in some learned journals and let someone else develop them commercially. And without him, old Arthur would have ended his days spinning cloth for a declin-

ing market. As it is, well, look around you, Mr. Pascoe.
One of the biggest independent pharmaceutical companies in the EEC and, so long as lads like my David keep
coming up with the goods, likely to continue so."

Pascoe, taking the instruction to look around literally, said, "This Maisterhouse, just exactly what is it?"

"Used to belong to the village squire. Arthur bought
it way back when his mill got going and the money
started rolling in. It had a name of its own but the
millworkers soon started calling it the Maisterhouse.
There was a nice piece of parkland with it, and when
the business went into rapid expansion after the last
war this was the obvious, i.e., cheapest, way to come.
Arthur Grindal was no sentimentalist and he wanted to
knock the old place down but they wouldn't let him.
Listed building, they said, you can't touch it. Right,
said Arthur, I won't. But I'll do what I want with my
own bloody land! And as you can see, he did. There
were very few restrictions on industrial development in
those days. So now we use the Maisterhouse for reception and entertainment, and there's accommodation for
the family and the odd distinguished guest who needs
to be right on top of things. Heritage folk want to come
sniffing around from time to time. It takes them a lot
longer to get through the main gate than it did you, I
can warrant you!"

Pascoe joined in his laugh. Keep on the right side of
the customer till you'd got his money. And in any case,
was he not also of this same hard Yorkshire stock,
traceable back to this very village? It was an idea that
was taking some getting used to.

He said, "Now about Wanwood House, sir. As you
know, some bones were discovered by some
women . . ."

"Yes, yes. Blasted animal protesters," said Batty. "I
can't imagine why you lot don't just round them all up
and put 'em away."

He sounded as if he meant "down."

Pascoe said, "Where a crime has been committed . . ."

Batty interrupted, "Crime? They killed a security guard up at Redcar, didn't they? Isn't murder a crime anymore?"

"That was tragic, though whether a murder charge would be sustainable, I'm not sure . . ."

"He died, didn't he? As a result of action by those lunatics. What would you call it? These people are a menace and need to be pursued to the extremity of the law."

"This means you will definitely be prosecuting for trespass?" said Pascoe, wondering how Dalziel would react to seeing his inamorata hauled up before a court, if that indeed was what she was.

"What? No, probably not," said Batty.

"Oh? I understood that your son, Dr. Batty, was determined . . ."

"David looks after research, mine is the final say-so in matters of general policy," said Batty sharply. "The state of the courts nowadays, prosecution's a waste of time and money. All it does is buy us bad publicity, and these bones could give us enough of that without pursuing more."

There was some muddled thinking here. Or maybe being able to adhere to three contrary opinions at the same time was a sine qua non of the captaincy of industry.

Pascoe said, "Yes, the bones. If I could have a look at the documents relating to your purchase of Wanwood House . . ."

"What period are you interested in?"

"We're not precisely sure yet, but as I explained on the phone, there's certainly no question of these remains having been buried there during ALBA's occupation of the premises."

"Yes, I understand that. I've had photocopies made of the relevant passages from the conveyance. As you'll see, it had in fact been used as a private hospital or clinic, some such thing, which is what attracted us. I mean we weren't starting from scratch in converting it from residential to scientific use. Also the location not too distant from the head office here, yet obscure enough, so we hoped, to be concealed from the attention of these lunatic protest groups. It didn't take them long to track us down. People are big on mouth and short on loyalty these days."

"Yes. I see from the conveyance you were dealing with a trustee in bankruptcy. How did a private hospital manage to go bankrupt in this day and age?"

"Healthcare is a business like any other, Mr. Pascoe. Expansion has its dangers as much as recession. Let yourself get overextended, and give your enemies a glimpse of your jugular, and you'd be amazed how quickly they're in there, slashing and sucking. Of course, a hospital is the kind of place you'd expect to find a few old bones. Couldn't just be that they didn't follow the regulations about the disposal of amputated limbs very closely, could it?"

Pascoe considered this macabre suggestion, or rather considered whether Batty was making it seriously.

He said, "Unless they did an operation there involving the removal of the complete cranium, I very much doubt it. How long had it been a hospital, do you know?"

"Oh seventy, eighty years," said Batty vaguely. "A hell of a long time, that's for sure. Does that help you?"

"Not a lot," said Pascoe. "Private family ownership's one thing. You've some chance of checking up on reports of missing persons, rumors of family quarrels. But when you think how many people, patients, relations, staff, must have been connected with even a small hospital over that period. And of course, the remains may have nothing to do with what went on inside the place. Someone just thought it was a handy bit of woodland to dump a body."

"Doesn't sound hopeful."

"Not unless we get a precise dating. Or failing that, a cutoff point somewhere the other side of sixty, preferably seventy years. Then, even if foul play is proved, there'd be so little chance of a result, we'd be able to stick it in the Open-But-Shut drawer."

Batty said, "Cut your losses, eh? Same in business. The art of good management is knowing when to say, far enough, let's forget it."

His tone and manner were pleasantly sympathetic. So why, wondered Pascoe, do I get a sense of . . . calculation?

He said, "Thank you for your time anyway, Mr. Batty."

"Not at all. Though you do seem to have had a long trip for little reward. We could have faxed you these papers."

"Oh, it's good to get out and about, actually see the wheel turning."

As they talked, Batty was moving him through the door and along the landing, but at the head of the staircase he halted. There were two women coming up, one a small sprightly woman in late middle age, the other younger and wearing what was unmistakably though not inelegantly a nurse's uniform.

"Janet," said Batty. "Say hello to Detective Chief Inspector Pascoe. Mr. Pascoe, my wife, Janet."

The older woman halted, said, "I'll be with you in a minute," to the nurse, who continued up the next flight of stairs, then extended her hand to Pascoe and said, "How do you do?"

The handshake was firm enough and the tone level

enough, but was he imagining a degree of unease? If so, it was probably no more than the common stormy petrel reaction to finding a copper on the premises. No one sees a policeman at the door and thinks, oh, my premium bonds must have come up.

But she didn't ask what he was doing here. Meaning she knew? Or that, like a good corporate wife, she knew better than to ask before her husband gave the signal?

"No one is ill, I hope?" said Pascoe, letting his gaze drift after the vanishing nurse.

"Oh no," said Batty. "We maintain a small first-aid unit in case of emergencies."

"Well, at least it should be well stocked." Pascoe smiled.

"What? Oh yes, of course. I'll see you in a moment, dear."

"Goodbye, Mr. Pascoe. Nice to have met you," said Janet Batty.

They continued their descent and a few moments later stepped back into the twentieth century.

"I suspect this would come as a bit of a shock to the original owner," said Pascoe, himself taken aback by the contrast between what he'd left behind and the whole messy complex stretched out before them.

"Possibly. On the other hand I daresay he looked out on his fields and flocks and forests and thought, all this is mine, this is what keeps me and my family in comfort, exactly as I do today. We're pragmatists up here in Yorkshire, Mr. Pascoe. You're from the South originally, I gather?"

Now where on earth did you gather that? wondered Pascoe. No, change the question. He'd no doubt that Batty could plug into the same Yorkshire internet that gave Dalziel his local omniscience. More interesting was, why should Batty have bothered to check him out?

A mischievous desire to let the man know that his system wasn't infallible made Pascoe say, "Originally? No, not the South. In fact my family are local, Mr. Batty. As local as yours. My grandmother was born in this very village, when it still was a village. Perhaps you've noticed some Pascoes in the church."

For some reason the suggestion seemed really to offend Batty. His face changed color and his studied good humor melted like snow off a dike.

"No," he said shortly. "Can't say I have but I don't pay much attention to the relics of the dead."

"Not even when they turn up on your own doorstep?" murmured Pascoe, interested to probe this reaction.

But the old Batty was back in control.

"Then least of all," he said, smiling. "Goodbye, Mr. Pascoe."

They shook hands and Pascoe got into his car.

"One more thing," he said through the open window. "I've been puzzling over your firm's name. ALBA. All I could come up with was some connection with the color white. You know, as in albino."

Batty grinned and said, "It's both more and less prosaic. When the two sides of the family united in business between the wars, or rather when old Arthur decided that the real future lay in pharmaceuticals rather than cloth, like any down-to-earth Yorkshireman he called the firm what it was, putting himself first, of course, Grindal and Batty. But in the fifties when we went public and the selling became as important as the manufacturing, if we were going to compete in the big time, some of us thought that something a bit snappier was needed."

He paused, as if his words had conjured up other images of those distant days.

"Some of us included you?" prompted Pascoe.

"I was in my early twenties, just back from business

school in the States. Oh yes, I was all for change," admitted Batty. "Not that anyone took much notice of me back in those days. Nobbut a lad, they said. My father was running the business by then with Uncle Bert, that's my wife's father, Herbert Grindal. They weren't much for change, Dad because he was naturally cautious, and Uncle Bert because being under old Arthur's thumb all his life hadn't left him much room for original thinking."

"Old Arthur?" said Pascoe still uncertain why a man who didn't pay much attention to the relicts of the dead should be so keen to share his family's history. "He must have been a ripe old age?"

"In his nineties," said Batty. "He'd finally retired in forty-eight on his ninetieth birthday, but he still cracked the whip when he wanted. And surprisingly he was all for a change, mainly because Janet, who was the apple of his eye, came up with this brilliant idea. That description was hers, but once her grandfather agreed, we all went along. And it was a pretty good idea, after all."

"The idea being ALBA?" said Pascoe, still puzzled.

"GrindAL BAtty," said Batty, stressing the relevant syllables. "Gerrit? And Arthur still went along even when Janet, who was only seventeen then and a real romantic, announced that an alba was some sort of medieval dawn chorus. Two for the price of one, he said. The firm's old partners, the company's new dawn. Practical or poetic, take your pick."

Pascoe looked westward to where the October sun was little more than a pallid aureole around the looming dome of a huge storage tank.

Of course on a summer morning with the sun rising behind the Maisterhouse it might all look very different. A new dawn, a new day . . .

. . . I watched the dawn lighten the sky beyond Sanctuary Wood—sounds nice and romantic put like that—except the sky was black with rain clouds —and Sanctuary were barely more than a bristle of blasted stumps—and this dawn would send us forward for a new big push.

Six weeks too fucking late Pete—said Jammy— this should have happened straight after Messines while Fritz was still on the back foot and the weather was set fair. Funny how up in the Line things look so obvious that them buggers back at Base just cant see.

Were not in the first wave thank God which is why Ive got time to write. Trouble is it gives more time to think too and more time to snap. Id like to say Im more worried about Gertie than me except Im not. But I am worried about him. The lads have taken to him ever since the night he were inspecting the sentries and came across Chuffy Chandler bashing his bishop—I were there too and I thought— sleeping at your posts a topping offence—God knows what they do to you for this—But all Gertie said was—corporal whatever youre feeding that man see that I get some too!

The lads loved this and Ive got to give it to him— he knows how to speak to them—friendly but firm with it—like a real officer. Its that word like that bothers me but—sometimes it sounds to me like hes speaking lines from a play—which isnt so easy to do when the curtain really goes up.

No chance to write for nearly a week—and the first four days it rained and rained and rained non stop —I bet this has been a famous victory in the papers back home—but were still here in Sanctuary only at the far side now so weve made some progress—it started all right—by the time we went forward the

*first attack had flushed out Fritz from his positions
on the eastern edge of the wood. Gertie were so keen
to get up there and fight that we were hard set to
keep up with him—I knew from Jammy that the bat-
talions orders were to deploy left to keep the line
between Sanctuary and Chateau Wood which had
been taken pretty quick—only with the ground so
churned up—and the smoke and the rain—and Gertie rushing on like a stallion thats got a whiff of the
mares—we crossed in front of our support to the
right and came out of Sanctuary on the wrong side
of the north eastern corner. Gertie waves his left arm
and says—theres Chateau—and starts sending us
out to take up our positions—I didnt think owt was
wrong but Jammy whose got the kind of sense of
direction that can find a pub in a desert says—no sir
thats Glencorse—and Gertie shouts—nonsense sergeant—and sets out after number one section.
Jammy tells the rest of the platoon to hold fast—but
I keep going after Gertie who reaches the Menin
Road when all hell breaks loose out of the wood
opposite and thats number one section gone—just
like that—now you see them now you dont—and
Gertie miraculously untouched just stands there like
a hen with gapes—mouth open nothing coming out.
I got to him first—hit him like a rugby league full
back—and heard the Hun bullets hissing overhead.
Then Jammy was with me and together we managed
to drag him back like a sack of coal.*

*Well that might have got Gertie a real kick in the
arse from above—except there were more bollocks
that day than youd see at a tinkers wedding including a whole brigade getting the false message that
Glencorse had been taken and this time the Huns
waiting till they were all across the road before they
snapped the trap shut.*

So all Gertie had done was get a few of us killed

which nobody blamed him too much for—but Id seen his face when it happened—and I said to Jammy—weve got real trouble here sarge—and he turned that great slab of a face to me and said—it were you saved his life lad—so Id say he were your responsibility now—wouldn't you? Wouldn't you?

"Mr. Pascoe. Hello. Are you all right?"

Pascoe looked up into the puzzled face of Thomas Batty.

"Sorry," he said. "I was just thinking, it looks like rain. Goodbye now."

And he drove off toward the setting sun.

VIII

THEY FOUND WENDY WALKER in Intensive Care.

The prognosis was not good.

"In fact," explained the doctor, who to Dalziel's aging eye looked like a schoolboy in disguise, "it's a miracle she's alive at all."

She'd been found in a drainage ditch alongside Ludd Lane, a narrow country road running parallel to the ring road just west of the university. It looked as if she'd been hit with such force that she'd been sent flying into the ditch, cracking her head against a stone and ending up facedown in six inches of water. What had saved her from drowning was that the water was actually moving, not all that fast, but downstream from her face, and her body had wedged itself in such a way that the anorak she was wearing formed a partial dam, lowering the level around her face sufficiently for her to breathe. But her skull was cracked and she'd been lying for several hours in near freezing temperatures before a passing farmer in his tractor noticed not her body but her bike, which had somersaulted into the hedge some thirty feet farther on. She'd had no identification on her and it wasn't till Annabel Jacklin came on duty at midday that her identity was established.

A uniformed team from Traffic had been out to the scene and their report was emphatic, that on that straight and narrow stretch of road on what had been a cold clear night, whoever had hit her must have known he'd hit her.

"So will she make it?" asked Dalziel.

The doctor shrugged, the impatient shrug of the professional being asked the impossible by the objectionable.

"All systems had just about shut down when she came in," he said. "Bit like an animal going into hibernation. Whether we can start them up again is the question. And if we do, with that skull damage and the possible inhibition of oxygen flow to the brain, would she want them started up again?"

He was foolish enough to make this last remark in hearing distance of Cap Marvell.

"Listen, you noisome little erk," she hissed. "She'd better recover consciousness, because if she doesn't, I'll make sure there's the most probing inquiry you ever saw into the resuscitation policies of this department. Do you understand me, Dr. God?"

Dalziel looked on with the approving admiration of a fellow artisan. This was good technique, he acknowledged. This was real piss-your-pants stuff.

When the doctor had retired looking shell-shocked, Cap turned to him and said, "And what are you doing hanging around here, Andy? Don't you get paid good public money for arresting madmen like this bastard who left Wendy for dead? That road would be the obvious quiet route home for any drunk at the university party living out west. You saw the amount of drink some of that lot were putting away."

This from one who during her brief stay at the party had managed to consume enough gin to fell a Flying Dutchman, seemed a touch rich. Also there was the question of being taught how to suck eggs. But Dalziel saw that this was not the time for formal debate and merely inscribed the points in the mental balance sheet he was building up on the question of which way to go with Amanda Marvell.

He said, "Hit-and-run, if they're local, we'll get 'em. If they're not . . ."

He shrugged. She said, "You mean you just give up?"

"I mean, it's harder. Look, luv, it's nasty, but it doesn't put the driver on the Ten Most Wanted list. And I don't see why you're getting so het up. From what I've seen, you and Walker weren't exactly best mates."

She studied him as if she'd just turned up a stone, but when she answered he realized it was his question she'd been studying.

"I suppose guilt has a lot to do with it," she said finally. "Much of the time she was a pain in the arse, always demanding why we didn't take a much harder line, torch a few fur shops, bomb scientific researchers' cars, that sort of thing. I told her if that's what she wanted she should join another group, and she said soon as she found one with a bit more commitment, she'd be off. And I said, good, with a bit of luck she might blow herself up too, and then we'd all get a bit of peace. I really would have been glad to see the back of her. And now perhaps I have."

Her eyes were moist. Dalziel said, "Nay, lass, tha's likely got enough to feel guilty about without piling this lot on top too. It's nowt to do with you, and you know it. Interesting, but. The other night at Wanwood

House, by the time I got there, it were you making all the fuss and Walker coming over all cooperative."

"Perhaps just our natural reactions to your powerful personality," said Cap.

"I'd not disagree, except she'd already made a statement to George Headingley and he's got as much personality as a park bench."

"For heaven's sake, can't you stop being a policeman just for a moment?" she said with a flash of irritation which reminded him once more just how upset this business with Walker had left her. Time to get her to lighten up.

"Just now you were moaning I weren't doing what I get paid for," he complained. "I can thole a woman being illogical so long as she's consistent with it."

She regarded him quite sweetly and said, "Andy, what am I going to do with you?"

"Owt you like, long as it doesn't draw blood," said Andy Dalziel. "But not in this place. Shortage of beds, so they tell me. I'll ring you later."

"I'll hang on here awhile," said Cap. "Where will you be?"

"Not had me lunch yet, remember? I'll likely head down to the Black Bull for a pint and a real pork pie."

She laughed at his ability to joke about food at a time of crisis, and before he could turn away gave him a vigorous farewell kiss which he recalled with some pleasure fifteen minutes later as he sank his teeth into a juicy meat pie in the lounge bar of the Bull. But he also recalled with uneasy curiosity the inconsistencies of her attitude to Wendy Walker.

Apart from giving DC Dennis Seymour a watching brief to keep an eye on Traffic's investigations, there was little more he could do at this stage to assist or accelerate things. If the lass recovered, then maybe her evidence would help. If she didn't, then it became homicide, and the involvement of the head of CID would not be remarkable.

Just as he was finishing his second pint and thinking about leaving, the door opened to admit Sergeant Wield.

"What fettle?" inquired Dalziel genially. "Looking for me, are you?"

"Looking for a spot of lunch actually, sir," said Wield.

"Well, you might as well get me another pint while you're ordering," said the Fat Man magnanimously. "Then you can tell me how you've been filling the long weary hours since last we met."

He's in a good mood with himself, thought Wield. Something must be going his way.

He set the drinks on the table and sat down.

"Had a chat with Jimmy Howard this morning," he said.

"Oh aye? And what did he tell you? That TecSec's a cover for the White Slave Trade?"

Though very ready to sing his sergeants' praises to others, Dalziel found that a touch of mocking skepticism was an excellent stimulant when they were working out some original idea of their own.

"Forgot to ask him about that, sir," said Wield. "No, told me nothing much except that he hadn't come across anything iffy since he joined the firm, but that had only been since August. In fact he told me three times at least that he only joined in August."

"So what does that mean?" asked Dalziel.

"Maybe just that he joined in August," said Wield. "I leaned on him just a little and made him promise to give us a bell if he does notice anything that worries him."

"And you think he will?"

"Could be he'll just go running to his old mate, Patten. Or could be he'll be fly and keep his options open."

"His old mate?" said Dalziel.

"I got the collator to run the two of them through her machine to see if any link came up. Couple of years back, there was a fracas at the old Lighthouse Club. You remember the place, sir, went under when we opposed their license because there were so many complaints about noise and nuisance. There was usually a pretty heavy game going on in their back room, and this night it ended up with one guy kicked half to death. Patten was involved there as a witness, didn't really see anything, it all happened so fast and the guy who did the damage, a stranger, had it away on his toes before the police arrived. Well, the police who arrived was initially Jimmy Howard. And there were some whispers that Patten should have been the main face in the frame. Only Howard's version of what he found propped up Patten's story and no one else was willing to say out loud what they were happy to whisper."

"So Howard's a bit bent and Patten's a hard man. You got owt I don't know?" said Dalziel.

Unfazed, Wield went on, "I got a breakdown of all the jobs TecSec have been hired to do since they were founded eighteen months ago. Until they picked up the ALBA contract three months back, it amounted to next to nowt."

"So what? Not easy getting a new company off the ground these days," said Dalziel with all the political authority of a man who'd once been too drunk to switch off *Question Time*.

"Yes, sir. Still doesn't explain how a shoestring outfit like TecSec picked up a contract like that. As for ALBA, they're big, but not yet international like Fraser-Greenleaf who are basically American. Word among the moneymen is that FG have been taking a greedy look towards ALBA for some time, but so far the

ALBA board have been able to convince their biggest shareholders that they'll make less money out of annexation than they will out of hanging on. There's rumors of some big breakthrough which will net billions and take over a big slice of FG's market share."

"Sounds like a bloody war," grunted Dalziel. "Okay, so yon weird mate of yours in the City Squad knows his businesses. But did he come up with anything really dodgy?"

"No, sir," Wield admitted.

"I bet he didn't. And I can tell you how TecSec got the job. Bossman there, Captain bloody Sanderson, is an old school chum of Dr. bloody Batty. That's how the world wanks, Wieldy. And as more of the folk you and me went to school with are in clink than in the cabinet or the City, that's why I'm no one's hot tip for commissioner, and you're not even short-listed for Queen of the May."

"What about Patten? He's a partner, remember."

"Sanderson's not daft, realizes most army officers are only as good as their NCO's, and Patten was a bloody good one. So when they get dumped together—"

"Didn't," interrupted Wield bravely. "Patten got out six months before the captain's demob and didn't team up with him till three months after that."

"Right little mole, aren't you, lad?" said Dalziel. "So they meet at some reunion, Sanderson says, what are you doing now, Sergeant? Patten says, not a lot. Sanderson says, I could use a good man to organize the practical side of things while I do the selling. How do you fancy the job?"

"He's a partner," repeated Wield.

"So he invests his severance pay. Everyone gets a lump sum these days."

"All gone," said Wield. "Nowt left."

"How do you know that? You've not been playing

with them buttons again, have you? Hacking into bank statements?"

"No, sir. Had a word with Mr. Charlesworth. He had a word with some of his friends."

Arnie Charlesworth was one of the town's leading bookies and an old drinking chum of Dalziel's.

"Not been taking my name in vain I hope, lad," he said suspiciously.

"Not in vain, sir. Mr. Charlesworth's affectionate respect for you proved very useful. Seems Patten spent his first couple of months out of the army trying to parlay his lump sum into a large fortune by way of various complicated bets. Got pretty close too, but in the end there was always a horse fell, or ate a dodgy carrot or something. You know how bookies hate the thought of losing. He paid up. It was either that or intensive care. Then he vanished from the local gambling scene for a few months till the summer when he showed up again as partner in TecSec with money in his pocket."

"So he went off somewhere the bookies didn't know him, hit a lucky streak, and worked his leavings back into enough to buy the partnership. Wieldy, you're really straining at this one."

"You want me to drop it, sir?"

Dalziel finished his pint and looked reflectively into the bottom of his glass.

"You still think there's summat there, do you?" he said.

Taking this not to be solely a hint that another drink would be welcome, Wield said, "Could be not much in the end, but something, yes."

"Then keep prodding. I've put a feeler out to see if this Sanderson had any strikes against him in the army."

"Officially, sir?" said Wield, concealing his pleasure at this retrospective evidence of the Fat Man's confidence.

"Officially's no use. Bloody army starts singing 'On-ward, Christian Soldiers' if any civilian starts asking questions about one of its own. No, this is personal contact stuff. Anything comes up I'll let you know. Meanwhile mebbe I can have half your attention back on this bones-in-the-wood thing. Just because you've dumped a few tons of sludge on Dr. Death doesn't mean you can wash your hands and forget about it."

"No, sir. Almost forgot. Just before I left the factory, there was a message for you from the Forensic Lab. Seems Dr. Gentry's sluices have come up with something."

"Useful?" said Dalziel hopefully.

Wield shrugged. *Useful* wasn't a word that Gentry used a lot. He saw his job as making discoveries. The use they were put to was in the purview of coarser life forms, like detective superintendents.

"Okay, Wieldy, why don't you shoot along there . . ."

"Sorry, sir," said the sergeant firmly. "I'm off this afternoon. Should have finished more than an hour ago. Unless you're authorizing overtime . . . ?"

"Only if you'll take washers," said Dalziel. "Where the hell's Peter? He's the only one can get any sense out of Death. I knew I should never have let him bunk off to Kirkton. I bet the bugger's sneaking around there, trying to prove he's descended from the lords of the fucking manor."

Though not following the reference, Wield sprang to Pascoe's defence.

"The DCI 'ud not waste time, sir," he said reprovingly. "Whatever he's doing, you can bet your last penny it'll need done."

"Yes, okay, Wieldy," said the Fat Man. "But whatever he's doing, it's not worth it if it means I've got to go and talk to yon walking corpse, Gentry!"

THE CHURCH DOOR WAS LOCKED.

A man in search of sanctuary, or even just a bit of shelter from the rain, was out of luck in modern Kirkton.

Pascoe turned up his coat collar and leaned against the ancient woodwork. He'd managed to find two Pascoe headstones in the unkempt graveyard before the first spots had signaled that the sad old sun had lost its struggle against the creeping barrage of cloud from the west.

The first stone had been one of the many leaning up against the churchyard wall, presumably not so much signaling the last resting place of those named thereon as that they were somewhere in the vicinity. Many were rendered illegible by the impious abrasion of time, but fortunately the mason who had inscribed the Pasco (sic) stone had struck deep, and though the sharp edges of the lettering had long since been rounded by the wind and rain and moss and frost, the message from the grave remained clear.

Here lye ye earthly relics of Walter Pasco shoemaker of this parish passed away in ye fifty third year of his life, April 16 1742 "His soul at last amended"

Soul. Last. Mended, thought Pascoe. Someone had had a sense of humor. Modern vicars got rather uptight about what they thought of as unsuitable inscriptions, but surely something like this could only have been devised by people genuinely fond of the dead man who didn't doubt that he was sharing the final joke with them.

The second memorial had still been in place, but

even though a century and a half younger, its softer stone and shallower chiseling had rendered it much more difficult to read. No jokes here, just the necessary information and pious exhortation.

Samuel Pascoe, struck down by Providence in his thirty sixth year, April 29th 1898. BE YE READY ALSO.

April, noted Pascoe, definitely seemed to be the cruelest month as far as the Pascoes were concerned. So much for Ellie's mockery of his refusal to let a mild Easter lull him into discarding his undervest too soon. *Be ye ready also.* He must remember that as a clincher next time discussion of his natural caution came up.

Of course it was possible that neither of these Pascoes was any relation. He'd need to look at something more detailed like the parish records to be sure of that.

"Help you?" said a voice.

A small man in a large suit was peering at him from over a clerical collar just visible beneath a bushy beard, and from under a golfing umbrella bearing the legend *And on the seventh day God played golf.*

"If you can open this door, you can offer me shelter from the rain," said Pascoe.

"Certainly."

The man produced a bunch of keys, three of which were necessary before the door swung open.

"Vandals," he explained apologetically. "Did my other church over at Mackley, so thought it best to kill two birds. Prevention better than. Jonathan Wood, by the way. Vicar of this."

He was very young, thought Pascoe, which probably meant the beard was an attempt at instant aging. He'd either been very ill and lost a lot of weight or he shopped at Oxfam. As for the brolly . . .

"Gift from my last. Curate there. Jolly lot," said the vicar, following his gaze. "And you?"

Mr. Jingle seemed an unlikely role model, so Pascoe guessed that his abbreviated conversational style was devotional rather than literary in origin, deriving perhaps from a sense of the transience of things. Did he carry it over into his services? *Dearly beloved. Gathered in the presence. Do you take. Pronounce you man.*

"Pascoe," he said. "Peter Pascoe. I'm on an ancestor hunt. We came from round here a couple of generations back. I've found some gravestones with the name on. Latest was Samuel Pascoe, died April 1898, aged thirty-six. I was wondering if there were any records of births, marriages, deaths. . . ."

His style was obviously too circumlocutory for the Reverend Wood, who cut in, "This way. Back to seventeenth. Before that, civil war."

Pascoe followed him down the aisle. It was a gloomy little church, with everything in it, font, altar, pulpit, pews, seeming disproportionately large, and the three stained-glass windows, with their central depiction of St. Laurence on the gridiron flanked by two other exceedingly grisly martyrdoms, did little to uplift his soul.

The vestry was better in that there was a bright electric light and no memento mori other than a box file of church records which Wood placed before him.

"Photocopied," he explained. "Originals safely stowed . . . '98 you said?"

He worked as rapidly as he spoke and in no time at all, or at least considerably less than Pascoe would have taken unaided, he found himself looking at an entry recording the death and burial of Samuel Pascoe in 1898. The entrant had been a conscientious man and there was the bonus of other information not included on the headstone. Sam Pascoe had died from injuries sustained in an accident at Grindal's Mill and he had left behind a widow, Ada, and a son, Peter. That just about clinched it, though it left unsolved the mystery of the name changes. But even as the thought passed through his mind, quick-fire Wood who had been riffling through the record sheets like the wild west wind came up with part of the answer.

"Here we are, to Saml. and Ada Pascoe, 13 Miter Lane, Kirkton, a son, Peter, July 15th, 1892. Swithin's Day. Wonder, did it rain? Not the first. Little note. 4/7/11. Leap forward. Yes. Wedding. Peter Pascoe of this, to Alice Clark spinster of."

Clark. It made sense. Alice Pascoe, out of . . . what? shame? fear? pride? . . . had reverted to her maiden name and passed it on to her daughter, Ada. Who by coincidence had married someone called Pascoe and so restored the family name. Coincidence? He recalled what Dalziel said about coincidence. "No such bloody thing. If it happens to you, it's good detection. If it happens to someone in the frame, it's a bloody lie." It didn't really apply here except in general terms. Don't trust coincidence.

Wood hadn't finished.

"Fast forward. 12/13/12. To Peter and Alice Pascoe a daughter, Ada. What's this? Same month. To Stephen and Mary Pascoe a son, Stephen George Colin. Where'd they come from? Back nine . . . whoa! No need. Jump gun. August 28th. Stephen Pascoe, 13 Miter Lane to Mary Quiggins, 3 High Street. Cut it fine. A connection? Miter Lane. Common family groupings."

"Possibly. I don't know. Miter Lane, does it still exist?"

"Name does. But blocks of flats. Sixties. Ghastly. No Pascoes I know of."

"Any Clarks?"

"Can't recall any. But Quiggins. Unusual name. There's old Mrs. Quiggins still lives with her daughter in High Street. Number three, I think. Original. Just over from church. Across cobbles. All that's left. Any use?"

"You've been most helpful," said Pascoe. "Just one

thing, you said something about not the first, a little note . . . ?"

"That's right. Someone else interested. Pencil. Keeping track. Look. Naughty, but only copies, so no harm. Other relative?"

"Most probably," said Pascoe. "Thanks again. I think it's stopped raining."

"Good. Brolly down. Old parishioners touchy."

It occurred to Pascoe that he might be wiser to change his umbrella rather than rely on the sun in his efforts to avoid giving offense. But he knew better than to come between a vicar and his God.

Outside, the cobbles were glistening blackly, like a still from an old French movie. This too was a salient, it occurred to him, this stretch of the old High Street and the church, a piece of the past bulging into the present, overlooked on all sides and rammed up hard against that impregnable defensive wall of the ALBA complex. He crossed the street carefully and looked for number 3.

The woman who came to the door looked as if she'd fallen on hard times, or more precisely as if hard times had fallen on her, leaving her bent and misshapen under their weight. Her torso formed a right angle with her spavined legs and she supported her body weight on a thick blackthorn stick. Twisting her head to one side so that one bright suspicious eye glared up at Pascoe from waist level, she said, "We've had it, we've got it, we don't want it," and prepared to close the door, evidently feeling that this rubric covered all possible contingencies.

"Mrs. Quiggins?" said Pascoe quickly. "I wonder if I might have a word."

"Mother, who is it?" demanded another female voice from within.

"It's only the tally-man. I've sent him packing," screeched the angulated woman whose bent body gave

Pascoe a clear view into the parlor, which opened direct onto the street. From a door in direct line with the street door and which his acquaintance with the topography of such houses told him probably led into the kitchen, a second woman emerged, younger in the sense that she was fiftyish to the other woman's indeterminate antiquity and still solidly upright, but with an unmistakable familial resemblance in the way her unblinking two eyes fixed him as she said, "Mother, come out of the way," giving Pascoe the impression she wasn't so much clearing the air for apology as the decks for action.

"Miss Quiggins?" he said.

"Who's asking?"

It was time for a quick decision. Friendly stranger seeking information about his family, or impersonal cop making impersonal inquiries?

He would have preferred to stay with the truth but instinct told him that boyish charm was no route to the inner counsels of this unwelcoming pair.

He produced his warrant card, flashed it—too quick he hoped for them to register his name—and said, "Police. We're trying to trace a family called Pascoe used to live in this area. The vicar said you might be able to help."

"Did he? What the hell does he know?" said the younger woman scornfully.

"He brings me fags," said Mrs. Quiggins, looking at Pascoe with hopeful greed.

Dalziel would have produced a packet instantly. Pascoe smiled apologetically and said, "So, can you help us, Miss Quiggins?"

"Mrs. Lyall. Was Miss Quiggins a long time back."

There was a note of nostalgia in her voice which suggested the altered state had not been altogether to her taste.

"So, Mrs. Lyall, about these Pascoes, do you know anyone of that name?" said Pascoe crisply.

Mrs. Lyall had moved her mother out of the way by main force, and now her bulk filled the door in a manner which suggested he was not about to be invited in.

"No one round here of that name," she said authoritatively. "What've they done?"

"Just helping with inquiries," said Pascoe dislocatively.

"Well, we can't. Sorry."

The door began to close. Then the old woman, presumably pissed off at being pulled out of the front line, cried invisibly, "What's he saying? Pascoes? Is he asking about them bloody Pascoes?"

"Oh, give it a rest, Mother!" yelled Mrs. Lyall over her shoulder. And to Pascoe she said, "She wanders. Pay no heed."

"She seems to recognize the name," said Pascoe.

"You reckon? Well, I live with her and I tell you she recognizes nowt. See this little bit of street here? Same as it was a hundred years back. That she recognizes, 'cos that's where she's lived all of her life. Take her fifty yards down the road to where it's all changed and she starts screaming like she's dropped off the end of the world. So if she recognizes the name it's because it belonged to someone who's long gone and likely long dead."

"Nonetheless," said Pascoe. The word affected the woman in much the same way as it affected Dalziel, bringing on a look of irritated resignation.

"If you've got time to waste, that's up to you. Me, I've got work to do. See you don't let her out!"

So saying, she turned and retreated to the kitchen, leaving Pascoe uncertain whether he'd been invited in or was expected merely to remain as guardian of the port.

He compromised by stepping over the threshold but remaining in the open doorway.

"Do you recall a family called Pascoe?" he said gently to the old lady.

"In trouble are they?" said Mrs. Quiggins.

There was a note of hope in the old woman's voice which made him think that that confirmation was more likely to move him forward than reassurance.

"I'm afraid so. We need to get hold of them urgently. So anything you can tell us about their whereabouts . . ."

She shook her head vigorously and said, "Find that whore and you'll find him. All rotten, every last one of them."

"That whore? Who do you mean?" he asked.

"Her! That cow! The one who was married to the other, the windy one who ran away and let his men get killed so they tied him up and shot him. All the same, it's in the blood, a bad lot."

She was a crazy old woman, her mind as crooked as her body, Pascoe told himself. And I'm almost as crazy to be standing here, listening to her ramblings. Call it a day. Go home. Cultivate your garden. Play with your kid. Make love to your wife.

He said steadily, "Would that be Peter you mean?"

"Aye, that's the one. Stuck-up bugger. Ideas above his station. And his mam no better than she ought to have been. And that other cow, so proud he were a sergeant, and all the time him plotting to kill the king!"

This was very lunacy! But he couldn't turn away from it now.

He said, "And the other, the one who ran off with the . . . whore?"

"Uncle bloody Steve, of course! Just upped and offed wi' her. Never a word more to Auntie Mary. Never a thought for the young 'un though he turned out as bad wi' that blood in him. The army said he'd gone to

America, but we knew where he was. Oh yes, we knew!"

He had to get it absolutely clear. Even malicious craziness needs to be recorded if it is to be refuted.

He said, "And the . . . whore as you call her, she was the cousin's wife, Peter Pascoe's wife?"

"That's right. Alice Clark as was. She knew how to pick 'em, didn't she? Spreading her legs to one stinking deserter while t'other she's married to is getting shot by his own side!"

The daughter had emerged from the kitchen and was standing watching Pascoe with growing puzzlement.

"You did take in what I said, didn't you?" she interposed. "All these ramblings of hers are stuff that happened a lifetime ago?"

"You've heard them before?"

"I could join in word for word! This and a dozen other tales she comes out with six times a day like it just happened yesterday."

"You said you didn't know any Pascoes?"

"Nor I do, not living. Nor her either if truth be told. She were a kid when all this were happening, if it did happen. She picked it all up from letting her lugs flap and keeping her mouth shut. When I first heard it way back, her aunt Mary weren't the virgin white she's become since, but the older she gets, the older her memories get too, and all she recalls now is what she picked up when she were six or seven."

"You shut up, our Madge," ordered the old woman. "I know more than I ever let on."

"I don't know about that, Mother, but you certainly let on a lot more than most on us want to know. Are you done, mister? 'Cos if you are, I'll shut that door and try to hang on to the bit of heat you've not let out already."

Pascoe let the injustice of this pass and said, "So you

can confirm at least from your own recollections of family tradition the truth of what your mother says?"

"That was the tale in our family. Auntie Mary's man had run off with his cousin's wife who got shot for a coward or something in the war. But there wasn't a Pascoe round here when I was a girl, and there's none now to my knowledge. You never let on it was history you was after."

She was now openly suspicious. It was, Pascoe felt, time to go. He couldn't resist one last question, suggested mainly because of the confusion of names in his own family.

"Why is your mother called Mrs. Quiggins? I mean, shouldn't that be her maiden name?"

It was a mistake he saw at once, implying knowledge there was no reason for him to have.

The daughter looked at him coldly for a moment, then said, "Not that it's any business of yours, but she managed to have me without benefit of clergy, so the Mrs. is sort of honorary, ain't that right, Mother? Never had much luck with men, the Quigginses. Now, are you done?"

"Yes," said Pascoe. "I'm done. Thank you for your help."

He stepped back into the cobbled street, feeling the damp cold air like a blessed relief.

Behind him, as if resenting the escape of her audience and trying to lure him back with juicier bait, the old woman's voice screeched, "I could tell you stories about them Pascoes! Should have shot the whole lot of 'em! Bad blood, that's what they were. Bad blood!"

And even with the door closed and the distance between them growing with each step, he could still hear the woman's eldritch screech as he got into his car.

"Bad blood! Bad blood!"

X

THE SLUICES OF DEATH filtered slowly, but they filtered exceeding small, and Gentry displayed his trawl with a smile of satisfaction like moonlight on the Aral Sea.

"Doesn't look much," said Dalziel.

He was right. On the table were four dishes, three containing coins and one containing some small pieces of metal.

"You are right," said Gentry, "though the paucity of material may be in itself as significant as a plenitude."

"Eh?" said Dalziel with the scornful suspicion of a man being offered a cut-price diamond tiara at a car-boot sale.

"First, the coins," said Gentry. "Quite a span. Here we have a real antiquity, a Jacobean groat, that is, a fourpenny piece, possibly quite valuable. And here at the other end of the temporal scale, a 1955 penny, with in-between and perhaps most interesting of all, seven gold sovereigns."

He paused for effect.

Dalziel said, "Fucking marvelous. I'll get on to Missing Persons and see if they've got owt on a three-hundred-year-old miser who's gone walkabout."

Gentry, whose established response to Dalziel's sarcasm was to take it literally, though whether this was a gambit or just natural pedantry no one had ever determined, said, "To assume that all these coins, or indeed any of them, spilled from the pockets of the deceased would be rashly predicative. Particularly in view of the evident absence of any pockets."

"You what?"

"The search of the telluric material continues, but I

think I can confidently predict that we are not about to find any traces of the various fiber and fasteners invariably present in human attire, not even any of the nails, leather, or lace eyelets component in footwear."

Dalziel digested this, then said, "Champion! So it's a very old miser who went around bollock naked and presumably kept his money up his jacksie!"

"Eductions are your department, Superintendent," said Gentry. "I merely present discoveries and facts."

"Oh aye? What's these facts then?" said Dalziel, peering down at the final dish.

"As you can see there are two pieces of metal. This one is quite clearly part of the clasp of a small purse or wallet or some such receptacle. The other is a mere shard, of what it is not possible to say, though a preliminary examination suggests it may have become fragmented from its original mass by explosive pressure."

"You mean, like part of a bullet or something?" said Dalziel without enthusiasm.

"If I had meant that, I would have said that," said Gentry. "The only other discovery that may or may not be pertinent is of various pieces of masonry which were removed separately, of course, not sluiced. Preliminary examination of the remnants of mortar suggests a structure of some antiquity."

"Haven't come across an inscription, have you?" asked Dalziel hopefully. "Something like, Here Lies Old Tom, God Rest His Rotten Soul?"

"An interesting speculation but no, we have seen nothing to suggest this was a tomb."

"And that's the lot?"

"Except of course for the bones."

"Bones? I don't see no bones."

"As instructed, I dispatched all osseous and organic matter directly to Mr. Longbottom," said Gentry frostily.

"Did that include a jawbone?"

"Indeed it did."

"Well, thank God for small mercies. You got a phone?"

He rang the Path Lab but all he got via an assistant who'd been instructed to pass it on verbatim was the message that he would be told what there was to tell as soon as there was anything to tell, and that was likely to be later rather than sooner if the necessary work was further interrupted by unnecessary phone calls.

"Tell him, up yours too," said Dalziel, banging down the phone and glowering at Gentry. His inclination was to exit on a piece of fine abuse but he didn't bother. Why fire Parthian shots at a brick wall?

He went back to his office, finding occasion to shout at nearly everyone he met on his route through the building, which wasn't a great number, as the first bellow created a shock wave which sent all who heard it scurrying for cover.

Why was he in such a foul mood? he asked himself. A possible murder case that was moving too slow for his liking? Hardly. He'd had far more fretful cases than this, with Desperate Dan on his back and blood and guts everywhere! In fact at the moment, Wanwood apart, there was precious little of any import apart from the usual break-ins, muggings, and assaults, on CID's books.

So what was the problem?

Cap Marvell was the problem, just as she'd been this morning. Then he'd resolved not to go round to her flat for lunch, but somehow he'd ended up going, and he'd got his jollies, which he had no complaint about—which in fact were of such a quality that a man might spend a long weekend in Bangkok without finding their equal—but also, without intending to, against all his intentions, and despite his continued silence on the subject of her whisky, he'd got in deeper.

In a way, that bloody Walker lass was to blame.

Without her intervention, it would have been interesting to see if the after-bed afterglow would have survived another vegetarian lunch. Instead he'd finished up at the hospital being given orders like he was a . . . what? Husband? . . . Hardly! Toyboy? . . . Jesus! . . . Partner? . . . That's what they called 'em nowadays, wasn't it? . . . Sounded like some tax-fiddling dodge in an iffy company. . . . How about, friend?

Nowt wrong with that, was there? A man needed friends. What was he making all the fuss about any road? Two mature people—she were near on old as he was—both knowing the score—no need to be mooning around like some kid whose balls had just dropped.

He found he was feeling guilty now about his uncharitable thoughts about Wendy Walker. Where the hell was all this guilt coming from? If I go on like this I'll be kissing the pope's ring, he told himself.

It seemed easier to salve the sore by picking up the phone and ringing the hospital to see how Wendy was.

Still hadn't recovered consciousness, they told him. Prognosis unchanged, except that the longer the worse. Next he got hold of Dennis Seymour, who also had little to report except the possibly significant negative that there were no signs of hard braking on Ludd Lane, suggesting whoever hit her hadn't responded at all to the contact.

"Could be he was so well pissed he didn't even notice," said Seymour.

"That makes it better, does it?" growled Dalziel. "Keep me posted."

An hour later the CID fax machine pumped out Troll Longbottom's preliminary report on the Wanwood bones.

Aided by Dr. Death's sluices, he had got together an almost complete skeleton with the exception of the left fibula, the right ulna, and various phalanges, the absence of which was probably down to the depradation of the local fauna.

The skeleton was of a man, five feet eight or nine inches tall, slight build, in his twenties, with some evidence of calcium deficiency suggesting dietary limitations in childhood but stopping well short of the level of deprivation which would have caused rickets.

The skull fracture already noted was confirmed as a possible cause of death, though by no means certain. There was evidence of other recently healed damage to the left leg, rib cage, and shoulder such as may have been occasioned by a severe beating, but which was certainly not cotemporal with death. The damage to the shoulder was such as would have severely limited movement of the left arm.

The jawbone was less helpful than might have been hoped. There had been three extractions and there was some sign of decay in one or two of the surviving teeth, but no filling work which would have helped with the dating. This suggested that the man had lived in an era, and possibly a class, in which extraction was the first rather than the last option when toothache struck.

On the basis of the general condition of the bones and such other evidence as they presented, Longbottom put the date of death at somewhere between forty-five and ninety years.

"Shit and derision!" exclaimed Dalziel. "The bugger's doing it on purpose!"

He rang the lab again and this time refused to be fobbed off.

"What the devil do you want now, Andy?" demanded the pathologist. "You've got my report."

"Preliminary, it says."

"There are other tests, but I don't anticipate any major changes."

"Not even the lower limit? Up it from forty-five to fifty, say? Or better still, sixty? Or cause of death.

Couldn't you be even vaguer? Mention the possibility of natural causes?"

"Andy, I can understand your anxiety to shift this one out of the realm of the investigable, but at the moment that's really the best I can do. Hasn't Gentry come up with anything which could point to a more precise date?"

Glumly Dalziel described Dr. Death's findings.

"Interesting," said Longbottom. "You know it used to be claimed that in I think it was King Alfred's time a naked virgin carrying a bag of gold could walk the length of England unmolested. Perhaps this chappie was trying to repeat the experiment and made it as far as Mid-Yorkshire before he failed. Wouldn't be the first refugee from the South it happened to."

"Very funny," said Dalziel. "Except that, if the sovereigns are his, he didn't fail, did he? I mean, he wasn't robbed. And it doesn't look as if he had them concealed about his person."

"True. Well, there's your line. If the sovs were his, that could help date him. If I'm right, they had gone out of general circulation by the twenties, so we'd be getting to the far end of my limits. And if he wasn't robbed, then one motive for fatal assault goes. Perhaps he was a naturist bathing in some woodland pool when he had an accident. Perhaps he'd been up at the big house rogering the mistress when the master came home. Wouldn't be the first Jack the Lad to exit in the buff, clutching the family jewels in one hand and whatever he valued second highest in the other."

"You've been reading too many dirty books," said Dalziel. "Dental records, they'd help, right?"

"To confirm identification, of course they would. Except that you don't have any identification to confirm, and in any case, if as seems probable, this chap is prewar, I doubt if his records are still lying about, even

supposing he didn't just have his extractions done by
the local vet in the first place."

"Thanks a lot," said Dalziel. "I can see why you specialize in dead 'uns, Troll. Don't have to worry about
cheering them up."

He put down the phone. It rang almost immediately.

"Seymour, sir. We've just had word on Walker's
bike from Forensic. No sign of any paint or other traces
from the contact vehicle, but the front wheel had damage consistent with being run over by a car wheel."

"Great, that helps a lot," said Dalziel.

"Yes, sir. I mean, no. I mean, maybe . . . look, the
thing is, sir, if the car actually ran over the bike, how
come we found it in the dike thirty feet away from the
woman?"

"Bugger who hit her threw it there so's anyone else
passing wouldn't notice the accident," suggested
Dalziel.

"Yes, sir. Except that as I explained earlier, there
aren't any traces on the road of a car braking violently.
And if the vehicle did actually run over the bike, it
would have been dragged along the surface, leaving
very distinct marks in the tarmac."

"So what is it you're suggesting, lad?"

"Well, maybe Wendy Walker was knocked down
somewhere else and the driver decided he'd rather she
were found a lot farther away from his home, say.
Or . . ."

"Let's have it, lad."

"Or she wasn't knocked down at all, but someone
would like it to look like that."

XI

FOR A WHILE ON THE JOURNEY back from Kirkton, Peter Pascoe got ahead of the rain. But always its dirty gray clouds came bubbling up in his rearview mirror and suddenly they were above and beyond him, spilling huge greasy drops to burst like insects on his screen. The dual carriageway he was on was crowded and soon driving began to feel like crawling along the bed of a filthy canal littered with the rubbish of a consumer-gorged society.

At the first opportunity he turned onto a country road, often his preferred route in good weather because of the pleasant rolling countryside it wound its way through. But today there was little hope of enjoying the view. Indeed, as if provoked by his attempt at escape, the clouds now darkened to black and exploded in such fury over his head that he could hardly see the road let alone the landscape. He dropped his speed to twenty but even then almost overshot a sharp bend, and deciding enough was enough, he pulled off the road onto a cart track and came to a halt in the shelter of a small clump of trees.

He turned on his radio but the rain was making it crackle and fizz so unpleasantly that he soon turned it off. He was, he realized, curiously disturbed by his encounter with the ghastly Quiggins women. Not just by the abuse the old one had showered on his family but also by the sense they'd given him of how claustrophobic life in a village like Kirkton must have been only a couple of generations ago. Perhaps still was! And this was his heritage, this was where he came from.

He almost wished that when he'd discovered that

the Wyfies' barracks had been knocked down he had simply scattered the ashes on the site and carried on home. What did it matter where your remains came to rest? If I should die, think only this of me: That there's some corner of a short-stay car park that is forever Ada!

He managed a smile at the parody but it didn't change things. He'd gone into the museum, met the major, and now he was stuck with knowledge he couldn't ignore.

The rain showed no sign of letting up. Pity he hadn't bought a newspaper. But there was reading matter in his glove compartment, and not inappropriate. It was the volume on World War I which Major Studholme had loaned him. He opened it and turned to the chapter on Passchendaele.

It was a brisk scholarly account, concentrating on giving detail rather than drawing conclusions. Not that this was a felt deficiency, as the simple facts spoke eloquently for themselves.

After the opening assaults on the last day of July, the opposing armies settled in their new lines, which weren't all that much different from the old, and shelled and bombed and skirmished with each other while the intermittent sun dried the surface of the bogland sufficiently for the Allied High Command to contemplate the next major push. Main objectives were the village of Langemarck on the left of the salient and Glencorse Wood on the right. August 13 was the chosen day for the attacks to start. On August 11 it started to rain again, and rained, and rained, and rained . . .

. . . and rained! After the opening attack wed come out of the line—weather had improved a bit then—sunshine and showers—and Gertie was back to his old form. I knew how he were feeling—first time under fire and youve survived—you feel like youve just

come out of the dentists—it were hell but its over and everythings going to be alright from now on.

Except that its not—youve got to do it again—and again—and again—and it never gets any better—and its when you realize that that the real test comes.

But for now Gertie felt like a hero. Bank Holiday back home, Pascoe—he said—everyone off to the coast. Wish I were with them sir—I said.

No you dont—he said—better off here. Think how they put up the price of ice cream on a Bank Holiday.

Well it were all very jolly for a while—but I knew that the longer the sun shone the more certain it was thered be another push—and sure enough on the 10th we went back into reserve—and sure enough on the 11th the rain started again.

Word is the bombardment has really got Jerry on the back foot up in Glencorse—said Gertie—doubt if well even be called forward this time.

I caught Jammy looking at me to see if Id agree—I said nothing—all I knew was the Huns had got more pillboxes than Doctor Dick in Glencorse and that Id never been in reserve yet but what we were called forward.

But still you hope against hope—when you hear the whistles and see the flares and know that up ahead the far side of Sanctuary its started—mebbe this time itll go to plan. We are cold and wet in our mud filled holes—but nobodys complaining—up there in Glencorse therell be heat enough from bombs and bullets—and men lying in the wet crying for water. Mebbe this time we wont be called—but I know we will—I know what Gerties still got to learn—that theres no such thing as worst—theres always more—and the only way to get Fritz out of his con-

crete pillboxes is to pile our dead so high in front of
them he cant see out to fire.

It took longer than I thought afore we were called
forward—not because things went better but because things were so bad hardly anybody was left to
send the news back.

In a battle you only know later what youve been
doing—while youre doing it all you know is what
you can see right ahead of you—and when this is a
sodden pockmarked desolation with a bristle of pathetic stumps that had once been trees—and theres
no glimmer of sun to give you a hint of direction—
then you might as well be anywhere—except there
was something to give us a hint—bodies—this was
where the first attack had gone in no doubt—like a
trail dropped in a paperchase the bodies of our own
dead showed us the way—we even trod on them—
no helping it—and besides they kept you out of the
mud.

I could hear Gertie jabbering away—lots of en-
couraging words like he was at a football match—
but a bit too high—a bit too fast—then suddenly
they stopped and I thought—hes bought it! But
when I looked along the line I saw hed just come to
a halt—just like that first time—mouth open like a
hen with gapes—staring at a head which had got
blown clean off some poor devils shoulders and
landed squat on the end of one of those blasted
stumps.

I saw Jammy give him a push—then when that
didnt work a real jab in the kidneys—that woke him
up and off he went again—only he wasnt shouting
any more—Jerry had been pretty quiet up till now—
maybe to let us get close—but suddenly he opened
up from those bloody boxes we all went down so
quick it must have been hard to say whod been hit

who not—only when we started to move and slither into better protection it soon became clear—Johnny Cadger was hit—hed always been looking for a Blighty but from the awful bubbling screams he was letting out hed overdone it—a lot of others too—but worst of all Jammy had taken one in the chest. Steve was close by him and had managed to drag him into cover—somehow I wriggled across to join them— Gertie was in the same hole—he looked so bad I felt sure he mustve caught one too—but Steve said—no hes all right but the sergeants bad—Jammy looked up at me and said—acting sergeant now Pete— mebbe permanent from the way I feel—I said—nay Jammy—miserable sod like you wouldnt do owt nice like dying on us—he tried to smile then said—Hows the platoon?—Fine—I said—He said—Get them back soon as its dark—thats the order right sir?— We all looked at Gertie who made an effort and nodded—Then Jammy said youd best lead Pete—Mr Grindal ull bring up the rear—I could see his point —Gertie was likely to lead us straight to the nearest pillbox—but I didnt like leaving Jammy—Steve said —itll be right Pete me and the lieutenant ull bring the sarge along—so I set off crawling to see what was left of the platoon.

Dark came soon and off we set back—soon as we started moving Jerry sent flares up and started shooting—but we kept going till we came to the end of the stumps of Glencorse and were looking across the open stretch between us and our lines in Sanctuary. We closed up here. There were more of us left than Id feared at first. In fact I saw a couple of faces— including Doyles—that Id not seen for some time— and I wondered if theyd been lying low looking for a chance to get back unscathed. Well I wasnt going to bubble them. All that concerned me was that Jammy was still with us—held up between Steve and the lieutenant—I began to feel almost hopeful.

I offered to take Gerties place—but Steve said— No hes better with something to do—so I went back to leading—would it have made any difference if Id insisted?—Maybe—but at least I got the others back safe despite a flurry of flares and bullets as we crawled the last hundred yards.

But there was a long pause after the last squaddie reached Sanctuary—then Gertie appeared by himself.

Where are the others?—I yelled. They caught it— he said—back there—it was hopeless—theyre dead.

I almost hit him—would have done if Chuffy hadnt grabbed my arm—not cos I didnt believe him —but cos I felt it were my fault—trusting him. Just as well I didn't connect as Cap Evenlode the adjutant showed up just then—dont know what hed seen but he gave us an old fashioned look. Word is he dont much like Gertie—typical stuck up family— likely thinks the Grindals are trade—and when he took Gertie aside with him to make his report I bet he gave him a rollocking too about controlling his men. But I didnt have time to worry about that—I was listening to a voice shouting somewhere out towards Glencorse—nothing unusual in the Salient— the air was full of voices calling screaming sobbing —it was the mud—once you were wounded and by yourself you soon got stuck fast—stretcher bearers did all they could but it often needed half a dozen men to pull one out—God knows how many died that might have been saved if they could have made it to a dressing station—so when I said—listen— thats Steve—they all thought I was being delirious— but I knew that voice—and besides now he was calling my name—Pete—Pete—so I didnt stop to think but went back out of the trench before anyone could

*try to stop me. I werent being brave—I just knew I
could never go back to Kirkton and tell the usual
lies about him dying like a hero if Id left him to a
long slow drowning in that mud.*

*I had a piece of rope coiled round my waist—that
was one thing wed learned in that first attack on
Sanctuary—Jammy had managed to scavenge a
whole coil while we were in rest—and everyone in
the platoon got a length—and I had a field dressing
pack—those apart I had nowt—I hadnt even bothered to bring my bondook—I wasnt going out there
to kill anyone—but there were plenty who had other
ideas.*

*From time to time a flare went up from either side
making me think of the shepherds in the field when
glory shone around. It were like that glory too—
meaning that for a short while you saw everything
perfectly clear, then darkness came rushing back
worse than before and I had to lie still till I got my
night sight back again. But oh the sights I saw under
that floating white light—wed fought back and forth
over this ground for more than a week and there was
scarcely a shell hole I looked into in search of Steve
that didnt have its occupant. Desperate now to find
Steve even if only to know for certain he were dead I
turned corpses over—and sometimes they were men
I knew—and sometimes they were men their own
mothers would not have known—but none was
Steve.*

*Id not dared call his name for fear of letting Fritz
know I were out here—but in the end anything were
better than slithering endlessly through this hell so I
yelled his name—and discovered that even a man at
the extreme of fear can still be made to jump when a
reply came back so close it seemed almost in my ear.
I turned my head and peered into the gloom of a
deep hole—after a while something moved down*

there—a darkness moving against a darkness—then a tiny gleam—a sliver of whiteness—gave me a point to focus on—it was an eye—and as I looked a face formed around it—and Steves voice said—You took your fucking time.

Gertie said you and the sarge had bought it—I said—He could be right—said Steve—he certainly is about the sarge—Oh shit—I said—Where is he Steve? Wheres Jammy?—I think Im standing on him—he said.

By now I could make out he were in a bad way— never mind what wounds he had—the left side of his head lay on the surface of the mud and of his body only his right arm and shoulder were still not covered. I threw him the end of my rope and he grasped it in his hand then twisted it round and round his wrist till it were held tight and I started to pull. The piece of ground I was lying on was full of debris so it provided a firmer base than anywhere else Id crawled that night—but not even this advantage could give me enough purchase to haul him free— and all his struggles to help himself did was sink him deeper.

Its no good, Pete, he said—Im a goner. Tell Mary, she can play around all she likes now but if she doesnt do right by little Steve Ill come back to haunt her so help me God.

Wed never talked of it before but I knew then that he knew what all the lads from Kirkton know—that his Mary wasnt exactly saving herself for her heroes return.

I said—don't talk daft—Ill get some help—well soon have you out of there—And he said—for God's sake dont leave me like this—put a bullet through my head before you go. Cant do that—I said—I came out without my bondook—Thats a hanging offence—he said—why dont you get some practise in?

*Ill put this rope round my neck and you heave on
your end and see if youve got enough strength to
strangle me.*

*God help us—I dont think he was joking—but
before I could decide what to do—and what I would
have decided Ill never know—another flare went up
and by its light I saw that God had taken the power
of decision away from me. On the far side of the
shell hole four German soldiers were crouched—
three with rifles and one—the officer—with a pistol
pointed straight at me.*

*I thought of running—and I thought of surrender-
ing—and I thought of Alice and Ada and Kirkton—
and while I was thinking of all these things I held up
the end of the rope and pointed at Steve and said—
Mein Bruder.*

*I didnt know the German for cousin and maybe if
I had it wouldnt have been so effective—but* Bruder
*made them pause just long enough for the officer to
say something. The expected rattle of gunfire didnt
come—Slowly the flare faded—I remained quite still
—where would I run to?—and when I got my sight
back they were at my side.*

*I think they checked that I had no weapon—just
a medical pack—perhaps they thought I was a non
combatant stretcher bearer or something like that—
perhaps the officer had a brother in the trenches—he
was young—same age as our Gertie Id say—with
the sunken shadowed eyes that mark all of us whove
been too long at the Front—what else is there to say
about him?—Nothing—and everything—I wouldnt
recognize him if I met him in the street—but I wish
him well and safely home—for he spoke again to his
men and they took the rope from me and began to
pull—and slowly Steve came out of that dreadful
hole.*

I think there may have been a moment when he

wondered whether to take us prisoner—words were spoken—the officer looked from me to Steve who was lying semi conscious at my side—and I would guess he said that taking us back with them was likely to prove a lot more dangerous than leaving us to our own devices.

Whatever—he spoke to me in English—the one phrase—Good luck—then they moved off—and Steve and I were by ourselves without a care in the world except how the two of us—one wounded—one exhausted—were to get back to our trenches without getting drowned—blown up—or shot by either side.

But get back we did—and by one last miracle almost to the very point where Id slipped over the top. Dawn was lightening the east and the lads were on stand-to—so I risked a shout which was less of a risk than being taken for a sneak attack—and a few moments later I was drinking a mug of tea while Steve was being stretchered to the rear.

It were funny—when news reached the remnants of the platoon that he should be OK though hed got a Blighty one he quickly changed from poor bastard to lucky bastard. What really caught the lads interest was our encounter with the Huns—as word got around about this—I found men from other platoons were coming up to me and asking me about it—out here we never hated the Hun like they do back home—too much sense that hes in the same bleeding boat—and this story of mine mebbe set them dreaming that somehow wed do out here what clearly they couldnt do back there and strike our own private peace.

I didnt know how I was going to react when I saw Gertie—or how he was going to react when he saw me. The way Steve told it he could have genuinely believed Jammy and him were both dead—so I gave him the benefit of the doubt—and he looked me straight in the eyes and said how glad he was hed been wrong about Steve—and how sad he was about Jammy—then he told me to sew another stripe on as he was recommending I got made up to sergeant in Jammys place.

Only once did I let my control slip—back in rest again I was sorting out the days Orders with him when he said—word of advice sergeant—go easy on spreading tales about friendly Huns—adjutant must have heard something—told me very pointed this morning that fraternizing with the enemy is regarded very seriously back at Base.

I said—Fraternizing?—They saved our fucking lives!—And he said—Exactly—so how do you feel about shooting Germans now?—And I said—them Germans?—if I knew it was them Id not shoot—in fact theres a lot of our own lot back at base Id sooner shoot than any of them Germans! Gertie said —for Christ sake Peter be careful what you say—you know how they feel about agitators just now—anyone else hears you talking like that and youre in real trouble—mutiny trouble—weve got to do our duty— follow orders—theres no other way—dont you see?

Well hes right of course—and the brass are right —and that German officer was right—and Im right too—and if every buggers so bloody right why arent we all back home moaning about the price of ice cream on a bank holiday instead of being stuck in the middle of this stinking mudhole where everythings so fucking wrong?

Why? Why? WHY!

The rain was slackening off just as it had slackened off early in September all those years ago, to be replaced by a gusty wind drying up the ground and with it any hopes that the brass might decide that the fixture was rained off. Not that, on past performance, there'd ever been much chance of that anyway.

Pascoe looked up at the trees, almost leafless now in October, but still tall and shapely with all the latent promise of spring's renewal in the supple swaying of their boughs. As he looked, his inward eye, which was the curse of solitude, stripped them of everything till they were mere black lifeless stumps. Through Glencorse and into Polygon. Every small advance doing nothing but put a few more yards of ravaged ground between you and whatever mockery of peace remained to the rear. And after Polygon, with the winter rains settling in, weeks more of the endless crawl through the yellow mud up the shallow ridge where stood, or rather lay, the ruined village of Passchendaele.

Pascoe forced himself back to the present by looking at his watch till at last the time registered. What had Pottle said? A window between four and five?

That's what I need, thought Pascoe. A window, nice and high, looking out across a sunlit pastoral landscape.

He was getting the sun at least. The storm had overtaken him and was moving east. Westward the dying sun rimmed the horizon with red and the sky was clear. Could be a frost tonight, he thought. Always something to look forward to.

He started the engine and went in pursuit of the retreating clouds.

PART THREE

POLYGON

I have a Garden of my own,
But so with Roses overgrown,
And Lilies, that you would it guess
To be a little Wilderness.

I

EDGAR WIELD LOOKED OUT of the frost-crazed kitchen window as he waited for the kettle to boil and recalled his certainties of endless Indian summer just a couple of mornings earlier.

Never bet with a farmer about weather, a woman about weddings, or a miner about whippets. Where did that bit of homely advice spring from? Someone who knew his stuff, so it couldn't have been a CID sergeant.

He was passing through an uncharacteristic period of self-doubt, swinging between suspicion that he was wasting his time with his blindman probings of TecSec and certainty that he was missing something as obvious as a drunk at a church fete. Curiously this doubt didn't make him unhappy. These last few months he had spent living in Corpse Cottage in Enscombe had relaxed and released him somehow, bringing the whole spectrum of emotional coloration within his reach for the first time in more years than he cared to remember. And if at one end dark self-doubt was the price he had to pay for bright self-awareness at the other, then that was okay. More than okay, a real bargain.

The kettle was boiling. He mashed the tea, some odd Chinese blend that Edwin insisted on. It was, he had said rather sniffily, an acquired taste. So, Wield had pointed out, was the strong stewed stuff he preferred—acquired through years of no choice—and he saw no cause to brag about that.

So they danced and fenced and sometimes fought around each other, every encounter a learning process, most outcomes leaving them a little bit closer.

He set the tray with two china mugs, a fresh-sliced lemon, a bowl of sugar, and carried it upstairs.

Edwin Digweed was sitting up in bed reading. It sometimes seemed to Wield that where'er his partner walked, old books immediately crowded into a shade. He looked suspiciously at the pile on the bedside table. It looked to be at least three volumes higher than the previous morning. Digweed's secondhand and anti-quarian bookshop in the village was often quite audibly groaning beneath the weight of words piled high on every surface. When he'd moved out to Corpse Cottage, the books had rushed in to occupy what had pre-viously been his living space above the shop, like water into a foundering ship. This was the one uncrossable line Wield drew. Books on bookshelves he didn't mind. But books on sills and stairs, in kitchen cupboards and bathroom cabinets, under sinks and over wardrobes, books breeding books in every nook, cranny, and empty space, was not his idea of interior decoration. A good book might be the precious lifeblood for a master spirit, but that didn't mean you wanted to drown in the stuff.

"You're up early," said Digweed. "Bad con-science?"

"Not so's you'd notice," said Wield, climbing back into bed. "Just this TecSec thing."

His first impulse when he and Edwin had joined forces was to continue what had been his iron rule for twenty years—to keep his professional and private lives completely separate. But he had discovered in himself a great weariness for living out of compartments, so he had started talking about his work, not even making a big thing about confidentiality. In his experience a man you needed to swear to secrecy was the last person on earth to share anything with.

He didn't tell everything, but if anything was so adhesive that the drive up the valley of the Een didn't wash it off, then he felt Digweed was entitled to know. Not that his partner gave any sign of feeling this was a right worth demonstrating over, his interest frequently being engaged by elements that were peripheral if not eccentric.

"Wanwood," he had said when Wield first aired his obsession (for so he acknowledged it to himself) about TecSec. "After Wanwood Forest, no doubt. Let me see."

And yet another book had appeared to be pored over before being discarded on one of the rampant piles.

"Yes, here we are. Wanwood House, originally a hunting lodge in the royal forest of Wanwood which in medieval times stretched from Mid-Yorkshire almost as far south as Doncaster. Given with land by Henry Seven to Sir Jeffrey Truman for loyal service at Bosworth. Family prospered during next three centuries but went into decline in eighteenth. House currently ruinous—and this was written, let me see, in 1866. What does it look like?"

"The house? Big and square. Like an old railway station."

"Victorian, you mean? Probably a nineteenth-century rebuilding. And you say the woodland surrounding it has been ripped up for security reasons? One of the last remnants of the old forest of Wanwood? My God, that's really criminal!"

But occasionally Digweed's long-submerged training as a lawyer surfaced and he expressed a proper forensic interest.

"Ah yes," he said now, putting a thin slice of lemon into his tea. "Your intuition. Or to put it another way, your irrational unsubstantiated gut feeling. How do you intend to proceed?"

"Don't know. Another go at Patten maybe."

"What about his partner?"

"Captain Sanderson? No, Mr. Dalziel's getting the dirt on him."

"I see. Class divide. Sergeants investigate sergeants, captains are left to the brass."

Wield laughed.

"Don't think either Sanderson or Fat Andy 'ud thank you for lumping them in the same class," he said.

"No. Now I bring your great leader to mind, or at least as much of him as I can cram into my fairly elastic imagination, I see what you mean. By have 'another go' do you mean electrodes on genitals or just the wet knotted towel?"

"Psychological pressure we call it when it doesn't leave marks," said Wield.

"Really? Fascinating. We really must consider bringing out a small booklet of police definitions. No, don't look offended."

"I wasn't. And how would you know?" said Wield. "Any road, this must be a big bore when you've got a book on early American presses in your hand."

"No, honestly, far from being bored, I'm fascinated. Let me prove it. It seems to me that two things occurred which, if connected, may give body to your somewhat ethereal suspicions. Firstly, the man Patten joined the firm. Secondly, the firm got its first substantial contract, working for ALBA."

"And if there's no connection?"

"Then I should concentrate on helping old ladies across the road."

"Well, thanks a lot," said Wield. "That's a big help. No, I mean it."

"You mean, you mean to be kind rather than satirical, perhaps. But I'm not finished. Once engage the attention of Sherlock Holmes and he applies the full might of his intellect to even the most trivial of details. A detail which may or may not be trivial seems to me to be the matter of what Patten was doing in the months between pouring his severance pay into the pockets of the bookmakers and becoming Captain Sanderson's partner."

"Yeah, I know. In fact I think I said that to you myself," said Wield.

"Hoity-toity," said Digweed. "Yes, indeed you did. But what you said was that you'd like to know what possibly nefarious activity Patten had got up to which earned him enough money to buy in. I think perhaps you ought to be asking why he should want to buy in? Or perhaps why Sanderson would want to let him buy in? Or even whether indeed he bought in at all in the strictly financial sense?"

"Eh? You're losing me."

"I do hope not. All right, let me put it simply. Suppose Patten bought in with blackmail? He knew something about Sanderson's past which the good captain preferred kept out of the papers? Or suppose he bought in with information? He knew something about ALBA which would help TecSec get taken on there?"

Wield sought for a reply that wouldn't be a put-down. These were the kind of airy-fairy speculations he was happy to take from Peter Pascoe because he knew that behind them all was a real cop's mind, centered on the need for proof.

"Not a great deal I can do to check them ideas out, but," he said. "Thanks all the same."

"You could check out whether in fact Patten during his dead time took a perfectly ordinary job to keep the wolf from the door," suggested Digweed. "It sometimes seems to me that you chaps are so busy digging the dirt that you forget to look around you at clear eye level."

Having delivered himself of this Holmesian utterance, Digweed returned his attention to his book.

Wield supped his tea and grimaced. Still had a lot of acquiring to do. But Edwin had a point about the job. Not that it would help much if it turned out Patten spent six months on a checkout at Sainsbury's. But if, as Wield suspected, there was a complete blank, then that would prove . . . nothing. But it would be a big encouragement!

Bravely he swallowed the rest of his tea and got out of bed again.

"Off so soon?" said Digweed.

"Aye, I've got some checking to do. And before you start looking so smug, think on. I've counted the books in that pile. There's nine counting the one you're reading. Gets to double figures and it's bonfire time. Right?"

"You're a hard man, Sergeant. And don't forget that this is a meatless day."

This was a weekly lowlight of the Corpse Cottage dietary regime.

"I didn't know what unnatural practices meant till I met you," said Wield.

Once he got to the station his checking didn't take long, which was just as well, as the outcome didn't seem worth waiting for. He'd shortcut official channels by ringing a contact in Social Security Investigations and asking her to punch up Patten's National Insurance number and checking on employment from November

the previous year till June this. The answer was so obvious that Wield felt a pang of resentment toward
Digweed, as if his partner had deliberately wasted his
time.

Patten, feeling the pinch when his gambling had
emptied his account, had looked for a job to suit his
talents and training, and been taken on by Task Force
Five, the Manchester-based security firm which, from
small beginnings in 1979, had burgeoned with the
eighties crime figures into one of the top three national
firms.

"So he's done their training course, and had seven
months to see how they get things done, when he runs
into Sanderson who's got a business he'd like to turn
into the next TFF," growled Dalziel. "Makes him a
good man to hire."

"Didn't get hired, became a partner," said Wield ob-
stinately.

"So he'd had a bit of luck with the bookies somewhere out of Mid-Yorkshire. Or maybe making him a
partner was compensation for not being able to afford
to pay him wages. How much does it cost to buy into
nowt anyway? This all you've got, Wieldy?"

"There's Rosso, that's Les Rosthwaite."

"Who the hell's he when he's at home?"

Wield told him.

Dalziel said, "Am I missing something here? Sanderson's batman came out with him and worked for
TecSec till he got himself killed in a car accident?"

"That's right, sir," said Wield, uneasily aware that
Dalziel, more than anyone, recognized the sound of the
bottom of a barrel being scraped.

"Anything suspicious?"

"Well, no, actually. I checked with Traffic. He was
more than twice over the limit and he'd got previous
for drunk and disorderly . . ."

"Thank God for that. I thought you were going to

say they found curare in his bloodstream and somehow I'd missed hearing about it. Are you done now?"

"Yes, sir, I'm done. Are you saying I should drop it now?"

"You've got to have got hold of summat afore you can drop it, lad," said Dalziel. "As far as TecSec goes, we've got nowt. Okay, it's odds on that there was some kind of fiddle went on for Sanderson to get the ALBA contract. Old Boys' network with mebbe a bit of Old Boys' blackmail thrown in, but without a complaint there's nowt criminal in that. So let's fry the fish that are in the pan, eh? The women in ANIMA who went on the raid, I want them all interviewed again."

Wield examined this, then said reasonably, "I thought we'd decided there was no way they could have anything to do with the remains, except finding them . . ."

"Don't start telling me what I know, Wieldy," said Dalziel irritably. "This is something else. You've not heard? No, of course, you were off enjoying yourself yesterday afternoon. It's a bloody good job there's someone round here puts in an honest day's work. It's Wendy Walker."

He told Wield the story.

"How's she doing?" asked the sergeant.

"Still unconscious," said Dalziel. "If she wakes up, mebbe she'll be able to tell us exactly what happened. Until then all we can be sure of is she weren't knocked down the way someone tried to make it look she was knocked down."

"Could be the driver just wanted to shift the scene of the accident a bit farther from home."

"Yeah, even Seymour managed to work that one out," snapped the Fat Man. "Well, that's a serious crime in itself. It would mean the driver knew she was alive still. And the way she was dumped facedown in a ditch full of water suggests he didn't much care if she stayed that way. So it could be attempted murder we're dealing with."

"So we're interviewing all known associates to see if we can pick up any pointers," said Wield.

"By gum, you're sharp today, Sergeant. I've got Seymour checking out her fellow lodgers in the house she lives in. Some kind of lefty commune by the sounds of it, so I doubt we'll get much cooperation there. And the other major bunch of contacts we know about are the ANIMA women, so if you can spare a bit of your precious time, Sergeant . . ."

The probable cause of Dalziel's bad temper was beginning to be clear, but Wield liked to have things completely clear.

"Does that include Ms. Marvell, sir?"

"She's one of them, isn't she?"

"Yes, but I thought, mebbe knowing her personally . . ."

He faltered under a gaze as obstructive as a roadblock.

"That's why I'm telling you off to do it," said Dalziel softly. "Unless you've got any objection?"

"Not the least in the world, sir," said Wield. Then he thought, hey, that sounds more like Edwin speaking than me. But the Fat Man didn't seem to have noticed. He was looking at his watch.

"You seen Peter this morning?" he asked.

"No, but I may have missed him. I didn't look in his room. . . ."

"Don't go all defensive cover-up on me, Wieldy," said Dalziel. "I doubt if I've seen him for more than two minutes since he got back from his gran's funeral. He claims he didn't kop for owt, but the way he's acting, you'd think he'd turned into a gent of independent means! I don't know what's happening to this department, but it's coming apart at the seams, and I'm the bugger to stitch it up again, even if it means drawing a

bit of blood in the process. So put that into your grape-
vine and spread it, lad."

"Yes, sir," said Wield. "I'll spread it like marga-
rine."

II

PETER PASCOE AWOKE.

It was black dark and the darkness pressed on him
like a wall of dank earth which a very little undermin-
ing would bring sliding down on top of him. His nos-
trils flared and his mouth drew in desperate drafts of
air, and he turned on his side and reached out his hand
in search of he knew not what possible comfort. His
fingers found flesh, still, cold, naked. He cried out in
shock and tried to withdraw his hand, but before he
could, it was seized in a grip irresistibly strong and out
of the darkness a voice said, "You've kicked the sodding duvet off again. God, I'm frozen solid!"

Then Ellie drew him close and held him across her
shivering body.

"Purely thermal," she murmured warningly. "Don't
get any ideas."

He didn't answer and after a while she became
aware that his shivering wasn't all down to tempera-
ture.

"Hey, are you okay?" she said.

"Yes. Just a bad dream."

"Don't tell me. This court-martial thing still?"

"Sort of . . . in a way . . . not about it though
. . . about me . . . I feel like I'm there . . . in the
Salient . . ."

"For Christ's sake, Peter," she exclaimed, sitting up.

"I know I said I thought you should go on with this, but if this is what it's doing to you, don't you think you should give it up?"

"Don't think it would make any difference. Thing is, this Salient feeling, it's not new . . . I've been there before . . . feeling out at the limit, exposed, utterly vulnerable."

"You're talking about after Burrthorpe, aren't you? And Chung?"

Ellie's belief in open government started at home.

"I suppose so. But other times too. In some ways all of my life. I've always looked for . . . strength. Maybe that's why I joined the Force. Married you even."

Attempt at lightness? Or truth in jest?

"You mean, me and Fat Andy are on a par? Thanks a bundle! Peter, I know there've been rough times, but we talked . . . at least I thought we talked, I thought we'd got things sorted."

"No, please, understand me, this has nothing to do with you . . . without what we've got, God knows where I'd be."

"But you've never told me, not fully. I thought we'd agreed to share everything. . . ."

"We do. But that doesn't mean just unloading all the time. You've had bad times too without unloading all your stuff on me."

She was silent for a while then said, "Sounds to me maybe I was. Pete, I know you've talked to Pottle in the past and it helped. Have you thought of trying him again?"

"I called to see him last night, on my way back from Kirkton."

He could feel her hurt at what must come over as another exclusion, but all she said was, "So what happened?"

"He listened, then said—it seems to me that what we've got here is stress related directly to an investigation, a not uncommon syndrome in your profession. The successful conclusion of the investigation usually solves the problem of the stress also. Let us hope it does so here."

He caught exactly the precise tone of the psychiatrist's pronouncement, emerging from the usual cloud of cigarette smoke which he justified by saying—if I gave up this one disgusting habit, who knows what others would rush in to fill the gap?

Normally Ellie might have been amused by the closeness of his mimicry. Now all she said was, "But what is it you're investigating, Pete? Do you really know?"

"That, I suspect, is Pottle's point. Look, I was going to tell you all this last night, when we got to talking about it. Then you came up with your alternative therapy. . . ."

After seeing Pottle he hadn't bothered to go in to the station, justifying himself with the argument that if there was anything more important waiting for him there than the usual pile of paperwork on his desk, the radio would have been foaming with his call sign all afternoon.

At home there hadn't been a chance to talk with Ellie about his day till Rosie was safely stowed in bed. She'd demanded a further episode of a bloodthirsty serial Pascoe had been inventing intermittently for longer than either could remember. Rosie sometimes went weeks without wanting a further episode but when she did, she had total recall of every detail of plot and personnel, and any variation was instantly and savagely corrected. With her editorial help he'd steered the latest installment to its usual cliff-hanging conclusion and she'd smiled up at him blissfully, murmured, "Fucking great, Dad," and fallen asleep.

"Ellie, we need to do something about this swearing thing," he'd said when he got downstairs.

"I'm seeing Ms. Martindale tomorrow," said Ellie.

This was Rosie's head teacher, a charming, smiling young woman, who came across as cooperative and conciliatory till you collided with her will of steel.

"Best of luck," said Pascoe.

"So how was your day?" she asked.

"I'll tell you over dinner," he said.

He'd started lightheartedly, making her laugh as he recounted his meeting with Poll Pollinger. But when he tried to carry on the mood into his account of his visit to Kirkton, he failed miserably.

"Let me get this straight," said Ellie. "Your great-grandfather, Peter, was married to Alice Clark, both of Kirkton."

"Yes."

"Also living in Kirkton was his cousin, Stephen Pascoe, who was married to Mary Quiggins."

"Yes."

"And this Stephen was making it with Alice and when Peter was executed for cowardice on the Western Front, Stephen left his wife and child and ran off with Alice."

"So the old Quiggins woman claims. The other one is too young to have any personal knowledge, but she confirms that was the family tradition."

"Did Ada ever say anything about having a new dad? Or an uncle called Stephen?"

"Not that I heard."

"And why did she grow up with the name Clark, her mother's maiden name? If Alice was shacking up with a man who had the same name as her husband's, wouldn't it have been easier just to carry on as Mrs. Pascoe?"

"I'd thought about that before all this came up. I was theorizing that she'd gone off and changed her name out of shock and shame. From what I've seen of Kirkton, it can't have been much fun living round there once it got out that your man had been executed by his own side for cowardice. But if she ran off with Stephen, she might have a double reason for changing her name. Shame, and the police."

"Why the police?" asked Ellie puzzled.

"Because la Quiggins called Stephen a deserter. I know from what Studholme said that he was wounded during the Ypres campaign in 1917. Presumably if he had recovered enough to be having an affair with Alice by late autumn, he'd recovered enough to be returned to duty. Perhaps he didn't fancy it."

"Hold on," said Ellie. "Before you start tarring all the Pascoes with the same brush, Studholme didn't say anything about this Stephen being a deserter, did he?"

"No."

"Don't you think he'd have mentioned that? Perhaps he ran off with Alice, had a couple of days with her, then when it was time to report back, he went off like a good little soldier back to the Front and got killed."

"Why do you say that?"

"Because clearly he didn't go back to his wife and family, and equally clearly, if Ada's silence means anything, he didn't go back to Alice. So, unless he was a real shit and treated his fancy woman like he treated his wife, it seems likely he didn't make it."

"Yeah, maybe."

Pascoe passed his hand over his face as if trying to rub something off, a gesture of weary despondency Ellie recognized and deplored. It meant that, quite unnecessarily in her view, he was letting this ancient history get to him in a big way. Damn Ada, she thought. What right did she have to let her life's obsession spill over into her grandson's?

This was the point at which Pascoe had felt ready to bring up his visit to Pottle, but before he could start Ellie excused herself and went into the kitchen, returning a moment later with an open bottle of his precious Nuits-Saint-Georges which she set alongside the already half-finished Hungarian Chardonnay.

Pascoe raised an eyebrow and said, "Thirsty?"

"You could say. You know how a big red oils my wheels."

"I can't say I'd noticed them creaking."

"That's because you're not close enough to listen yet," she said sultrily. She was very good at sultry when the mood was on her.

They finished the bottle in bed. Of all the teetering tightropes alcohol sets a man to tread, that between desire and performance is perhaps the most perilous, but it seemed to Peter Pascoe that for once he'd got the balance perfectly right, moving forward steady as Blondin, till the air exploded in a blast of nuclear light, sending him plunging joyfully over the edge into what had been a welcome and welcoming darkness.

Then had come that other darkness, and the waking dream which was not all a dream . . . but at least it had sparked off this talk. . . . He felt better now . . . Ellie had turned away from him, snuggling into the reclaimed duvet. He put his arms round her and cupped her breasts . . . twin salients these but full of comfort and promise . . . I too am Homo Saliens, he thought, Salient Man posted here for the duration. . . .

"Hey, I said no ideas," Ellie murmured drowsily. "Far too early . . . your hands are cold . . . let us sleep now . . ."

Next time he awoke it was to the sound of the postman whose way with a doorbell marked him as a frustrated fireman. He sat up quickly, wished he hadn't, looked at the alarm clock, wished he hadn't done that either, and rolled out of bed, dragging the duvet with him.

"For God's sake," said Ellie. "You're doing it again."

"We've slept in," he said. "I'm late for work, Rosie's late for school, and you're late for . . . something."

"Life," she groaned. "Jesus, what do those fucking Frogs put in their booze?"

Catch her unawares and she could be deliciously politically incorrect. But no time now to enjoy the sound, not to mention the sight of her, sprawled across the bed in a state of naked abandon which even in his present haste brought the familiar lustful tightness to his throat.

The doorbell had long stopped ringing. He dragged on his dressing gown and staggered onto the landing, shouting, "Rosie, love, get up, will you? You're late."

"No, I'm not," said his daughter from the foot of the stairs. "I've had my breakfast and I've been making yours."

She was all dressed ready for school, neat and tidy as could be, and in the kitchen the percolator was bubbling, the toaster toasting, and two bowls of muesli sat on the table.

By his there was a bulky package.

"I had to sign for it," said Rosie proudly. "The postman said really you or Mummy should sign but I said you were busy."

That at least was something, thought Pascoe. On recent evidence, he'd not have been surprised if she'd told the man her parents were pissed out of their minds and probably bonking their eyeballs out.

He said, "You've done really well, darling. But you should have waited. You know you oughtn't to be playing around with electrical things in the kitchen."

She regarded him with the scorn of one who'd been born knowing how to program a VCR, and said, "Skimmed milk or Gold Top?"

Pascoe examined the package. The label told him it was from Barbara Lomax, Ada's solicitor. He'd phoned her office to say that he'd carried out Ada's instructions with regard to disposing her ashes, and would be interested to know what other duties his role as executor required of him. He'd expected there might be a few papers to sign, but this package looked like serious work.

Well, it would have to wait. Legal duties were important, but he had a greater master than the Law to serve.

He shoveled in his muesli, slurped down his coffee, refused (much to Rosie's distress) his toast, and on his way up to the bathroom passed Ellie on her way down.

"Bloody red wine," she growled at him. "You know it doesn't agree with me."

"It wasn't my idea," he called, but she was already out of earshot.

He went out of the door at a run but she caught him as he backed the car out of the garage.

"But it was worth it," she murmured, bending to kiss him through the window. Then rather spoiled it by adding doubtfully, "At least I think it was . . . never mind, it'll probably all come back later."

As he drove too fast along the road into town, he found himself like a tardy schoolboy rehearsing excuses. Maybe I should have asked Rosie to write me a note! he mocked himself. Just tell the fat old sod the truth. Which was? That I slept in. Why? Because I slept too well. Also because I slept too badly. Which? Both. How come? I slept well because we wined and dined and . . . exhausted ourselves. And I slept badly because I've got this maggot in my mind like one of those maggots which grew fat on all those thousands of bodies out there in the Salient, corners now of foreign fields, compost and bonemeal, long plowed under, to set the green shoots reaching for the sun, for beasts to graze on and finally create those mountains of excess for which the EEC is the jest and riddle of the known world.

No! Better Rosie's note than this rambling truth. Dear Mr. Dalziel, my daddy is late because he and Mummy got pissed last night. I will try to make sure it doesn't happen again.

His radio crackled. Control, which in this case meant Dalziel, wanted to know his location. He was approaching a roundabout. Straight on would take him to his desk in about fifteen minutes. Exit right and the ring road would bring him within striking distance of Wanwood House in about the same time.

A bit of advice from his younger detective days sprang into his mine. *Never be late, always be somewhere else.* Could even have been the Fat Man himself.

He kept going round the roundabout.

Into his radio mike he said, "Location Wanwood House following up yesterday's inquiries at ALBA HQ."

What he was going to do when he got there he had no idea. This was an absurd schoolboyish way for a mature DCI to be behaving. But when you thought about all those young boys who back in 1914 had lied themselves to death, perhaps there was a balance to be redressed, and every act of mature childishness was a tiny chipping at that greatest mountain of European waste, the Everest of unused youth.

Perhaps. Or perhaps he was just following a well-worn track into the male midlife crisis.

Whatever, he'd better start thinking of a reason for visiting Wanwood or he might find crisis coming a little early this year.

III

WIELD USUALLY GOT ON well with women. After they got over the twin barriers of his looks and his profession, they found his presence so unthreatening that even the most nervous were able to relax, though only the most perceptive, such as Ellie Pascoe, got beyond the face and the job into the penetralium of his mystery, and worked out that the cause of their comfort was his gayness. Like sometimes cancels out like, however, and it soon became apparent he wasn't going to get anything out of the first two ANIMA women he interviewed, Meg Jenkins and Donna Linsey, who ran a pet shop and their lives together. He doubted if they'd have sold him a goldfish and was glad to put their musty, musky premises behind him.

The next three were much more unbending but not to any great effect other than a consensus that what Wendy Walker did outside the group was a mystery. This in itself was not uninteresting, in that to keep yourself to yourself within any group of Yorkshire women required an act of will beyond the reach of all but the most dedicated. But Wield had been too long at his last to cobble significance out of secrecy. He knew better than most that the habit of discretion was harder to divest than the reasons for it. Like the old adage said, once a nun, always a nun.

Annabel Jacklin happily was as un-nunlike as you can get without starring in *The Sound of Music*. This was Jacksie, the buxom blonde whose descent into the crater had prefaced the discovery of the buried bones. Previously Wield had only glimpsed her sodden wet, mud-streaked, and deeply shocked. Fully recovered from her experience, she now made the most of a not too distant resemblance in both looks and bounce to Marilyn Monroe at her peak in *Some Like It Hot,* a movie which an old partner of Wield's had once made him sit through three times. This was not an experience likely to be repeated in company of Edwin Digweed, who was fervent in his belief that the only good films ever made were square-shaped, grainy, and usually silent, which left Wield nothing to do but shrug and say, "Nobody's perfect."

But any hint of flirtatious flaunt at finding a strange man on her doorstep vanished the moment Wield identified the reason for his visit.

"I nearly fainted when I realized who it was they'd got in Intensive Care," she said. "First time it's happened to me, someone I knew personally I mean, and it's a real shock, you know, you're in a kind of different mode when you're at work, sort of detached, you've got to be, in our job, and seeing someone you know sort of jolts you back to what you are normally, do you know what I mean?"

"Yes," said Wield. "Same in my line."

"I can imagine. How is she, do you know? It's my day off but I was going to call round and see how she was doing."

"Still unconscious, I believe. But they're doing their best. Sorry. Here's me telling you. What I need's a bit of background, Miss Jacklin. Had you known Miss Walker long? Were you close friends?"

"Yes. Well, I think so. I don't know. I mean, I knew her . . . know her . . . we were friends but not for all that long. . . ."

"You mean, you got on well but you hadn't known her long enough really to know a lot about her?" said Wield.

"That's right. Hey, why don't you answer all the

questions as well as ask them?" said the woman, her earlier sparkle reasserting itself.

"Does that mean you met outside the group?"

"Couple of times, yeah. It was her who kept me in the group really. When she joined I was feeling pretty pissed off. Not with helping the animals and things, I've always done that since a kid, you know, RSPCA, donkey sanctuaries, animal shelters, then I got into signing petitions, and marches, and protests . . ."

"Then you joined ANIMA," inserted Wield.

"That's right. Woman who worked in the same place as me who I sometimes saw at demos took me along. It was all right as long as she was there, then she left. Husband got a job down south. After that it wasn't so good."

"How?"

"Well, the others, I don't know, treated me like I was still a kid. They all think the sun shines out of Cap's bum . . ."

"And you don't?"

"Oh, she's fine. It wasn't her. I mean, it was in a way 'cos she's so single-minded and I could tell she got exasperated a couple of times when I did something clumsy. I don't mean to, but they make me a bit nervous. Anyway I didn't mind Cap, she's the leader, but I couldn't see how this gave any of the others the right to patronize me."

"And that made you want to leave?"

"Partly, but what really pissed me off was when I found I was being left out of things. Someone said something, and I realized they were talking about an op I hadn't been on. I asked Cap and she said vaguely that she'd tried to contact me but I hadn't been available, which was crap. And I thought if it's happened once, how many more times?"

"When was this?" asked Wield.

"Oh, earlier in the year. So I was ready to tell them

all to stuff it when Wendy joined. At first I thought, what the hell's this? I mean, first time you meet her, she comes over a bit weird. But once I got talking, we really hit it off."

"Had a lot in common, did you?" asked Wield.

"Not much," admitted Jacksie. "But she was outside the inner circle too and that made a real difference. She said some really saucy things to some of the others, and behind their backs . . . well, I couldn't tell you what she said, not to a man."

She smiled and waited to be pressed. Wield said, "So what else did you talk about when you weren't slagging off the others?"

She looked ready to bridle, then perhaps recollected what had brought him looking for her.

"Oh, she went on a bit about miners and women's rights and things," she said with the light dismissiveness of one whose worldview was experientially myopic. "And she told me about getting wed when she was seventeen and what a prick he turned out to be."

"Did she mention any other men, you know, boyfriends?"

"No one special. She told me a few stories about fellows, you know, funny stories, the stupid way they go on when they're doing it. Sometimes though I thought she might be a bit sort of both ways, if you follow me, and that was why she liked me."

"Did she try anything?" said Wield with what he hoped was heterosexual sternness.

"Oh no. You don't have to look hard to see I'm not that way inclined," said Jacksie with the naive and cruel certainty that anyone as attractive as herself must be straight. "Not that it bothered that Donna from making a pass once—you should have seen the looks Meg gave me!—so mebbe I'm wrong about Wendy. Anyway, it never came up. Girls, I mean. Just men."

"So what else did you talk about?"

"The group, mainly. I told her about being pissed off and she said they did seem as go-ahead as the activities committee of the WI and wasn't there other groups with a bit more go that we could join?"

"And are there?"

"Oh yes, a few. You get to hear things at big demos, recognize faces."

"Did you make any contacts then?"

Suddenly she was looking at him with eyes whose blue had more of storm trooper than baby doll in them, and her body language had changed from fancy-a-slice-of-this? to where-the-hell-are-you-coming-from?

"What's all this got to do with Wendy being knocked down?" she asked coldly.

"Just trying to put together a picture," said Wield.

"Is that right? You mean, seeing as you were here and this stupid cow's all shook up because her friend's in hospital, you might as well see if you can get her to incriminate anybody while she's not looking."

It wasn't altogether true, but true enough to mean the interview had just about run its course.

"Sorry," said Wield. "And I'm really sorry about Wendy. We'll do our best to get the bastard. I'm off to see Ms. Marvell now. I gather she's really cut up about what's happened."

If he'd asked another direct question he suspected he'd have been told to get stuffed, but the obliquity got him his answer.

"Don't see why she should be, they were always at each other's throats. Wendy's fault as much as Cap's."

"Because she thought you should be a more hard-nosed group?"

"Yes, generally. Though it's funny, that last row they had, the night we found the bones . . ."

"Yes?"

Jacksie checked what she was going to say to make sure it didn't contain anything that could be used in evidence against anybody, then went on, "It were the other way round. They were the last to be brought into that room where they locked us up till you lot arrived. When they came in they were going at it hammer and tongs. Wendy said, 'What the hell were you going to do, Cap? Take his head off? And Cap said, 'Why not? They've been hired to protect those bastards cutting up the animals, so that makes them the enemy too.' Funny that. And now if you don't mind I've wasted enough time yacking to you. I'm going to the hospital to see how Wendy is for myself."

Which brought him finally and he had to admit reluctantly to Cap Marvell's door. It was one thing to mock the Fat Man's fancy behind his back, another to be put in a situation where there was no avoiding close contemplation of its implications. In most things Dalziel was a law unto himself, but that only worked so long as he was, without fear or favor, *the* Law unto others. For a cop to screw someone likely to be called as a witness in a case he was working on was foolhardy. For a cop to screw anyone likely to end up in the dock was folly. Okay, so Cap Marvell looked unlikely to be prosecuted by ALBA in connection with the raid on Wanwood, but sooner or later she was going to be prosecuted for something! Dalziel had obviously judged this a risk worth taking, assuming of course that judgment figured at all in matters sexual. But even he must have been taken aback by the speed with which it had proved necessary for Cap to be interviewed again in connection with a criminal matter. Not that it seemed probable she would have anything to contribute to the Walker inquiry other than the necessary comments of a known associate. Perhaps it would turn out to be a fortuitous early warning, making Dalziel step back before he got in too deep.

Shit, thought Wield with sudden self-disgust. How mealy-minded could you get! A few months of what felt like a stable partnership had turned him into Mrs. Grundy! If randy Andy thought he'd found true love, then the old sod 'ud be mad not to grab it with both hands while it was before him.

The door opened and he found himself looking at what, if salacious speculation were correct, the old sod had probably grabbed at with both hands already.

"Sergeant Wield, I presume. You'd better come in."

This was the only hint that she had been forewarned of his visit, but it was enough. If Dalziel were stepping back, it was the merest shuffle rather than a bloody great step.

She listened to his preamble with courteous patience, then said, "I assume this means that you feel there is a chance that whoever knocked Wendy down may have been known to her, perhaps even had a motive for wishing her harm, and you are therefore collating information on her habits, background, and associates?"

Sharp lady. Or mebbe she'd had this spelled out to her already and was just wanting to get it on the official record to avoid a slipup which might embarrass her great protector.

"That's it, spot on," said Wield. "So owt you can tell us . . ."

He got the story much as before, though angled slightly differently. Walker had joined the group about two months earlier. She had proved an active and energetic colleague, but hadn't seemed interested in forging links outside the group's main activities . . . "regarding which, as you will understand, I am not about to give you any details, Sergeant," she concluded.

"I got the impression she and Miss Jacklin were pretty friendly," said Wield.

"I suppose they were. Are," said Cap, regarding him speculatively. "But as to their meeting outside the group, you'd really have to ask Annabel. I know nothing about the social life of either of them."

"I'd have thought in your line of business you'd have wanted to know quite a lot about your associates, Ms. Marvell," said Wield.

"Personal introduction is the principle I work on," said Cap. "Someone I trust introduces someone she trusts. That's step one. Then I watch and evaluate."

"I gather someone who moved away introduced Miss Jacklin," said Wield. "So who introduced Wendy Walker?"

She hesitated. She's told Dalziel, Wield guessed, but doesn't know if he's told me. Who the heck is it they're making such a song and dance about? The chief constable's grannie?

This flight of fancy put the real answer in his mind even as Cap Marvell said, "It was Ellie Pascoe, your Mr. Pascoe's wife."

She looked as if she were thinking about adding something else but if she was, she changed her mind.

Saving it for pillow talk, thought Wield churlishly.

"So what grade did you give Miss Walker?" he asked.

"Sorry?"

"You said you watched and evaluated," said Wield.

"That's right. As I said, she was full of energy. And ideas. Never afraid of putting her point of view forward."

"Which was different from yours?"

"Why do you say that?"

Wield could have answered that every other member of ANIMA had mentioned, with varying degrees of approval, Wendy's aggressive contribution to debate. Instead he said, "Not much point in putting her viewpoint if all she were doing was agreeing with you. And she doesn't sound like the apple-for-the-teacher type."

Cap smiled.

"Not unless it had a bomb in it," she agreed. "Yes, we often locked horns, from our first encounter almost. That's one of the things I liked about her. She didn't let anything pass unchallenged. Made you think about what you thought. I'm sorry. I'm talking about her in the past tense. I don't mean to."

"It happens. So what were the main areas of disagreement?" asked Wield, adding reassuringly, "It's all right. Anything you say won't be taken down and used in evidence against you."

"I hope it may be used *for* me," she replied. "Wendy was hot for direct action; not just animal release, but active sabotage, serious damage, hitting the bastards where it hurts, I quote, which is in the pocket."

"You mean arson? explosions? that sort of thing."

Cap nodded.

"And people? How did she feel about harming people?"

"She said that those who inflicted suffering should be prepared to suffer themselves."

"And you?"

She gazed at him with wide-eyed seriousness.

"I said that my first and only aim was to alleviate animal suffering and as long as I was in charge of ANIMA, this would be our sole guiding light."

"Meaning no bombs or sabotage or attacks on individuals?"

"Meaning just that, Sergeant."

"And yet even though she disagreed so much, Wendy stayed?"

"Yes. Interesting that. I expect she was merely biding her time till she got a better offer."

"Aren't we all?" said Edgar Wield. But he didn't mean it.

IV

LAST TIME PASCOE HAD BEEN at Wanwood House the old woodland had been whole. Nothing he'd heard about the cordon sanitaire had prepared him for the swath of muddy desolation now ripped through its heart.

He stopped the car and got out to take a closer look, venturing onto a duckboard, but starting back sharply as it threatened to sink beneath him.

"Morning sir," said a voice.

He turned to find a man in TecSec's green uniform watching him.

"Morning," said Pascoe. "My God, did we really send men to fight in this?"

"Aye, and things haven't changed so much in eighty years that the bastards wouldn't do it again if the need arose. Thank God for choppers and tactical nukes, say I."

Pascoe looked with interest at this man who'd so easily picked up his reference. The scarred face returned his gaze unblinkingly.

"DCI Pascoe, here to see Dr. Batty," he said, offering his hand.

"Yes, I know. They rang from the gate. Patten, in charge of security. When you didn't show in half a minute, I thought I'd better check."

"In case I got bogged down?" Pascoe smiled, disengaging from the handshake which threatened to become macho. "You interested in the Great War? I noticed you picked up the reference to Passchendaele."

"Kigg. General Kiggell, Haig's CGS," said Patten. "My granddad quoted it so often, I'd be ashamed not to know it. Ended up claiming he was actually there when it was said, but I doubt it. He was certainly in the battle though, if that's what you can call it."

"Which mob?"

"Wyfies."

"Good lord. My great-grandfather too."

"Oh yes? Mebbe they knew each other," said Patten indifferently. "Dr. Batty's in a staff meeting just now but shouldn't be long. Wondered if you'd fancy a coffee with me and my partner, Captain Sanderson."

"That would be nice," said Pascoe as they got into the car. "Captain, you say. Military or naval?"

"Army. Same mob as me."

"Would that be the Wyfies too? I mean the York-shire Fusiliers since the reorganization."

"That's right," said Patten.

"So you're keeping up the family tradition, Mr. Patten?"

"Aye. Fourth generation of service. Not that it counted for much when they started slimming down. Loyalty's still one-way traffic, Mr. Pascoe. Like it was at Passchendaele."

"Wasn't it always so?"

"No. Time was when soldiers loved their generals. Alexander, Caesar, the old Iron Duke even, and he was a right bastard by all accounts. Not because they didn't get the lads killed, or have them lashed, or feed them weevils, but 'cos when push came to shove, the generals were on the same side as the men, often *at* their side, up to their knees in the same fucking mud."

"And they weren't in the Great War?" prompted Pascoe.

"Not the way my granddad told it, and not the way the old boys at the reunions remembered it. Politicians and profiteers ran that show, and the generals, most on 'em, were in their pockets, or too damn scared or stupid to stand up and say, enough's enough. After it were over, they made Haig an earl and gave him a hundred thousand pounds. A florin a head for the lads who were dead, my granddad used to say. He was no politician, old Doug, but by Christ he made his profit."

"But lessons were learned, weren't they?" urged Pascoe, curious to see how far this ex-soldier's resentment would take him.

"Some," admitted Patten grudgingly. "Last lot were better by all accounts. But it's still the politicos that call the shots. Or when they need us, like the Falklands, it's all Land of Hope and Glory and thank you, Mr. Atkins, but two minutes' peace and the word comes from Westminster, start sacking the sods."

"Being made redundant and being sent over the top in the Salient aren't quite the same thing," said Pascoe gently.

"Same kind of people not giving a fuck who gets hurt or how many," retorted Patten. "If they'd tried it on with the Iron Duke, he'd have sent the Guards down Whitehall with bayonets fixed. Nothing like cold steel when there's a shortage of backbone. Might still work too, if only we had someone with the guts to try it."

Pascoe made a mental recording of all this for later retailing to Ellie as yet another example of how an apparently shared indignation could lead to such disparate ends. Patten's revulsion at the unnecessary slaughter of Passchendaele led him to advocate a military dictatorship! While his own led him to . . . what? Pacifism? No. He believed he would fight in a just cause. Antimilitarism then? Certainly, but not of the knee-jerk variety. The country needed its armed forces, so long, of course, as they were kept under the control of the democratically elected government. In other words, politicians. In other words, the kind of "control" which, in Patten's eyes, led directly to the carnage at Passchendaele. . . .

"We're here, sir," said Patten.

They had arrived at the front of the house. Pascoe realized he had parked the car on automatic pilot and was now sitting staring vacantly out of the window and into his thoughts, while the TecSec man stood waiting by the open door.

"Yes, of course. Sorry." He got out and looked up at the lowering facade. "Not a very welcoming place, is it? I can see why it didn't survive as a private hospital. Perhaps that's where those bones came from. Patient trying to escape."

"Anything more on that, sir?"

"Oh, inquiries are proceeding," said Pascoe vaguely.

"Oh yes?" Patten smiled cynically. "Used to get that kind of bromide in the army, usually meaning 'we're lost.' "

"I wouldn't say lost," said Pascoe. "But certainly still feeling our way."

"Well, if you're serious about that body mebbe having something to do with the hospital, then you've come to the right spot," said Patten, leading him round the side of the house.

"I doubt it. Not unless you've got their records stashed away in a cellar."

"That's more or less what I do mean," replied Patten to his surprise. "Can't swear it's the records, but I do know that when we were checking the place over last summer with a view to making it secure, I found a cellar full of rusty old filing cabinets jammed full of junk."

"Really?" said Pascoe. "Now, that I would like to see. If it could be arranged."

"No problem. But let's have that coffee first."

He ushered Pascoe through a side door and into the TecSec office where a rather old-fashionedly smooth man he guessed to be Captain Sanderson was sitting behind a desk. He rose smiling and offered his hand.

"Peter Pascoe, I presume. Heard about you. Had the

pleasure of meeting your boss yesterday. Broke the mold making him, I should think."

He raised one eyebrow quizzically, a trick Pascoe guessed he practiced in front of the mirror.

"Mr. Dalziel, you mean? He is certainly unique."

"And you're certainly diplomatic," laughed Sanderson. "Des, why don't you rustle us up some coffee?"

Partners they might be, but it was still the sergeant who brewed up, Pascoe noted.

"Take a seat, Mr. Pascoe. Tell me, does a visit from a superintendent one day and a chief inspector the next mean that things are getting better or worse?"

"Depends what things you had in mind," said Pascoe.

"Bones-in-the-wood sort of things," said Sanderson.

"I see. Then it depends what you mean by *better* and *worse*."

"Well, from my point of view, having the contract for security here at Wanwood, *better* would be if you told me that you'd decided the bones belonged to some old tramp who'd dossed down in the wood and passed away from natural causes. *Worse* would be if you decided there was a crime here which needed investigation. And worst of all would be if you suspected there might be more bodies out there and were planning to instigate a full-scale excavation program."

Patten put a cup of coffee in front of Pascoe and offered him milk and sugar. He shook his head and sipped the bitter black liquid.

"In other words, the less publicity the better?"

"You've got it."

"Why worry? I should have thought that your only real quarrel was with the animal rights people, and from that point of view, ALBA's little secret has been out since the raid in the summer."

"True," said Sanderson. "But as you probably know from police experience, there's a difference between a target and a symbol. Aldermaston, Portlon Down, Greenham Common, none of them unique in what went on there, but they each became a symbol for the whole and thus the object of continuous attention from the protesters. We can deal with the occasional hassle, but we don't want to end up as everyone's favorite target."

"I'm pleased to meet such concern for an employer," murmured Pascoe. "A more cynical approach might have been to rub your hands and say, the more hassle ALBA get, the more they'll need to shell out on security. After all there's still a fair stretch of ground untouched out there. Plenty of room for a moat, say. Or a hundred-foot wall."

"Oh dear. Do I detect disapproval of what we've done to the wood?" said Sanderson, smiling.

"I'm fond of trees," admitted Pascoe.

"And animals too, I daresay. How do you feel about their use in medical research, Chief Inspector? I only ask because as an old army man, I appreciate how difficult it can be sometimes when there's tension between personal feelings and official orders."

The tone was sympathetic and sincere but nonetheless Pascoe knew he was being mocked.

He finished his coffee and said carefully, "Such a question might have been pertinent last summer when I was here investigating the raid on the labs which resulted in your firm's employment, Captain Sanderson. But as my present investigation is concerned only with the remains discovered in the wood, and the head of ALBA himself has assured me he has no wish to prosecute the animal rights group involved, your question is, in one sense at least, impertinent."

"Slap goes my wrist," said Sanderson, untroubled. "But we mustn't keep you from your duties, Chief Inspector. Are you looking for Dr. Batty? He seems a trifle busy just now."

He glanced at the bank of TV screens, on one of which Batty could be seen at work with several other white-coated figures in a lab.

"No hurry," said Pascoe. "Mr. Patten, you said something about a cellar . . . ?"

Sanderson shot Patten an inquiring glance.

"Them old filing cabinets," explained the ex-sergeant. "Mr. Pascoe's interested in the place when it were a hospital."

"Ah yes. Because of the bones. Good thinking, though I fear you'll find it dusty work. Perhaps you'd care to borrow one of our uniforms?"

"No, thanks," said Pascoe. "I tend to think more clearly in plain clothes."

Ten minutes later he was regretting his smart answer; in fact he was regretting that Patten had ever mentioned the cabinets. He'd feared the worst when the man had led him via progressively deteriorating corridors out of the high-tech reconstructed regions of the house into what was a pretty well untouched Victorian back kitchen overlooking a bin-strewn yard. Memories of the Wyfies museum in Leeds came to his mind, and when the TecSec man pushed open a cellar door, he wouldn't have been surprised to hear the crump of shells and the stutter of machine-gun fire drifting up the dark steps. In the event he found himself surrounded by the past in a different form, a henge of rusty filing cabinets coated in dust, debris, and spiders' webs, and lit by a single bulb in a low ceiling.

He took a deep breath of the dank air in an effort to control his incipient claustrophobia. Patten had promised to tell him as soon as Batty became available. He hoped to hell it wouldn't be long.

He pulled open a drawer at random and found himself looking at a pile of shredded paper. This cabinet had rusted so badly that mice or, worse, rats had been able to force a way through the decaying metal and chew away to their hearts' content. He turned to another. The same. Ah well, he thought, at least I tried. One more like this and I'm out of here.

But the third, alas, had held fast and the files were complete. He opened one and read *Major Quinnel David Andrew Admitted August 30th 1916.*

Jesus wept! he thought. Did everything lead back to this fucking war?

He read on. These were case notes. The major had received severe damage to both legs in a shell blast near Albert, been treated first at a field hospital, then transferred to a base hospital near Boulogne for preliminary surgery, returned to London for more work at the Charing Cross, and finally been shipped up to Yorkshire for postoperative treatment and convalescence.

All the other notes were concerned with injured officers too and Pascoe had guessed what the situation was even before he hit upon the earliest files of them all.

One of the many areas of unpreparedness in the Great War had been in medical provision. Not even the most Jeremianic of prophets had foreseen the tidal wave of wounded men which would swamp the country for four long years. All over the British Isles the upper classes had seen where their patriotic duty lay and had offered their second, and even their third, though rarely their fourth, houses as temporary hospitals, clinics, and rest homes. And not just the upper classes. The nineteenth century had seen the rise of a new and powerful class, the captains of industry who, having imitated their betters in the purchase or construction of their own country houses, were not slow to follow this new aristocratic example.

One noble art they had not yet learned, because its breeding ground is assurance rather than aspiration, was that of doing good by stealth, and all the early correspondence on the transformation of Wanwood House from country seat to hospital for wounded officers contained a modest reference to the generosity of its owner.

"Well well well," said Peter Pascoe as he read the owner's name.

"Indeed I hope that's how I find you, Detective Chief Inspector," said a voice from the doorway.

Startled, he turned and found himself looking into the smiling face of David Batty.

"They told me you were down here," said the doctor. "So I thought I'd descend and see if I could help you."

"Not unless you've been superefficient and had all the info on these files transferred to discs."

"Sorry. Nothing to do with us, this lot. I've been meaning to get these cellars cleaned out ever since we got established here. We could do with the storage space. What are you hoping to find anyway? Reports of a missing patient who might have wandered off and snuffed it in the woods?"

"Something like that. But I think I'll leave it to someone with a more clerical cast of mind and less fear of dark confined places."

He pushed the drawer shut and joined Batty at the door. As they went up the stairs, the doctor said, "You did sound as if something had caught your attention just now. All those *well*s."

"Just a name. Funny, you come across a name you haven't heard before, then lo and behold, up it pops again almost immediately."

"And the name?"

They had emerged into the stone-flagged rear hallway from which the cellar steps descended. A shaft of daylight streamed through a high window and Pascoe positioned himself beneath it like a pitman stepping into a shower.

"Grindal," he said. "Arthur Grindal. Your great-grandfather, I believe."

"Old Arthur. Ah yes, of course, you were talking to my father yesterday, weren't you? And you came across the name again in those files? How interesting, though not perhaps all that surprising in the circumstances."

"The circumstances being that Wanwood belonged to Arthur Grindal before it became a hospital? You don't seem to have mentioned this to anyone. And your father certainly never mentioned it to me yesterday."

Batty took his arm and gently urged him out of the hallway into the renovated part of the house.

"For my part, there's been no occasion to mention it. Why should I? It's got no significance, has it? As for Father, he belongs to the old Yorkshire school of thought which recommends keeping yourself to yourself, especially when it comes to family matters."

"Is that so? He spoke fairly freely about the family, if I remember right."

"Only what he saw no harm in telling you, I expect," chuckled Batty, pushing open the door of his office. "Have a seat. Care for a coffee? Or do your tastes follow your leader's?"

He flourished a bottle of Glenmorangie.

"No, thanks. Nothing for me. So what harm could there be in telling me about the family connection with the house?"

"No harm, in any immediate sense. But it's a tale which doesn't altogether redound to the family credit. If you've the time and the inclination, I'll tell you it, though of course I shall deny having uttered a word if my father ever gets wind of my indiscretion."

He sat down and poured himself a little whisky.

"Hope you don't mind, but a good story deserves a good telling. Just say if you change your mind. Cheers."

He tossed the drink back and smiled. He was, thought Pascoe, a rather attractive guy, easy to talk to once you established that you weren't hired help to be ordered around, not bad-looking, very outgoing, yet there was that something—he recalled it from their previous encounters during the summer—that made him feel just a touch uneasy, like a dog on the edge of a thunderstorm.

"Right. Here goes. Sure you want to hear this? Okay. Old Arthur founded the family fortunes on that old Yorkshire staple, wool. You'll have seen the remnants of the old mill at Kirkton yesterday."

"Yes, and your father did tell me how the two interests of the family came together, the Batty medical innovations and the Grindal entrepreneurship."

"Oh yes, he would. Not above a bit of discreet boasting. But there would be things he kept quiet about. Old Arthur's social ambitions, for one thing. He belonged to the Yorkshire school of economics which believes you can buy owt if you've got the brass. He bought the Wanwood estate and boasted he got his money back by chopping down most of what was left of the ancient Wanwood Forest except the bit immediately around the house, and selling off first the timber, then the cleared land. The old Elizabethan manor was in a state of disrepair so he knocked that down and built his own baronial hall. And he sat back and waited for the county set to treat him like they treated the old Truman family who'd been here for five hundred years."

"What happened to them?"

"Fell on hard times. Great War wiped the last two out, I believe, but the parish church is full of mentions both inside and out, which can't have improved Arthur's state of mind as it dawned on him that the county wasn't going to come calling. Bought another place in London and one at Cromer when that turned fashionable, and used Wanwood less and less. But he still had his eye on making a social mark, getting some kind of title if he could, and when he caught on that top people were offering their country houses for hospitals in the war, he jumped on that bandwagon."

"You make it sound very cynical."

"Do I? Well, I rather think it was. It got him noticed and also provided somewhere for my other great-grandfather, Sam Batty, to try out his medical innovations without too much comeback if they went wrong."

"So even then the Battys were into animal experiments at Wanwood," said Pascoe.

"Very sharp." Batty laughed. "Yes, I recall last time we met thinking, here's a one to watch. Does it help if I tell you that the animals being experimented on back then were exclusively officer class? Old Arthur reckoned that by sticking to officers there was more chance of winning the notice and gratitude of families with influence. Don't misunderstand me. The old boy was as virulently patriotic as everyone else was in those days. He wanted to do his bit, and more than his bit. But he reckoned the laborer was worthy of his hire and he estimated his own worth as a knighthood. I can just imagine what he felt like when his name appeared with hundreds of others in the new honors list, and he found he'd got an OBE!"

"Devastating," observed Pascoe.

"The family story is he wanted to tell them to stuff it, but calmer counsel prevailed and he set about getting in peace what he hadn't managed in war. Contributions to party funds, being in the right places on the right committees at the right times—he even gave Wanwood to the nation as a hospital. That made a big splash."

"That was generous," admitted Pascoe.

"Not really." Batty smiled. "What actually happened was some of the medical staff who worked there during the war approached him with a view to making it a permanent clinic. He didn't much care for the place anymore, it was going to cost a bomb to refurbish it to domestic habitability, so he did a deal and sold them a ninety-nine-year lease. Only somehow it came out in the papers that he'd given the place away."

"And it was a private clinic, right? Hardly a gift to the nation."

"There were public beds for qualifying locals. It did quite well I believe till the NHS got under way. Then it might have gone under if an independent company hadn't taken it over. A company in which purely by chance old Arthur had a controlling share."

He watched Pascoe's reaction almost gleefully. Why's he doing this? wondered Pascoe. Paying off some old score against his dad who clearly wanted to keep all this under his hat? And what's it got to do with anything anyway?

He said, "Dr. Batty . . ."

"David. Do call me David. Your elephantoid boss does and I see no reason why I should be on less familiar terms with the civilized face of policing than with its rump."

Pascoe smiled, not just at the joke though it wasn't bad, but at the value judgment it contained. You'd think a doctor of all people would know the dangers of underestimating a rump.

"David, this is all very interesting, but the fact that your great-grandfather was a wily old bird hardly seems relevant to my inquiries. Though of course if what you're saying is that somehow ALBA bought what it in fact owned already, the DTI might be interested . . ."

"I thought I made it clear. ALBA didn't own it. This other company did. True, old Arthur's shares in it were inherited by my . . . mother, so when the company, that's ALBA, decided that Wanwood would make an ideal site for its research center, there was little problem about putting the clinic, which was already in terminal decline, into liquidation. It was all perfectly legal and aboveboard. You saw the papers yourself."

Pascoe had registered but could see no significance in the curious little hesitation about Mrs. Batty's ownership of the controlling share. Perhaps that's where the weakest point of the fiddle lay. Not that he believed there was one chance in a million of proving an illegality. This was peanuts compared with the billions that vanished every year in the great world of commerce, leaving no trace but the anguish of impoverished shareholders and the frustration of the Serious Fraud Squad. But for all that, he knew what common sense, not to mention common decency, told him, that there had been a fiddle.

"Yes, I saw the papers. But I saw nothing there to indicate ALBA was buying what the wife of its chairman owned already and had helped put into receivership in order to facilitate her husband's acquisition," said Pascoe coldly.

"Well, you wouldn't, would you? As for my father, he's got rather the same ambitions as old Arthur, and this is one skeleton he prefers to keep buried deep in the family cupboard. Why he should worry I don't know. In the present climate a history of good old honest sleaze is probably a recommendation!"

"Sleaze? Would you care to be a little more specific without of course incriminating yourself."

"Nice one, Peter," said Batty, chuckling. "Well, you see, by 1930 Arthur was becoming really impatient. He reckoned he'd dropped enough strong, and expensive, hints. So he entered into direct negotiation for what, after all, he truly believed was no more than his due. And everyone was at it. Alas, he'd waited too long. He found himself caught up in the wave of indignation and investigation which ended up with Maundy Gregory's conviction in '33 for touting honors. That was it. He escaped prosecution himself, but his name was attainted forevermore. You can see why my father would prefer that old story wasn't dredged up when he's so close to the short list himself."

No, thought Pascoe. I can't really. And I can't see why I've spent so much time sitting here listening to this sordid saga of life in the commercial fast lane.

He said, "Will you have any objection to one of my men coming along and taking a closer look at those files in your cellar?"

"No, of course not," said Batty. "If you care to take them away and burn them when you're finished I'd have no objection to that either. So tell me, Peter, what was it you actually wanted to see me about?"

"Well, about the files, I suppose," said Pascoe.

"But you didn't know the files existed till you got here," said Batty, amused.

Pascoe smiled too.

"ESP," he said. "I'm famous for it, didn't you know?"

V

ELLIE PASCOE'S APPOINTMENT with Miss Martindale was at midday. She wasn't looking forward to it. Not many people intimidated her, but Miss Martindale was high on the short list.

In appearance the head teacher was far from formidable. With her flowered dresses, flattish shoes, bare legs, bobbed hair, and round, smiling, glowing, almost makeup-less face, she wouldn't have been out of place at a Betjeman tennis tourney. But when you tried to stick labels on her, that healthy pink skin was like Teflon.

Politically, from loony left to rabid right, nothing fitted. Socially she moved with an automatic gearbox up
and down the classes. Sexually she gave no clue
whether she was vestal or vicious, straight or gay. Her
manner was easy and friendly yet she observed the for-
malities as rigidly as any old-fashioned schoolmarm. To
Ellie's invitation at an earlier meeting to use her first
name she'd replied, smiling, "I'll think of you as Ellie
but in the interests of consistency it had better stay
Mrs. Pascoe."

"And how shall I think of you?" inquired Ellie.

"If all goes well, I hope as little as possible," had
come the reply. So, difficult to lay a glove on. But if she
floated like a butterfly, she could also sting like a bee.

"After we spoke on the phone, I had a word with
Rose's class teacher, who couldn't recall a single instance of Rose using inappropriate language."

No language was "bad" of course. On that at least
they were agreed.

"Perhaps," said Ellie, "because in reference to the
learning situation no occasion arose when it would
seem appropriate."

"We have also monitored as far as is humanly possible her speech outside of the classroom. In play. During fairly fierce disputes with her friends about some
point of information or order. The same."

"What are you saying, Ms. Martindale?" The *Ms.*
was the closest Ellie could get to establishing some
control of the relationship. "That I'm imagining this
inappropriate language?"

"Of course not." That natural irresistible smile.
"Simply that you and your husband are, to the best of
our knowledge so far, the only ones who have shared
an occasion on which Rose felt the language in question was appropriate."

It took Ellie an incredulous microsecond to pick the
bones out of this.

"You mean it's our fault?"

"Please, Mrs. Pascoe, I didn't think we were talking faults here. I thought we were meeting to discuss what you see as a problem, not to deal with what others might see as a complaint."

Ellie pulled herself together.

"You're quite right," she said. "I *do* see it as a problem. And if, as seems likely, the problem originates here, then yes again, I *am* making a complaint."

"Fair enough. The complaint being that your daughter is learning new words and phrases at school?"

Ellie stiffened in her seat and pursed her lips. Then she thought in horror, I don't purse my lips! That's what Mum used to do when she felt a fit of righteous indignation coming on!

She saw Miss Martindale regarding her gravely but with just the hint of a held-back smile on that generous mouth. Their gazes locked. And gradually the tension ebbed from Ellie's shoulder muscles and she relaxed in her chair.

"Oh shit," she said.

"Is that exclamatory or descriptive?"

"It just seemed the appropriate thing to say."

Miss Martindale considered and the smile broke loose.

"Bugger me," she said, "if I don't believe you're right."

When she left ten minutes later, Ellie offered her hand and said, "Thank you, Miss Martindale."

The smile flickered in acknowledgment of the *Miss*.

"Always a pleasure, Ms. Pascoe," she said.

As she drove away, Ellie was still smiling. That was something you tended to forget about Miss Martindale. You rarely came away from an interview feeling victorious. But you usually came away feeling good. She drove into the town center. Street-level parking was almost impossible and she disliked the multistory. On impulse she turned into the Black Bull car park. This was CID's favorite drinking hole and normally she'd have steered clear, but today the thought of bumping into the gang didn't bother her, and she might even be lucky enough to catch Peter there by himself, though of course he claimed it was only the iron grip of Fat Andy that dragged him into the place. The other attraction was that for the price of a sandwich and a beer, plus a nice smile at Jolly Jack the lugubrious landlord, she could get free parking while she did her afternoon shopping.

She was rather disappointed to find the place almost empty.

"Long time no see," said the landlord as she curled her long legs round a bar stool. "Thought you must've left him."

"I can see how my absence has aged you," she replied. "Half of best and a beef and mustard please."

There was a copy of last night's *Evening Post* on the bar and she glanced at it idly as she waited. Then a name caught her eye.

And for the second time that morning, "Oh shit!" seemed the only appropriate response.

She slid off the stool and headed for the telephone by the door. The infirmary number had been etched into her memory bank during the time Peter had been in there recovering from his injuries down Burrthorpe mine. She got through straightaway.

"I'm ringing about a friend who's in intensive care," she said. "Wendy Walker."

There was a hesitation, then a new voice asked, "Are you a relative?"

"No. A friend."

"Could I have your name, please?"

For a moment she came close to explosion.

Then she said, "Is this just mindless bureaucracy or a police job?"

That did it.

"Is that Mrs. Pascoe? Dennis Seymour here."

"Dennis, great. How is she?"

"She's still not recovered consciousness yet, Mrs. Pascoe, but they're hopeful. Er, is it yourself you're ringing for or the guv'nor?"

"It's myself, Dennis. The guv'nor, as you so archaically call him, hasn't seen fit to mention Wendy's accident."

That was unfair. Of course Peter would have told her if he'd known.

She said, "What exactly happened, Dennis?"

"Oh, looks like hit and run," he said vaguely. "Knocked her off her bike."

"It said in the *Post* it was on Ludd Lane."

"That's right."

Ellie considered. There was something not right here.

She said, "Dennis, what are you doing there?"

"Just waiting. Mr. Dalziel said he wanted to know soon as she woke up."

"Oh yes." Which was really English for the more expressive American "Oh yeah?" She knew her Dalziel and he didn't waste valuable CID time letting his officers hang around hospitals waiting for traffic accident victims to wake up. Not even when it was hit-and-run. That was a job which even PC Hector, Mid-Yorkshire's contribution to Care in the Community, could manage with a more than even chance of success.

She knew it wasn't fair to browbeat Seymour into telling more than he should, but if that's what it took to get at the truth . . .

Then behind her she heard a voice say, "Jack, one Scotch pie and some mushy peas, and a lettuce sandwich for my rabbit."

Ellie said, "Thanks, Dennis. Regards to Bernadette. See you."

She turned to see Andy Dalziel inserting his buttocks into the only chair in the pub fit to receive such a generous offering. With him was Wield. The landlord was already advancing from the bar with a foaming pint in either hand. Not even a cabinet minister at the Ritz could command better service.

"That lettuce, Mr. Wield, you want something with it?"

"Tomato 'ud be nice, Jack. And mebbe a slice of onion."

"Jesus, just because you're living like a vegetable, there's no need to eat the bloody things," said Dalziel in disgust. "Well, hello, lass, is that you? By God you're looking well. Take heed, Wieldy. You don't fill your jeans like that on peas and parsnips!"

"Hello, Andy. Don't get up. Hi, Wieldy."

Wield, who had half risen, sank back into his seat, smiling. Dalziel, who hadn't moved, said, "Take the weight off your feet, lass. Have you got a drink?"

He's only spoken a couple of sentences, thought Ellie, and twice he's implied I'm getting fat!

"I've ordered something. Oh, thanks, Jack."

The landlord had arrived with her gill and sandwich.

"Is that the beef?" said Dalziel. "Jack, tha's not been buying them carcasses from the Ministry vet again, have you?"

Quickly Ellie bit into her sandwich.

"It's fine," she said. "Andy, what's going off about Wendy Walker? I'd ask Peter . . ."

"Aye. Didn't he once used to work for me? How's he finding retirement?"

". . . only as he didn't mention it last night, I assume he knows nothing about it."

"Surprised it's taken you so long to catch on. Happened the night afore last, same evening as that university do. Didn't you say you thought she'd be coming?

Well, she were found knocked off her bike in Ludd Lane, so mebbe she was on her way."

"Not from home, she wasn't," said Ellie. "Her place is in exactly the opposite direction. And she said she wasn't coming on her bike because she wanted a lift back."

"Lift back don't mean you can't arrive on a bike," objected Dalziel.

Ellie said quietly, "Andy, what's going on? She's my friend. Why're you playing with me?"

"Nay," said the Fat Man, taking a long pull at his beer. "Seems to me like it's you doing the playing. Friend gets knocked down, you don't start thinking foul play, not without reason. Now, in polite conversation, it's ladies first. And in police conversation, it's witnesses first. Either way, that's you, luv."

It's not fair, thought Ellie. Only two people who can outpunch me, and I've got to take 'em both on in the same day!

Wield said, "Hello, Pete. Get you a drink?"

A hand touched her shoulder and she looked up to see her husband's pleased but puzzled face. She smiled at him and he stooped to kiss her.

"So where've you been then?" said Dalziel menacingly. "Somewhere interesting I hope?"

"I thought so," said Pascoe, sitting down. "Jack's bringing me a pint, Wieldy. Incidentally, I've got a nice little job, right up your street. Out at Wanwood House. Which is where I've spent a not uninteresting morning."

"It'll keep," said Dalziel. "We were just talking about Wendy Walker's accident."

"Good lord. What happened?" asked Pascoe, glancing anxiously at his wife.

She'd never doubted his ignorance but it was good to have it confirmed nonetheless.

Dalziel gave the bare facts, paused, then went on.

"But we've got reason to think it's mebbe more than a simple hit-and-run. Could be she were hit, in one sense or another, a long way off Ludd Lane, and just dumped there to die."

He's decided best way to get me talking is to give it straight, thought Ellie. And as usual the fat bastard's right! Well, I just hope he likes it when he hears it.

She said quietly, "I may have some information which can help."

Pascoe looked at her in surprise. Dalziel said, "All contributions gratefully received."

"Wendy came to see me the afternoon of the uni party. She had something she wanted to tell me, or at least talk over with me. But it wasn't convenient then."

She glanced at her husband, who was wearing that little frown of concentration which made him look like Thomas Aquinas. Should she have waited till they were alone before telling him this? In other words, was she doing that most unwifely thing of making your husband look foolish in front of his peers? She didn't think so, but there were still areas of the male psyche which remained terra incognita. Too late to draw back now. And in any case all she'd really have done talking to him privately would have been to offload the perilous task of putting Andy in a quandary.

She went on, "Walker is Wendy's married name. She kept it when she split with her husband partly because she liked the alliteration but mainly because she had no desire to relive the childhood embarrassment of her family name. Shufflebottom."

She paused and looked at the three men. Pascoe frowned a little harder. Dalziel said, "Nowt wrong wi' Shufflebottom. Good honest Yorkshire name."

Yes, thought Ellie. If you're a good honest Yorkshire lad, with shoulders like an ox yoke and fists like hams.

And Wield, whose mind sorted out connections like

Bradshaw, said "Same name as that guard that got killed up at Redcar."

"Wendy's brother," said Ellie. "Worked down Burrthorpe Main from leaving school till after the strike. But when they started cutting back and cutting back, he was one of the first to accept terms and go. They fell out over it. Wendy said that none of them should let themselves be bought off. Mark said that he had a wife and three small children to think about. He took the money, got a job as a security guard and moved up to Redcar. Wendy didn't see him again till after they closed Burrthorpe completely. Then it struck her that she was letting those bastards at Westminster cut her off from her own flesh and blood too. So she went visiting. Earlier this year. It was fatted-calf time. They made her more than welcome. The kids were delighted to get their auntie back. Her sister-in-law, who is completely apolitical, was delighted to have an ally in the old Yorkshire struggle to keep the man of the house in his rightful place. And Mark wanted her to move up to the northeast and start her life again. She went back to Burrthorpe and spent a few weeks thinking about it, but she'd just made her mind up to go when the news came about the animal rights raid. And Mark's death."

She paused to take a sip of beer.

Dalziel was staring at her unblinkingly. He sees where this is going, she thought.

"She was devastated. Naturally. She'd found her brother again, and lost him forever, all within a matter of weeks. She wasn't all that much concerned with who'd killed him, not at first. For someone with her background she had surprising confidence in the police. They'd get someone, he'd be tried, convicted, sent down for ten years maybe. It wouldn't stop her sister-in-law from being a widow or her nephews from being fatherless. Or herself from being adrift in a world which no longer made much sense. It wasn't till the second raid, the one at Wanwood in the summer, which the papers said bore all the hallmarks of the same group, that it really got to her that whoever killed her brother was alive, and well, and carrying on business as usual. She read Peter's name in the paper as the officer in charge of the investigation. And she came to see me."

She was addressing herself purely to Peter now.

"I hadn't had any contact with her since . . . not for ages. All she wanted now was to know if there was any hope of an arrest. I said I couldn't talk about your work with anyone not in the Force. She told me why she wanted to know. Then I said I'd ask you."

"And did you?" he asked.

"Didn't need to. You came home that night really down. Said you were getting nowhere and that Andy here had told you to wind things down and put it on the shelf till something broke to reactivate it. If I'd *had* to ask, or if the case was going on, I'd have told you everything then. But there was no need."

No need to bring up Wendy Walker and Burrthorpe and all its attendant pain.

"So I saw Wendy again and told her, no, there wasn't likely to be an arrest. She went away. A few days later she was back. She asked me if I had any contact with anyone in the animal rights movement. I said, yes, I knew a couple of people, but not the sort who'd be involved in violence, if that's what she meant. She said, it didn't matter. All she wanted was an introduction. She wanted to get in, establish her credentials, get a reputation as an extremist, and hopefully pick up some lead to the group which had killed her brother. She was convinced it was Yorkshire-based, with the two known raids being where they were."

"And you encouraged her in this?" said Pascoe.

"I told her it was crazy. And pointless. I told her that almost certainly the police would have their own undercover operators in the movement already, and if they hadn't come up with a lead, what chance was there that she would? But she was adamant. This is what she wanted, all that she wanted. I could see that she needed something. Like I say, she was totally adrift. Everything had gone . . ."

"She still had her brother's family," said Pascoe.

"She'd been back to see them," said Ellie. "There was a fellow there, helping with the garden, that kind of thing. Not living in, in fact nothing else happening yet, her sister-in-law assured her. But she didn't deny she had hopes. They spoke honestly, woman to woman. Wendy couldn't blame her, as a woman. But as a sister . . . well, at the very least she felt this was yet another development which left her on the outside. She needed something to keep her life moving forward. So I said I'd have a word with someone I knew. And I spoke to Cap Marvell."

Dalziel said, "Are you saying you told her all this? Any of this?"

"No. I told her everything else about Wendy's background but nothing of this. I told her that Wendy was disillusioned with politics and left-wing radicalism and wanted a new cause without all the human ambiguities of the old one. Cap said to send her along. That's all I did. Except that I promised Wendy to keep this to myself. And in return she promised if ever anything broke or looked like breaking, she'd contact me before pursuing it further."

She leaned forward and said directly to Peter, "In the remote contingency she did find out something, I wanted to make sure that nothing could happen which might embarrass or compromise you."

He smiled and drooped the eyelid farthest from Dalziel in a wink which said, *It's okay, I know that.*

"And what did she find out?" asked Dalziel.

She gave him her full attention now.

"I've no idea. Like I said, she called the day after they found those bones at Wanwood. I got the impression something had come up the previous night, or maybe it had been confirmed the previous night—"

"Something?" he interrupted.

"Nothing as firm as definite proof, else she'd have come straight out with it," Ellie assured him. "But something she wanted to talk over with me, a piece of behavior perhaps, or something she'd overheard one of the others say . . . I really don't know. . . ."

"But something definitely connected to the previous night?" he insisted.

Ellie put her fingers over her eyes in the effort of remembering.

"I thought she looked pale . . . well, paler than usual, and I suggested that finding those bones must have shaken her up . . . and she said, no it wasn't that . . . and she mentioned when they got inside the building, something about Cap Marvell running riot . . . then Peter came in. But she did say before she left it was probably all in her imagination."

Reassurance! Why the hell was she offering the Fat Man reassurance. Like telling a pit bull you weren't going to hurt him!

He said, "And you were expecting to see her at the party? To talk about this?"

"Right. Well, not at the party maybe, but I'm sure while I was giving her a lift home, she'd have brought it up. . . ."

"Did you say owt about this to anyone else?"

"No! Well, except . . ."

"Yes?"

"I may have said something to Cap about Wendy wanting to talk to me. I mean, look, to be honest, I never felt altogether right about landing Wendy on her as a kind of spy. Okay, Cap's not a close friend, and this kind of stuff she's got herself into strikes me as a diversion from much more serious issues—get the big things right, and we get everything right—but for all that, it worried me because it was a bit . . . sneaky. Sorry, that sounds childish, but it's the right, the appropriate word."

A picture of Miss Martindale's wry smile flashed into her mind.

"So you were paving the way for a full admission in case anything Wendy might have come up with brought the whole business into the open," said Peter.

Oh, how well you know me, my husband. But no need to spell out my moral ambiguity quite so plainly!

"Right," she said.

"But clearly," he went on, "at no point did it ever enter your mind that Cap Marvell herself might be an object of Wendy's suspicions? Otherwise she's the last person you'd have said anything to. Right?"

So he too was in the reassure-Dalziel business. Oh, that tender blossom, that rathe primrose, needing protection from the cold blasts of suspicion playing on his newfound ladylove. Could Cap Marvell really be mixed up in the Redcar business? Could antic chance have made her introduce Wendy to the woman who'd killed her brother? Dafter things happened on television. And what did she really know about Cap anyway? Wasn't her gut reaction that she was nonviolent based more on social assumption that ladies of Marvell's class didn't go around breaking skulls than any real psychological insight? And how would Andy Dalziel react to the growing suspicion that he might have been banging away where he should have been banging up?

Like vulcanologists sailing off Krakatoa, they watched, poised between flight and fascination.

Slowly the great head turned, the slab features and blank eyes concealing whatever lavatic emotions surged and bubbled within, his gaze passing like a dark shadow over Wield and Ellie and Peter, till it came to rest on the bar.

"Jack!" he bellowed. "Are you exhuming that pie, or what?"

VI

SERGEANT WIELD GROANED as he pulled open the first filing cabinet drawer and released a gust of that scent of old damp paper which permeated Digweed's shop and which he was determined was not going to tinge the air of Corpse Cottage.

At least, unlike Pascoe, he had come dressed for the job in a white police-issue overall with surgical gloves. Patten had laughed when he saw him and said, "What's this? Frankenstein meets the Abominable Snowman?"

Patten's good spirits and the fact that he was the one who'd drawn Pascoe's attention to the cabinets convinced Wield that whatever else he found down here, it wasn't going to have any bearing on any scam TecSec was involved in. Of course, it could be he was completely wrong and TecSec was as clean as a whistle. Unlike Dalziel, Wield had no religious faith in his gut. If licking toads or chewing exotic mushrooms could conjure up visions, no reason why a bit of ripe cheese or dodgy kebab shouldn't provoke a dyspeptic hunch.

But the way that Jimmy Howard had jumped when he bumped into them just now, as Patten was showing Wield the way to the cellar, kept his rumblings loud and clear.

For the moment, however, despite the smell, he was not altogether displeased to be down here out of harm's way. Unfortunately he hadn't had time to give an account of his morning's work to Dalziel before Ellie Pascoe's revelations, which meant that when he did get round to it, every reference to the antagonism between Walker and Marvell came out like another straw on the camel's back.

"And Cap herself, what did you make of her?" Pascoe had asked, before Dalziel could, or couldn't, as the case might be. This was after Ellie had taken her leave.

Nothing to do but give the same answer he'd have given if Dalziel had been able to resist handling the fruit.

"Tough," he said. "Able to look after herself, and anything else she cares to look after. Not the kind that you could put anything across, or at least, not for long."

"You mean, she might have had some suspicions about Wendy Walker?"

"About her real commitment? Yes, it wouldn't surprise me. Though of course the issue was clouded by Walker sounding off about the need for more direct, i.e., violent action."

"And Marvell's attitude to more direct action?"

"My impression was, she probably wouldn't set out to hurt anyone, but if it happened more or less by accident, I think she could deal with it."

"And the others?"

"Jacklin and Walker apart, I reckon she's dominant enough for them to go along with her."

"Why not Jacklin? She doesn't sound like one of society's strong wills."

"That's mebbe the trouble."

He gave details of Jacksie's relationship with the group.

"And being a nurse, of course, night duty means she's not as freely available as the others for evening activities. Cuts both ways. Means that sometimes she misses out, but also that if Cap wanted, it would be easy to miss her out."

"Arrange something for a night you know she couldn't make it?" said Pascoe. "Might be interesting to check if she was on duty the nights of the Redcar raid, and the first one at Wanwood."

"To prove what?" said Dalziel.

"Oh, just dotting the *i's* and crossing the *t's*," said Pascoe vaguely.

"As in shit!" snarled Dalziel. He drained his pint and banged his glass on the table with a crash which would have had many landlords grabbing for their baseball bats, but only got Jolly Jack reaching for the pump.

"All right. Do it," said Dalziel. "Owt else from your little tit-a-tit wi' Miss Jacklin."

It ill behooved a man with his unconcealed mammary obsession with Cap Marvell to make breast jokes with regard to any other woman, thought Wield primly. Perhaps it was time for the little people to stop tippytoeing around the man mountain.

He said, "Yes, there was, as a matter of fact. That night at Wanwood when they ran amok inside, Jacksie got the impression that Cap knew exactly where she was running to. And she was struck by the way she and Walker seemed to have swapped attitudes when they were locked up together later."

Taking out his notebook, he quoted Jacksie's precise words.

Dalziel flapped his hand in a dismissive gesture which in central Asia would have destroyed whole fleets of flies.

"She explained that, swinging them wire cutters. Yon bugger Patten suddenly appeared in front of her. Reflex defense. I'd have done the same myself."

And if a man lay dead at your feet after you'd done it, what then? wondered Wield.

"What about knowing her way around, sir?" he asked. "I checked the TecSec statements. She almost made it to the labs."

Pascoe rode to the rescue.

"She sounds to me exactly the kind of person who'd research anything she planned to do very carefully, not just act on girlish impulse."

His intention was simply to offer another reasonable explanation of the woman's apparent knowledge of the geography of Wanwood, but he realized even as the words were still coming out that their application went far beyond that.

Both Wield and the Fat Man had turned on him gazes which were at once inscrutable and eloquent.

And that was when he said hastily, "Oh, by the by, talking of Wanwood . . ." and told them of his adventures among the filing cabinets.

Now Wield started using that gift which God has dished out to some humans with great generosity because, like a blind man with a jigsaw puzzle, He has only limited use for it Himself—the gift of creating order out of chaos.

First he established which cabinets had not been penetrated by ravening rodents. Using an indelible black marker he put the sign of the cross on those which were beyond his human skills.

Next he divided the others into their two main categories, patients' records and admin correspondence, marking this on the cabinets. And finally he established the date parameters of each set of files and marked this on the side also. With many gaps, they ranged from 1915 to 1946. Pascoe, with that serendipity with which God sometimes compensates those who are Marys rather than Marthas, had stumbled on the earliest almost immediately. His news about the original ownership of Wanwood had been interesting, but Wield couldn't see how it related to their inquiries, nor did he really have any idea what it might be that Pascoe had set him looking for down here. But as a team the three of them, himself, and fat Andy, and Peter, had long since come to rely on each other's peculiar talents to the extent that each could lead the others a long way down his particular road before they cried, Hold! Enough!

Physically, the cabinets relating to the war years 1915–19 were the most accessible. Wield guessed that this was because they were the first to be dumped down here, after the war when the hospital administrators started looking forward to a period of peace and profit. Whoever had lugged them down the stairs had seen no reason to go deeper into the cellar than he needed, so had left them close by the entrance.

After 1945, perhaps something to do with the establishment of the National Health Service, other means of disposing of outdated records had been found.

Wield read through the early admin stuff and glanced at some of the medical records. If the bones had anything to do with the hospital, and if these cabinets contained any clue to this connection, there were two ways of doing this. One was the Wield way, which meant reading through everything and taking notes and hoping that out of such a careful cold collation some piece of nutritious information might emerge. The other was the lucky Pascoe way of putting in your thumb at random and hoping you pulled out a nice juicy plum.

He closed his eyes, jerked open a drawer, reached in, and grabbed a file.

"Well, bugger me," he said. "But not too much."

A good policeman knows that coincidences though always suspicious are not invariably significant.

The file he had in his hand belonged to Second Lieutenant Herbert Grindal of the West Yorkshire Fusiliers.

So what did it mean? Wield asked himself.

That Arthur Grindal who had so generously donated his country house to his nation's needs had also contributed a son (or nephew maybe?) to his country's defense, and that when this same youth was wounded, he'd ended up at Wanwood Hospital for treatment. Nothing surprising or sinister in that. Nothing, considering the casualty rate in that mass mayhem, particularly ironic either. As for tragic, he riffled through the file, saw that Grindal had been invalided in September 1917 suffering from a broken arm and neurasthenia and had been passed fit for service by a Medical Board the following January. So, a happy ending, assuming of course that he made it through to the end of the war.

He dropped the file back into its drawer and glanced at his watch. He'd been here long enough, he decided. He'd tell Pascoe precisely what he'd found and done, and hope that maybe he'd get a bit more precision in return about where to look for what.

He didn't suffer from claustrophobia but it was a relief to get out of that cellar and back to daylight. Not that there was much left this October afternoon, and only a tiny fraction of that filtered through the grubby panes of the only window admitting on this old back kitchen. But he stood by it, his eyes drinking in the bright gloom.

There was nothing much to see. The back kitchen formed a bay protruding from the rear of the house, and the window was set in the wall looking sideways across a cobbled yard littered with dustbins to a matching bay about thirty feet away. There was a door in that wall and now there was something to see. The door opened fractionally but no one came out. Then a figure came round the corner of the house, looked right and left and right again like a good boy crossing the road, then moved swiftly to the open door.

It was Jimmy Howard. He paused in the doorway. It was too far and too dusky to see who was inside, and in any case the TecSec man blocked most of the view. But Wield got an impression of a white-clad arm reaching out and Howard taking something which he slipped into his pocket. Then the door was closed and Howard was walking swiftly away.

Wield moved swiftly too. He had the kind of mind which had automatically mapped every area of Wanwood House that he'd walked through. A locked door delayed him for a few seconds while he made a detour, but he was still quick enough to reach a corridor leading toward the lab area as a white-coated figure passed through a door at the other end.

No problem even from behind. It was the radiantly beautiful research assistant, Jane Ambler.

That was half the puzzle solved. He turned round and headed back the way he'd come, diverting before he reached the back kitchen to head toward the TecSec office. But as he passed a window opening onto the staff car park, he glimpsed Howard getting into an old Escort and driving away.

So despite knowing that Wield was onto him, the dickhead was still driving himself to work. Perhaps he thought a deal had been done. If so, he was soon going to find out all bets were off.

Wield went out to his own car and picked up his radio mike.

"DS Wield," he said. "I've got a job for any car you might have in the vicinity of the west linkway."

He gave details of Howard's car and number, noted from his earlier researches into the status of the ex-cop's license. Privately, the kind of mind which forgot nothing could sometimes be a real pain, but professionally it came in very useful.

"I think you'll find the driver doesn't have a current license," he said. "I'd like him booked and held till I get there. But don't mention my name. Oh, and by the way, he's ex-job and will probably be asking favors. We're right out of them, okay?"

As he peeled off his overall, Patten came out of the house and walked toward him.

"Any luck?" he said.

"Sorry?"

"With them files. Any missing bodies or bones?"

"Not yet. But we'll keep on looking."

"Rather you than me," said Patten. "Cheers."

He smiled, crinkling his scar, and returned to the house.

Why's he so happy I'm spending my time here in that filthy cellar? wondered Wield. Perhaps Jimmy Howard had the answer.

He went to find out.

At the station, Charley Slocum, the custody sergeant, greeted his arrival without much enthusiasm.

"Yes, we've got him. He's making a lot of noise and asking for you. Seems to think you can get him out of this. I hope you're going to disabuse him, Wieldy. If this is some clever little CID scheme, you should have kept him to yourself. He's in the system now, and that means, no deals."

"Fine, Charley. Got a list of his belongings?"

He checked through the list. All legit.

Wield said, "Where's his car?"

"Out back."

"Give us a moment? I need a witness."

They went out to the Escort. Wield opened the driver's door and checked in the glove shelf and the door wallets. Nothing except the usual array of maps, dusters, etc. He paused, then stooped and lifted the rubber footmat.

A small white envelope lay revealed.

"What's that?" asked Slocum.

"How should I know?" said Wield, picking it up by one corner and dropping it in an evidence bag. "But if you wheel Howard out for me, I'll ask him."

VII

AFTER WIELD HAD LEFT THE BLACK BULL, Pascoe and Dalziel had sat in silence for a while.

"Another pint, sir?" Pascoe finally ventured.

"Don't think so," said the Fat Man. "Enough's enough."

This was like God resting on the fourth day.

"Can I have that on tape?" said Pascoe.

Dalziel frowned and said, "You got no work to do?"

Pascoe said, "I thought I'd go to the hospital. See how Walker is. And I guess that's where Ellie will be."

"Aye. Hope she's not doing owt daft like blaming herself. There's no future in it, blaming yourself."

"No one knows yet there's anything for anyone to blame themselves for," said Pascoe.

"Oh, there's always summat, lad. There's always summat," said Dalziel. "Off you go, see how she is. Both on 'em."

"What'll you do, sir?"

"Start back where I should've started in the first place," said Dalziel. "At the crime."

"The bones, you mean?"

"Nay, lad. Still don't know if there's a crime in them or not. No, it's unlawful entry, criminal damage, threatening behavior I mean. Them's the crimes we do know about. I let 'em go too easy because . . ."

"Because you had, potentially at least, a much more

serious investigation on your hands," interjected Pascoe. "And because ALBA didn't want to prosecute."

". . . because I had other fish to fry," said Dalziel ambiguously. "Should have made sure I filleted 'em first. Still, only one thing to do when you get a bone stuck . . ."

"And what's that?"

"Take a big bite of summat, chew it hard and swallow it down!"

Pascoe contained his smile till he got outside, then immediately felt guilty.

Even a man engaged in a less prurient profession might have entertained himself deconstructing such an image, he assured himself defensively as he drove away. Has my life in the police locker room rendered me perceptibly coarser? One for Ellie.

But not just now, he thought when he saw her in the hospital waiting room.

"No change?" he said.

"She's moved up a level of consciousness, they reckon," said Ellie. "But no one's making any forecasts."

"You know what doctors are," said Pascoe lightly. "Won't tell you the time in case they get sued. Listen, love, this isn't down to you, any of it."

"I should never have introduced her to Cap. Or kept it from you. I should have made her talk when she came round to see me, but . . ."

"But I came in."

"No! I wasn't going to blame you, not this time. Most other times, yes, but not this one." She managed a smile. "All I was thinking was, we'd just been about to go to bed and it wasn't going to happen now. And I was looking forward to our evening in, and that wasn't going to happen either. All because of sodding Wendy Walker!"

"And now you feel guilty. Without knowing anything about what happened. Listen, Wendy lying un-conscious up there may have, in fact very probably does have, nothing to do with you or any of this busi-ness about her brother. So just wait and see, eh? And no need to wait here. Who's up there with her?"

"Dennis Seymour."

"Fine. So any news, we'll be the first to get it. Now let's go home."

She said hesitantly, "Yes, you're right, I know it . . . but would you mind if I stay just a bit longer? What I mean is, could you pick Rosie up from school? Sorry. I'm being selfish. I know you've got work to do . . ."

"Nothing that any other three or four ordinary detectives couldn't manage in a month," he said. "Of course I'll pick Rosie up. By the way, how'd you get on with little Miss Martinet?"

"It was fine. Well, sort of. Basically she seems to think that Rose only swears in front of us because she feels it's a kind of password admitting her to the fam-ily's innermost sanctum. In other words, it's us she's learned from, but as for the most part it's only when we're by ourselves that we use these words, she thinks they belong to our special language."

"Shit," said Pascoe.

"My response in a nutshell. Which makes you think, doesn't it?"

"So what do we do?"

"Watch our language. Stuff her ears with bread pel-lets. I don't know. I certainly don't want to introduce her to the concept of censorship at this stage in her development."

"Oh good. I'll go and dig out that old Bible you hid in the attic, shall I? Only joking. Only just joking, I mean. Don't be too long, eh?"

He kissed her. She responded hard, giving him some tongue. He enjoyed it, then drew away.

"One thing Old Virgin Bottom has guaranteed you won't find in these places is a spare bed," he said. "We really should go private."

Rosie greeted his appearance at the school gate with some suspicion.

"Why's Mummy not here?" she demanded.

"Well, you know how she feels about stereotypical behavior," he said, swinging her high.

Home, he provided her with a cheese and jam sandwich and a glass of apple juice with a squeeze of tomato puree and left her watching a cartoon on television while he sat down and opened the package from Ada's lawyer.

In it he found another carefully bound packet with his name on it and a covering note from the lawyer.

Dear Mr. Pascoe,

Your grandmother left instructions that once I had heard from you that her wishes regarding the disposal of her ashes had been carried out, I was to dispatch to you the enclosed packet. I have no knowledge of its contents other than assurance that they are Mrs. Pascoe's family papers of no testimonial interest to us as executors of her will. Should they prove not to be the case, however, or if there is any doubt, I am sure you will contact me for professional advice.

Yours sincerely,
Barbara Lomax

He took a paper knife and carefully cut through the layers of tape swathing the packet, noting with amusement that Ada had scrawled her name across the main junctions of tape, thus making it almost impossible to remove and replace them undetected.

Like a sensible Yorkshire woman, she obviously felt that only fools and gods put those they trusted most in way of temptation.

The packet contained another envelope addressed to him in Ada's hand, a plastic folder stuffed with documents and letters, an old exercise book, and yet another package wrapped in a piece of chamois leather so dry that it cracked as he tried to unfold it. What emerged, as though from the fragments of a very old eggshell, was another book, about the size of a World's Classics volume. It had a leather cover and was clearly homemade, with exercise book paper cut down and sewn together with oiled thread and a soldier's careful stitch. Each page was crammed with minute writing in faded pencil. Pascoe rose and got the Sherlock Holmes magnifying glass which had been a joke birthday present many years ago. He examined a page at random. . . .

New years Day—its snowing—we all moan but not much—a man can thole cold—in fact theres talk of a fellow in 3 platoon deliberately let his left foot get frostbitten so as hed lose a couple of toes and get Blightied—could be true seeing as words gone up on Orders that not taking proper precautions against frostbite is an offense—next thing not ducking a bullet will be an offense! One things for sure but—it can get as cold as it likes but nobody wants the winter over—like little Harry Holmes whos got a way with words and a not half bad voice either sings— The flowers that bloom in the Spring trala are bottomed in bonemeal and blood And the brasshats are starting to sing trala Lets attack dear old Fritzes left wing trala And straighten our line through that wood So thats what we mean when we say or we

sing Fuck off to the flowers that bloom in the Spring!
—Happy New Year to everybody—everybody who
wants this war to finish I mean—British or German.
Happy New Year.

He put the glass aside. His hand was trembling
slightly. This was that other Peter Pascoe's war journal,
this little book carefully constructed to fit snugly in
some pack or pocket, bound in leather and wrapped in
shammy to keep out the damp. Where had it come
from? Did he really want to read it?

He tore open the envelope and found what he'd expected, a letter from Ada.

Dear Peter,

What to do with all the enclosed papers has puzzled
me greatly in recent years. They are after all a record of
a life's obsession which I have been at pains not to
inflict on my family. Perhaps I was wrong in this. Cer-
tainly I could not conceal its most obvious effects, and
I know that my hatred of uniform, based as it seemed
to be merely on suffering what many millions of others
suffered, the loss of a father in the Great War, came
across as mere eccentricity bordering on dottiness. Per-
haps if I had been more open, my relationship with
your father might have been different, and his with his
children. Who knows?

The truth is, as you will see, that my father did not
have the doubtful privilege of dying for his country but
suffered the ultimate indignity of being murdered by his
country.

My mother, God bless her, though she felt the pain
of this more than any of us can ever guess, also felt the
shame of it more than any of us can ever understand
who were not adult in that most vilely jingoistic age.
That he was incapable of doing anything deserving of

such a fate she was certain, but then she had also been certain that her Peter could never harm another living creature, and yet he had gone out there to France for the sole purpose of shooting Germans dead. In that time, believing several impossible things at the same time must have been almost a condition of survival, and feeling both pride and shame simultaneously was far from uncommon.

Whether she would ever have spoken of these things voluntarily I do not know, but I had got into my twenties before there came the knock on the door that brought it all out in the open. That was a terrible day with everyone full of anger and accusation. Who would have guessed that out of it would come the greatest joy of my life, though that too was to last only a few years till those madmen who rule our lives snatched it away again. But even at the height of my indignation, I won't conceal from you that I too, like my mother, felt a pang of shame though I hated myself for it. And there was resentment too that I'd been forced to confront the ignominy which attended his death. I'd surely been better off before with nothing but an old photo and a memory of him on his last leave, playing on the piano he bought soon after I was born, so that I too like the children of the rich could grow up with music at my fingertips. Well, he would have been disappointed there as you know! But once I got over that egotistical reaction, I was determined for his sake and for my own to find out as much as I could of the truth of things. Two of us living together both with our appointed quests—I used to say we should call our house Camelot! It seemed impossible back then with youth and vigor on our side that we shouldn't be successful. But history has its own agenda and the Powers That Be, in and out of uniform, in the protection of themselves at least are superb strategists.

So the truth about my father remains hidden. Per-

haps it will stay so forever. Certainly I no longer feel it matters. Whatever he did or did not do, I do not believe any power on earth had the right to tie its own citizens to a stake after the sketchiest formality of a trial, and shoot them dead. I have read the many books written in recent years on the subject, and I believe that most right thinking people agree with me that a terrible mistake was made, though naturally our political leaders refuse to acknowledge it.

Therefore it seems proper to me now that I should pass on to you, my executor, not the fever of my obsession, but its clinical record, because it is part of our family heritage. Perhaps it has even made us what we are today, which, if true, I am not very proud of.

Forgive me for the silly test I have set you before these papers came into your possession. But a doubt remained, and this was a way of making a token gesture toward satisfying it. Therefore I shall instruct Barbara that if she has the slightest suspicion that you have merely scattered my ashes in the nearest ditch (and who would blame you?) then she should consign these documents to the fire.

And forgive me also, if you feel it necessary, or possible, for being what I am. Here in part you may find some of the reasons for it.

> *Your loving grandmother,*
> *Ada.*

He put the letter down and checked on Rosie. She was lying on her stomach, completely absorbed in some sci-fi cartoon adventure. He said, "No more after this, okay?" and smiled as she impatiently waved him away.

Now he opened the exercise book.

On the first page, written in the careful almost child-ish hand of a man not much used to penmanship, and light-years away from the fluent minuscule scrawl of the leather-bound journal, he read:

April 16 1913 Mr Cartwright at the Institute reckons it ud help me with writing and reading and also with discussing new ideas if I wrote about something that I knew a lot about—I asked him what—and he said —what about yourself—your life. I said—whod want to read that? And he said—how about your daughter when she grows up? So here it is Ada for you—if it turns into owt worth the keeping that is. MY LIFE.

Peter Pascoe turned the page.

VIII

"ANDY. I thought it might be you. Come on in."

Cap Marvell led him into her living room. On the coffee table stood the bottle of the paint-stripping Scotch, open with a full glass beside it. On the hi-fi a woman was singing agitatedly in German.

"You'll join me?" said Cap.

"No, thanks," said Dalziel. "Still going on about the war, is she?"

"No. She's saying that she would never have let the children go out in such filthy weather. They've died, you see. Mahler wrote a whole group of songs about children dying."

"Right bundle of fun, weren't he?" said Dalziel.

"He had his moments." She smiled. "You know,

though, this song could be about war. All wars. Sending children out where the bullets rattle like hail and the shell blasts carve swaths through forests and folk.''

The song ended. She switched the player off.

"You keep on going on like you lost your lad in the Falklands," said Dalziel.

"In a way I did," she said. "In his place I got a hero, which isn't quite the same thing. I had dinner with him last night, by the way."

"Oh aye? Takes his spurs and sword off before he sits down to eat, does he?"

She frowned and said, "Andy, from time to time I may be mildly satirical about my son but it is a privilege I don't extend to my friends."

Dalziel scratched his left jowl like a chef tenderizing a T-bone.

"Well, that's me pricked in the pecking order," he said. "With such a bad attack of the maternals, I don't suppose you earned your snout pay."

"Of course I did," she said. "In fact it was surprisingly easy. With so much conversational no-man's-land between us, Piers always seizes avidly on any acceptable topic which does present itself and never lets it go till he's torn it to shreds. Buster Sanderson saw us happily through our entree and well into the petit fours."

"Buster?"

"As in Keaton. He is evidently quite unflappable and the Mess, even when deploring his escapades, was united in admiration of the aplomb with which he met both discovery and disaster."

"For instance?"

"Night exercise in Germany. The CO returned unexpectedly early to his caravan and found his bunk occupied by Buster on top of a Fräulein. Without interrupting his stroke, the captain looked up and said, 'Interrogation, sir. Give me another minute and I'll have it out of her.' Or during a mortar attack on their barracks in Northern Ireland, Buster was on the phone trying to persuade his bookie to extend his credit. Everyone else dived for cover. When they emerged Buster was still on the phone saying, 'Bangs? What bangs? Look, another five hundred is all I'm asking.' "

"So, he's a randy dickhead," said Dalziel, unimpressed. "But is he a crook?"

"He had a reputation for being—how did Piers put it?—unsound in matters of finance or the heart. But when it came to a fight, you couldn't ask for a better chap in your corner. He came dangerously close on several occasions to being cashiered or whatever it is they do to gentlemen that steal the Mess silver or cheat at snap. And though the CO claimed that he was never consulted about the regiment's redundancies, nobody was surprised when Buster's name came out of the hat. Or his man's."

"His man's? You mean, Patten?"

"No, of course not. Sergeant Patten had left some months before Buster. I'd have thought you'd have known that."

At this point a real snout would have found himself levitated by his collar, banged very hard against a wall, and advised that unless he had comprehensive medical insurance, it was unwise to get clever.

Dalziel said, "Aye, I did know that. Who then?"

"His batman. Private Rosthwaite. Rosso. Took care of all of Buster's needs."

"You sound like that means more than bulling his boots."

Cap smiled and sipped her Scotch without flinching or foaming at the mouth.

"Piers had to be pressed. There are some things a hero does not talk about with his mother. I thought he was being a bit coy about admitting what didn't take a mastermind to guess, that a good officer's servant would do a bit of pandering on the side. But I finally got it out of him that Rosso, when time and place and circumstances made the procurement of female company difficult or dangerous, was reputed to supply the deficiency itself."

"You mean he took it up the jacksie?" said Dalziel, thinking he could see where the Hero got his coyness from. "Buster's AC/DC?"

"It would seem so."

"Thought they kicked you out of the army for that."

"Perhaps, among other things, they did."

She didn't seem to know Rosso was dead, thought Dalziel. Why should she? He himself hadn't known anything about it till Wield had mentioned the accident. Did the fact that Sanderson might have used him for soldier's comforts make his death any more significant? No reason why. But mebbe he shouldn't have been quite so dismissive of the sergeant when he'd been trying to flesh out his wispy suspicions of TecSec.

"So what did the . . . your son have to say about Patten?"

"Not a great deal. It seems he had a reputation for being a bit of a hard man, the kind of NCO who might have made it to the very top except that from time to time he'd cross the very wavy line which even the army draws between honesty and dishonesty, discipline and brutality, and get busted. Of course, the army, being the army, knows the value of such men and very rapidly he'd always be promoted once more to his former rank. Rather like the police, I daresay."

"No," said Dalziel. "You get reduced in the force, you'd need more luck than Lazarus to make it back up. That it then?"

"That's it," said Cap. "Have I earned my thirty pieces of silver?"

"Nay, lass, that 'ud make you both Judas and the Virgin Mary. Can't have it both ways. Not unless you're Captain Sanderson."

They sat in silence now. She knows it wasn't this that I've come about, thought Dalziel. Since Wield's visit she's been expecting me. Why? He could think of reasons. And he knew enough of human complexities to know there could be reasons he couldn't think of.

He said, "You've not asked about Wendy."

"I rang the hospital just before you turned up. Still no change."

She sounded genuinely concerned. But then she would be, either way.

He said, "Get on okay with Sergeant Wield, did you?"

"He was . . . interesting. I liked him. He made me feel at ease."

"Any reason why you shouldn't feel at ease?"

"Only my guilty knowledge that I was screwing his boss," said Cap. "I use the imperfect tense advisedly. I get a distinct impression that you haven't come here to have your wicked way with me, Andy."

"Why do you think I have come?" he asked.

"Something about Wendy's accident. The questions your sergeant asked . . . oh, don't misunderstand me, he gave away nothing. But I've been asked questions by quite a lot of policeman over the last ten years, and I know the difference between routine inquiries and purposeful probing."

"Why should we be asking you questions about Walker's accident?" he said.

It was a crap question, not even justifiable as cat-and-mouse. There, each advance and apparent retreat was purposeful, leaving you a little farther forward. But this did nowt, except fill in time while he tried to make his mind up which way to go. Such uncertainty was not a state of mind he normally brought to the interrogation room.

She didn't bother to reply, her silence confirming the status of the question.

She knows this is hard for me, he thought. So the clever thing is to make her think it's harder than it is.

"Look," he said. "This is hard for me. I should mebbe have sent someone else."

"You did," she said. "Mr. Wield."

"I meant someone senior. My DCI, Pete Pascoe."

"Why didn't you?"

"Because I owe it to you—to both of us—to come myself. You understand?"

Tempting her to agree, to acknowledge she knew what this was all about.

She sipped her drink.

"Yes, I think so," she said slowly.

Jesus. Why didn't his heart leap as it usually did at the first sign of a hairline crack? Why did this part he was acting of the reluctant inquisitor feel so sodding real?

She went on, "I understand that there's something about Wendy's accident bothering you. Well, there would be of course. It was hit-and-run. And from the way you're going on, Andy, incredible though it seems, I can only assume you've got me—how do you put it? —in the frame. Is that right?"

She was looking at him with a wide-eyed, innocent sincerity which could have got her a job as a token woman in a Tory cabinet.

His heart hardened. Guilty, she was playing hard to get. Innocent, well, she had nothing to fear, did she?

Cards-on-the-table time. She knew what they were, or she didn't. Either way, continued concealment was a waste of time.

He said, "We think the hit-and-run might be just a cover-up, and Walker could have been attacked and left to die."

Her reaction was perfect. Shock, incredulity, outrage, each perfectly proportioned, as first the fact then the implication of what he was saying hit her.

"You bastard!" she said. "Oh, you bastard!"

"Hang about," he said in an injured tone. "Second ago you were all philosophical, now all of a sudden I'm a bastard. What's changed?"

"Hit-and-run's one thing. Someone reports a Discovery near the scene, a number like mine, you've got to look into it. But this is cold-blooded murder you're talking about!"

"Attempted murder," he reminded her gently. "Walker can still open her eyes and put everything right."

She didn't look like she found this a comfort, but then, he generously allowed, he doubted if he'd find it much of a comfort to be told that proving his innocence might depend on someone coming out of a coma.

She refilled her glass and emptied it immediately. She must have a pot-glazed gullet. Her eyes still said *Bastard!* but when she spoke her voice was controlled.

"Andy, there must be reasons why you're questioning me like this. Do I get to hear them?"

"Why not?" he said. "Walker's Mark Shufflebottom's brother."

"Who?"

Bad, he thought. Anyone in the animal rights movement had to know the name, and in any case, hadn't he mentioned it to her himself only a couple of days ago?

"Not the guard at the FG plant at Redcar?" she went on. "Is that who you mean?"

Good recovery. He was firmly into his interrogation mode now. Be absolute for guilt, that was the only way. That was what Wally Tallantire, his first CID boss, had taught him. *In court they're innocent till proved guilty, Andy*, he'd said. *In here* (tapping his head) *they're guilty till proved innocent.*

"That's the one. Walker reckoned the only way she was going to find who killed her brother was to do it herself. That's why she joined your lot."

"Because she thought we had something to do with it?" said Cap incredulously.

Very good. If this was acting, then it were Old Vic standard. Made you wonder about them yells she'd let out on the bed yesterday afternoon. He suddenly felt old and grubby.

"Not necessarily. She wanted an in and you were it."

"Because she knew Ellie Pascoe and Ellie knew me?"

Slightly betrayed. Not too much, seeing there were more important issues on the agenda here. This really was a class act. If it was.

"That's it. And once in, she set about getting herself a name as a hard case and trying to make contacts with real extremists at meetings and demos."

"I thought she was wrong for us from the start. Far too pushy."

He believed her, but that didn't make her innocent. Cap Marvell's extremism would be the kind that required unquestioning obedience, not individual acts of derring-do.

She went on, "So what happened, Andy, that got me from being Wendy's way-in to being number one suspect?"

He said, "Summat happened that night at Wanwood. When I first saw you, you were the one being all aggressive, Walker was meek and mild and cooperating like mad. I've read the TecSec statements. Seems like you were the one wanted to take the guards' heads off with your wire cutters. In fact it was Walker stopped you doing serious damage."

"They said that?"

"Yeah. Not true?"

She shrugged and said, "Not the way you put it. That one with the scar, he just stood there with a macho fancy-your-chances sneer on his face. I don't deny it would have been quite pleasant to wipe it off. But even without Wendy's interference, I'd have banged him in the goolies, not tried to split his skull."

"You're all heart," said Dalziel.

"I see it's been a mistake," she replied. "So the theory is that somehow I let it slip that I was the mad killer of Redcar and decided that Wendy had to be silenced before she could spread the word? It would make a lousy movie. I mean, first of all, I'd have had to find out what Wendy was really up to, wouldn't I? How did I manage that?"

"She said something that got you thinking."

"Oh yes. And that was enough?"

"Enough to set you off checking her out a bit more thoroughly than you'd done before."

"The next day, you mean? Well, I have an alibi for most of that if you recall, spending it as I did in the company of a pillar of the community . . . oh shit, Andy. You think that's what I was doing with you? You think I opened my legs to get you to open your mouth? Oh shit."

Her distress nearly got to him. He wished he had a drink, even the paint stripper. But this was no time to relent.

"You wanted to get me talking about her, I recall. And she'd just been to see you and you'd had a row. But you didn't dare try to get the truth out of her then and there 'cos you knew I might turn up any moment."

She regarded him with amazement.

"You heard that?" she said. "But you said nothing . . ."

"Nothing to say," he replied. "Then, I just thought it were girls' talk . . ."

"And now it's all down to her suspecting I'm her brother's killer. And me suspecting that she's onto me . . . so how am I supposed to have found out the truth about her? If you were eavesdropping, you know that

nothing was said about Redcar and Mark Shufflebottom, nothing at all!"

Aggressive defense, often a sign that you were getting there. But also a natural reaction, he reminded
himself. Reassured himself.

"That's true," he admitted. "You can't have been
certain. Not by a long shot. You'd have needed to talk
to her again. When you learned she was going to have a
heart-to-heart with Ellie Pascoe, could be the alarm
really started sounding."

"I don't believe this," she almost whispered. "Andy,
you're talking as if you're certain that . . ."

"Nay, lass, don't take on," he said. "It's just a way
of putting things. I do it all the time. It's routine, this is
all routine. I'm just covering myself, covering both of
us. I've got to be thorough. Like the first time I came
here, I asked where you were the dates of the Redcar
raid and the first raid on Wanwood."

"Yes, and I told you."

"I know. Only now I need lots of detail of dates,
times, witnesses. For the record."

She rose and left the room, returning a moment later
with her diary. He smiled at her encouragingly. It was
half sincere, half an act, and he couldn't tell the boundary line. Surely it was better to play the right bastard
rather than continue with this hot/cold pressure?

She looked quite relaxed for a moment as she flicked
through the pages of her diary. Then she looked up,
eyes huge with bewilderment, and said, "Andy, why are
you making me do this? I know you say it's your job,
it's just routine, but I still can't really believe that even
for the sake of appearances you've got to act as if it
were truly possible that I tried to kill Wendy Walker the
other night. For God's sake, we were at the university
party together."

"You left early."

"To watch the telly interview. I asked you to come with me."

"You knew I wouldn't."

"How the hell did I know that?"

He gave her a conspiratorial grin and said, "It's easy done when you've had the practice."

She said, "You mean, I manipulated you?"

"Why not? You've a way with words. Like if you hung around outside till you saw Walker arrive, I doubt you'd have had any problem persuading her to get into that van of yours for a little chat to sort her doubts and difficulties out. Plenty of room for the bike too."

He dropped the bike in casually. The bike was a bit of a puzzle. Walker had told Ellie she was coming to the party by bus and would like a lift home. If she did come on the bus, then Cap would have had to go back to her squat to pick up the bike. Questions had already been asked there with the kind of result to be expected from folk who trusted the police like politicians. The driver of the bus whose arrival most closely coincided with Cap's departure from the party thought he did recollect someone answering Wendy's description, but as further questioning elicited the judgment that all female students wore jeans, anoraks, and trainers, and most of them were skinny and pale and undernourished, this was far from conclusive.

So he watched Cap carefully to see if she reacted at all to his assumption that Wendy had come to the party on her bike. She didn't.

She said, "And having got her into the Discovery and realizing she knew my guilty secret, I'm supposed to have knocked her unconscious, then driven out along Ludd Lane where I staged an accident and left her in a ditch to drown?"

Drown. She said *drown*, not *die*. Had he talked to her about the stream in the ditch and the way Walker's waterproof had formed a dam and saved her from drowning? It was possible. There'd been no reason not to. He'd been deep into trust then. He recalled another bit of Wally's wisdom. *Trust no bugger save your own mam. And not till you've checked her record first.*

He said, "If you didn't do that, what did you do?"

"What I've told you, of course. I went straight home and poured myself a drink and sat and admired myself on television."

"Any witnesses? You didn't stop off for petrol on the way home? Or pop out to buy a bottle of yon Mex ale or a packet of crisps?"

Here was her chance to trump his hidden ace before he even played it, to offer some explanation as to how ten minutes after the program she'd allegedly rushed off to see had ended, he saw her coming from her garage and going into her unlit flat.

"No, Andy. I went straight home, settled down in front of the box, and that was it." She spoke with a fervor that might almost have convinced him if he hadn't had the personal ocular proof that she was lying.

Part of him was tempted to challenge her straightway, but that was the part that wasn't a cop, and while not totally disenfranchised, it had certainly been a minority vote for longer than he could recall.

No, this was one you saved up for court, or at least for when you'd got her in an interview room with the tape running.

There was a double ring at the doorbell.

He said, "That'll be for me. We'll need your garage and car keys."

She looked at him sadly and said, "Oh, Andy. Isn't this where you say something about only obeying orders?"

"Nay, lass," he said, holding out his huge hand. "Giving them. Now let's be having them keys."

IX

"BEFORE YOU SWITCH THAT THING ON, I thought we had a deal," said Jimmy Howard.

"That was before we found this," said Wield, holding up the plastic bag containing the envelope from Howard's car. "Press the switch, Shirley."

Detective Constable Shirley Novello started the recorder and Wield recited the litany of date, time, and those present.

"Do you recognize this envelope, Jimmy?" asked Wield.

"Well, I can see it's an envelope, but one envelope looks much like another, doesn't it?"

"Take a closer look," said Wield.

"No, doesn't ring any bells."

"We found it in your car, Jimmy."

"Nothing to do with me. Where'd you find it?"

"Under the rubber matting by the driver's seat."

"There you are then. Could have been there ever since I got the heap."

"Don't give it a good clean every Sunday then?"

"Not really."

"So, if it's nothing to do with you, there's no chance it'll have your prints on it?"

"Well, it might do now, seeing as I've just had a good look at it."

"Don't get clever, Jimmy. For the tape, the envelope is in a tamper-proof evidence bag, sealed, with time and date certified. There's something in the envelope, Jimmy. Some tablets. We've taken one out and sent it to the lab for analysis. And idea what we'll find?"

"Aspirin?" said Howard. "Look, I don't know

what's in that envelope and I don't know how it got in my car, if that was where you found it. And I can't see how my fingerprints can be on it, unless they were on it before whoever planted it in my car planted it there. I mean, it looks like an ordinary brown envelope like we've got lying around the office. I could handle any number of those each day."

"And who do you think might have planted it?" asked Wield.

"Any number of people. When you've been a cop you make enemies, you must know that. Might even be you, Sergeant Wield."

DC Novello looked at Wield anxiously. This was the first time she'd sat in on one of his interviews, in fact it was her first formal interview since her transfer to plainclothes. Everyone had told her she was mad to put her future in Fat Andy's gift. She'd appeared on her first day, face scrubbed, hair bound tightly back, wearing jeans and a baggy sweater. Dalziel had looked her up and down and said, "You got no skirts or lipstick? Place is full of scruffy buggers already." The others had laughed and settled down to treating her with varying degrees of caution and condescension till they saw what she was made of. Only Wield, so far as she could judge, simply accepted her as one of the team, no tags attached. This, plus his reputation as an implacable interviewer of suspects, gave her two good reasons for feeling anxious about the way things were going.

"Why do you say that, Jimmy?" asked Wield.

"Well, you came to see me the other day, didn't you? Trying to pressure me to say bad things about my employers. When I wouldn't, you warned me to watch out, ex-cop with a drunk-driving charge against his name should know better than to turn his back on his old mates. I told you to get stuffed and leave me alone."

It was good, Wield had to admit. He'd underestimated Howard, forgetting that the guy had been a cop for a long time, and the kind of cop who knew how everything worked. The second he saw the envelope he knew that all deals were off. And, knowing that taped interviews could work both ways as evidence, he was busy getting his retaliation in first.

What he didn't know was that Wield had witnessed the envelope being handed over by Jane Ambler. The Drug Squad were organizing simultaneous searches of her flat and Howard's house. This involved their total manpower, leaving Wield to have first bite at the ex-policeman.

Now he surprised both Howard and DC Novello by saying, "I think that's enough for now. Interview terminated at eighteen forty-three p.m."

Reaching across the table he flicked off the tape switch, stood up, yawned, and said, "Long day, Jimmy. For you too. I'll see you back to your cell."

As they walked along the corridor he said, "Jimmy, you should have had your solicitor there. Could have saved you a lot of grief. Stopped you digging yourself in deeper."

"What's that mean? Getting worried, Wieldy? You should be. There's going to be so much shit flying around, some of it's bound to stick."

"About me pressurizing you, you mean? No way. Not when Jane Ambler coughs the lot."

He paused to see the effect of the name on Howard. The man looked like he'd unexpectedly bitten into a chili.

"All you've done, lad, is put a load of crap on tape. I mean, it'll be no good now saying you didn't know what were in the envelope she gave you, not when you've lied your socks off claiming you never saw it. Nay, Jimmy, a good brief would have advised you to say nowt till you knew what it was you were up against. Didn't your time in the Force teach you anything?"

They had reached the cell. He opened the door and pushed Howard ahead of him. The man turned and put his hand against the door to prevent it being closed.

He said urgently, "Look, Sarge, is there nowt we can do?"

"Not my case now, Jimmy. That were just for the record. Drug Squad takes over now."

"Shit. Look, suppose I'd been going to tell you about Janey Ambler, as part of our deal, only I didn't have time to get round to it?"

Wield laughed like a coffee grinder.

"You're own mam 'ud find that one hard to credit, Jimmy."

"Yeah, but, look, Sarge, anything you could say about me cooperating, sort of working undercover for you, would help. I mean, at least it would sow a doubt about the drugs, wouldn't it? You wouldn't have to say you believe me or not, just stay neutral, long as you could say I was cooperating fully on the other business."

"What other business is that, Jimmy?"

Howard hesitated. Whatever he knows, thought Wield, he knows that once it's out, the bargaining's over.

He said, "Jimmy, I'd like to help you, but you see my problem. I've got to chat up them hard bastards in the Drug Squad to get them to go easy. And to do that I'd need to be waving something at them a lot bigger than a little drug bust. But I don't know what it is I'd be waving, do I? In other words, I can't do a deal till I know what we're dealing with."

"Yeah, and the minute I tell you, where's the need for you to do any deal anyway?" snarled Howard.

It was an old circle and Wield had had long practice in breaking out of it. But before he could urge his arguments, he heard footsteps down the corridor and the custody sergeant's voice saying, "Here he is, Mr. Beasley. And this is Detective Sergeant Wield who's just been interviewing him."

Into the cell came a fresh-faced young man in an elegantly cut gray suit.

He said, "I hope the interview isn't continuing outside of the properly designated room, Sergeant? You know how the courts frown on such breaches of PACE."

"Who are you?" said Wield.

"Mr. Beasley's Mr. Howard's solicitor," said Charley Slocum.

"That right, Jimmy?" said Wield, looking at the prisoner, whose face gave little sign of recognition.

"I'm employed by TecSec actually," said Beasley. "Mrs. Howard rang the office as soon as she heard about Mr. Howard's spot of bother and Captain Sanderson, having a good old military sense of responsibility for his chaps, instructed me to come along and offer my services. On the firm, of course, Mr. Howard."

Wield said, "That's big on him. Jimmy, it's up to you."

Howard hesitated, then said, "You did say I ought to have spoke with a solicitor, Sarge. Never too late, eh?"

Wield shrugged and stepped out into the corridor.

Over his shoulder he said, "I'll see you in court, Jimmy. For some folk it's always too late. From the very day they're born."

My name is Peter Pascoe.

I were born on Swithins Day in the year 1892—a ten-month babby giving my mam great pain which when she complained of they said was no wonder as shed given birth to a giant with his head already hard as any rock—which is why she called me Peter —knowing her Bible well though no other book.

My mother had been Mrs Grindals maid up at the Maisterhouse—but on getting pregnant and marrying she had to leave of course and settled down in No 13 Miter Lane which is where I were born.

My father were a chargehand at Grindals mill. He was I think a good man though fond of drink— which they pointed to when he had his accident— the crowner saying no blame attached to the overseers or manager. I were five years old then—old enough to hear talk of compensation though not to understand what it might mean—and when I asked I were told it meant starving or not starving. I recall asking my mam if we were to starve and she said she hoped God would provide—and next day we heard that Mrs Grindal had given birth to a son and Mr Grindal was sending her out to the big new house hed built in the mid county for the better air —and mam were sent for to go with her as nursemaid. I think they did not want me to go too but my mother said she could not leave me behind and then they said I could go—which all the men said was because of this compensation and some tried to persuade my mother not to go—but I was glad when she said she would go as I did not care to starve.

The new house was called Wanwood and I lived in the coachhouse with the grooms while my mother stayed in the nursery to be close to the babby. He were a poor mewling thing she said—many times in the first months they feared for his life—and I think none feared as much as I since the grooms told me if he did die then my mother and I must go back to Kirkton where wed surely starve.

I prayed hard to save his life but knew I were

*really praying to save my own so did not know if
this would count. Then Mrs Grindals brother Mr
Sam Batty came to stay—who they said was a very
great man of science with knowledge of all kinds of
potions and ointments—and he quarrelled with the
doctor—who walked off saying that if owt happened
to the boy they knew where to lay the blame—but
nothing did happen and in a sennight the lad were
putting on weight and colour—whether in thanks to
my prayers or Mr Sams powders or even the old doctors medicines I did not know or much care. All I
cared was I could stay at Wanwood and see my
mother at least once every day and have a good
meal twice as often.*

*I got a start at education too for they made me
walk five miles to the village school each day—my
fellow pupils did not make me welcome being nothing but a stupid townie in their eyes but six years
growing in Kirkton had taught me to look out for
myself and when they saw I could bite they soon
learned to leave me be.*

*So here I lived happily for five or six years—till
such time as I was told it was time for me to earn
my living which I might do as boy-of-all-work in the
household—and so training up to footman or some
such—or I could be set on at the mill in Kirkton.*

*I asked my mother what I should choose—expect-
ing she would be warm for the household—but she
surprised me saying it was an ill life always at her
mistress whim and depending on her moods—and
specially so for a man who must find it hard work
winning a mans respect as a servant.*

*I was young but not so young as not to know this
must have been hard for her to say—Wanwood being more than thirty miles from Kirkton where indeed they still kept up the Maisterhouse but Mrs
Grindal rarely went there these days dividing her*

time between Wanwood and the London house they had bought and a house they leased by the sea near a place called Cromer which was where the fashionable people went. These last two I never visited staying behind under the care of the housekeeper at Wanwood—which truth to tell was no care at all—so though I missed my mother it was small pain otherwise to be left behind—my own master to roam at will.

This being used to being left alone added to what my mother said made me resolve to work at the mill —two days later I travelled to Kirkton in the coach with Mr Grindal himself who spent most of his time at the Maisterhouse—in those days he seemed a giant with brows like a ploughed field that used to turn black when he lost his temper which was quick and terrible. But he spoke kindly to me on the journey seeming surprised at my choice but pleased too —saying that I was a sharp lad and if I kept my nose clean there was no reason I shouldnt prosper.

But oh I had no reason to think of prospering during those first months at the mill where my main job was to crawl beneath the machines as they were working and sweep up the waste—I cannot think of anything worse than the noise and the close air and the terrible fear in my young heart that I underwent in those first endless days when you may imagine scarce a moment passed that I did not bitterly regret my choice to leave the safe servitude of Wanwood. Whatever life may bring me I shall never forget those long long seemingly endless hours of hopeless terror that filled my daily existence and my nightly dreams . . .

But what cant be cured must be endured and a man is a rare adaptable creature particularly a young one—and eventually what seemed at first but meaningless or even malevolent chaos came to have

some shape and order—and I began to feel that
mebbe after all I had some control.

I was lodged at my uncle Georges house—that is
my fathers younger brother whose wife my aunt Sara
was worn out with having had seven children—but
only one surviving—my cousin Stephen who was
two years younger than me—but such a weany lad
he might have been five.

At first Stephen did not care to have an older boy
above him—for though he was the son of the house
with lads it is always size and strength that sets the
order—but I think that when he saw how lonely and
unhappy I was in those first days he made up his
mind I werent no threat and one evening on my way
home from the mill I came on some bigger boys tor-
menting him and I gave one such a buffet on the
nose I think it may have been broke—and the others
ran off with him—and after that I could do no
wrong in Stephens eyes.

Uncle George was the timekeeper at the mill—he
was very bitter about the manner of my father's
death but dare not say over much because he feared
to lose what was regarded as a good and easy post.

But there were others who spoke more boldly—
Union men—not just about my father which was old
business—but about conditions and pay and such
things—Mr Grindal hated unions and would not
have employed any man who came to him openly
saying he was a member—but the Union men knowing this had worked secretly at their recruitment till
by the time he became aware of them they were far
too many to be dismissed without bringing the
whole mill to a standstill—and with it perhaps many
others in the area which would not have won him
much thanks from the other owners.

Uncle George despite him being so bitter about
his brothers death was no lover of the Union which

*he said had done precious little in the matter of
compensation—he warned me about getting mixed
up with them—saying that he reckoned Mr Grindal
had his eye on me for advancement—but Id not get
far if he thought I were mixed up with the Union
men. Being still a boy and working only a boys
hours and earning a boys pay I was not able yet for
full membership—so I cunningly gave the Union
men the impression I would join when I got of age
and Uncle George the impression that I was keeping
them at arms length—and so I contrived to live at
ease with everyone during those early years.*

*I knew Alice Clark right from the start of living
back in Kirkton. I mean I knew she existed—one of
two sisters living two doors up from Uncle Georges
—but she were Stephens age—nobbut a child—so I
paid her no more heed than I did the coalmans
horse that I saw as often and admired a lot more. It
werent till I were near on eighteen and shed been
working at the mill herself for more than a year that
I started taking notice. She were filling out nicely
and had such a way of walking—as if she were by
herself strolling under the trees by the river rather
than passing down the aisle between them rattling
machines—that I found myself going out of my way
just for the pleasure of looking at her. From looking
it were a short step to talking—nothing out of the
way—just a few words if we met on the way to the
mill or on leaving it—which we seemed to do more
and more often that summer. It were a long way off
courting—I still told myself she were only a child—
and I had no thought that anyone would have noticed my interest—in fact I dont think I really understood it myself—I mean I were interested in girls
and had been for the past two years or so—but little
Alice didnt belong in the same class as the big bo-*

somed wicked tongued women us growing lads lusted after.

It were Stephen who got things started without meaning it. We were sitting eating our bait one day when he said slyly—There goes thy light o love our Peter. I looked up and saw Alice walking with some other lasses quite close. I felt myself blush a bit—without knowing why—and I said—now stop thy laking—I dont know what tha means.

It were likely my awkwardness that made some of the others laugh—and one of them—a big solid brute of a fellow called Archie Doyle—with a reputation for beating his wife—said—Tell us then young Pascoe hasta shagged her yet?

Now a silence fell—not because any of them were shocked—this kind of question passes for wit in a mill—but to see how I would take it. If you let yourself get angered—then thas done forever—fair game for any who want to get a rise. I took my time—chewing on a crust of bread—then I said—Whysta want to know Archie? Ist so long since tha did it thasel—thas forgotten how?

That got them laughing—all but Doyle who jumped to his feet and came towards me fists clenched. Id seen him in action and I knew what he could do—I jumped up too thinking of running—but I knew I couldnt run forever and hed always be looking for me. So I grabbed up a length of four-by-two lying around for use in wedging the machine gate open—and I held it before me like a club—and I said—Listen Archie—Ill put up wi thy filthy tongue cos that knows no better. But if ever tha lays a finger on me Ill split thy skull wide open so help me God.

He stopped in his tracks but I could see he wasnt going to back down not unless he had a way out—and he were too thick to think of one—and I was wrought too tight to give him one—then one of the *others—Tommy Mather one of the Union men—said —No need to get thy dander up Pete. Archie ud never have spoke like he did if hed known tha was really courting the lass—would you Archie?—and Doyle said—No. How was I to know?—and I said— Thats all right then. Just then the hooter went and as we went back to work Mather said to me—Best start making up to the girl for the next week or so at least young Pascoe—just till Archie gets used to the idea.*

I didnt answer but I found myself thinking about it all through the shift. The truth was—and Im almost ashamed to write it—that Doyles foul minded question had got me thinking about Alice not as a growing child but as a grown woman. Its funny the way God twists things—turning bad to good and sometimes so it seems good to bad.

So thats how I started courting Alice and she told me later to my surprise that shed been waiting ever so long for me to ask and had almost begun to fear I never would!

We were in no rush to get wed—partly because we wanted something behind us—and partly because so sure were we of each other neither felt the need to tie us together with church knots. As for those strong fleshly urgings which some women use to lead a resisting man to the altar—so alike were we in this that soon we were giving and taking gladly—confident that what we did was holy without need of parson preaching his solemn words.

Another reason was that I was getting on so well in the job. Id long moved on from being a crawling boy and rapidly moved up through most of the jobs on the machines—too rapid for some like Archie Doyle who started sneering at me as the bosses pet. In the end I did what I mebbe shouldve done that first time and told him to put up or shut up—and when he put up I split his head open. He still got one or two blows in and gave me a cracked rib or two but there was no doubting the result and after that no one said owt about my rapid advance. In fact Doyle suffered unjustly—though not before time —because I knew in my heart that it werent no peculiar merit that was getting me on—though I quickly mastered everything I turned my hand to— but Mr Grindals special interest.

By this time the Union men had just about given up on me—not that I argued against them but rather I twisted and turned and ducked and dodged— knowing as I did that my progress would hit a brick wall if ever Mr Grindal got it in his head I was mixed up with them. Sometimes I talked of this with Alice whose father was hot for the Union—she played the submissive maidens part saying it were mens business and beyond her—but there was nowt submissive about her when her dad told her that no bosses man was going to marry his daughter— whereupon she told him that no Union man was going to tell her who she could wed or not!

For all that he might have been an obstacle to us till she came of age—which I had rather waited for than what did happen—which was an outbreak of typhoid fever in Kirkton that carried several off including Mr Clark among the first. Alice too was touched and I feared for her life but when I told Mr Grindal of this—who till now I had kept dark about my hopes for marriage not knowing how he might view them—he immediately got his brother-in-law Mr Sam Batty to consult with her doctor. Mr Sam was now quite famous for his patent ointments and stomach draughts which he would probably have given away for free if Mr Grindal had not set him up in works on a piece of land he owned just over the river from the mill. I have heard Mr Grindal say his brother-in-law knew more about the workings of the human system than any doctor in England but less about the workings of the capital system than any grocer in Leeds. I know not what he prescribed or said but do know that under his advice Alice quickly recovered—for which I am more grateful to him than any man living.

So now with no father to object and with Mr Grindals approval—for once he met Alice he could see for himself that she was apt to make a wife and helpmeet fit for any man—we had the banns called and married in the Spring of 1911—and the following year little Ada was born.

By now I was off the mill floor and into the counting house—a proper clerk with good prospects and enough money coming in to keep his wife and family properly—I even bought a piano because Alice hoped that Ada would turn out musical—and to my surprise I found that I was gifted that way myself—never before having any chance to discover this—and in no time I was able to pick out the ragtime tunes which were all the rage.

Mr Grindals trust in me grew daily—and when he decided that his son—young Bertie should spend his summer holiday emptying his head of all the fancy notions he was picking up from his mother and his expensive school it was to my care that he entrusted him.

He was a good looking boy in a rather girlish way with long soft light brown hair—which when he was advised to take care of it catching in the machines he tied back with a red silk kerchief—after which everyone called him Gertie though never in Mr Grindals earshot.

He said he recalled me from when he was a baby and he talked of my mother most affectionately—whom I had not seen for more than a twelvemonth.

She had been taken ill while the family were in the house at Cromer and remained there when they moved on—unable even to travel to see her grandchild. I had accepted reassurance that it was a slight and temporary illness but from some hints that young Gertie carelessly let drop I began to fear it might be something much worse—but to my shame I did nowt about it. This apart there was little to trouble my life—and when Mr Grindal recommended that I should go to the Institute to take courses in bookkeeping and generally improve myself I looked into the future—working for the best of firms in the best of countries—and saw nothing but peace and prosperity on the horizon.

Mr Cartwright asked me last night how my autobiography was going on—I answered pretty well—though in truth I have neglected it for many months now—and he asked if he might see it when I felt it was ready—I said there was a long way to go—but what I meant was I do not think I will let him or anyone see it—save it be Alice and one day our little Ada.

Mr Cartwright told me that Mr Philip Snowden the Member of Parliament was coming to speak at the Institute tomorrow and said I might be interested to hear what he had to say. I have read about him in the newspapers. Also I have heard Mr Grindal speak of him—he thinks he is a disgrace to Yorkshire and to England and ought to be hanged! So perhaps I will go—but well muffled up against discovery.

Its many weeks since I wrote and much has happened—my mother is dead, thats the worst and the saddest thing—and they say there is to be a war but no one is sure when.

I went to hear Mr Snowden that night and I came

*away with my head reeling with ideas. Id listened in
the past to our Union men talking of course—and
also to the likes of Mr Cartwright at the Institute—
but all they had to say seemed so local and domestic
and concerned with battling against bosses who
didnt have the interests of their worker at heart like
Mr Grindal did—or so I thought he did.*

*Mr Snowden wasnt just talking about Leeds but
—he was talking about the whole of the world and
what it meant to be a working man wherever you
were. I were bursting to tell Alice all Id heard
and she listened—sometimes nodding—sometimes
frowning—and when Id done she said it all sounded
grand but Id best not to go sounding off round the
mill next day—which was good advice except that it
turned out that somehow Mr Grindal knew Id been
at the meeting—I can only guess that there were police spies there and one of them knew my face—and
he asked me straight out what did I think? Shouldnt
this man Snowden be transported to Germany where
all the other enemies of the King were concentrated?
I said I had not heard anything that sounded like
treason to me and did he care to look at a new
scheme I had devised for the more efficient billing of
creditors? This distracted him and soon after he had
to go away on business—now I took the chance of
talking to Tommy Mather who I guessed would have
been at the meeting too—though I had not seen
him. I was right—and we had a good talk about
what had been said—so good that it could not be
finished on the mill floor in view of everyone—so we
met later to continue.*

*This was the first of many talks I had with
Tommy—real talks these—not me half listening to
his recruiting propaganda as our exchanges had
mostly been in the past.*

By the time Mr Grindal came back from London a week later I was a paid up member of the Union.

When Mr Grindal came into the counting house and asked me to step into his office he looked so grave of face that my heart fell—thinking as I did that he had heard the news and was going to sack me—now here would be a chance to test this solidarity of my new comrades I had heard so much about—instead he told me that Mrs Grindal had had news from Cromer that my mother was much worse and asking to see me.

He gave me leave to go at once—I had never travelled so far on the train before nor wish to do so again—though I must admit it were a grand sight to see the sea all sparking mile after mile under a sky as blue as a painted ceiling.

I found my mother on point of death alone and uncared for—oh there was a housekeeper there to see to her needs—but she was a strange close unwelcoming creature providing as much in the way of company as a splintery yard brush. As for care and tender loving kindness—I dont doubt she was fed regularly and the doctor called to attend when she seemed worse—but thats no more than youd give to a sick animal.

How long has she been like this? I asked—More than a week—And how long since you let your mistress know in London?—The same.

So Mrs Grindal had known my mothers state well before her husbands trip yet made no attempt to tell me—And he had known of it from the start of his visit—yet waited till his return to pass it on. But both would think they had treated her well—almost as one of the family.

This was the sad heart of service which my mother had warned me away from—work should be defined by a wage contract not by the patronage of *the employer. Guilt fanned my anger. I should have paid more heed—asked more questions. I sat by her bedside holding her cold hand—the doctor came— shook his head—and left—I sat with her five hours —she gave a little sign—I thought the life had gone out of her and squeezed her hand to bring it back— too hard for she grimaced with pain and said—Getting bearing leaving—you always were a painful child—then she was gone.*

So that was it—a strange life she led—looking after others children—not looking after or being looked after by her own—till we parted at last knowing as little as we knew about each other when I first went to Kirkton to set on at the mill.

I had stopped being angry when I travelled back home or at least Id stopped showing it—anger is a good fuel but a wasteful flame—but I knew now where my loyalties lay.

Back in Kirkton I found Mr Grindal in a mood which was almost frenzied—the war was coming he said and we must be ready for it—he made it sound like patriotic zeal but I overheard him say to his brother-in-law one night when he thought they were alone in the office—It may last only a matter of months and unless were in at the start it will be too late to reap the full benefit—this sounded more like profiting than patriotism to me.

He was spending more and more time energy and money on developing Mr Sams medicine works and had already started converting part of the mill to machines for the production of bandage and dressings. I asked him if it was wise to rush into such a limited market which would require injuries on an unimaginable scale to make it worthwhile—he laughed and said I should forget about the horsemen Id seen with their bright sabres exercising on Ilkley Moor—he had been in Germany the previous year and seen the German army at its exercise—this was going to be a war fought not with horses and lances but with machine guns each worth a whole rifle companys fire power—with artillery that could throw shells twenty miles—with bombs and mines that could blow a hole in the ground big enough to sink a church in.

I spoke with Tommy Mather and told him that it seemed to me to be wrong that a workers union should be engaged in preparing in any way for a war which must involve our comrades killing and being killed by men just like us in foreign countries. He said that with no unemployed men left in Kirkton and no love of the Germans in Yorkshire he doubted such a view would get much support but hed call a meeting anyway as the members ought to know what was going on.

He was right—Archie Doyle got the biggest cheer when he said—Likely there wont be a war so lets make hay while the sun shines—and if by chance there were a war he for one wouldnt mind seeing a bit of these furren parts everyone said were so grand—and knocking a couple of Germans on the head while he was there.

When I spoke there was silence except for one voice—probably Doyles—which called—Dost Mr Grindal know thas out by thysen lad?—which got the biggest laugh of the meeting.

Mr Grindal werent laughing when I saw him next day—He said—What the hell do you think your playing at? Ive fetched you up from nowt and here you are acting like some socialist agitator with a chip on his shoulder.

I might have known hed have his ears even at a Union meeting.

I tried to explain but he was in no mood to listen—all he said was—Well Im glad the rest have got

*more sense—They soon gave you your answer—And
I said—Aye and theyll likely give you yours—all the
working men of this country—if you really do get
your war. You'll need men to fight it and you wont
find them in the Unions that I can tell you.*

*It were stupid to say that really—temper talking
which is a sad waste of good breath.*

*He said—Suppose youre wrong Pascoe—suppose
there is a war and your mates show more stomach
for a fight than you do? What'll you do then? Sit at
home and complain about it?*

*And I said—If the Labour Movement doesnt op-
pose the war and lets its members go to fight then
never worry—I wont let my mates go off alone.*

*It was a proud boastful sort of thing to say—but
it was true as well—I was no pacifist opposed to all
wars—if there was just cause I saw nothing wrong
in fighting and much in not fighting—so if everyone
else voted me in the wrong Id not stand against that
—Id go.*

*I expected Mr Grindal to keep on yelling at me
but what I said seemed to put him in a better mood
—all he did was smile and say—Ill not let thee forget you said that Pascoe. Now lets get some work
done.*

*And I think that was the very first moment I truly
believed that there would be a war.*

XI

WHEN ELLIE PASCOE GOT HOME she burst into the house
like an SAS hostage rescue team.

"Hello, Mum," said Rosie, sitting cross-legged on

the sofa with an open tin of biscuits by her side and her eyes glued on the TV screen where John Wayne was trying not to be provoked into a fight in a saloon.

Ellie did not answer but moved through the open door into the dining room where her husband was sitting at a paper-strewn table.

"Peter," she said. "Do you know what time it is?"

He glanced at his watch.

"Late as that? You haven't been at the hospital all this time, have you?"

"Yes, I have. And I tried to ring you three times but all I could get was the answering machine."

"Sorry. I must have forgotten to switch it off."

"The bloody phone still rings, Peter!" she cried in exasperation.

"Yes, but only twice when the machine's engaged," he said reasonably. He ran his fingers through his hair and went on, "I got carried away . . . this stuff. You wouldn't believe it."

"Probably not. What I did believe was something dreadful must have happened for you and Rosie not to be at home. And what the hell is that she's watching on the box?"

Pascoe rose and peered through into the lounge. Wayne's good intentions had been thwarted and the saloon brawl was in full swing.

"Sorry," he said. "But you'll understand when you read this lot."

"What is it?" she said, glancing at the table. "Jesus, not more bloody Great War gunk? Have you lost all interest in the here and now? Such as, what your child's doing to her mind? And what's happening in Intensive Care?"

"I'm sorry, I'm sorry. Rosie, switch that off. And how's Wendy? Any change?"

"Yes. That's what I rang to say the first time. She's regained consciousness."

"That's great. What's she say? Does she recall what happened to her?"

Ellie shook her head.

"She's barely awake. They're still not certain how much her brain might have been affected. They let me in to see her briefly. At first I thought she recognized me but then she said, "Cap, Cap, Cap . . . oh why, why why?" I would have stayed longer but I was getting really worried about not being able to get through here."

Pascoe took her in his arms and said, "Sorry, sorry."

Over her shoulder he saw that the saloon fight had finished and the hero and heroine were embracing. Rosie, deciding that flesh and blood had it over flat image, zapped them to oblivion and turned to watch her parents. I bet if we started punching each other, she'd give up telly altogether, thought Pascoe.

He said, "Okay, you sit down. I'll get you something to eat and organize this one for bed. Like a drink to be going on with?"

"That would be great."

He poured her a gin, put a couple of lasagnes in the microwave to defrost, and hustled his daughter upstairs.

She said, "What about my tea?"

"Oh God, haven't you had anything?" he asked guiltily.

"Yes, I helped myself," she said, grinning.

Breakfast and tea in a single day. Thank God for school dinners, he thought.

He said, "Don't tell your mother."

"Don't tell her what?" said Ellie from the doorway.

"That I got into trouble today for throwing stones in the playground," said Rosie promptly, leaving Pascoe pleased to be off the hook but aghast at the convincing ease with which she lied.

Alone with his daughter, he tried to remonstrate with her.

"Yes, but I did get into trouble for throwing stones," she said. "So it wasn't a lie, was it?" This was turning into a problem in logic rather than ethics.

"Even the truth can be a lie sometimes?" he heard himself saying sententiously.

"But can't a lie be better than the truth sometimes?" she argued.

This piece of precocity took his breath away. Having a bright kid was one thing, but childhood could be a long and bumpy road for a smart-ass.

Then Rosie yawned and added, "Like swearing."

"Have you been talking to Miss Martindale?" asked Pascoe.

"Yes. I got sent to her for throwing the stones. And she said sometimes bad things could be good. Like telling lies. But you have to be careful."

"And swearing?"

"She said if you dropped something heavy on your toe, it was good to have a special word you could shout out to get the pain out of you, and that's why some words were bad unless you had a pain to get out."

She was almost asleep now. At the door he paused and said, "Why were you throwing stones?"

"There was this man walking past the playground with a dog and it wouldn't do as it was told so he started hitting it with the lead and it was yelling. So I threw a stone and then he yelled too."

Downstairs he saw Ellie at the dining room table with the exercise book journal open in front of her. As he watched she knuckled a tear out of her eyes. Quietly he went into the kitchen, turned the microwave up, made a green salad, poured a couple of glasses of wine and brought the meal through on a tray.

Ellie said, brightly, "He's got your attitude to punctuation. When in doubt, miss it out."

"Him and Bernard Shaw."

"And his writing's worse than yours. I can't make head or tail of this."

She indicated the small leather-bound volume.

"You need a glass. It's his trench journal. So far as I can make out it stops in spring 1917 when he was home on leave. He probably left it at home for safe-keeping and started a new one back in Flanders. God knows what happened to that."

"And these?" said Ellie, indicating the document folder.

"I haven't sorted them yet, but it looks like a record of Ada's efforts to get some real information about what actually happened to her father. Letters to the War Office, MPs, that sort of thing. And their replies. A record of frustration. But the earlier documents are the ones that signify. Here. Imagine that dropping through your letterbox."

He extracted a folded and faded sheet of paper and laid it before her. It was from the Infantry Records Office, dated November 1917.

Dear Mrs. Pascoe

I am directed to inform you that a report has been received from the War Office that your husband, Sergeant Pascoe, Peter, was sentenced by court-martial to suffer death by being shot, and this sentence was duly executed on November 20th 1917.

I am madam,
Your obedient servant,

The signature was illegible.

"Oh God," said Ellie. "I can't believe they really sent things like that."

"Only about three hundred of them," said Pascoe.

"The bastards, oh the bastards," said Ellie.

"It was all a long time ago, and what's three hundred against the millions who died in those years," said Pascoe. "I paraphrase."

"Don't get clever," she said fiercely. "We've barely enough time and energy to fight the here-and-now battles without busting our guts to right old wrongs. But this isn't a principle in here, Peter. This is a person. This is a whole sodding family!"

She banged her hand down on the open exercise book.

"Yeah. Ironic, eh?" said Pascoe. "Sorry, I'm not doing an I-told-you-so. I've found myself wishing that Ada had done what she felt tempted to do and burnt the whole bloody lot instead of dumping it in my lap."

"She might as well have done. It's not as if you're going to be able to get beyond the dead end she hit, are you?"

"I don't know. All I know is that somehow I seem to be right in the middle of it. You know what the house was called where Peter was brought up? Wanwood. And the family his mother nursemaided for were the Grindals. And this medical genius Sam Batty, his descendants and the Grindals still run the company. Look, there's a letter here from Herbert Grindal, commiserating with my great-grandmother. He was an officer in the Wyfies, and when I was looking though the old records at Wanwood this morning I came across his name as a patient there when it was a hospital during the war. I tell you, it's like being out in the Salient with shit coming at you from all sides!"

Ellie hacked a piece out of her lasagne, glad to be back in her role of the voice of reason.

"No shit, just good story lines for a Victorian novel," she said. "Where does it get you? Nowhere. Ada hit a barrier. You're going to need more than a bit of creepy coincidence to get you over it."

"There's always Poll Pollinger."

"Details of the trial, you mean? Don't build up your hopes. From the sound of it, these things weren't exactly conducted in ideal circumstances with a stenographer making a verbatim record. You know what he was charged with, you know he was found guilty. I suspect that even if Poll manages to wheedle a transcript out of her bent colonel, it'll occupy half a sheet of paper and won't tell you much more. This is personal, Peter. Keep it that way. Read his journals. From what I've seen so far, he sounds the kind of man you can be proud to be descended from. And if the war and the system broke him, then pray that you and yours will never be tested to breaking point. Every day I look at the telly and see things that make me think, that is beyond my endurance. Do that to me, and I would go under. Maybe we can change some of those things. Meanwhile, be proud, be hopeful, and eat your lasagne."

"Well, bugger me, as our daughter might have said before Miss Martindale waved her magic wand," said Pascoe. "I married a philosopher. Here's looking at you, Socrates."

He raised his glass. The phone rang.

"Shit," said Pascoe, feeling Miss Martindale would have approved.

He got up and went through into the hallway. Ellie heard his voice distantly but deliberately made no effort to organize sound into sense.

She saw by his face when he returned that she'd been right. This was not something she wanted to know.

"What?" she asked.

"It was Andy," he said. "Wendy Walker's died. And they've arrested Cap Marvell."

XII

BY FRIDAY LUNCHTIME, Ada's funeral seemed a long, long way away. Presumably Dalziel felt the distance he had traveled in the days between to be just as great if not greater.

Late that Monday night he had set eyes for the very first time on Cap Marvell. During the next couple of days he had, if rumor were right, entered into a meaningful relationship with her.

And on the evening of the third day, he had read her her rights.

The case against her was so far mainly circumstantial. They had found in her Discovery a bicycle clip matching the one found on Wendy Walker's right ankle, plus traces of oil and rust matching those on her cycle. Marvell explained these by claiming that on several occasions she'd given Walker and her bike a lift. In order to fit the machine into the storage area, Walker had removed the front wheel, thus possibly dislodging a considerable amount of rust and oil.

They had also found traces of blood on a rear seat. It was the same group as Walker's. Marvell recalled that one of the group had cut herself on a demo to which they'd been ferried in the Discovery. Tested, this woman proved to be Group O also.

There was a fresh scratch on the front bumper of the Discovery, which might have been caused by running over the front wheel of a bicycle, and debris collected

from the front tire treads was being subjected to every
test known to Dr. Death in an effort to establish a
transfer link with either the bike or Ludd Lane.

Cap Marvell's claims to have been at a wedding in
Scarborough on the date of the Redcar raid had been
substantiated. But closer inquiry had produced the information that a fair proportion of the official guests
had been political activists of one sort or another, including Meg Jenkins and Donna Linsey from ANIMA.
As for the extra unrecorded guests who turned up for
the pub party after the ceremony, it could be assumed
though not proven that the proportion here was even
higher.

"How far's Scarborough from Redcar. About fifty
miles?" said Pascoe.

"Hour's run on a quiet evening in a fast car," said
Wield.

"So someone says, 'This party's a bit dead, who fancies a bit of action? Let's head up the coast and liberate
a few downtrodden animals.' "

"That would explain the way they acted once they
got inside, you know, running riot and wrecking the
place. And with the luck of the half pissed they got
away scot-free."

"After giving poor Mark Shufflebottom a friendly
tap on the head to keep him quiet."

"Only, being half pissed, the tap was a bit harder
than intended and the poor sod keels over dead."

"Not realizing this, they head back down to the
party which has picked up again and goes on till the
break of day."

"Which is when they get the news on the radio, after
which they split, after taking a vow that everyone in the
group can recall seeing everyone else every minute of
the party, from the first champagne cork popping till
the last piss artist puking."

The elaboration of lack of intent was for Dalziel's benefit, but the basic scenario had a lot to commend it.

"What about the raid on Wanwood in the summer?" asked Pascoe. "Same style, lot of vandalism, animals just turned loose to roam the countryside. Does this mean they were pissed again?"

"Why not? Marvell says she had dinner with her son that night. From what you say, sir, that could have seen her well oiled by the time they parted."

By common consent, they had decided that there was no point in pussyfooting around Dalziel. Okay, if they saw a chance to suggest that Marvell's putative fatal assault upon the guard had been accidental rather than premeditated, there was no harm in taking it. But they both knew the Fat Man well enough to guess that any hint on their part that they were marking time on this one would have only served to force him into the painful task of doing the dirty work himself.

He nodded now and said, "Aye, that's about the strength of it. How about t'others in the group?"

"Alibis for that night? All tight, except for Jenkins and Linsey. The same two as went to the Scarborough wedding. They say they can't really recall so far back, but they think they had a quiet night in."

"What's one of them when it's at home?" said Dalziel with tautology that came close to pathos.

Pascoe said brightly, "Okay, so let's look at what we've got. What might or might not have been a dying declaration which fortunately Seymour had the wit to get on tape."

He pressed the button on the cassette deck on the table before them.

First Ellie's voice.

Wendy, it's okay, you're in hospital. It's so great to see your eyes open. Wendy, this is Ellie Pascoe. Can you hear me?

Then Wendy Walker.

Cap, Cap, Cap . . . oh why, why why?

The note of bewilderment was almost unbearable.

Pascoe resumed briskly. "On top of this we've got our knowledge of what Wendy was up to, the evidence of Marvell's propensity for violence in the TecSec statements, her lack of alibi for the dates of the Redcar raid and the first Wanwood raid, the physical traces of Walker's bike in the Discovery . . ."

There was a tap on the door followed by Seymour's bright red hair round it.

"Sorry," he said. "But we've found a witness. Terence Oliphant. Lives in one of them bungalows between Ludd Lane and the bypass. He was taking his dog for a walk in the field behind his house—that's the big meadow that abuts on Ludd Lane, when he saw the lights of a stationary vehicle in the lane. As he watched it took off moving very fast eastwards. He says he can't be sure about the make except that it was higher than an ordinary car, more like some kind of van. We showed him the silhouette of a Discovery and he said, yes, that could have been it."

"Why'd he not come forward himself?" growled Dalziel. "Doesn't he read the papers?"

"Yes, that was the trouble. All the reports of where the body was found with the bike beyond it suggested she'd been hit by a car traveling westwards so he couldn't see how this might have had anything to do with it."

"God help us when the sodding citizenry become detectives," said Dalziel. "Time?"

"Half nine-ish."

It fitted.

Pascoe said, "Good work, Dennis. Thanks."

When the door had closed he said, "Okay, another piece of circumstantial, but we're still a long way from anything that's going to impress the CPS. We need something more. . . ."

"There is something more," said Dalziel tonelessly.

Oh shit, thought Pascoe. Not pillow talk, this last indignity of a noble tec.

"She says she left the university party early to go home and watch her interview on telly. Well, I watched it with Bog-eye at the party. And soon as it were done, I drove off to Marvell's flat. Only it were in darkness. Then I saw her coming from the garage block where she parks her vehicle and go into the building."

"What did you do then, sir?" asked Pascoe.

"Drove off home."

Pascoe let out a sigh of relief. CID CHIEF BONKS KILLER HOT FROM SCENE OF CRIME was not a headline he cared to envisage.

"Have you put this to her, sir?" asked Wield.

"Not yet. But she's been asked every which way if she went straight home from the party and watched the interview. She says yes every time."

"It's got to be put to her direct, sir," urged Pascoe.

"Teach your grandmother," snarled the Fat Man. Then he passed his hand over his face, putting Pascoe in mind of an eclipse of the moon.

"Sorry," said Dalziel. "I were just trying to think how I'd use it if it weren't me but some independent witness that had come forward with the story. I think I'd have still hung on. But I can't be sure. Pete, time I did what I should have done a lot earlier. You take over the running of this case. Okay?"

"Good lord, sir, your memory's going," said Pascoe. "You disqualified yourself from being in charge yesterday lunchtime, the minute that Ellie told us what Walker had been up to. It was only at my personal insistence that you interviewed Ms. Marvell yesterday afternoon, because I felt that the personal link would be conducive to getting to the truth. Don't you remember, Wieldy?"

"That's right," said Wield. "I mean, any fool 'ud

know a man of your experience wouldn't compromise the handling of a case where he was personally involved."

Dalziel regarded them both blankly for a moment, then gave a faint smile.

"Must be mixing my drinks is making me forgetful. I'll cut down on the water," he said. "So what's your plan, Chief Inspector?"

"Question first, sir. This Cap Marvell, I've not yet met her. All I know about her is what I've heard from my wife, and from you. So tell me, in your opinion, could she have done this?"

"By God, give some buggers a little bit of power and it goes right to their heads," said Dalziel. But there was no force in it. Pascoe could tell he was seriously pondering the question. As presumably he had been seriously pondering it for the past twenty-four hours.

He said, "Hitting a guard in the heat of the moment and accidentally killing him. Aye, I could see her doing that. Could see meself doing that. You too, Wieldy. Mebbe not you, Peter, though I don't know. But if you did, you'd likely be running forward to confess and make amends."

"And Ms. Marvell?" insisted Pascoe.

"No. Like me she'd think that what's done is done, and why rush forward to suffer for what you didn't intend and can't change? And she'd be bloody good at covering her tracks too. No Lady Macbeth stuff."

Pity, thought Pascoe. Lady Mac meets Falstaff. Would have made a great play.

He said, "And if we move on from accident? You say she'd be good at covering her tracks. How far might she go? Cold-blooded murder?"

Dalziel said, "Two days back I'd have said impossible."

"And two days on?"

The Fat Man didn't hesitate.

"As a man, still impossible. But I've seen too many poor sods thinking with their cocks to be impressed. As a cop, the old rule's got to apply. Guilty till proved innocent. That's what I hope you'll prove, lad. And because I hope it so fucking much, that's why I've handed things over to you. I need a run off."

He rose and left the room.

Pascoe said, "Set that to music and you'd have one of the greatest romantic arias of all time."

"Aye, and I know just the guy to sing the part."

"Who?"

"Pavarotti," said Wield. "Mind you, he'd have to put on a bit of weight."

Dalziel in the corridor heard them laughing. He didn't mind, even if they were laughing at him or his predicament.

Man of my age gets his bollocks in the mangle, he deserves laughing at, he reflected. And they were good lads, eager to do their best to aid the disenmanglement with minimum pain.

Feeling somewhat comforted, he headed to the loo.

XIII

JIMMY HOWARD WAS STILL in police custody, but only just.

After the arrival of the TecSec solicitor he had made a statement which completely denied any knowledge of the contents of the envelope found in his car.

In fact when the lab analysis was complete, it turned out that Howard might have been pretty safe even without his denial, as the capsules contained ketamine hydrochloride, a mild hallucinogenic which, known as

Special K, had a moderate street value, but hadn't yet made it to the banned drugs list.

The small Mid-Yorks Drug Squad had tossed the case back at Wield, saying they had enough on their plate without wasting time on what looked at best like a case of simple theft and receiving stolen property.

The lab assistant, Jane Ambler, had been interviewed in her home the previous night. She had denied handing any envelope to Howard and showed no reaction to talk of fingerprints, a calmness confirmed when examination revealed only one usable thumbprint on the envelope. This was definitely Howard's and provided Wield with the thin thread by which he kept the ex-constable tethered in custody.

Search of both the woman's home and Howard's had failed to throw up any supporting evidence.

Wield ran it all in front of Peter Pascoe, who said, "Looks like a politician's promise to me. Prick it and what have you got? Your evidence that you saw a person who *might* have been Ambler handing Howard an envelope that *might* have been the one found in his car containing a legal drug. Without an admission, this one's a no-no."

"I was doing fine with Howard till that likely lad sent by TecSec turned up," said Wield gloomily.

"Staff perks," said Pascoe. "But he's going to find it hard to carry on at Wanwood without being able to drive out there. This should mean his license goes for at least another year."

"Yeah. Great result," said Wield.

"What about Ambler? No cracks there?"

"Butter wouldn't melt."

"In her mouth?"

"In her anything," said Wield savagely.

"You don't like her?"

"I saw her injecting a little monkey."

Pascoe raised his eyebrows at this nonprofessional

reaction from the man he'd always regarded as the acme of professionalism. Perhaps Dalziel was right and the sergeant had undergone some sea change in Enscombe.

"Anyway it'll clear the decks, and we'll need plenty of space to get this business with Marvell sorted."

"Finding out who killed Walker, you mean," emended Wield gently.

"Yes, that's what I meant. Listen I reckon it's time I met the famous Cap. Why don't you see if you can make contact with Walker's sister-in-law, the widow in Redcar, see if she'd heard anything recently. Someone ought to tell her the news anyway."

"I think mebbe I'll leave that to the locals," said Wield. "But I will have a word myself. After I've been back to Wanwood."

"Wanwood? Look, forget those files for the time being. We've more important fish to fry."

"Not the files. I wanted to have a word with Dr. Batty about drug records and staff supervision. He was busy this morning so I didn't like to press."

Pascoe grinned and said, "Meaning you reckon you can keep Jimmy banged up so long as you're still pursuing inquiries. When's his first twenty-four hours up? About teatime? I don't think anyone's going to give you an extension."

"Me neither," said Wield. "How's Ellie?"

"Fine. Why?"

"Walker was a mate, wasn't she? And from what she told us yesterday, it strikes me she could easy start blaming herself."

The same thought had occurred to Pascoe the previous night, but there'd been little sign of breast-beating from his wife so he'd thought it best to let sleeping dogs lie. Wield's concern still came as a reproach.

"She's fine. I'm just going to give her a ring actually."

The phone was answered on the second ring as if Ellie had been expecting a call.

He said, "Hi, love. How are you?"

"Pretty well. Anything happening?"

"Just proceeding with inquiries. Which means that Cap's spent most of the morning with her solicitor while we've been checking everything twice."

"And?"

"And she's still in the frame. Good news is, Andy's out of it. I'm in charge now."

"Good God. What did you use? A bulldozer?"

"He went like a lamb. You sure you're okay?"

"Yes. Well, still a bit numb. Listen, if you're worried I think it's all my fault, well, I do, a bit. But I'm not sure how much till you idle sods find out what really happened. Like the man said, guilt without responsibility is the prerogative of the masochist throughout the ages. And while I don't mind a bit of biting by way of erotic arousal, I draw the line at the whip. But I'm glad you rang. I've just had Poll Pollinger on the line."

"Oh yes. Any luck?"

"Well, she's seen the file on the court-martial, but says that her pet colonel reckoned the Ministry of D would make whatever she can do to him seem painless if he let her make photocopies. What she did though was make pretty comprehensive notes of the things she thought you'd want to know. Even these are a bit risky and she wanted to make sure that either you or I were around before she faxed them here. Even as we speak the modern marvel which turns your house into a litter bin is starting to talk. Hang on a sec. I'll just check to make sure it is Poll's notes and not some double-glazing handout."

There was a pause then she resumed, "Yes, it is. Field General Court Martial of Sergeant Peter Pascoe convened at Zillebeke November 1917, Officer Presiding—"

"Yes, fine," interrupted Pascoe. "I'll see it all later. Not sure when. If I'm going to be late, I'll try to let you know. . . ."

"Hang on, Peter. Before you go. That chap who called the other night, the rather charming military gent with bits missing. What was his name?"

"Studholme. Major Hilary Studholme. Why?"

"Well, just a coincidence perhaps, but your great-granddad's Prisoner's Friend, which Poll glosses as untrained defense counsel, is down here as Captain Thomas Hilary Studholme of the West Yorkshire Fusiliers. Interesting, huh?"

For a moment Pascoe was back in the museum mock-up of the front line trench with the lifelike dummy reclining on the camp bed, open on his breast a copy of *The Wood Beyond the World* inscribed *To Hillie from Mummy*.

"Peter, you still there?"

"Yes," he said. "I am. And you're right. Very interesting indeed."

When Wield arrived at Wanwood, Des Patten was waiting for him.

"What's the word on Jimmy Howard?" he asked.

"Helping with inquiries," said Wield.

"You gonna do him for drugs? No, don't look like that. It's not a guilty secret. Tony Beasley gave the captain a bell."

"So much for client confidentiality. Would it bother you if we did?"

"I'd have to hire a replacement."

"So, not personally?"

Patten shrugged.

"I hate to see anyone getting into bother, but there's bother and bother. Like in the mob, one of your men gets himself in trouble for nutting some shortchanging barman or shagging some local scrubber, you rally round, send him on a course, say he was on guard duty that night. He gets in bother with stealing a mate's dosh, or flogging his ring down the park, then that's it. He's out, and good riddance."

"How about a drugs charge?"

"Out. In both cases. In the mob, no one wants a hophead backing you up."

"And in TecSec?"

"We're very particular. Get a criminal record and it's goodbye."

"Not bothered by driving over the limit though? Or driving without a license?"

Patten frowned.

"Over the limit can happen to anyone," he said. "But not having a license . . . that's plain stupid. I didn't know. We sometimes do driving jobs. That could have got us in big bother."

"He's got himself in it, certainly. But the way it's looking, that might be all he's facing. No way your clever young brief's going to get him off that."

"Beasley was the captain's idea. Very paternalistic, the captain. Good quality in an officer, getting close to the men. That's why they have NCOs make sure they don't take it too far."

"Like with Rosso?"

Dalziel had passed on Piers Pitt-Evenlode's revelations about Buster Sanderson's interesting military career.

"What's that mean?" said Patten, very alert.

"Just that he must have been very upset by the accident."

"He was," said Patten. "Very upset. Dr. Batty's waiting for you. I'd tread careful. He's not in a very good mood today."

He turned smartly on his heel and marched away.

Dismissed, thought Wield.

Batty jumped up from his armchair as Wield entered

the staff sitting room. He looked pale and drawn as if he hadn't slept much last night.

"Sergeant," he said, running his hand through his soft brown hair. "What's all this about Jane Ambler?"

"Do you use ketamine hydrochloride in your labs, sir?" said Wield.

"K? Why, yes. Sometimes. What's that got to do with anything?"

"What do you use it for, sir?"

"As a relaxant. In certain circumstances as an anaesthetic. It was developed by the Americans for veterinary purposes initially, and because our experimental animals are used in tests which can involve anything from new drugs to surgery we have to have available a wide variety of control techniques so we can be quite sure whatever tests we're conducting on a new drug, say, aren't being affected by an existing drug. . . ."

"I'm with you," said Wield. "So would it be possible for you to check your supplies of K and see if any is missing?"

"How much are we talking?"

"Twelve capsules."

Batty shook his head in irritation as if Wield had said something stupid.

Who's been rattling his cage? wondered the sergeant.

"We make up our own capsules here if we need them, so it's not just a matter of counting. Twelve you say? Couple of grams tops. Well, we'd know of course how much has been used and where it's been used. But if anyone cared to change the proportions slightly, or if a spillage was reported . . ."

"Spillage? What do you mean?"

"For heavens sake, don't you speak English?" snapped Batty. "These are animals we are dealing with here, Sergeant. Some of them quite large and strong. They don't all just lie there and take it, you know.

Quite often there will be some wastage as we administer a dosage. Of course then we start again from scratch. A spillage will be sluiced away, not swept up and used again."

He gave a little shudder as though offended by the thought.

"Very hygienic, I'm sure," murmured Wield. "Can we take a look?"

They took a look. The records and the amount of the drug remaining checked exactly. There were, however, three reported spillages involving Jane Ambler.

"Butterfingers," said Wield.

"Even these amounts wouldn't be enough for twelve capsules," objected Batty.

"Then mebbe she put a bit aside for herself whenever she used the drug," said Wield.

"But that might have had an effect on some of our experiments!" said Batty indignantly.

"I assume, if it were being used as an anaesthetic, it wouldn't have been very pleasant for the poor animals either," retorted Wield.

Batty eyed him narrowly.

"Sergeant Wield, I assure you we have the very highest regard for the welfare of our animals. Now before we go further I insist you tell me what precise evidence you have against Miss Ambler or any other member of my staff."

"Not enough to bring charges, not yet," Wield replied. "But enough to make me suggest, sir, that you take a very thorough inventory of the drugs in your care and review your security procedures in respect of them."

It sounded pretty neutral to him but Batty was clearly at the end of his short fuse.

He said harshly, "I don't need you to tell me how to run my labs, Sergeant. Not when you can't organize a piss-up in your own brewery."

"Don't follow, sir," said Wield, conventionally stolid.

"You're acting like you're one hundred percent sure that a crime's been committed here but you're telling me there's nothing you can do about it," he sneered. "What a way to run a police force! Well, if you can't act, I can. Good day to you, Sergeant."

He turned and marched away.

Dismissed again, thought Wield.

As he unlocked his car, Patten appeared again, smiling.

"Warned you not to upset the doc, didn't I? He can be really vindictive."

"How do you know what I've been doing?"

"Watching you on closed-circuit of course. It's all right, it's not wired for sound but I could tell you weren't whispering sweet nothings in his ear. Look, I should mebbe have warned you, you could be on a hiding to nothing bad-mouthing Miss Fridgidaire. They're very close, know what I mean?"

He gave an exaggerated pelvic thrust.

Wield looked at him in surprise. He hadn't got the feeling that Batty felt particularly protective to Jane Ambler. On the contrary.

"How do you know this?" he asked.

"The old CCTV again. Like Nixon and them tapes, you get so used to a thing you forget it's still working even when you don't want it. Saw them at it right there where they keep the animals. Makes you wonder who should be in cages, doesn't it?"

"No competition. This system, was it running the night those women ran wild?"

"Sure."

"Why'd you not mention it?"

"Why the hell should I? No crime, no damage, no charges, what's to mention? If you'd asked you could have seen it. And don't say you didn't know. The cameras are there for all to see and you've seen the monitors."

"Fair point. Like to see it now but if it's not been wiped."

"We do a five-day cycle so you should be just in time. Anything in particular?"

"When you cornered Marvell and she looked set to take a swing with the wire cutters."

"You keep on about that. Why so interested? There was no harm done."

"Not this time."

It was a silly thing to say. The old silent Wield wouldn't have let it slip. The sweet relaxing air of Enscombe wasn't all beneficial.

He could see Patten's sharp mind working.

"This time . . . eh, you're never trying to tie that old bird in with that poor devil those bastards topped at FraserGreenleaf?"

He laughed his derision out loud.

"Suppose that old bird *had* taken a swing," said Wield. "And your head *had* got in the way?"

Patten considered and his expression became serious.

"Yeah, well, she's certainly got the upper body development to get that thing moving . . . and there was a moment when I thought she was going to have to go for sure . . . but look, there has to be something else behind all this. I mean, you can piss around with the likes of Jimmy Howard because it suits you, but someone who talks like her . . ."

It was a crude but not altogether inaccurate analysis of what Pascoe would call the social dynamic of police investigation.

Wield said carefully, "We should have checked the TV tapes earlier. That was an oversight. All I'm doing now is covering my back. And I would be particularly interested if you could watch with me and try to recall exactly what was being said."

"Always keen to cooperate with the police, Sergeant," said Patten. "Let's go take a look."

XIV

"IF A CONDEMNED MAN has bad toothache on the eve of his execution, what does he spend the night thinking about?"

"Sorry, Pete?" said Lionel Harris. "Is this relevant?"

"Oh yes," said Pascoe. Doubly so. First, it dramatized his own dilemma in that ever since his conversation with Ellie, despite being landed with an inquiry which looked like tying in Andy Dalziel with a double killer, all he could think of was Hilary Studholme, junior and senior. He recalled his feeling the night the major called round that the man had had more to say, or not to say. Would he have come running so quickly merely to confirm that the Sergeant Pascoe his father had so unsuccessfully defended was Ada's father if that was all he knew? And why hadn't he mentioned his own family involvement?

No, there had to be more. There might be a clue in Poll Pollinger's digest, but Pascoe guessed it was going to take another trip to the regimental museum to get to the real bottom of this.

On a quieter day he might have bunked off, but today he owed it to Dalziel to keep his nose to the grindstone. If only he could keep his mind there too!

Then he'd been told that Cap Marvell's brief wanted

a word and when he saw who it was, he'd known he needed all his wits about him.

Lionel Harris, familiarly known as "Bomber," might be grayer round the temples and roomier round the waist than on their first encounter many years ago, but he was still the same sharp little man who'd made Pascoe look a twit (and without him noticing it!) on the young DC's very first appearance in a Mid-Yorkshire court.

So he chucked his disguised dilemma at the solicitor's head in an effort to wrong-foot him as soon as he came through the door.

"I've never come across a case of suicide while the balance of the molars was disturbed, so I assume that on the whole the greater fear would dominate the lesser pain."

"I wonder," said Pascoe thoughtfully. "Still, it's always good to get a legal perspective. So how can I help you, Lionel?"

They had become friends, or at least friendly foes, over the years. But each knew the other had a different bottom line.

"I just wanted a word, off the record, about the position of my client, Amanda Marvell. You know how I hate making an official fuss . . ."

"Oh yes. Printed in block capitals on the file we keep on you," murmured Pascoe. " 'Hates making a fuss.' "

". . . but in this case my client has cooperated fully. Nay, in my opinion she has cooperated to excess, making no complaint when she was kept in custody overnight, offering no threat of action for false imprisonment, refusing to let news of her maltreatment be released to the media, quietly answering all your questions, and enduring with restraint and dignity all the indignities heaped upon her. But enough is enough . . ."

"There we have no argument," interrupted Pascoe. "In fact, I doubt if I've ever heard you say a truer word. Enough is indisputably enough. But as I'm in charge of this case, it would seem a dereliction of my duty if I let Ms. Marvell go without personally ascertaining that everything has been done by the book."

"I'm sorry?" said Harris, alert. "You say you're in charge, Peter? I thought Mr. Dalziel . . ."

"Disqualified himself immediately on the grounds of personal involvement," said Pascoe. "But because he and Ms. Marvell know each other socially, I thought it might make matters less stressful for her if she spoke to the superintendent to start with, under my supervision of course. I hope Ms. Marvell hasn't found anything to upset her in this mode of procedure?"

"Well, no," said Harris, who Pascoe guessed had been saving up his complaint about Dalziel's involvement as a final body blow. That he would know about the relationship, Pascoe was sure. From what Ellie had told him there had been too many of Mid-Yorkshire's great and good at the university party for Cap Marvell's escort not to have set their collective imagination reeling.

"Good. Then let's have the lady in, shall we?"

He had seen her distantly before, but never spoken to her. Close up, he found her rather heavy features untouched by makeup after her night in the cell disappointed any expectation he had of sharing Dalziel's sense of attraction. Okay, she had great knockers if your fancy erred toward field sports, but she didn't light his touch paper.

"I'm sorry if I'm a disappointment," she said. "But at least we neither of us can be accused of concealment, can we?"

He felt himself blushing. It was as if she'd overheard his pathetically macho thoughts. She'd certainly read his reaction on his face.

"I do hope not," he managed in recovery. "In fact, to make absolutely sure, I'd like to go over one or two things with you once more."

Her steady wide-eyed gaze reminded him of someone, Miss Martindale, that was who. No other resemblance of age, figure, or coloring, but that same sense of being in the presence of someone whose actions were based on rock-hard certainties. Would Miss Martindale take a swing at anyone she felt was in the way of her duty to her pupils? Metaphorically, without doubt. Literally? If the kids were locked in cages and being experimented upon, yes, very probably. But the parallel was inexact. You couldn't compare kids and animals. Like Rosie, he might be tempted to hurl a stone at someone beating a dog, but it would take someone beating Rosie to turn him homicidal.

"You have a son, Ms. Marvell," he said.

"Yes."

"I don't see what my client's family has to do with this," said Harris.

"Really? But you must be aware that Colonel Pitt-Evenlode provides the alibi for one of the dates we're interested in? Surely you don't object to my referring to witnesses?"

"No, of course not . . ."

It was nice to bomb Bomber, thought Pascoe.

"Your son confirms your dinner engagement on the night in question. Neither of you were able to be very precise about the time you finished. Fortunately the restaurant credit card system records time of transaction among all the other details. And even more fortunately they maintain their records. The colonel paid the bill at nine thirty-two p.m. This is rather earlier than either of your estimates. The colonel's was tennish, if I recall. And yours was, let me see, ten to ten-thirty, plus another fifteen minutes to go to the cloakroom, get your coat et cetera, and make your way to the exit where your son had called a taxi."

"Is there a point you are laboring towards, Peter?" asked Harris.

"Simply this. Ms. Marvell's original estimate that she arrived home about eleven p.m. made it difficult for her to have changed—I presume that she would have changed—and driven out to Wanwood House to be involved in a break-in there, which the night watchman, who as you will recall was locked in his room with the telephone wires cut, recorded as commencing at a quarter past eleven."

He was pleased to see his orotund style was irritating Harris. But an irritated Bomber is not a man you want to be in the same room as.

"Perhaps you could clear up a small point for me," he said. "On both these occasions my client had been wining and dining. No doubt, through bills at the restaurant and witnesses at the wedding, you can ascertain just how much wine. Hardly the best preparation for an expedition such as you allege."

"Not if planned," agreed Pascoe. "But if spontaneous, alcohol could be a contributory factor rather than a point in rebuttal."

Hint of a deal there. Diminished responsibility? Well, why not?

Bomber was smiling.

"My point is that while a trio of tipsy ladies might have effected entry to Wanwood, which at the time in question was I gather secured only by one man and his dog, I really can't see how even the luck of the drunk could have got them undetected into FraserGreenleaf's plant, which had much more sophisticated protection from a top national security firm."

The same point had already struck Pascoe.

He said weakly, "I daresay an hour's drive had sobered them up."

"Indeed. And even on your short acquaintance with Ms. Marvell, you must have concluded that she is a very sensible woman. Sober, would she have proceeded with such an insanely stupid action?"

Cap Marvell coughed gently but compellingly.

"I am still here," she said mildly. "And while I'm pleased to have your advice, Mr. Harris, I think it might speed matters up if Mr. Pascoe is allowed to ask his questions and I to answer them as best I can."

This is the world upside down, thought Pascoe. Suspect rebukes the brief and offers full unaggressive co-operation to the fuzz! Time to join in the daftness.

He said, "Ms. Marvell, why are you being so calm and cooperative?"

She turned that wide candid gaze upon him and this time he felt some of her power of attraction.

"Because I feel I owe Superintendent Dalziel this. Because when I walk out of here, which I hope will be sooner rather than later, I want to feel certain that I have left you no excuse to haul me back in. Because, you should understand, Mr. Pascoe, that this is your one free shot. After this it's press, television, letters to my MP, claims for damages, barristers, High Court, European Court, the lot. So do carry on."

Pascoe glanced at Harris. The solicitor gave him a sympathetic smile and a sorry-I-can't-help-you shrug, then settled back in his chair to enjoy the show.

Bastard, thought Pascoe. All those years, and he still lets me talk myself into trouble!

He said, "These occasions when you claim you gave Ms. Walker and her bicycle a lift in your car, let's take another look at them . . ."

"So you've let her go?" said Ellie.

"Had to."

"Threatening noises off from the Hero?"

"No. Evidently Lieutenant Colonel Pitt-Evenlode is

taking it all in his stride. But then he is still under the impression that mummy is merely being investigated for another of her silly little free-the-wee-beasties stunts."

"Why didn't you put Andy's sighting of her the night of the party to her?"

"Because at the moment it's all we've got, and if she looked a jury straight in the eye and said, 'He's lying,' I'm not sure who they'd believe."

"You're sure who *you* believe?"

"Of course," he said. "But I'd like a bit of support so that a simple denial won't get her off the hook. All we want is a firm sighting of her Discovery driving around when she says she was watching telly. Or even someone from one of the other flats noticing the time of her return."

"But do you really think she did it?" said Ellie.

Pascoe shrugged and said, "Open mind, but Bomber's point about a bunch of drunks getting past Security at Redcar is a good one."

"I didn't ask if you thought she killed that guard," said Ellie. "Do you think she might have killed Wendy?"

"But if the two are linked . . ."

"Could be they're not. Could be that she had some completely different motive for getting rid of Wendy and she's laughing her socks off at the unedifying sight of you and fat Andy barking up the wrong tree."

Pascoe shook his head in admiration of his wife's devious thought processes. Perhaps it took a woman to suss out a woman. Perhaps he should hand this one over to WDC Novello.

He said, "You think she might have done it then?"

"For the right reason, perhaps. What I'm certain of is she's very manipulative. One way or another she's good at getting people to dance to her tune. But I see

I'm boring you. What you really want is to take a look at Poll's fax, isn't it?"

"I'm trying not to want it," said Pascoe wearily. "And no, love, you don't bore me. Ever."

He gave her a kiss to prove it. But when she led him to the dining room where she'd arranged the fax sheets on the table, he didn't resist.

Poll's covering note was admirably terse and to the point.

> The record of your great grandfather's trial consists of (1) the official court-martial papers detailing the charge (2) the names of those taking part (3) the president's notes on witnesses' statements and any cross-questioning (4) written evidence presented (5) defence (6) sentence and recommendations (7) written comments from C.O. on character and record (8) written opinions from brigade, corps, and army commanders on whether the sentence should be commuted or carried out (9) Army Form B 122 which is your g. grandfather's conduct sheet (10) the commander in chief's signature confirming his agreement with sentence. I am sending you my notes as I made them, no embellishments. I know that what you want is simply the facts.

There was no signature. Poll didn't believe in taking more chances than she had to.

Pascoe turned to the notes.

> (1) cowardice in face of the enemy—September 26 1917 in Polygon Wood—during advance, assaulted platoon commander Lt. Grindal—told survivors of platoon their orders were to with-

draw—and led them back to their starting line on
south edge of wood. NB authorities spoilt for
choice—striking SO, quitting post, disobedience,
casting away arms, mutiny, all capital.

(2) President—Major Arthur Lippman plus
Captain John Partridge and Lieutenant Lionel
Holliday. Prosecuting officer—Captain Hartley
Evenlode (Adj. WYF)—Prisoner's friend—Cap-
tain Thomas Hilary Studholme.

(3) First witness for pros. Major Vernon—Australian—came across small group of men shelter-
ing in trench—asked what they were doing—one
of them—Private Doyle—said they were sole survivors of 2 platoon WYFs and had been ordered
back. Vernon asked, By whom? Doyle said sergeant had relayed order. Where sergeant? Gone
further back with wounded officer. Where weapons? Ordered to throw them away by sergeant.
Vernon made note of names and unit. Own duties
didn't leave time for further investigation.

Second witness Sergeant Mackie, Field Ambulance Unit on duty at Advanced Aid Station. Sergeant Pascoe appeared with Lieutenant Grindal—
half carrying him, though Lt. was conscious. P.
put him down and asked Mackie to take a look at
him. He went to sit a few yards away and lit a
cigarette. Mackie examined Lt. and found no sign
of injury other than severe bruising to jaw. Pres.
asked if any theory about cause and Mackie said,
as if he'd been punched. Mackie said he asked
Sergeant P. if he was injured and he said no, he'd
be going back forward shortly, he just wanted to
make sure the Lt. was all right.

Third witness, Captain Ainstable, Staff Officer.
Gathering info on progress of assault on Polygon.

Noticed Sergeant P. Asked if he was getting
treated, told no. Asked what he was doing there.
Told he was having a smoke. Asked why he
wasn't with his unit. Told that most of them were
dead and if he, the Capt., didn't believe it, he was
free to go into the wood and take a look for himself. Capt. then ordered his arrest—for insubordination initially, but on checking with Mackie on
suspicion of desertion. (Yet another poss.
charge!)

Fourth witness, Private Doyle. Said the platoon
took very heavy casualties during advance
through Polygon. Heard Sergt. P continually
urging Lt. Grindal to slow down and take cover.
Pres asked if this came across as military advice
from old experienced soldier to young officer.
Doyle said no, impression he got was Sergt. P.
was shit scared. Pres: Which you weren't? Doyle:
Oh yes. But like most of the rest of them it was
his job to keep going till ordered to stop, not to
tell other people what to do. (NB Clearly impressed Pres. as honest answer from good English
yeoman) Finally came under heavy fire from pillbox. Many of platoon killed at this point. Last
saw Lt. standing up with revolver in hand. Got
impression he was pointing it at sergt. and urging
him forwards. Then there was shell blast. When
smoke and debris cleared, Lt. and sergt. no longer
visible but shortly afterwards sergt. appeared,
said Lt. was injured and that they should withdraw. Doyle asked on whose authority. Sergt.
said Lt. had passed on order just before he was
injured by shell blast. Said he would see to Lt.
himself, but others followed and when he saw
them, sergt. ordered them to throw away their
rifles and give him a hand. When they demurred

he said, OK if you'd rather be dead with a gun than live without one, that's your business. Pres: but you did throw your weapons away? Doyle: only so we could help the Lt. out of wood with Lt. recovering use of legs a bit. Sergt. said that others should take cover while he saw Lt. safely back to aid post. Pres: what did you do after Major Vernon spoke to you? Doyle: what we'd been on the point of doing when he arrived. Went forward again to recover our weapons and make contact with rest of battalion. Which Capt. Evenlode (pros.) said he could confirm Doyle eventually did, the other two both having been killed en route. Capt. Evenlode also threw in that on an earlier occasion he had personally witnessed defendant acting threateningly towards Lt. Grindal and he'd only been deterred from putting him on charge by Lt.'s vigorous opposition.

Fifth witness Major Winander RAMC. On duty at Advanced Casualty Clearing Post. Examined Lt. Grindal, confirmed Mackie's diagnosis, no wounds except for contusion on jaw but severely dazed and deafened probably from shell blast. Later examined Sergt. Pascoe. Confirmed uninjured except for lacerations on knuckles of right hand. Pres: as if acquired by punching something? Major: yes. Pascoe was by then in custody of military police. Grindal was sent to casualty clearing station but unfortunately the ambulance he was travelling in was blown over by a shell. Lt. sustained broken arm and ribs. But major reaffirmed that prior to this he had no injuries except to his jaw.

(NB No record of Prisoner's Friend having asked any questions of these witnesses. This not unusual. Being too clever could antagonize court and implication of cross-examination was that pres. of court was not doing his job properly.)

(4) This kind of written evidence unusual. Explains delay between offence and FGCM. Lt. Grindal's evidence dictated to his father Arthur Grindal because of difficulty with writing with broken arm, and sent from UK. Lt. said that during attack he could recall sergt. declaring that the tactics were misconceived and would achieve nothing but all their deaths. Casualties were indeed heavy though to some extent this could be put down to slow progress caused by sergt.'s extreme caution, thus giving enemy time to get a line on them. Way blocked by pillbox. Essential they took it at any cost, but sergt. said it was madness, they must go back. He remonstrated with sergt. then something hit him on the jaw and everything went black. Remembers nothing more till arrival at dressing station. Definitely gave no order to withdraw because he received no order to withdraw. Deeply conscious that any man could snap in heat of battle and begged court to show compassion to Sergt. Pascoe who had been showing signs of being under strain for some time.

Accompanying letter from Arthur Grindal. Says that despite son's desire to cover up for Sergt. Pascoe, he feels it his duty to speak out if only to prevent others from being put at risk by future association with the sergt. who used to be in his, Grindal's, employ before war. Despite many favours shown, he proved to be an unreliable workman, preferring to associate with union and socialist freethinkers rather than advancing

his family and his firm's interests by putting in an
honest day's work for a good day's pay. Even on
his recent leave he had been observed at a socialist rally in Leeds which advocated following the
Russian example of insurrection against the legal
authorities and replacing the king and parliament
by a council of workers, as well as withdrawing
all troops from the Front and leaving the enemies
of our country to deal with France as they wished.
Nevertheless Grindal hoped that the army might
temper justice with mercy etc. (If there'd been
any doubt about verdict, which there probably
wasn't, this letter was the clincher. It was never
read out in court, not being strictly speaking relevant to the facts of the case. Lt. Grindals letter
was read out.)

(5) Sergt. Pascoe made a statement saying that
after the shell blast had left Lt. Grindal unfit to
give orders, command of platoon had fallen on
him and he'd judged it best to get Lt. back to aid
post, suspecting that he might have internal injuries as well as evident shock. Admitted striking
Lt. to restrain him from blundering forward to
certain death from pillbox machine guns. After
depositing Lt. it was his intention to go forward
again after a short rest to make contact with Battalion HQ and get further orders. Pres. asked why
he'd told remnants of platoon that Lt. had communicated order to withdraw. Replied, if he'd
given it himself men might have been put in bad
light when explaining actions later, but by implying it was Batt. HQ order, he'd put them in clear.
Pres made note saying it was clear sergt. knew he
was doing wrong. Asked him why after Lt. inca-
pacitated by shell blast he didn't attempt to contact battalion officers on either flank. Sergt. said

he'd no idea who was still alive and after what he'd seen in his section it wasn't likely to be many. Pres: was that a criticism of the tactics involved in the assault? Sergt: it was a criticism of the whole fucking campaign. Reproved for swearing. Pres: you are aware that the assault on Polygon Wood was a success and at the end of the attack the wood was firmly in the hands of the comrades you turned your back on? Sergt. replied, but it wasn't a wood. He wished to hell they'd all stop calling things names that no longer fitted. A wood was a place with trees and undergrowth, with green shade and birds singing and mossy tracks and maybe rabbits and deer playing around. These so-called woods he'd spent the last few weeks watching good men die over were nowt but blasted stumps sticking up out of churned up ground where your only solid footing was like to be a dead man's bones, and if you nailed a crosspiece on every stump to turn them into grave markers, there'd still not be enough for all the men who'd died to take or defend them. And there was none of them worth it, not one of these so-called sodding woods, whatever picture it might give folk back home of cavalry trotting under oak and beech. Their names were a deceit. The whole campaign in the Salient was a deceit. Every fighting man in the army, including those in this court, knew that the taking of Polygon Wood, and of the other pathetic two or three miles of muddy hell that had been covered these last few weeks, wouldn't bring the end of the war a day nearer. If after this the leaders on both sides couldn't see how futile the whole business was, then what was to stop them fighting on till they ran out of men to fight with?

(Pres made what look like verbatim notes of all this. Must have scribbled furiously. Perhaps he felt that prisoner's personal statement merited close consideration. Only comment at end was SANITY? Not an issue, of course. Catch-22 had always applied. If Arthur Grindal's letter clinched verdict, this outburst probably put lid on any hope of a strong recommendation to mercy.)

This was end of defence. No witnesses called, everyone possible having been called by prosecution.

(6) Verdict guilty, sentence death, no recommendation to mercy.

(7) C.O. says sergt. had shown many good qualities as soldier but recently stories had been circulating that he was centre of disaffection based on idea that working men with pacifist inclinations on both sides should unite in refusing to fight any more. Lt. Grindal had given assurances from personal knowledge of sergt. that he could keep him straight. C.O.'s sense that Lt. had suffered personal betrayal meant he could not demur from court's verdict.

(8) After such comments at battalion level, verdict was rubber-stamped approved all way up the line of command.

(9) B 122 exemplary. Shows what a lot of fucking notice they took of that!

(10) Confirmed. Signed Douglas Haig CiC.

(That's it. Apart from sergt.'s spirited outburst, it's pretty well par for the course. Evidence as it stands made it almost impossible for F.G.C.M. not to bring in guilty verdict. But in terms of basic legal and human rights—and I mean those which were accepted and operative in civvy courts in 1917—the whole shebang is a mess which you wouldn't shoot a dingo on. Absence of ref. to Prisoner's Friend doesn't necessarily mean the poor bastard didn't do his best, but only that Pres. of Court, possibly out of kindness to a fellow officer because he knew that senior eyes which got bloodshot at any hint of a troublemaker would be scanning these records, didn't feel the need to record his efforts. Not much here for your comfort but then you didn't expect any, did you? One last thing. After you've read, marked and learned this, would you quite literally inwardly digest it, or destroy it by some other means. See you!)

Pascoe finished reading, then gathered the papers up and took them through to the lounge where Ellie was sitting in front of the fire, nursing a glass of Scotch.

"Hi. All done?"

He knelt beside her and laid the fax sheets on the flames.

"I wish I could feel that was symbolic," said Ellie. "Shall I pour you a Scotch?"

"Better not," said Pascoe.

"That doesn't mean what I think it means, I hope."

"I need to see Studholme and I doubt if I'll have time tomorrow."

"They've invented this thing called the telephone."

"I need to see him," repeated Pascoe.

She didn't argue but rose and went out into the hall. He heard her using the telephone. When she returned he looked at her inquiringly.

"Just fixing a baby-sitter. Hit lucky with Myrtle down the road. She'll be here in ten minutes. Any objection?"

"Yes," he said, smiling. "If you hadn't been so quick getting stuck into that whisky, you could have done the driving too."

XV

"YOU WON'T BE LATE?" said Edwin Digweed.

"Definitely not."

"Good, because Dora's promised us something really special."

"I'm practically on my way," said Wield.

He put down the phone and returned his attention to the TV screen. Behind him he heard the door of the CID audiovisual room open.

"Working late," said Dalziel. "Or do you just get lousy reception out in the sticks?"

Wield shifted sideways to give a clear view of the screen. On it a frozen frame over Des Patten's shoulder of Cap Marvell, lightly crouched, holding the heavy wire cutters at her side like a broadsword in a double-handed grip. Her expression was calm, with the calmness of concentration rather than repose, and her unblinking gaze was focused on the man before her.

Wield pressed his remote control and let the tape move forward frame by frame. The left foot advanced, the chest and arm muscles bunched visibly as the shoulders began to turn, taking the cutters behind her, like a tennis player winding up for a double-handed forehand drive. Then as she reached the furthermost point of her backswing, Wendy Walker came into the picture, putting her skinny body between the woman and the security guard, her back to Cap, her arms spread wide to inhibit any blow. Behind her they saw

Marvell slowly relax. Then Wendy turned to face her, putting her hands on her upper arms and clearly speaking to her. They saw Cap's mouth open in reply, her expression relaxing into exaggerated surprise. Then Jimmy Howard appeared behind them and took the cutters from Cap's unresisting hands.

Up to this point Patten hadn't moved. Now he stepped forward and spoke. And the two women closely escorted by Patten and Howard moved out of shot through a door.

"So what do you think, sir," said Wield, glancing at Dalziel for the first time. If the Fat Man had needed a moment to control his expression, he'd put it to good use.

"It's okay but it's not Disney," he said. "We could do with subtitles."

"Yes. I asked Patten what were said and he could only give a general idea. So I thought I'd get Howard up here to see if his memory were any better. Novello's gone to fetch him."

Dalziel looked surprised.

"Chancing your arm a bit, Wieldy. You told his brief? I'm sure he'll be able to quote something in PACE that makes taking a prisoner from the cells to chat about another case without telling his brief a capital offense."

"Probably," said Wield. "Except he's not a prisoner. There's nowt'll stick except driving when disqualified. So Novello's processing him out, then inviting him as an ex-colleague and a fellow professional in the security business to lend us a hand here."

"Oh aye. Very green."

"Sorry?"

"Recycling rubbish," said Dalziel scornfully.

"We've got to take help where we can find it," said Wield. "I gather we've let Ms. Marvell go?"

"Aye. Like Howard, nowt to hold her on."

"Difference is, we know Howard's guilty, sir," said Wield gently.

"And after watching them pictures, you reckon she's off the hook, do you?"

Wield was saved from reply by the opening of the door to admit WDC Novello and Jimmy Howard.

"Hello, Jimmy. Nice of you to give us a hand," said Wield.

"You've got a nerve after banging me up like that," said Howard. But there was little force in his protest as he took in the brooding presence of Dalziel, who'd spread himself across a chair which didn't look like it was enjoying his proximity either.

"Just take a look at this tape of what happened the other night, Jimmy, and see if you can recollect exactly what was said. Not just you. Everyone," instructed Wield.

He wound the tape back and ran it through at normal speed.

"Bloody hell," said Howard. "You're not still going on about this, are you? I mean, what's the problem?"

"No problem, Jimmy. Just try to recall what was said," urged Wield.

Once more he ran the sequence, this time in slow motion.

"I've been through all this," said Howard. "Okay, when I came in after the skinny lass, t'other, her with the headlights, she's standing in front of Des, looking like she's just about to swing yon cutters at him . . ."

"How do you work that out?" said Wield. "You must have been looking at her back."

"Aye, but you could see she was getting ready for a swing. I mean, just look at the pictures. There it goes, she's not getting ready for a clog dance, is she?"

"Any words spoken?"

"Des said something like, *Easy now.* She said nowt, but she were breathing pretty hard."

"Then what?"

"Skinny lass is in front of me. We've both stopped short when we saw what was happening . . ."

"I'm sorry. Why was that? You stopping, I mean."

"Well, it's like bursting into a room and finding someone with a knife at someone else's throat. You pause to take stock, don't you?"

"You felt there was as real a threat as that, did you?" said Wield, glancing at the Fat Man, who yawned and looked at his watch.

"You could have cut the air," said Howard. "Then the skinny lass shoots forward and jumps between the two of them."

"What's she saying at this point?"

Howard stared at the screen, then said, "*Hold it, Cap.* Something like that."

"And when she turns round?" said Wield, letting the tape run on.

"She said, *Cool, Cap. We don't want anyone getting hurt here, do we, not without cause.* Something like that."

"And did Marvell say anything in reply? She seems to open her mouth there."

"Yeah. She said *Jesus,* sort of long drawn out on her breath, like she just couldn't believe her ears. But she relaxed and me and Des moved forward and got them sorted, no more trouble. Look, what's the point of this? No one's pressing charges, are they?"

"Not about the break-in, no," said Wield.

"About what then? I mean, what odds can it make to anyone who said what? You need a formal complaint for threatening behavior."

"Not always," said Wield. "And especially not when it's threatening with a deadly weapon."

"That thing? Deadly?" Howard laughed.

Wield regarded him seriously and said, "It's intent that counts, Jimmy, thought you'd have remembered that. And swung hard enough at your head, that thing could kill you, which in my book makes it deadly."

"Kill . . . ? Like up at Redcar you mean? You still harping on about that?"

"Mustn't leave any stones unturned even if it means turning some of them twice," said Wield. "So you're sure that's all you can remember of what was said."

"Yeah. Sure. Why don't you ask them as did the talking anyway?"

"Well, we have. As far as possible."

"What's that mean?" asked Howard suspiciously.

"It means you can't talk to the dead," boomed Dalziel. "Sergeant, get this scrote out of here. He were no use to us in the Force, why the hell should he be any use to us out of it?"

Howard wasn't bothering with even a token indignation, Wield noticed. There was quite a different expression on his face. The sergeant nodded at Novello, who also looked as if she wanted to say something. But Dalziel rose and stretched himself and the movement, though free of menace, set the WDC urging an unresisting Howard through the door.

"No further forward then, Wieldy," said the Fat Man, scratching his neck as though it contained something he would like to get out.

"No, sir," said Wield. He wanted to add that Dalziel's dismissal had got rid of Howard before he'd finished with him, but felt that the moment was so unripe he could break a tooth on it.

"Peter gone home?"

"Yes, sir. He'd just gone when I got back with this tape."

"And you didn't reckon it were important enough to call him back to take a look at? Well, you were dead right, weren't you? The lad'll learn more watching *Coronation Street* than this. So, Howard set loose, Cap Marvell set loose, no more useless revelations from

Troll Longbottom or Dr. Death, we might as well hang the VACANCIES sign outside the cells and head off to enjoy the weekend. Wieldy, fancy a pint?"

"No thanks, sir. Better get back."

"Quite right. Mustn't let your dinner spoil. What's it tonight? Parsnip pie?"

Provoked by the sneer, Wield said, "Meatless day were yesterday, sir. Day after, we always get Dora Creed go to town on a nice bit of lamb or mebbe a rib of beef. You remember Miss Creed, sir? Runs the Wayside Cafe?"

A glint of interest and envy touched Dalziel's eyes as he recollected the superb nosh Dora Creed dished up for hungry travelers out at Enscombe.

"Sounds like your ship's really come home at last, Wieldy. I'm glad for you. No one deserves it more. Goodnight then."

He turned and left the room. Wield stood in thought for a moment.

Sympathy to the Fat Man was like flashing *The Satanic Verses* at a mullah. Clever thing was to head on home and let the memory of Dalziel's unhappiness season his own content. But while his partner, Edwin, might have the shot-silk sensibility to enjoy such a refined Gallic pleasure, his heart was Yorkshire homespun.

He went into the corridor and called after the retreating figure. "Mebbe just a pint then, sir."

XVI

CAP MARVELL SAT in front of the television with a glass
of her ersatz whisky in one hand and the remote control in the other, zapping across the channels in search
of one which might lead her out of the dark maze of
her mind for a few minutes. Vain hope, even with the
service which vaingloriously trumpets itself as the best
in the world.

She turned off the sound but left the picture on for
the sake of the shifting images and flickering colors
which brought the illusion of life into the room.

She had had a good decade and more in which to
find herself, and now here she was, feeling completely
lost again. That was real progress! But she had to be
practical. Was there anything that could be saved from
the situation? Only herself, perhaps; and the way she
was feeling now, she wasn't sure she was worth the
effort.

Fuck that fat bastard! Five days ago she hadn't
known him and she had felt unassailable in mind,
spirit, and conscience. Now here she was, feeling as
adrift as she had felt all those years ago when she had
seen the first cracks filigreeing the delicate eggshell
structure of her life as Mrs. Rupert Pitt-Evenlode.

She sucked on her whisky. She had seen him flinch
as he tasted it, and now she drained the glass in defiant
affirmation of her own identity which had felt so whole
and permanent till he showed up. And would do again.
That was the only possible response to this crisis. To
survive, to carry on. To show the bastard!

She found herself smiling at her own illogicality. As
lovers all over the world know (and how many have

not been lovers?), showing you don't care is evidence incontrovertible that you do. But it was a start. Not the showing, but the smiling. Life after Dalziel was a real possibility.

But the bastard, oh the bastard!

Jimmy Howard was also drinking Scotch. It had come out of a pub optic and he neither knew nor cared about the brand. The pub was situated on the far side of town from where he lived and he'd never been in it before. Even so, he had found himself the remotest shadiest corner. He wanted to sit in peace, with minimal risk of being recognized or approached.

There were things to work out, decisions to be made. The trouble with decisions was that they tended to be decisive. His mind went back to that first occasion, not so distant in real time, but light-years away in perceived, when he had taken his first silencer. *Mr. Howard* (he was still Mr. Howard then, the police constable being addressed respectfully by the ingratiating suspect), *Mr. Howard, can't we talk this over like sensible men? Sit down like friends even, over a drink.* There had been an unmistakable stress on the word *drink.* And that had been the moment when a step in one direction would have kept him firmly in the fold, while a step in the other . . . But he had genuinely thought you could step out, then step back in again, with no real harm done, and he'd replied, *It would need to be a bloody large drink.*

Now here he was again at a crossroads. Different ins, perhaps, and different outs . . . oh yes, certainly the possibility of very different outs!

He rose and went to the bar, feeling the need of more Scotch.

As the barman set the glass in front of him, "I'll get that one, Jimmy," said a voice.

* * *

Dalziel said, "Pete seems happy enough these days. Him and his missus I mean. Don't think he'll ever feel safe, mind. Way yon Ellie's mind works, a good cop can never feel safe with her. But secure, aye, I'd say he's feeling pretty secure just now. Kiddie helps, of course. Harder to walk out on a kiddie. Aye, a kiddie might have helped."

Wield for once had refused to submit to Dalziel's eleventh commandment which stated, *When I drink, every bugger drinks.* He had sat nursing his glass, rising obediently whenever the Fat Man said, "Your shout, lad," and getting another pint and whisky chaser. On his own shout, Dalziel ignored the sergeant's demur and always returned with two pints and chasers, both of which he supped almost absentmindedly as Wield hung on to his initial drink.

One thing you weren't likely to get with the Fat Man was a maudlin let-it-all-hang-out, I'll-be-sorry-I-said-this-in-the-morning-but-not-as-sorry-as-you'll-be-you-heard-it confession. But Wield knew from long experience that, as the drink took hold, he might give you a quick flash of the truth of his heart through a gauzy veil of obliquities.

"She's a grand lass, Ellie, but," said Wield, who was a considerable fan of Ellie Pascoe.

"I know that, but trouble, you can't deny that. Mebbe it doesn't matter, but, if the rest's all right."

He waved a glass vaguely to comprehend "the rest," then emptied it and picked up one of Wield's.

"There was this lass I once knew, a while back, a widow, just after Pete got wed . . . were you at the wedding, Wieldy?"

"No sir. Recovering from having my appendix out."

"Oh aye. Well, like I say, I had a bit of a holiday after, got friendly with this lass. Got pretty close. Looked like it might come to summat. You get these daft ideas, seeing the lad get wed, all that stuff. . . ."

He looked reflectively into his glass and Wield took the chance to look reflectively at the clock he could see in the bar mirror. Shit. Edwin's not going to be pleased, he thought.

"Not boring you, am I, Wieldy?" said Dalziel sharply, as if the sergeant had pulled out a pocket watch and held it to his ear.

"Never came to anything then?" said Wield, refusing to be diverted into defense.

"We had our moments," said Dalziel. "But there was summat a bit iffy about the way her husband had died . . . I didn't think I could take a chance. . . ."

"In case she topped you as well, sir?" Wield couldn't resist saying.

"In case I had to finger her collar," retorted the Fat Man. "I was right, wasn't I?"

"You must have thought you were," said Wield.

"I knew I was, as a cop. And I was fifty-fifty sure as a man. . . ."

"Sounds like a landslide majority to me," said Wield.

"Aye, but suppose I'd not been so sure as a man? Suppose I'd felt eighty-twenty she were in the clear? Would I still have been right?"

Crunch time, thought Wield.

"Depends what's most important," he said steadily. "I mean, generally. If it's the job number one always, and the rest runners up, then that makes things easy, even when they're hard."

"Yeah? You reckon Peter would jack the job then, if Ellie gave him an either-or?"

"I'd say so. Mebbe it's knowing that that makes her not do it," said Wield.

"You sound like you've been getting your nose stuck into some of your mate's *Reader's Digest*s," mocked Dalziel. "Talking of which, how about you? Desperate

Dan says get yourself out of Brigadoon and back into your bachelor flat in town, what do you do?"

While Dalziel was as far from mealymouthed as you could get without injections of Pentothal, he'd never before come so close to inviting discussion of Wield's domestic situation.

"Easy," said Wield. "I'd take early retirement."

And it *was* easy now he'd said it. He felt the constraints of the job which had always been at the very center of his life slip away like silk off a stripper. Hey, I'm a swan after all, he thought.

"Them twitchings of your lip, you grinning or having a fit?" inquired Dalziel.

"Sorry, sir. It's a matter of priorities, I'd say. You were right not to let things go any further with yon widow if what you felt was, when things went wrong, you'd be fingering her collar."

"What would be the alternative?" demanded Dalziel.

"Helping her pack her suitcase and buying two tickets to Rio?" suggested Wield. "And, no. I won't have another drink, sir. It's time I got off home."

Knowing how expert the other was at delaying tactics, he rose even as he spoke and headed for the door. But before he reached it, a hand grasped his sleeve and he glanced aside to find himself looking at Detective Constable Novello.

"Buy you a drink, Sarge?" she said.

"Some other time, thanks," he said. "I'm a bit late."

She released his sleeve but remained at his side, looking at him.

Something she wants to talk about, he thought, but not important enough to spit it right out. Therefore not important enough to drop me even deeper in it with Edwin.

He jerked his head toward the table where Dalziel

was sitting apparently deep in contemplation of the shirt button straining over his navel.

"Super's in a drinking mood, but," he said.

Her gaze moved to the monumental figure, then back.

"I've not drunk enough myself," she said. "Goodnight then, Sarge."

Feeling both a heel and a hero that at last he'd put the job second, Wield went out into the night.

Away to the west in Leeds, Peter Pascoe too was being offered a drink.

He shook his head but Ellie said, "Yes, please. As it comes," and Hilary Studholme smiled at her almost gratefully as he poured a measure large enough to please a detective superintendent.

He'd expressed no surprise when he'd opened the door and seen the Pascoes. It was late-night opening at the supermarket and through the automatic doors, almost continuously open under the steady stream of shoppers, drifted a thin line of disco music, broken now and then by a plummy voice urging customers not to miss the unmissable bargains to be found at the delicatessen counter. Lights blazed above, around, and from within the building, and through the unearthly glow cast by the sodium lamps which ringed the car park drifted a no-man's-land brume of October mist and deadly exhaust gases.

"Amazing," Ellie breathed as she took in the contrast between the world represented by that garish bustle and the narrow high Victorian museum. And when she stepped inside and the heavy door blanked out the 1990s like a candle snuffer, "Amazing," she said again.

She would have liked to linger in the museum, but this was Peter's show and she had accompanied the two men silently up the steep staircases to the major's tiny flat. At least there was to be no forensic fencing,

Studholme coming straight to the point with military directness.

"You found out about my father," he said as he poured himself a Scotch. "I didn't know whether to tell you or not. I almost did, then I thought, if he's really set on digging up the past, he'll find out himself and come back to me."

"Everyone seems set on giving me little tests," said Pascoe. "Pass them, and I'm allowed to move on a little further. I presume you got your own knowledge from your father's war journal?"

"Yes. That's why Pascoe rang a bell. Then you said it wouldn't have been Pascoe. Then I found that old photo and it looked so like you, I just had to check."

"But there's more, isn't there? Not just the name. That wouldn't be enough to leave you so agitated. There has to be something else."

The major glanced at Ellie and smiled again.

"Living with someone who's always put two and two together must present its problems," he said.

"His arithmetic's not always that hot," said Ellie.

"What else is there?" said Pascoe, refusing to be lured into these mood-lightening exchanges.

The major regarded him with his one bright eye, sighed, rose and went to an old bureau not a million miles in style from Ada's secretaire.

From a drawer he took a book stylishly bound in tooled leather.

"My father's diary," he said. "I had it bound to stop it falling apart. When I die, it will have its place in the museum, but till then . . . well, it was his personal record, and if it was meant for anyone else's eyes, I like to think it was mine."

Expertly he opened it with his one hand at a place marked by a pipe spill.

"This is what he wrote about Sergeant Pascoe's trial.

You can look at it yourself if you like, but I warn you, his hand is almost illegible to the untutored eye."

"Why don't you read it to us," said Ellie.

"Very well. Could you pass me my glasses?"

Ellie picked up a pair of wire-rimmed spectacles lying on the table next to the whisky decanter, approached the major, and without any hesitation placed them on his nose.

"Thank you, my dear," he said with another flash of that charming smile.

"My pleasure," said Ellie.

Jesus, thought Pascoe. Thank God the old sod isn't ten years younger!

"I'll do a little bit of editing as I go," said Studholme. "But nothing relevant, I assure you."

He coughed twice to clear his throat and began reading. He adopted an old-fashioned public-speaking style, much heavier than his normal mode, like a man called upon to read a lesson at a carol service.

"October 1917. Date fixed for Pascoe's court-martial at last. Delay caused by Grindal's absence. Minor physical injuries, so everyone thought he'd be back in matter of weeks. CO got report saying neurasthenia diagnosed with no prospect of rapid return, so it has been decided to admit written account as evidence. Evenlode sneered at mention of neurasthenia which he calls shirkers' cramp. Says that temporary gents are particularly susceptible, by which he means Grindal because his family are trade."

"This Evenlode," interrupted Ellie. "Any relation to the Pitt-Evenlodes?"

"Oh yes. Name got modified when his cousin, the baron, married the only child of Sir Chesney Pitt who was keen to preserve his own family name. The Evenlodes felt that the distaff side, being inferior, should come second, but the story is that Sir Chesney said that if they called themselves Evenlode-Pitt, it would be like having a coal mine in the family. Their grandson, Piers, is serving in the regiment currently, just gazetted lieutenant colonel. Do you know them?"

"A nodding acquaintance," said Ellie, who could sound regally condescending when she wanted.

"Evenlode was the adjutant, right?" said Pascoe, determined to cut through the coziness.

"Right. And from what my father wrote, he had a distaste for Sergeant Pascoe which outweighed even his dislike of Lieutenant Grindal. Where was I? Oh yes, here we are. *Evenlode raised no objection to using written evidence however. Never liked the way Pascoe stuck up for his men. Recall him telling poor old Hurley that an infantry platoon needed good NCOs not trouble-stirring shop stewards. And since that business of Pascoe being helped by Fritz to rescue his cousin, he's really had him marked down as one of these Bolshevik agitators everyone's been talking about since the spring. From my knowledge of both Pascoe and Grindal, I'd have bet on the sergeant being much the steadier of the two. But no one's asking me.*"

He paused to turn the page.

Pascoe said, "This Evenlode, he was the prosecuting officer, yes?"

"That's right. It was usually the adjutant from the prisoner's unit who took that role. Kept it in the family, so to speak, and also meant that he would have a personal knowledge of the individuals involved. It was generally thought to work to the prisoner's advantage."

"Generally. Meaning, like a general? Very apt," sneered Pascoe.

Ellie quickly said, "The cousin, what was his name, Steve Pascoe, right? What became of him?"

"I told you what those women at Kirkton said," began Pascoe, irritated at the interruption.

"Yes, I know. Ran off with his cousin's widow. What I mean is, if he deserted too, how come he never got caught? And how come, if Peter reported you right, Major, the only mention of him in the regimental records is that he got wounded in the Salient?"

"Ah yes. Private Stephen Pascoe, I did check naturally once I realized my father's involvement," said Studholme. "It was rather a sad case. Technically he did desert. His uniform and identity discs were found bundled up at the railway station in Liverpool and it was assumed he'd either stowed away or otherwise obtained a passage to America. The thing was that though he made a fair recovery from the injuries he sustained in August, the medical records show that the movement of his left upper arm and shoulder was going to be permanently impaired. On the day he took off, he'd been before a Medical Board to assess his condition. This was normal practice for all wounded men prior to returning them to their units—or, of course, advising further treatment. The Board examined him and made their recommendation, which was for discharge. He had no future as a fighting soldier and would be more use to the country in his old job."

"Nobody, of course, thought to tell him this on the spot," snapped Pascoe.

"That's not the way the army works, I'm afraid," said Studholme with genuine regret. "Proper channels are the thing. Presumably he went off thinking they were going to rubber-stamp his return to the Front and decided he'd had enough. Technically, as I say, he was still in the army till he received his official discharge. But no regiment likes to have desertions in its records and in this case to haul a chap back to try him on a capital offense when it had been decided he wasn't fit to fight anyway would have offended natural justice. So his discharge was quietly and quickly processed at the depot, which was here in Leeds, and the fact that he went AWOL for his last couple of weeks of service gently passed over."

"Well, I'm so glad another Pascoe's name wasn't allowed to besmirch your precious records," said Pascoe bitterly. "Let's get back to your father, shall we?"

"Of course. The next entry begins: *I should never have written 'But no one's asking me!' They just have, or rather, they've just told me, because naturally there's no saying no in such matters. I'm to be Pascoe's Friend. The CO told me it was a nasty job but he knew I'd do my best. Evenlode said that on the contrary it was a cushy number, the verdict was in no doubt, so all it meant was I spent a couple of days out of the line, keeping myself warm and dry and killing lice. I said, that must mean it's cushy for you too, rather sarcastic. But he missed my point, saying, oh yes, it's killing that one big louse that I'll particularly enjoy. He really is a nasty piece of work.*"

He paused again and said to Ellie, "Refill. Do help yourself."

"Gosh, have I drunk it? Thanks, I will."

She did. Pascoe said, "So what does your father say about the trial?"

"Well, before that he writes about his difficulty in getting Pascoe to talk about his defense: *He really doesn't seem to grasp the danger he's in. He admits freely he struck Grindal but says it was only to disable him from harming himself by continuing to advance in a dazed state, and then he describes leading the remnant of his platoon back to the jump-off point as if it were the most reasonable thing in the world to do. All he seems to have any regret about is being rude to a staff officer, and the reason he regrets this is that there's no point in losing your rag with dumb animals, which is unlikely to endear him to the court. Though on second thought, if they are all line officers, they may well take his point!*"

The major permitted himself a smile as he read this and Pascoe said, "How comforting that your father didn't lose his sense of humor in face of someone else's adversity."

"Peter, for heaven's sake," said Ellie.

"No, my fault, I'm sorry, Mr. Pascoe, this must be very painful for you. There's little more. He records that Sergeant Pascoe is clearly relying on the testimony of Lieutenant Grindal and of the members of his platoon to clear him, or at least reduce his punishment to loss of stripes. He regrets that his efforts to cross-question witnesses, in particular Private Doyle, are unproductive and cut short by the president. He tries to object to the admission of Grindal's written testimony because it didn't afford opportunity for cross-examination, but is told that these Chancery Lane tactics are entirely out of place here . . ."

"There's none of this in the trial record!" protested Pascoe.

The major's eye lit up with interest.

"You've seen it, have you?" he inquired.

Ellie bared her teeth at her husband, and said firmly to Studholme, "No, he hasn't. But we did get an unofficial digest from an influential friend, one condition of which was complete confidentiality."

"My lips are sealed," said Studholme. "I know how these things work. Mr. Pascoe, I can understand your feelings about my father's ineffectiveness. I shan't bore you with the details, but please believe me, he agonizes at some length about your great-grandfather's fate and despite knowing in his rational mind that there was nothing he could do to alter it, he felt, and continued to feel till the end of his days I believe, guilty that he should have played any part in it."

Pascoe refused to catch Ellie's eye and said nothing.

Studholme sighed and went on, "You will be relieved to hear my father had nothing to do with the actual execution, so I am spared the macabre task of reading out a description. He did however see Sergeant

Pascoe the day before, when he took on himself the task of bearing the news that there was no hope of mercy and the sentence was to be carried out the following morning."

He put down the book to take a sip of whisky, then picked it up again and began reading.

"The sergeant gave me a letter to his wife which he asked me to post. I said I would. Then after a little hesitation he produced a book consisting of several sheets of paper roughly sewn together between covers made from squares of rubber from an old ground sheet. This, he said, was a journal he'd been keeping. There'd been another book from the start of the war which he'd left at home on his last leave, thinking that either he'd be able to use it to recall these years for himself in later life, or if he fell, it would be a record for his family. But he is uncertain whether he should ask for these later leaves to be sent home also, because of the tragic material they contain. He asked me if I would take it and, when I had time, read it, then send it to his wife or not at my discretion. It was not a task I wanted, but equally it wasn't one I could refuse. Then we shook hands and he thanked me most courteously for what he called my kindness and help, and I left and walked around in the dark by myself for an hour or more for shame of being caught weeping."

Studholme put the book down and removed his glasses.

"There is a note added at a later date in which he says that he has read the journal with some difficulty and decided after much thought that Pascoe was right to be reluctant to have it passed on to his wife. He concludes, *There is little in here to heal and much to keep old wounds raw. R.I.P."*

"So what did he do with it then? Burn it?" demanded Pascoe.

"No, Mr. Pascoe, it is here."

He put his hand into the bureau drawer and produced a volume of the same surface dimensions as the one Pascoe had received from Ada, though much slimmer.

"I have glanced at it. It is difficult as my father implied, but what little I have managed to interpret seems to confirm he may have been right in his decision. But that was eighty years ago. Before you condemn him for interference, read it yourself and see if you would have wished him to act differently."

He handed the book over. Pascoe took it. It felt cold and clammy and the lights in the room seemed to dim as he recollected the circumstances in which his great-grandfather had last touched this volume.

Studholme went on, "Perhaps we can talk again when the perspectives are still longer. Mrs. Pascoe, it's been a pleasure meeting you again."

"For me too," said Ellie. "I'd like to look round your museum sometime."

"I look forward to being your guide."

They went down the stairs. At the door, Ellie dug an elbow into Pascoe's ribs and he said, "Thanks, Major. You've been very . . . well, thanks anyway."

"I'm sorry," said Studholme. "I really am."

"Me too," said Peter Pascoe.

XVII

IT WAS TWO O'CLOCK in the morning before Pascoe succeeded in reaching the end of the sergeant's journal. Haste of composition, agitation of spirit, and the fading of age had rendered much of the writing almost illegible, but again and again as it seemed he had reached an impasse, his mind found the way; almost, he might have said had he been a superstitious man, heard a voice speaking the obscure words and phrases out loud.

Ellie during all this time offered no reproach about the lateness of the hour, no comment upon the wisdom of the proceedings, but simply brought cups of strong coffee at regular intervals, and otherwise sat curled up on the sofa with a book which only later did he realize was the history of the Great War that Studholme had loaned him.

"Okay," he said finally. "You want to hear it?"

"I haven't sat up half the night in hope of hearing the nightingale," she replied. "But perhaps you can edit?"

"Of course. It's the assault in Polygon Wood that's central. Here's what he wrote afterwards, when he'd been arrested, but well before he admits to himself what serious crap he was in."

He coughed, recognized the echo of Studholme's introit, and forced himself to use his normal everyday tone as he started reading.

Gertie finally snapped today—Id seen the signs from the moment we were told of our place in the line— he were talking all the time and making jokes that werent near funny—and reminding me of the old days when I were a lad and him a nipper. Bit different from Wanwood—he kept saying—Remember those trees—thought they touched the sky like it says in the poem—not that you could see the sky— so many branches and leaves all moving in the wind it was like being on the bed of the sea with all that green surging overhead. That was one of your games remember? You were always good at inventing games to keep me amused.

Id best see what I can manage today then sir—I

said. And I did try. I think his main fear to start with
was that hed be too afraid to move—that when the
command came to go forward and we all rose up
and climbed out of our hole his legs wouldnt raise
him and hed simply be left lying there for all to see
and mock at. So I fed him rum—his ration my ration and a bit more besides till if hed had much
more he wouldnt have been able to move for being
stotious let alone being feart. It worked and when
the signal came I gave him a bit of a lift—then he
was up and off like someone on the cover of the
Boys Own—waving his pistol and yelling like he
were going to clear Jerry out of Polygon single
handed.

Didnt last of course—couldnt—I were hoping
maybe hed get a friendly Blighty—bullet through his
shoulder—bit of shrapnel in his leg—anything to
knock him over and give him an excuse to lie there
—but he seemed charmed—and while rest of us
were creeping forward bent double—or going down
never to creep again—he were prancing around like
a lad on a football field yelling at us to keep up with
him.

In old days it might have been alright—quick
charge on foot or horseback—scatter the enemy—all
over in half an hour or so. Bet that many a man
won his medal half seas over. But this lot goes on
forever—and gets nowhere. Hour—two hours—all
fucking day—you look around and where youve got
to looks no different from where you set off from—
same holes same mud—same pathetic stumps—
same bodies—same stench—same endless hopeless
senseless sameness.

Rum wears off—mind starts working again—realize that not all the courage nor all the cleverness in
the world can save you now—blind chance—long
odds—and if you do make it through this day noth-

ing to look forward to but another and another and another. Gertie slowed then stopped—still with charmed life—rest of platoon badly hit—all around men Id known and some Id loved dead and dying— but Gertie untouched—except inside—I was close— saw his face as he turned—saw the horror and the terror there—all right if hed just collapsed maybe— could always say knocked over by shell blast—but I saw him start to run.

Run? No running possible in that mud—floun- dering like weary swimmer close enough to bank to stand up—but definitely going back—no question if he met another officer what he was doing—hed even tell them what he was doing—hed hit them if they tried to stop him—and if he were seen by someone like Evenlode who hates his guts that ud be the end for him—cashiered—disgraced—maybe worse though they dont shoot so many officers.

He were moving away from me and I might never have caught him—then shell blast threw up a wall of mud in his path and turned him towards me. I hit him. Down he went. Couldn't leave him there— likely hed turn over into mud and drown—or recover and set off back again. I went to others in platoon— not many—said lieutenant were hit and we had or- ders to withdraw—they wanted to believe me—no- body asked questions—I told them to give me a hand with Gertie—off we went back—passed through next wave of attack—nobody said anything and I thought—good luck! Back at jump off point I told others to wait. Gertie was able to stumble along with a bit of help now and I took him back to Aid Post—sat there for a bit to get my wind—then I gave smart answer to Staff Officer. That were silly. Sensi- tive souls staff officers. Put me under arrest for in- subordination. Stupid sod doesnt realize what a favour hes doing me keeping me back here out of

*line. Maybe I should have started being in-
subordinate a long time back!*

*Not funny. Try to smile and feel happy but all I
can think of is all my mates—all the fellows I lived
with and should have looked after—lying dead and
dying broken and bleeding out there in Polygon
Wood. Thats where I ought to be not here cumfy and
safe—out there in Polygon Wood.*

Pascoe stopped reading and Ellie said, "Did he really
think he was safe?"

"Why do you ask?"

"It's just the way he describes things, the black
hopelessness of it all, he tries to put it off on Grindal—
and don't misunderstand me, I believe every word he
says about Grindal—but these are his own feelings he's
describing, aren't they?"

"Oh yes," said Pascoe passionately. "No doubt of
that. No doubt whatsoever."

Ellie gave him a puzzled look then went on. "And in
taking care of Gertie, which I'm sure he did, he also
takes care of himself. All the time I get this feeling that
he's using Gertie somehow to externalize his own fears,
and he ends up trying to persuade himself that having
got Gertie back safe somehow guarantees his own
safety. He must have known, surely, that with a battle
raging, you didn't get locked up away from the action
for a simple act of insubordination."

"Sharp little thing, aren't you?" said Pascoe.
"You're dead right. He knows that. But he doesn't
want to let himself know it. He's so much like me, Ellie. I see myself in him all the time, all his fears and
failings, all his little tricks to try and get by. He's so
much like me."

"One big difference," said Ellie, coming to stand behind his chair and draping her arms around his shoul-

ders. "You're alive. But the cat gets out of the bag later, does it?"

"Oh yes. During the trial. At first, like Studholme said, he put his trust in Gertie's testimony. He writes: 'Hes no fool Gertie—and hes basically a decent kind of man. A bit of peace and quiet will soon have him back to normal and hell work out what happened. Hell know theres no danger of him being charged because whos to give evidence against him except me? And hell know what Im saying happened because the captain has written to him—and hell send word that Ive got it dead right—so Im not worrying.' "

"Like hell," said Ellie.

"Like hell indeed," said Pascoe. "After he's heard Gertie's letter read out and realizes where this leaves him, there's obviously a gap when he doesn't write anything. Then he resumes after the verdict."

Maybe I shouldnt have burst out like I did but it made no difference. They are going to kill me whatever I say and they might as well hear the truth of what I think—though not the whole truth—for I will not tell them that Gertie broke and was running for they would not believe it except perhaps for the adjutant who is malicious enough to spread it around —thus catching us both in different ways. And even that is still not the whole truth—for though the true facts of the business have been hidden from them I am none the less guilty as charged—Gerties fear was my fear and when I saved him from running it was also to use him so as I could run myself. I told that staff officer that I was going back up the line as soon as Id finished my fag but would I have done so? And was not perhaps my insubordination a deliberate attempt to sting him to anger and thus get myself arrested? So if they are right to shoot cowards then they are right to think themselves right to shoot me.

> *But I know I am not a coward—nor I think is Gertie*
> *—so they are not right—or at least their vicious law*
> *isnt right. God help me that it has come to this. And*
> *God help Bertie Grindal when he realizes what it*
> *has come to.*

" 'God help Bertie Grindal when he realizes'!" echoed Ellie mockingly. "So what does he do? Sends a consoling letter and a bit of cash to the widow, then gets on with the rest of his privileged life. God, if she'd known the truth, I bet she'd have thrown that money back in his face!"

"Perhaps she did know the truth or some of it," said Pascoe. "Here near the end he writes: 'I shall give this to Mr. Studholme to do with as he sees fit, and a letter for him to send to Alice in which I shall simply say my goodbyes. And I have written to Stephen by the usual route so that he may know enough to stop Archie Doyles tongue if yon bastard starts blackening me about Kirkton.' "

"The usual route?"

"Someone going back on leave would post it in England. That way you jumped the censor," said Pascoe.

"I hope to God this thing between Steve and Alice didn't start till after he got that letter," said Ellie. "Pete, are you okay?"

He was sitting looking into space or rather through it as if he were seeing something beyond.

"I'm an idiot," he said. "This has all come piling on me so thick over the past couple of days I've lost sight of where it all started and the mystery of the names. Where's Ada's letter?"

He started sorting through the contents of the package he'd received from Barbara Lomax and then through the papers he'd brought back with him from Ada's cottage.

"Listen, she talks about a knock on the door which

brought everything out in the open. I just took it that there was a letter, perhaps something official about a pension or something her mother had been applying for, I don't know. But it was obviously a person. And when later she writes about *two of us living together both with our appointed quests,* it's not her and her mother, it's her and my grandfather Colin Pascoe."

"Hold on," said Ellie. "You're saying this Colin Pascoe is who? Stephen's son? But he was called Steve, I'm sure he's referred to in the diary."

"That's right. Stephen after his father which his mother couldn't bear the sound of after he allegedly upped and left her. And George after his paternal grandfather, which I daresay she didn't fancy either. And finally Colin probably after the Quiggins grandfather. That's what he grew up being called. It's here on Ada's marriage lines. Stephen George Colin Pascoe who, when he came of age and felt his independence, was determined to track his errant father down and had nothing to go on but the old family story that he'd run off with cousin Peter's widow. So naturally he went in search of the widow and somehow picked up her trail."

They sat in silence for a while thinking of the scene when the young Pascoe arrived at the Clark women's house.

"Must have been like having a bomb lobbed through the window," said Ellie. "No wonder she married him."

"Sorry?"

"A guy turns up accusing your mum of having it off with his dad while your dad was being executed in France, the only reason you don't kill him is you fancy him rotten."

Pascoe laughed and said, "I always said you and Ada had a lot in common. Too much maybe. God, look at the time. Let's head to bed, love. Mystery solved. One of them."

"No," said Ellie. "Mystery doubled. Before you were just bothered by what happened to one of your great-grandfathers. Now you've got another to worry about. Stephen didn't run off with Alice. Did he really take off to America and never make any attempt then or later to contact his son? Or . . ."

"Or?"

"Or did he head round to Alice's as soon as he got Peter's letter and find her sitting there with Herbert Antony Grindal's note of condolence in her one hand and his blood money in the other?"

And suddenly Pascoe saw seven golden sovereigns shining through the mud.

PART FOUR

WANWOOD

Among the beds of Lilyes, I
Have sought it oft, where it should lye;
Yet could not, till it self would rise,
Find it, although before mine Eyes.

I

"YOU WHA'?" said Andy Dalziel, packing enough incredulity into the two syllables to make Doubting Thomas sound like a planted question at Prime Minister's Question Time.

"You heard me," said Pascoe.

"Nay, lad, but I'm not certain I heard you right. You're saying that yon cranium you fetched me from old Death's sluices belonged to your own great-granddad who got shot by a firing squad in Flanders?"

"No," said Pascoe patiently. "That was my other great-grandfather, also called Pascoe. This is the one who got invalided home and when he found out what had happened to his cousin, he went out to Wanwood Hospital to have it out with Lieutenant Grindal."

"Oh aye. And this Grindal who's a patient there, suffering from war wounds and neurasthenia," said Dalziel, who'd clearly been paying much closer attention than he pretended, "he knocks your great-granddad down with his crutches then buries the body after stripping it of all its clothes which he then takes to

Liverpool to lay a false scent? He didn't meet a big bad wolf in the woods while he were at it, did he?"

"For fuck's sake, this is no joking matter!" exploded Pascoe.

Dalziel looked at him keenly then said, "Who's laughing? I'm just saying that as a working thesis I've seen better runners pulling milk floats."

"Perhaps so," said Pascoe, regretting his outburst. "At the very least I think the family know more than they're saying. I'd like to go back to Kirkton and have another talk with Batty senior."

"You'll do it in your own time then," said Dalziel sternly. "There's work to be done here and you've not exactly been pulling your weight lately."

Pascoe didn't argue. The Fat Man looked in no mood to be contradicted, and in any case there was more than a grain of truth in what he said.

Also he knew he was allowing his own concerns to mask the fact that Dalziel had personal problems just as deep and a great deal more immediate.

"Anything new on Wendy Walker?" he asked.

"Nowt."

"And is, er, Ms. Marvell still in the frame?"

Those hard bright eyes ran over his face like a security sensor, cataloguing each feature for future reference.

"No change," he said laconically, meaning, Pascoe interpreted, that nothing further had emerged either to incriminate or to exculpate the woman.

He said, "You like her a lot?" turning it from assertion to question in mid-utterance.

The eyes seemed to be measuring his inside-head dimensions this time.

"You planning to give me advice, Pete? I should warn you, I've already heard from the Sage of Enscombe."

"Well, I've started so I might as well finish," said

Pascoe. "Make your peace now *before* you're certain, otherwise either way, it'll make no difference. If you like her that much, that is."

"If I knew that, I'd not be listening to you and Old Mother Riley here," growled Dalziel, glancing toward Wield who had just come through the door. "What's up wi' you? Get your ticket punched for being late last night, did you?"

He was far advanced in the art of interpreting Wield's expression, which to Pascoe looked little different from that which registered amusement or delight.

"Got a woman downstairs playing merry hell, sir," said the sergeant.

Cap Marvell, thought Pascoe, and he saw that Dalziel thought the same.

"Mrs. Howard," continued the sergeant. "Wanting to know how long we're going to keep her man banged up."

"But I thought . . ." began Pascoe.

"That's right. We did, last night," said Wield. "No grounds for holding him longer."

"Then why didn't he go home?" said Pascoe.

"Fancy woman?" said Wield.

"Would you say he's the type?"

"There's no telling," said Wield, making sure his gaze didn't even touch Dalziel's penumbra. "But after talking to his missus . . . Could just have done a bunk, of course."

"Why?" said Dalziel. "That TecSec brief had got him right off the hook, and you don't run from a banned-driving charge. Peter, you talk to Mrs. Howard, ooze some of that boyish charm over her and see if she knows owt useful. Wieldy, you check out that lass you saw give him the envelope, and if there's no joy there, then get out to Wanwood and chat up your mate in TecSec. And on your way out, one of you send Novello in, will you?"

Wield passed on the message.

"Does he want a cup of tea?" asked Novello, only half satirically.

Wield said, "That chat you wanted last night, mebbe later, eh?"

"It's okay, I've slept on it, Sarge. Woke up and it seemed a lot of nothing."

She tapped on Dalziel's door and waited till she heard a bellow which might have been *Come in,* or the mating call of the African gorilla.

There was, however, nothing amatory about his expression.

"Sit," he said.

She perched right on the edge of a chair and he said, "Afraid of catching summat?"

"No, sir. Just didn't think I'd be staying long enough to get comfortable."

Did I really say that? she asked herself incredulously.

"Oh aye? Why's that?"

"Well, we haven't had a lot of . . ." The word that came into her mind was intercourse, but it didn't seem a good choice. ". . . talked a lot since I joined the department."

"Got something worth saying, have you?"

"Well, not really . . ."

"Good. Soon as you have, just knock and come in. Now, last evening you escorted yon scrote Jimmy Howard out of the building, right?"

"Yes, sir."

"Talk with him, did you?"

"Well, yes, a bit, but I don't think . . . I know I didn't tell him anything. . . ."

"Christ, lass, you must have a bigger guilt complex than Judas sodding Iscariot! It's Howard I'm interested in, not you. So what was the crack?"

She eased her buttocks more fully onto the seat of

the chair and said, "We talked about that video he'd been looking at. He asked me if it was true that the thin woman, Walker, was really dead, and I said yes, she was. And he asked how, and I didn't see any harm in telling him, I mean, it was in the local paper . . ."

"Do I look like the pope or summat, lass?" demanded Dalziel.

It occurred to Novello, who was a good Catholic, that given an ermined cloak and a flat red cap, Dalziel could very easily pass for one of the medieval fleshly school of cardinals she'd seen in paintings.

"You want to confess," he went on, "you go to see Father Kerrigan. Just tell me what went off!"

Given her assumption up to now that he was hardly aware of her existence, his knowledge that Father Kerrigan was her parish priest came as a jolt. If he knew that, what else . . . but his fingers were reshaping a paper knife which she took to be a sign of impatience.

"So I told him what I knew, I mean what was public knowledge about Walker's death. And he went on about her. How did she die? Why were we interested? And I told him that we were always interested in hit-and-run accidents, and he laughed and said . . . said things had changed since he was in the Force."

Dalziel had noticed the hesitation and said, "What you mean is he said something like, it took more than a mere hit-and-run to get yon fat bugger off his arse when I was in the Force. Right?"

There was a distant cousin of a smile playing round his lips, so she said, "*Bastard*, sir. He said fat bastard. And I said I knew nothing about that, but if he wanted to go and ask you himself, using the same form of words of course, I was happy to take him back upstairs. He refused my offer."

"He's not entirely brain-dead then," said Dalziel. "How'd he seem to you? I mean, what state of mind do you think he was in, asking these questions?"

She thought awhile then said, "Agitated. Maybe even scared. Certainly well off balance."

"And did he ask anything about Marvell, the other woman on the video?"

"No. Just Walker."

"Right. Thanks, lass."

She rose to go, her legs feeling absurdly weak with relief. Then he said, "You spoken to Sergeant Wield yet?"

"This morning? Just when he told me you wanted to see me, sir . . ."

"I know that. I mean, whatever it was you wanted to say to him last night, have you had time this morning?"

As many CID officers before, she began to wonder in which part of her anatomy he'd planted his bug.

"Oh, that. It was nothing, really . . ."

"In this department, luv, nothing is nothing till I say it's nowt. So tell me."

So she told him.

Pascoe, meanwhile, finding that getting sense out of Mrs. Howard was like getting straight answers out of a cabinet minister, abandoned charm and adopted the bludgeoning technique of a current affairs interviewer.

"Has he ever stayed away all night before?"

"Yeah, sometimes, on night shifts and such . . ."

"Not night shifts," he snapped. "We're not talking about night shifts, you know that, Mrs. Howard. Now, please answer the question. Has he ever stayed out all night before?"

"Yes. A couple of times, but I didn't half give him . . ."

"I'm not interested in what you gave him. Why did he stay out on these occasions? Another woman?"

"No! You think I'd put up with that . . ."

"Then *what*, Mrs. Howard? What did you put up with?"

"It was playing cards, usually. And drink. He'd get in a game and get a bit of drink down him, then he'd turn up next day, skint usually, and hardly able to walk."

"So that's what he might have been doing last night?"

"After you'd had him here all the previous night? No, all Jimmy would want would be to get home and wash the stink of them cells off him before he went out."

"You're saying he wouldn't even have popped in for a quick one?"

"Mebbe that. But no more. That was one thing about Jimmy, couldn't bear feeling mucky. Used to shower straight off when he came home from shift, both in the Force and in his new job."

So cleanliness if not godliness got him home, thought Pascoe.

He asked, "Like his new job, does he?"

"Well enough. It's something. Keeps him from getting under my feet."

Shower apart, thought Pascoe, looking at the broadly built, gaunt-faced, resentful-eyed woman before him, what else was there to lure Howard home?

He said, "I shouldn't worry too much, Mrs. Howard—"

"I don't need you to tell me how much I should worry," she interrupted. "Time was when I had to put up with patronizing pillocks like you for Jimmy's sake, but that at least's all behind us. All I want from you now is to tell me what's going off."

"Why, nothing," he said. "It was you who came to us, remember, asking about your husband . . ."

"Aye, and if you really just thought he'd gone on the booze, I'd not be sitting here talking to a chief inspector. I know how you lot work, and I know what you reckon to them you get rid of, and there's no way someone married to one of them 'ud get more than the time of day from a plod on the desk if there weren't something serious going off."

I really must pull myself together, Pascoe thought. Dalziel's righter than he knows. I've not been pulling my weight this week, and even when I'm going through the motions, I'm not really taking heed. Thick, unattractive termagant, that's how I've summed her up and that seemed enough. But she's not thick; and what the hell would I look like if I was in here worried sick about Ellie's whereabouts? As for termagant . . . "Lost your tongue or what?" she demanded . . . well, one out of three wasn't bad.

"Mrs. Howard," he said gently. "You're quite right. We *are* concerned about Jimmy, though without any firm reason for being so. If there were anything positive to tell you, I would, but there isn't. You know we had him in in connection with a possible drugs offense. There is no prospect of our charging him, which is why we let him go. But the drugs world is not a healthy place to be even on the fringes of. If there's anything at all you can tell us, if you have any reason yourself to believe Jimmy could be in danger, tell me. I'm not asking you to incriminate him. This is between you and me. No recording, no record even. For Jimmy's sake. Tell me."

There was no answer to Wield's ringing at Jane Ambler's flat. A neighbor emerged noncoincidentally just as he was about to give up and said, "She's probably gone to work."

"Always work on a Saturday, does she?"

"Sometimes. I just know she went out at her usual time this morning."

"No one staying with her just now, is there? Or visit her late last night?"

"Not that I know of. You police?"

"What makes you say that?"

"Well, you lot were round searching her place, weren't you? I asked her about it and she said it was all a mix-up. Still mixed up, are you?"

"Thanks for your help," said Wield.

It didn't sound promising, but as he was heading for Wanwood anyway, if she was there, he could kill two birds with one stone.

WDC Novello said, "It was that videotape you were looking at, sir. There was something . . . could we see it again?"

Might as well be hanged for a sheep as a lamb, she thought. And if what she imagined she'd noticed proved a chimera, then at least she'd be able to start her backtracking right off!

Dalziel rose and led the way to the audiovisual room. With Wield in charge of the tape, it was stored safely away in its catalogued place. He put it into the player and switched on. Nothing happened.

"Got to switch on the monitor as well, sir," suggested Novello helpfully.

"Wondered when you'd spot that," said Dalziel. "Here, you'd best have the remote, seeing as you're a technological genius."

They watched Cap Marvell's confrontation with Des Patten, saw the cutters begin to swing back, saw Wendy Walker's intervention . . .

"It's here," said Novello, slowing the frames down. "You all seemed to be watching the chesty dame . . ." Dalziel glanced at her narrowly. Could there really be someone in the Mid-Yorkshire Force who didn't know about his thing with Cap? ". . . looking to see if she were really going to swing those things at the security guard, right? But I was watching the skinny one. If you look at her, well, if you're trying to stop someone launching an attack, it's them you'd face, isn't it? It's them you'd look at as you were talking. But she stands in front of the fat lass with her back to her and her arms spread wide, almost like she was protecting her from the guard. And she never takes her eyes off the man, see?"

Dalziel realized that he'd done it again. He'd only had eyes for Cap. In slow motion he could see quite clearly the definition of her upper body muscles under the wet sweater as she swung the cutters back, the quiet resolution on that still, determined face. Not the expression of a woman in a murderous rage, he realized. Gentle tap between the legs to clear her path perhaps, but it came to him now that he knew beyond doubt she wasn't about to coldly and deliberately fracture someone's skull.

He ought to ring her. He ought to get up now and ring her and tell her, no, there wasn't any new evidence but he knew she was innocent, and even if she weren't, it didn't matter . . .

Novello said, uneasily, "What do you think, sir?"

Dalziel said, "Play it again, lass."

By the time Wield got to Wanwood, the weather which in town had merely seemed on the drizzly side of murky was wild and wintry and the wind roamed among the trees like a berserker who, having stripped his victims naked, is now bent on rending them limb from limb.

The guard on duty at the gate said, "You're out of luck if you want Dr. Batty. Not here."

"Oh. Place shuts down at the weekend, does it?"

"More or less. Get one or two people in usually. Got to be someone to take care of the animals, I suppose."

"I'm glad to hear it. Miss Ambler in?"

"Yeah. Mr. Patten said it was all right."

Brooding on this strange choice of words, Wield

drove up the drive and parked in front of the TecSec office next to a white Polo.

"Can't keep you away, can we?" said Patten as he entered on a blast of damp cold air. "What's it today? There's no one here except us chickens."

"I thought Jane Ambler was in?"

"That's right. There she is. If it's her you're after, she won't be long."

He spun his chair to face the bank of TV monitors and pointed at one. On it Wield saw Jane Ambler in what looked like a cloakroom removing articles from a locker and dropping them into a sports hold-all. At her side was a TecSec guard.

"What's going off?" asked Wield.

Patten spun back to face him.

"What? You don't know?"

"Know what?"

"She's been fired!"

"Eh? But you said that her and Batty . . ."

Over Patten's shoulder, he saw Ambler go to what looked like a storeroom and open the door. The TecSec man spoke to her, as if asking what business she had in there. She seemed to be urging him to go in and check for himself.

"Had a thing going? Yeah, but that's all it is to the randy doc, a thing. Puts his own thing about in a big way. Of course it did mean she could cause trouble for him at home if so inclined, but not any longer, not since the night before last."

The guard stood on the threshold of the storeroom. The woman gave him a sharp push, slammed the door behind him and turned the key.

Wield said, "What happened the night before last?"

Patten grinned, clearly enjoying himself.

"Seems the doc got home to find his clothes shoved into a lot of bin liners out on the lawn and the locks all changed. His wife was onto him at last and had chucked the poor sod out, sent him running home to mummy and daddy."

Ambler had left the room and vanished from the screen without appearing on another. The corridors weren't covered by the system, it appeared. Patten glanced round as if alerted by Wield's straying gaze.

"Finished, is she? Good, she'll come back this way and you can have your chat with her."

"I thought Batty was in a funny mood yesterday," said Wield. "But you didn't know about this when we talked, did you?"

"No. I was knocked right back when about an hour after you left, he called through to say that he'd just been on the phone to Ambler and told her she was fired and would I delete her authority to enter Wanwood."

"But she has entered," objected Wield. And was still entering. She had appeared on the screen showing what he thought was Batty's office and now she was unlocking a drawer in his desk.

"Turned up saying she wanted to clear her personal things out. Didn't want the embarrassment of coming back when everyone was in. So I gave her an escort and sent her through."

He glanced round again, just missing the woman's exit from the office after removing an envelope from the drawer and putting it into her hold-all.

"Do you think she reckoned that if Batty and his wife ever split up, the doctor would take up with her permanent?" asked Wield.

"Could be. Hey, you don't think she were the one bubbled Batty to his missus?" The idea seemed to delight Patten. "If that's right then it must have been a real sickener when, far from getting the man, all she gets is the sack!"

Ambler was now in one of the rooms in which the experimental animals were kept. She left the door wide-open, pushed open all the windows, then started unlocking the cages.

"So how did you find out about the split-up?" asked Wield, who could see where his duty lay but recalled the warnings in a recent policy communiqué about the dangers of overofficiousness. *Think before you act,* had been the advice. So now he was thinking.

"Rang the captain to tell him what was happening and he filled me in. He's a bit of a lad himself, and it did cross my mind that maybe he was giving Mrs. Batty one and had let it out that the doc was playing away too."

"Why would he do that? I mean, after all, your setup here depends on Dr. Batty's goodwill, doesn't it?"

"Business arrangement all signed and sealed." Patten grinned. "And goodwill goes out of the window when a good fuck comes through the door, eh, Sergeant?"

Jane Ambler had come through another door and was repeating her liberation tactics.

Reluctantly Wield resisted the temptation to debate Patten's interesting proposition. Thinking time was over and he had to speak before Patten noticed for himself.

He said, "RSPCA would be glad to see how well you exercise your animals."

"Eh?" Patten spun round. "Jesus! Why the hell didn't you say something sooner?"

He hammered a button which set an alarm screaming.

"Thought it might be part of her duties," said Wield, not trying very hard to sound convincing.

"Bollocks! And where the hell's that idiot I sent to keep an eye on her? Come on. We'd best get down there and sort this out."

"You want me? You think there's been a crime committed?"

But Patten wasn't playing any more games. He rushed past Wield and out of the office.

For a brief moment the sergeant stood and looked at the monitors, which showed him a variety of small animals emerging nervously from their cages and sniffing the air of freedom with every sign of doubt.

"Know just how you feel," Wield said. Then followed.

II

"THANK YOU," said Andy Dalziel into the phone. "Thank you very much indeed."

He banged the receiver down and turned his benevolent gaze upon WDC Novello who, doubting the evidence of her eyes, said uneasily, "Good news, sir?"

"I think so," he said. But before he could share it, if that was his intention, the door burst open and Pascoe came in.

"I think I've got something, sir," he said.

"If it's catching, bugger off," said the Fat Man.

"It's Mrs. Howard," said Pascoe, riding the familiar joke with an ease which Novello noted and registered. "She's dead certain there's something iffy about Tec-Sec. Says that her Jimmy used to drink a lot with Rosso, that's ex-Private Rosthwaite, Sanderson's old batman . . ."

"Yes, yes, I know who he is. Was," said Dalziel impatiently. "Are we getting close to the good stuff or have I missed it already?"

Again Novello noted the lack of reaction to the provocations. Was this the secret of survival?

"She says she used to go on about him, Rosso, I mean, because she reckoned he was such a piss artist, he was leading even Jimmy astray. Then they stopped going out together. She gloated—not her word but that's what she meant—and Jimmy told her to put a sock in it, it wasn't anything she'd said, it was just that it wasn't good policy, not for a man starting out on a new career."

"Meaning?"

"Perhaps that Rosso, pissed, was telling Jimmy things he didn't want to know. Mrs. Howard says that it was clear Rosso really resented the way that Patten had come into the company and got level billing while he was still very much the faithful retainer."

"Then he ran into a tree," said Dalziel.

"And Jimmy went very quiet after that."

"Old friend dies, it knocks you back."

"He wasn't grieving, not according to his missus. Or if he was, it was Jimmy he grieved for."

"That it?"

"More or less," said Pascoe rather sulkily. (So he *was* vulnerable, thought Novello.) "Anyway I can see that you've got something far more important and significant to tell me."

"Don't pout, else you'll have Wieldy sending you valentines. And what you've said fits nicely with what I've just found out. It were Ivor here who put me onto it."

Pascoe glanced at Novello, who gave him the bewildered smile of a United supporter who has strayed into a City pub and been bought a pint.

"Well done," he said.

"Aye, bloody well done," said Dalziel. "You've not been using her proper, Peter. Think on. I'll have no discrimination in my department. Ivor, go and fetch my

car round to the front, eh? We'll be down in two
shakes of a tart's tail.''

"So what's the startling revelation?" said Pascoe after the woman had gone.

Dalziel was busy dialing a number. He said "shit" as
he got the engaged tone, then pressed the *repeat redial*
button.

"We were asking the wrong question, lad," he said.
"It shouldn't have been whether or not Cap meant to
attack Patten, but why was Wendy Walker acting as
peacekeeper? I mean, she was a real fire-eater that one,
and we know her main aim was to get a reputation in
the animal protest game as an extremist, ready to go all
the way for the cause. Here was the perfect situation.
Scratch a few eyes out, smash a few windows, create
merry hell till she got arrested and had her day in
court. But what does she do? Pours oil on troubled
waters. Why?"

"You're going to tell me. Eventually," said Pascoe.

"Because she clocks Des Patten. It's not a face to
forget, is it? And she's seen it before."

"Oh yes. Where?"

"Wieldy checked Patten out, 'cos he thought he
might have been doing something dodgy between vanishing out of Mid-Yorkshire and reappearing as Sanderson's partner. He were disappointed to find that all
he'd been doing was working for Task Force Five, the
Manchester security company."

"Yes, I know who they are. So? Oh shit."

"Aye, lad," said Dalziel reproachfully. "You did the
liaising with Redcar when ALBA had their bit of bother
last summer. It's all in your file. FraserGreenleaf's security was looked after by Task Force Five."

"But I didn't know that Patten . . . I mean, TecSec
didn't come on the Wanwood scene till after my investigation, did they?"

"No matter, lad," said Dalziel magnanimously.

"Even Homer has to take a leak. I've just been on the bell to Redcar. They've checked. And yes, Des Patten was on the security staff at FraserGreenleaf. He had a disagreement about overtime payments and jacked it in about three weeks before the raid where Shufflebottom got killed."

"And Ellie said that Wendy had been up there on a visit not long before. You think she met him?"

"Saw him in a pub, maybe. Her brother says hello, tells her he's a colleague, and because of that scar, the face sticks. And then she sees him again."

"But why should that rouse her suspicions? He is in the business after all."

"Probably doesn't. Not at first. In fact she might be more worried he'd clock her and start asking questions. So she calms things down, cooperates to get away without any more hassle. But when she gets home she starts thinking. And when she catches on that we're asking questions about whether ANIMA could have been involved in the previous raid at Wanwood, which in its turn looked tied into the Redcar raid, bells start buzzing. She mebbe starts asking questions about TecSec, finds they got the contract as a result of that summer raid. It's still a long way even from firm suspicion, but unfortunately for her, Patten's cottoned on who she is."

"How?" asked Pascoe.

Dalziel scratched his neck punitively and said, "Me. First thing I did when I saw her was mention Burrthorpe. Patten were earwigging. He must've known Shufflebottom's background. Not summat he'd keep secret. Perhaps Wendy's face rang a bell with him too. And it wouldn't be difficult to check her maiden name."

"And he killed her on the off chance she was onto something?" said Pascoe incredulously.

"Why not? Soldier's creed, isn't it? You get 'em in

your sights, shoot. You may not have another chance. But mebbe there was more. She must have slept on it and woke up feeling worried whether she had summat or nowt. So she called on Cap Marvell for a chat . . ."

"But she didn't even like the woman," protested Pascoe.

"Walker was a bright lass," said Dalziel. "She knew there were other ways of looking at things than her own and she wouldn't let likes or dislikes get in the way of doing whatever she set out to do. She'd use anybody or anything she thought might be helpful."

He means Ellie too, thought Pascoe. Interesting idea. Could it be that it was the aboriginals converting the missionaries after all?

"Ms. Marvell told you this?"

"No. I overheard," said Dalziel. "Got nowhere. Cap didn't have the time so they had a row instead. Next Walker goes round to your place . . ."

"And gets nowhere again," said Pascoe. "But she arranged to see Ellie that night."

"Yeah, but she wasn't the kind to sit on her thumb all day when there were things she could be doing. Suppose she started nosing round the TecSec office in town, asking questions about Patten, and he found out. Then, being the way he is, he might think, better safe than sorry. And after Rosso, he could have got a taste for traffic accidents . . ."

"Rosso?"

"That's what you were suggesting, wasn't it? That Rosso became a liability so they knocked him off? Or did you have it down to Act of God?"

"Well, no, but it was just a hypothesis. . . . Look, if any of this is true, it all started because TecSec faked an animal rights raid on FG's plant at Redcar. Why?"

"Think about it," said Dalziel. "Suppose there's something another firm's got that you'd like a look at, without them knowing of course. And you talk about this with an old chum in the security business who then meets up with another old acquaintance who just happens to have left the outfit looking after security at the plant his chum's interested in. Suddenly it seems possible. In, out, make it look like animals libbers, wreck a couple of offices, and take some snaps of whatever it is chummy wants. Goes like a dream till Shufflebottom runs into Patten. And that's blown it altogether. I mean, no one's going to believe Des Patten is an animal rights protester! So he gets rid of the problem the only way he knows how. And again with Rosso, who's shooting his mouth off when he's pissed. And again with Walker. And mebbe again . . ."

". . . with Jimmy Howard if he started thinking he knew more than he ought and we had some kind of hold on him. Sir, shouldn't we get over to Wanwood and have a word? If Wieldy's there already and Patten gets the wrong idea . . ."

"Wieldy can take care of himself. But you're right. Let's go."

He rose and made for the door.

"Sir, your telephone . . . it's on repeat."

"Oh aye. Switch it off, will you?"

Before he did so, Pascoe looked at the number being printed on the display. It was local. He didn't recognize it but as he reached to press the cancel button the call was answered by a woman's voice saying simply, "Yes?"

Just one syllable, but he had no difficulty in recognizing Cap Marvell's voice. Which meant that either Dalziel was certain she was in the clear, or that for once he was taking Pascoe's advice.

He went to the door and looked into the corridor. No sign of the Fat Man, just the echo of his voice coming up the stairwell, ". . . bloody move on!"

He went back to the phone, pressed the *cancel* button, and hurried out after his great master.

III

BY THE TIME THEY REACHED THE LAB AREA it was as if Noah's Ark had struck an iceberg. There were terrified animals everywhere and through the open windows a rising gale was hurling blasts of icy air and volleys of horizontal hail. A couple of TecSec men, roused by the alarm, had arrived simultaneously.

"Don't just stand there," screamed Patten. "Grab those bloody things!"

"But take care," admonished Wield. "You never know what they've got."

The men, galvanized into activity by their boss's parade ground bellow, slowed visibly as the implications of Wield's warning struck them.

Patten shot him a furious glance and yelled, "It's okay. There's nothing communicable, Dr. Batty's word on it."

"Is that right or did you make it up?" asked Wield, the policeman in him reluctantly taking over. If any of the escaped beasts *did* have a communicable disease, then there could be a serious problem.

"Any that need special precautions when they're handled are kept in there," said Patten, indicating another door. "And it doesn't look like she's been in."

Wield tried the handle. It was still locked. Through the glass panel the cages appeared untampered with, though their inmates were setting up a tremendous racket as if in sympathy with their fleeing fellows.

"Well, at least she's got some sense," said Wield.

"More likely the bitch simply doesn't have a key," snarled Patten. "Come on, let's find her. Where the hell are you going?"

"To the car park," said Wield. "First off, I need to radio this in. And second, unless she's planning to walk all the way back to town, that's where the lass'll be heading too."

That was the trouble with the army, he thought. Good at doing things, not so good at thinking. Even Jimmy Howard would have worked this one out.

Which reminded him.

"You see anything of Jimmy Howard?" he asked as they hurried out of the building.

"Not since you arrested him. Isn't he still banged up then?"

Funny, thought Wield. Tony Beasley, the TecSec brief, had rung last evening to check that his client was being released as the law required. Perhaps he only communicated with Captain Sanderson.

"No, we had to let him go."

"Another police cock-up then? Done a runner, has he? Don't blame him. Once you lot get your teeth into someone, you'll keep crunching till you draw blood. Jimmy would know that . . . there she is. Stop, you fucking bitch!"

Ambler was opening the door of the white Polo. She saw them coming, chucked her hold-all onto the passenger seat, scrambled in after it, and with a speed which won Wield's admiration got her key in the ignition and started the engine. Even so, Patten had moved fast enough to get his hand on the door handle. Ambler banged down the locking pin and accelerated away. The TecSec man ran alongside, letting his grip on the handle tow him to Olympic sprint speed before he had to decide whether to let go or be dragged. He let go, but kept on running, shouting something over his shoulder. The wild wind whipped his words away, but Wield caught ". . . gates . . ." Presumably he meant the two security gates across the drive completing the boundaries of the cordon sanitaire. If these had been closed, they could still overtake the woman. Reluctantly he broke into a jog. He was still, thank God, wearing his light topcoat, but it didn't feel like it was going to offer any long-term protection. He wasn't motivated by any burning desire to arrest Ambler, but it didn't seem a good idea to leave the task to Patten, not the way he was acting.

He rounded the top bend of the drive and saw that the gates were shut. Presumably the man responsible had shut them as soon as he heard the alarm. But where was he? Chances were the stupid sod had then abandoned his post to help in the roundup of the animals.

Security companies . . . as much protection as a crocheted condom!

The Polo had screeched to a halt and Ambler was out, pulling at the bolt on the first gate and throwing her whole weight against it. Slowly it swung open. She ran back toward the car, hesitated, looked back toward the second gate.

She's had it, thought Wield. No way she can get the other gate open before Patten, who was thundering down the drive, reached her. He slowed down, thinking she might use the TecSec man's speed to dodge round him, in which case he'd have the job of acting as backstop.

Instead she turned and ran. There was nowhere to go. The gate ahead was unclimbable and on either side stretched that wide swath of desolation which TecSec had ripped through the noble old wood. Even dry it would have been unattractive terrain, but drenched by the autumn rains, its surface a morass of glutinous mud pocked with water-filled craters, only a madman, or one under threat from a madman, would advance across its treacherous surface.

Ambler paused and glanced back. Perhaps she was contemplating surrender. But whatever she saw in Pat-

ten's face persuaded her that an insane valor is sometimes the better part of a dangerous discretion.

She turned and ran into the wasteland.

For a second Wield thought that like some story-
book fay she was skimming lightfoot across the gelati-
nous mud, leaving nothing more than the merest splash
of water vapor to mark her path. Then he realized that
she must be following the line of unretrieved, perhaps
unretrievable, duckboards laid to facilitate passage to
the crater where Wendy Walker had encountered the
bones.

This was serious. With the removal of so much material for Dr. Death's sluices, the crater now was huge
and immersion there could lead to a fate far worse than
George Headingley's heavy cold.

Interestingly, the same thought seemed to have occurred to Patten. Rage drained from his face to be replaced by real concern, and he called after the fleeing
woman, "Jane, don't be daft, lass. There's nowhere to
go. Take care. Come on back, no one's going to harm
you."

It was impossible to tell if the woman heard him
above the howl of the storm. Wield came alongside and
added his voice to the plea.

"Miss Ambler," he bellowed, almost Dalziel-decibel
level. "It's okay. We know you've had real provocation.
There's no real harm done. Head on back here and
we'll soon sort it out."

The woman had stopped, whether because she'd
heard or merely reached the limit of the duckboards
was impossible to say. The surviving trees of
Wanwood, pressing like caged football supporters
against the nethermost security fence, rocked and
surged in a fury of sound which a fanciful mind might
have heard as a protest against the death of their fellows. A tremendous blast unsteadied the woman. She

staggered, recovered, staggered again. Then she was gone.

"Jesus!" exploded Patten. Then he was running along the duckboards, followed more cautiously by Wield.

The excavations had turned the crater into a small tarn filled with impenetrably brown water. As they reached its edge, the woman surfaced gasping for air and flailing her arms wildly. There were seven or eight feet of water beneath her, Wield guessed, bottomed by God knew what depth of sucking, clinging mud. That would be the killer. Get your feet stuck in that and there'd be no kicking free.

"Float," he yelled. "On your back. Just float!"

Perhaps she heard him, perhaps it was just exhaustion and the paralyzing effect of the cold water, but she stopped flailing and lay backward on the surface. Patten, on one knee like a Victorian suitor, reached out his right hand. Wield grabbed the other to give him support. Ambler saw the outstretched hand, reached for it, their index fingers touched like God's and Adam's, then the wind drove a small wave into her gasping mouth and she choked and vanished under once again.

Seconds passed. One. Two. Three . . .

"Shit," said Patten. "I'll have to go in."

He began kicking his shoes off. Thank God for action man! thought Wield fervently, withdrawing all his previous reservations about the breed. Then right in the center of the tarn he saw a movement in the waters, like the turbulence in the pool at Lourdes which presages the moment of miracle.

"There she is!" he screamed.

And next moment like some creature of the deep too violently aroused from its age-long slumber, Jane Ambler burst upward with such force that it seemed as if she was ambitious to stand on the surface of the water. It was a maneuver to win a gold medal at synchronized swimming; and incredibly, horribly, she was not disqualified by lack of a partner. In her arms was the figure of a man, his head flopping backward like a chrysanthemum on a broken stalk, and as the brown water drained through the sodden locks, Wield recognized Jimmy Howard.

He only had a split second to register the knowledge and the reason it gave for Patten's concern at seeing the girl plunge into the water. Then a clenched fist caught him on the back of his neck and he tumbled forward into the muddy depths.

As he sank, he thought, I should have worked harder to get Edwin out of his bad temper this morning. He'll think I got myself drowned on purpose just to spite him!

The thought was so absurd he might have laughed if that wouldn't have involved imbibing another gallon of this foul liquid. Instead he kicked out and burst to the surface, gasping in great mouthfuls of windy air. Jane Ambler was quite close. He was pleased to see she had jilted her grisly escort, and he reached out and took her in the prescribed lifesaving hold. Shock seemed to have rendered her catatonic and she made no attempt to struggle.

He glanced toward the duckboards. Patten was crouched there, his gaze fixed on them. It didn't need a novelist's imagination to read what was going through his mind. Was there any chance of getting away with sending them to join Jimmy Howard at the bottom of the crater? And with one down, and probably three others behind him, what did it matter how short the odds were anyway? That was the military mind. Limited by its elevation of death to a first rather than a last option.

He paddled to the far side of the crater and tried to get a supporting grip on the wall. Muddy clay came away in his hand. There was neither exit nor support there. The water was bitterly cold. He couldn't keep the pair of them afloat for long. It would have to be the duckboard and the hope that Patten's mind still had some hold on the realities of the situation.

The man had stood up and was looking back toward the drive. Perhaps he's just going to make a run for it, thought Wield hopefully. But no, he was kneeling down again, reaching out a threatening hand as Wield got closer. Grab it and jerk him into the water? thought the sergeant. Then drown the bastard!

He might have a chance. But he doubted if Ambler could survive if he let her go.

He was very close now.

Too close. As he opened his mouth to start the unpromising reasoning process, the hand shot out the extra inches and seized him by the collar. He drew in a huge breath of air, but instead of the expected thrust into the drowning depths, he felt himself being pulled alongside the duckboards.

God is all-powerful, he thought. He can make even the military mind see reason.

Then he turned his head sideways and saw that it wasn't seeing reason that had made Patten change his plans, it was the sight of Andy Dalziel and Peter Pascoe advancing along the boards like gods out of a machine.

Back on terra firma, with Patten cuffed and on his way to a cell, Wield, showered and dried and wearing the only clothes available, which was the hated TecSec uniform, drank a cup of tea liberally laced with Batty's Glenmorangie which Dalziel had liberated from the doctor's sideboard.

"He won't mind," said Dalziel. "Soul of generosity, that fellow."

"Has he been told what's gone off?" asked Wield.

"Not yet," said Dalziel. "Thought I'd leave it till I

see if we've got enough to nick him, then I won't need to be polite to the sod anymore."

He filled Wield in on the hypothesis he and Pascoe had put together.

"But it's not going to be easy to prove without an admission," he concluded.

"Or hard evidence."

"Oh aye. Or hard evidence." He regarded Wield shrewdly. "Got anything in mind?"

"Jane Ambler could be worth talking to," said Wield.

He hadn't had time yet to go into the details of the woman's sabotage.

"You reckon? Then let's go see her. She's lying down in the medical room with Novello waiting for the ambulance."

"I'll catch you up," said Wield. "Something I need from the car."

He went outside. Ambler's Polo had been driven back up to the house to clear the drive. He opened the passenger door and started searching through the hold-all on the seat. There wasn't a great deal in it—obviously "collecting her things" had merely been a ruse to get back inside Wanwood—and there was only one envelope. Handling it carefully, he glanced inside. It contained half a dozen film negatives. He held them up to the light and saw lines of type far too small to decipher. Replacing them, he started to close the car door and as he did so, he sensed rather than saw a movement beneath the seat.

Cautiously he stooped and peered under. A pair of bright small eyes peered fearfully back. He reached down and a little paw clutched at his outstretched finger. Gently he drew out a tiny monkey which could have been the one he'd seen Ambler injecting on their first meeting.

It must have crept into the car when the woman abandoned it at the first gate.

"Good move," said Wield. "You almost made it."

Suddenly it wriggled out of his grasp but didn't try to escape. Instead it jumped onto his shoulder and wrapped its arms around his neck, nuzzling at his ear.

Wield glanced around. No one in sight. He went quickly to his own car and opened the boot.

The little animal protested when he prized it free from his shoulder and set it down on an old traveling rug.

"You prefer a cage and hypos on the hour, you just say so," he said sternly.

The monkey went quiet and snuggled down into the rug.

"Right. I'll see you later," said Wield, gently closing the boot.

As he went back inside he heard a distant ambulance bell.

In the medical room he found Jane Ambler also wearing a TecSec uniform and looking reasonably well, considering what she'd been through. WDC Novello was sitting watchfully at her side while the looming figure of Dalziel blocked the light from the window.

She looked pleased to see him. With Dalziel doing his Hannibal-Lecter-at-the-Health-Farm impression, she'd probably have looked pleased to see King Kong.

"I want to thank you," she said weakly.

"My pleasure," said Wield. "Listen, luv, all this stuff you did to get your own back on Batty, I want you to know I've been there, I understand what you were feeling."

As he spoke he moved to put himself between the woman and the Fat Man.

"I reckon the court could understand that too," he went on. "Spur-of-the-moment revenge, anyone could do it. But taking them negatives, that's a bit different."

He held up the envelope.

"That could look like you were going to try a bit of blackmail," he said. "And once the court gets a sniff of premeditation . . ."

"I just wanted to frighten him," she said.

Wield dug his finger into his ear as if he hadn't quite caught the remark.

He said, "Of course if you'd been uneasy for some time that something not quite right was going off at ALBA, and you decided that as this was probably your last chance to get hold of the evidence, it was your duty as a good citizen to make sure these negatives came into our hands. . . ."

He could see her like a chess champion working out all the moves and their implications. He moved slightly to one side to reopen her view of Dalziel, which was a bit like Kasparov drawing an opponent's attention to the presence of a KGB bodyguard with his hand on his gun butt.

It clearly concentrated the mind wonderfully.

She said, "Okay. This is the way it was. David Batty and I were very close. It was his idea, he started it, but I admit I was happy to go along. He's a good-looking guy and I was flattered, young research assistant making it with the department chief. But eventually I started getting worried by some of the things he let slip about some aspects of our work."

"What aspects?" said Wield.

"Our main project ever since I joined has been work on a new treatment for rheumatoid arthritis. You should understand that the first company to make a breakthrough there is guaranteed billions. There are always plenty of rumors flying around and word started to get around that FraserGreenleaf were way ahead. David was really narked about this, particularly as the researcher I'd replaced had been headhunted by FG about eighteen months ago. Of course he was legally tied not to communicate anything he'd been working on here, but it's almost impossible to enforce that, and David had convinced himself that FG's breakthrough, if it came, would really be ALBA's."

She paused.

"So?" prompted Wield.

"So a few months back, in the summer, suddenly the direction of our research took a dramatic change," she said. "I couldn't see why. It didn't follow naturally out of what had gone before. And when I asked David why . . ."

She paused again, then looking past Wield to Dalziel she said, "I want it to be clearly understood that I have no firm knowledge of anything, only some guesses based on hints dropped by David Batty during the course of our . . . work. Unless I'm convinced you understand and accept this, I don't think I have anything more to say."

"I think mebbe you've said enough already," said Dalziel, giving her a hungry grin.

She grinned back and said, "Not under caution I haven't. And I certainly won't sign anything. Or give evidence in court. Not unless I see it in black and white that it's clearly understood that I am entirely an innocent party in all this."

"All what?" inquired Dalziel.

"How should I know, being entirely innocent?" she replied.

She was, acknowledged Wield, a real gladiator.

Suddenly Dalziel's hungry grin turned to Santa Claus beam.

"Nay, lass, tha's so squeaky clean it makes my eyes hurt just to look at you. Never fear, I'll stand up and tell the court you're the Virgin Mary. So what did Dr. Batty answer when you asked him about the new research?"

"He took some photographic negatives out of his

desk, waved them in the air and said, 'God moves in a mysterious way His wonders to perform, and so do I!' He was a bit drunk at the time.''

"And what did you understand by this?"

"That somehow he'd got information from somewhere about someone else's research."

"But you'd no idea how or whose?"

"None whatsoever. All I knew was that after he fired me, if I didn't take this last chance to get hold of those negatives, I might never find out the truth. I was of course going to hand them over to the authorities at the first opportunity."

"Which is right now, lass. And don't think we're not grateful," said Dalziel.

The door opened and Pascoe came in.

"Ambulance is here, sir."

"Grand. You fit enough to travel up front, miss?"

"I think so. Why?"

"Then we can get them to fit Jimmy Howard in the back, saves a double journey," said Dalziel genially. "Got to watch NHS finances these days, haven't we? Novello, you go with the lady. See she's taken care of."

The door closed behind them.

"There goes a real piece of work," said Dalziel not unadmiringly.

"Why? What's happened?" said Pascoe.

They told him. He said, "So you reckon these negatives are photos of FraserGreenleaf research papers, taken during the Redcar raid?"

"I'd put money on it. One way to find out. We'll get 'em printed then ask someone from FG to take a look. Have we got hold of Captain Sanderson?"

Pascoe shook his head.

"They just called in to say that there's no sign of him at his flat or at TecSec HQ."

"Bugger," said Dalziel. "I'd have liked to finger his

collar before he got wind that owt's gone wrong. What about Batty?''

"Blank there too, sir. Thought the simplest thing to do was ring his home and tell him a few of the animals had got loose and invite him out here, but all I got was his wife, who said she didn't know where he was. Didn't sound as if she cared much either, though I got the impression there was someone there.''

Wield coughed and said, "Could be that Mrs. Batty's chucked her husband out. Could even be that Captain Sanderson's round there, comforting her.''

Dalziel looked thoughtfully at the sergeant and said, "Total immersion turned you psychic or what, Wieldy?''

"No, sir. Just something Patten said.''

"Oh aye. Give you any ideas where the doctor might have ended up?''

"Gone home to mummy, he thought.''

"Where else?'' laughed the Fat Man. "Right, I'll go and see if I can catch the captain on the job; you, Wieldy, see to them photos, then get yourself down to the hospital and take Ambler's statement. She seems to fancy you. Oh, and while you're down there, get yourself checked out. I know since the Water Board got privatized, we've not had to be too choosy about what we drink, but I think even the chairman would think his millions hard-earned if he had to share his bath with Jimmy Howard.''

"What shall I do, sir?'' asked Pascoe.

"You, Pete? Why, I'd have thought you'd have signed off by now, having spared us a good couple of hours of your time today. Tell you what. You were going on about wanting an excuse to ask Tom Batty some more questions. Why don't you pop out to Kirkton and if you see your way to fitting it in, pick up Dr. David and bring him back for questioning. But only if it's not going to interfere with your own plans of course.''

Dalziel's ironic touch made Ian Paisley sound like Jane Austen.

"I'll do that, sir," said Pascoe.

"I'd be grateful. And do us a favor, lad. Try to keep at least one foot in the nineties!"

"I'll try," said Peter Pascoe.

IV

SLOW AND PERILOUS was the journey westward, with flooded roads and fallen trees. Three times the drapes of darkness swirling in his headlamps' beam were drawn back by the emergency services, and for a moment like the Venerable Bede's sparrow he passed through a salient of light across which stretcher bearers bore the wounded and the dead from the wreckage of their lives.

Kirkton lay in darkness. The power lines must have come down. Only the red glow of coal and the buttermilk light of candles limned the curtained windows. So must the village have looked when it still was a village eighty years ago. But an inflammation of the sky beyond the massive fortress wall told him that ALBA lived up to its name in this at least, summoning up the dawn of its own generators when the national grid failed.

They were expecting him at the Maisterhouse. Of course the gateman would have rung through. But as he entered the long sitting room and saw them grouped around the fireplace—Thomas Batty serious and watchful—Janet Batty, Bertie Grindal's daughter, uncertain and anxious—Dr. David, the main object of his visit, smiling and welcoming—he got a sense of expectancy deeper rooted than mere foreknowledge.

It was David Batty who spoke.

"Chief Inspector Pascoe . . . Peter . . . good to see you again. Take a pew. And take some tea too. No use offering anything stronger, I suppose?"

He seemed too genuinely at ease for it to be wholly an act, confirming Pascoe's feeling that their expectancy had nothing to do with what had happened at Wanwood—today, at least.

So don't break the mood, he thought as he sat down. Time enough to reveal his official purpose.

He said, "Nothing for me, thanks. Aren't you going to sit down too?"

They were still looming over him. David Batty grinned and slumped into a deep armchair while his parents perched awkwardly on the edge of a chaise longue which looked sculpted rather than upholstered.

Whatever they have to tell me, thought Pascoe, is going to be told through necessity not choice. They must be shown that I know too much now to be diverted from pursuing the whole truth.

He said, "Mr. Batty, last time we met I think I mentioned to you that I had a family connection with Kirkton. I had a slight suspicion then that you knew something more about the Pascoe connection than you were letting on, and that the knowledge that I was one of the Kirkton Pascoes came as a bit of a shock to you."

"No. Why should it?" the man said unconvincingly.

"Good question. I wondered about it myself. Then as I later discovered a fairly close connection between your family and mine a generation or so back, I thought perhaps you too were somehow aware of it. But it still didn't explain the intensity of your reaction. Then yesterday—or rather early this morning—"

He stifled an associative yawn as his words reminded him how little sleep he'd had.

"Sorry," he said. "I discovered or at least developed a strong suspicion of something quite extraordinary, to wit, that the bones discovered out at Wanwood belonged to my great-grandfather."

He saw on the older pair's faces the admission of knowledge, quickly suppressed on the man's, but its traces less easily erased from the woman's.

Leaning forward and concentrating on her, Pascoe said, "I mean of course the great-grandfather your father, Herbert Grindal, *actually* killed, not my other great-grandfather, the one he merely allowed to be executed in Flanders."

Tears filled her eyes. Her husband looked ready to work himself up into a fine fit of indignation, but as the tears started to stream down his wife's face, he seemed to acknowledge to himself that there was no point in trying to bluster a way out of this.

He said, "How . . . ?"

Pascoe said, "I have in my possession Sergeant Peter Pascoe's journal right up to the eve of his execution. Also I have seen the journal of the officer who acted as his Prisoner's Friend at the court-martial, and I know the details of the evidence given by your father, Mrs. Batty, and the letter accompanying it, written by your grandfather."

The implication that he'd got onto these last two via Studholme's journal seemed strong enough to keep faith with Poll Pollinger.

"What I want to do now," he went on, "is discover what more you can tell me about this business. I should warn you that the inquiry into the cause of death of Stephen Pascoe is still ongoing, and as things stand at the moment, I shall feel impelled to reveal at the inquest all that I have been able to discover."

Let 'em know that like any paranoid he'd go all the way!

"These are scarcely matters for the media, Mr. Pascoe," protested the older Batty. "Tabloid publicity wouldn't benefit anyone."

"You think not? I don't see how it could hurt my family," retorted Pascoe. "There's no way either of my ancestors could be stigmatized worse than they have been for the past eighty years."

"I really can't see what all the fuss is about, for God's sake," said David Batty impatiently. "It's history we're talking here! That's all your fat boss seemed worried about, Peter. Proving it all happened so long ago that it wouldn't either occupy his time or worsen his crime figures."

Pascoe regarded him coldly. This was a man with very little moral sense. Knowing that moved his pleasant easygoing manner into a new dimension.

But no reason not to use him. He forced a young conspirator's smile.

"That's right, David," he said. "But if I'm going to keep quiet, I need to know what exactly it is I'm keeping quiet about, so I don't let it out by accident."

This fallacious pragmatism fell on sympathetic ears.

"Let's show him," said David Batty. "Then he'll know we're all in it together."

His parents exchanged questioning glances, but their son, not waiting for an answer, rose and left the room. A moment later he returned with an old buff legal envelope.

"Here we go," he said, dropping it on Pascoe's lap. "This should fill in the gaps."

Pascoe opened it and took out a single sheet of foolscap covered by a neat copperplate hand. There was a heading printed in capitals. STATEMENT OF ARTHUR HERBERT GRINDAL NOVEMBER 30TH 1917.

Another voice from the past. When would it ever fall silent?

He began to read.

I, Arthur Herbert Grindal of Kirkton in the county of Yorkshire, being of sound mind, affirm and assert that the following is a true and accurate description of the circumstances surrounding the death of Stephen Pascoe, also of Kirkton.

On the evening of November 27th last I was visiting my son Bertie then being treated for wounds received in Flanders during military service at the Officers' Hospital situated at Wanwood House, Mid-Yorkshire. He was in a state of some distress having just learned that his former platoon sergeant, Peter Pascoe, cousin to the above mentioned Stephen Pascoe, had been executed by firing squad having been found guilty of cowardice in face of the enemy. Bertie, in a nervous condition diagnosed as neurasthenia brought on by long and continuous exposure to the danger of front line life, took upon himself some responsibility for the death of his sergeant, and had been deeply shocked by allegations made against him during the court-martial even though I understand that none of his other men or fellow officers had offered any but highest praise for his own conduct under fire. I calmed him down and when the time came to leave we went out to my car and, finding ourselves with much still to say to each other, took a turn down the drive to keep the blood circulating against the night frost. Here we were aware of a figure approaching which when it became identifiable in the moonlight, I recognized as Stephen Pascoe, who used to be in my employ. He was wearing a greatcoat over his private's uniform. I got the impression he had been drinking. As soon as he saw my son he cried, "Grindal, there you are, it's you I've come looking for. I know from my cousin what really happened out there and I'll find other lads to back up the true story when this lot's over, believe me. Meanwhile don't you dare go writing letters to Peter's wife, widow I mean, that's what you've made her, and as for your filthy money . . ." and here he hurled a leather purse full into Bertie's face and rushed at him with both hands outstretched as though he wanted to strangle him. I tried to intervene and got knocked aside for my pains. As I lay on the ground I saw Pascoe seize hold of Bertie, they spun around, moving off the drive into the trees, and there one of them caught his foot on a root and they both went down locked together. But only Bertie got up.

He helped me to my feet and I examined Pascoe. His head had hit a sharp edge of rock protruding from the earth and he was no longer breathing.

Bertie was in no condition to make decisions so I took control. What happened next was my sole decision and my sole responsibility. Together we lifted the body and carried it into the wood. There is an old icehouse there, built for the original old mansion and long disused, almost completely hidden beneath earth and undergrowth. Here we laid the body. Then I escorted Bertie back to the hospital where I told the matron his nerves had taken a turn for the worse and she administered a sleeping draught. After that I set off to drive home and in the lights of my car noticed the purse lying in the driveway. I stopped to pick it up and then got an idea of how I might throw the authorities off the scent when they began to look for the missing soldier. I went to the icehouse and stripped the body of all its military uniform and identifying discs. The purse with the gold sovereigns in it I tossed in beside the corpse. The clothes I put in my car and two days later when I was in Liverpool on business, I hid them where they would be found in the railway station there.

I am making this statement because, in the event of my death and the subsequent discovery of Stephen Pascoe's remains, it is possible that my son might, because of his nervous condition, give a false or partial account of events, laying himself open to criminal charges, perhaps even murder. I wish to make it quite clear that apart from aiding me in the concealment of the body (and that only because he was at that time incapable of not following my commands), Bertie has broken no law. My fear was, and is, that if his part in Pascoe's accidental death came to light, any rumours which might already be in circulation or subsequently arise about my son's conduct as an officer during the late campaign in Flanders could flare up and result in false accusation, and perhaps permanent nervous debility.

Nothing in this letter, nor in any contribution I may have made or may subsequently make, to the maintenance of Sergeant's Pascoe's family, should be taken as acknowledgment or admission of any responsibility in law for said family, or recognition of any allegations made concerning my own conduct or that of my son Herbert on active service. My purpose, as stated, is simply to assert the

bare facts of the unfortunate and accidental death
of Private Stephen Pascoe.

It was signed by Arthur Grindal with his signature
witnessed by a Leeds solicitor and his clerk.

Pascoe read it through three times. It should have
been moving—a man's desperate attempt to protect his
son—but something about it rang false as an atheist's
prayers.

"Does that satisfy you, Mr. Pascoe?" said Thomas
Batty. "A sad and tragic affair but long buried in the
past and best left that way."

"Like all the other mistakes made in those years, you
mean?" said Pascoe. "God, how the hell can this country go anywhere if it can't face the truth about itself?"

"That's a bit heavy," said Dr. David. "Okay, World
War One was a mess, but this isn't really anything to
do with it."

"It's everything to do with it! But let's just stick to
the fine detail then. First off, no allegations were made
against Bertie during the trial other than that he was
dazed, and possibly wounded by a shell blast and had
to be restrained from a single-handed assault on an enemy pillbox."

Batty considered then said, "Okay. So?"

"So Arthur Grindal could only have got the idea
that such allegations might be made from one source.
His own son, who must have poured his heart out, admitting that he was in a state of sheer terror most of
the time and would probably have run if the sergeant
hadn't taken control. I wonder what his *real* written
evidence would have sounded like?"

"What do you mean?" asked Thomas Batty.

"I mean that the evidence mainly responsible for
killing my great-grandfather was a deposition, allegedly
dictated to Arthur Grindal, in which Sergeant Pascoe's
actions were painted in the worst light possible. It was

supported by a covering letter in which Arthur depicted him as a socialist agitator of the worst kind. And you know what? None of these lies was necessary! My poor benighted great-grandfather was out there, lying through his teeth to protect his pathetic little officer's reputation!"

He stopped abruptly. Janet Batty's face had drained of color, leaving it pale and waxy as a lily. It's this woman's father I'm talking about, he thought. My own connection with all this is three generations old and I never knew the men involved, but it's this woman's father, and her pain must go at least as deep as my indignation.

He said, "Mrs. Batty, I'm sorry. I believe your father was as much a victim here as anyone else. I'm sure if he had ever known . . ."

"Oh, he knows," she burst out. "He knows!"

It took a few seconds for the tense to sink in.

"Knows?" he echoed.

He saw Thomas Batty's warning glance, David Batty's wry grin, remembered the nurse he'd seen going up the stairs on his first visit to the Maisterhouse.

"He's still alive?" he said incredulously. "He's here?"

He saw the answer in Janet's face. Illogically this somehow made it all far worse. When all concerned had shared their common end, whether it meant repose in a carefully tended family plot, or in a distant soldier's grave, or even in the sodden clay of a ravaged wood, there was a distancing which made the woman's living pain a great dissuader from further public rage and accusation.

But the thought that not only had this man enjoyed a long and comfortable life with all the blessings of family and fortune but was *still* enjoying it . . .

Or perhaps not. Forcing himself to speak evenly he said, "He must be very old."

"Oh yes," said David Batty almost mockingly. "We're all looking forward to the telegram from Her Majesty."

"He's very frail," said Janet Batty defensively. "But he's still got all his mental faculties."

"That must be a blessing to all concerned," said Pascoe savagely.

"We thought so. Till this week that is."

"He heard about it on television, didn't he?" said Pascoe. "He knew at once who it was, he didn't even need to wait for the details to come out. What was his reaction? That he wanted to make a clean breast after all these years? That's why you saw me personally, Mr. Batty, to stress that ALBA wouldn't be prosecuting the ANIMA women, to start putting the lid on things as firmly as you could. No wonder you jumped when I told you I was one of the Kirkton Pascoes! Felt like someone walking over your grave, did it?"

He rose to his feet. He was sick of all this. Time to do what he'd come to do and get out. He tried to suppress a deep-down tremor of pleasure at the unexpected revenge he was going to take on this family which had so comprehensively misshaped his own.

Thomas was up too, getting between him and the door.

"You can't see him, Mr. Pascoe," he said. "He's too frail to take it."

Pascoe regarded him with some irritation in which there was an element of pity. He didn't really believe that the elder Batty had been party to the raid of FraserGreenleaf, guessed that the news that his own son was an instigator of theft and an accessory to murder would destroy him.

"Why should you imagine I want to see your father-in-law?" he asked scornfully.

The question started rhetorical, but somewhere along the line it became real.

Why *should* Batty think he wanted to confront Gertie? Or rather, why was it he still got the feeling, especially from the senior Battys, that the bottom line in all this was still unread?

Arthur's statement. That feeling he had of something still requiring explication. The bottom line literally, or rather, the bottom lines.

"Your grandfather mentions contributions to the maintenance of the sergeant's family," he said to Mrs. Batty. "He never made any, I'm sure of that."

"He couldn't find them, no one could," she replied.

Young Colin Pascoe did, thought Pascoe. Only perhaps he looked harder.

He said, "But why should he feel the need even to try? He'd seen his son's efforts at help tossed back in his face."

She shrugged as if not trusting herself to speak.

Thomas Batty said, "It's time I think to let sleeping dogs lie. You're a reasonable man, Mr. Pascoe, and I'm sure you can see that . . ."

"What sleeping dog?" said Pascoe. "I thought we'd woken them all up. What sleeping dog?"

He picked up the handwritten statement again, reread the final paragraph. *Responsibility in law . . . allegations concerning my own conduct . . .* why should old Arthur have put in these apparently utterly redundant disclaimers? What responsibility in law could have been alleged against him . . . ?

He looked at Thomas Batty's blank unrevealing face, turned from it to Janet's pale stretched-out features out of which stared a pair of intent and very blue eyes, turned finally to David and met the same blue eyes in that narrow intelligent face whose features had always created in him an uncomfortable sense of near recognition.

He thought, *Not this!* He recalled that other Peter Pascoe's piece of self-improving autobiography which recounted how his mother had been in service with the Grindals up to the time she left to get married and give birth to her son, recalled the dreadful Quiggins woman's screamed accusation that she'd been no better than she ought to have been . . .

Not this!

He said, "I'm going to see him."

"What? No!" protested Thomas.

"Mrs. Batty," said Pascoe. "Feel free to go and prepare him as best you can, but I'm going up whatever any of you say. Don't you think I'm entitled?"

She didn't argue but rose at once and left the room.

David Batty laughed out loud and said, "Thought you'd get there in the end, Peter. Kind of mind that doesn't miss a trick. Takes a one to know a one!"

Pascoe left the room, stepping round Thomas, who didn't move.

He ran lightly up the stairs, saw an open door and made for it.

In a large airy bedroom giving a view out across the high boundary wall toward the church and old village of Kirkton, he saw Janet Batty sitting on the edge of a bed with her arm around the shoulders of an old man, propped up by pillows. His face was pared down almost to the skull, but a shock of soft white hair still fell over his brow and the eyes which fixed on Pascoe were bright blue and alert.

Then they began to fill with tears just as his daughter's had filled a little while earlier.

"Peter," he said brokenly. "It's you . . . after all this time . . . I didn't know . . . not then . . . I swear . . ."

He's not seeing me, thought Pascoe. He's seeing that other Peter who died for him.

"Didn't know what?" he asked, knowing the answer but needing to hear it from this ghost incarnate who could be himself a half century on.

"That we are brothers," said Bertie Grindal.

Brothers. Had the sergeant known? Had his mother said something to him on that visit to her deathbed in Cromer? Was this the reason that Arthur had so long delayed passing on the information about her illness? He would need to read the journals again and again to find answers to these questions. And perhaps they weren't there. And perhaps he didn't want to know them.

Janet Batty was speaking.

"He had to make a choice. Grandfather had to make a choice."

Between the legitimate heir and the left-wing bastard?

"No choice," said Pascoe, his eyes riveted on the old man in the bed.

"I've just been working it out," said David's voice from behind him. "Funny really, but because you've got an extra generation in, I must be something like your half uncle, once removed. Welcome to the family!"

Pascoe now let his gaze leave the old man and his pale-faced daughter, and turned slowly to take in David Batty with his father behind him on the landing.

He recalled his admission to Ellie . . . *I used to fantasize about discovering I was a changeling and I really had this completely different family I could make a fresh start with. . . .* And here it was, his new family to set alongside the old one which had proved so singularly unsuccessful. No point in hanging around. Time to make that fresh start . . .

A kind of wild laughter was welling up inside him at the black comedy of it all, and its repression made his shoulders shake.

"No need to take on," said David. "I won't insist on my right to be called uncle."

"Kind of you," said Peter Pascoe. "But a man

should cling to his rights. Why don't I tell you a few of yours?''

And without a backward glance at the old man in the bed, he took the puzzled David Batty by the arm and urged him down the stairs.

V

ANDY DALZIEL PARKED his car in the same spot opposite Cap Marvell's flat that he'd used four nights earlier.

It was almost the same time too and as he sat, unde-cided on his next move, he saw her again, only this time she was coming out of the apartment block and heading round to the garages.

Like a man who has screwed up his courage for a visit to the dentist's then finds the surgery closed, Dalziel didn't know whether he felt glad or disap-pointed.

Morning would be better, he decided. He'd had a long hard day, though not so long as Des Patten, Cap-tain Sanderson, and Dr. Batty. He'd found the captain at the doctor's house, wearing nothing but a kimono and a satisfied smile, both of which had been removed prior to his departure for the station. Later Pascoe had turned up with Batty and that had been the turning point. The two military men knew the value of keeping their mouths shut till they found a way to communicate and produce a consistent story. But Batty, once the string of deaths had been laid before him, had been almost overenthusiastic in his efforts to put clear blue water between himself and an accessory-to-murder charge. Yes, he'd paid Sanderson to steal the Fraser-Greenleaf research papers; yes, the second part of the deal had been for TecSec to get the Wanwood House contract after Patten had staged a raid there too, serving the double purpose of demonstrating the need to upgrade security and at the same time refocusing attention on the nonexistent animal rights extremists who'd killed the guard at Redcar. But no, he hadn't at any time had any knowledge, either prior or subsequent, of any of the other deaths now laid at TecSec's door, and he'd honestly believed the guard's death had been completely accidental.

Load of bollocks, proclaimed Dalziel. But the doctor's small volume of evidence was going to be invaluable in putting the other two away. So, cause for celebration. But Wield had long since headed off home, and as for Pascoe, the lad had been in a funny mood, quite unable to join in the general euphoria that usually attended the fingering of collars. In fact, if he were honest, Dalziel himself had to admit he'd needed to work on it. Always at the back of his mind was the sense of unfinished business with Cap Marvell.

But it would have to stay unfinished tonight. God knows where she was heading now at this hour, and he didn't want to risk finding out! Pointless trying to apologize for one misunderstanding with another already on the boil.

He switched on his engine, then realizing he would be driving past the entrance to the garage courtyard with the good chance that she'd drive out simultaneously and clock him, he switched off again. Best to let her go. And follow? No! Jesus Christ, if he was going to get anywhere with this woman, which he doubted, he'd have to stop acting like a cop.

But where the hell was she? Didn't take this long to start up a vehicle and drive out.

Suddenly he was worried. Could fate be so malevolent as to let Cap get mugged while he was sitting out here feeling like a nervous adolescent?

Too bloody right it could! he thought grimly.

He picked up the gift-wrapped cylinder lying on the passenger seat, gripped it like a club, and got out of the car. Moving with that lightness and stealth which often amazed those who'd never seen him in action, he crossed the road and went along the front of the block.

At the corner of the alley leading into the rear yard where the garages were, he paused. No sound . . . no . . . wait . . . a distant voice . . . female . . . low . . . pleading . . .

He launched himself forward again, still light-footed but now covering the ground with the surprising speed of a grizzly bear on the rampage. Teeth bared in fury and exertion, he rounded the corner. And stopped.

In the light cast out of an open garage door, Cap Marvell crouched, surrounded by cats feeding at half a dozen saucers piled high with scraps of meat. Several of the animals, alarmed by Dalziel's approach, retreated and the woman looked up angrily.

"Quiet!" she urged. "It's okay, my dears, nothing to worry about, back you come."

Slowly the cats returned and began to feed again. They were mainly lean ragged beasts with the scars of street warfare upon them.

"Bet the neighbors love you," said Dalziel.

"Bet the neighbors aren't starving," replied Cap.

"You do this regular, do you?"

"Most nights when I'm home. Watch the news, then it's suppertime. Nice to have a bit of order in a disordered universe. Why do you ask?"

Dalziel considered whether explanation would help his case, decided on the whole it wouldn't.

"No reason," he said. "Thought we should talk."

"We talked, remember?"

"Still things left to say."

"I don't think so, Andy."

"Brought you a present."

He offered her the cylinder. She didn't take it, so he tore off the wrapping to reveal a bottle of whisky.

"The Macallan," he said reverently. "Twelve years old. Single malt."

"Maybe it'll get married when it grows up," she said.

The cats had finished eating. She gathered up the saucers.

"Thought you might like to know what happened about Walker," he said.

"I'll read about it in the papers," she said. "Unless you've sat on them again?"

"No, it'll be there, eventually."

"Good," she said.

She put out the garage light, closed the door, and began to walk away.

"Hey, you're forgetting your malt."

"Never touch the stuff," she called over her shoulder.

He set it carefully on the ground.

"Well, it's there if you change your mind," he said.

"I won't." Her voice came out of the darkness. "But it's a nice gesture, Superintendent. You can plead it in mitigation. Nothing God likes better than a nice gesture."

He waited a moment then followed. She had gone into the apartment block when he reached the roadway. He paused, contemplated, then turned and went back down the alley. Bright eyes watched him hopefully from the darkness.

He raised two huge fingers, not to them but at the skies.

"Think on," he said. "*That's* a nice gesture. *This* is nigh on two and a half gills."

And picking up the bottle of whisky, he strode off to his car.

EPILOGUE

THE SHEEP FROM GEORGE CREED'S FLOCK at Enscombe were taken in the transporter to the Haig depot, where they remained in more or less comfortable conditions for twenty-four hours. Then they were reloaded into another unmarked transporter and driven south. Since the decision of most of the major ferry companies not to transport live animals to the Continent, other arrangements had to be made, and a container ship with surplus space had contracted to move the Haig consignment from Grimsby to Dunkirk. Severe weather conditions delayed the sailing and it was Friday morning before the ship docked in France. Dead or alive, British meat was never welcome in that country except in circumstances of dire emergency, and a group of French farmers, tipped off by a sympathetic customs official, ambushed the transporter a few miles inland. The driver was dumped in a ditch and the sheep, which by now had not been fed or watered for three days, were released. Some were shot or beaten to death by the ambushers, some savaged by their dogs, a few managed to escape. Twenty-four hours of high-level and high-sounding diplomatic exchange ensued. The usual track of indignation, exculpation, and compensation was trodden. By Saturday evening honor was declared satisfied at all levels on both sides. Meanwhile the surviving sheep had been rounded up and a less provocative route to the ultimate destination of the great Federal Republic of Germany worked out. And on Sunday morning, which also happened to be Armistice Day, as the bugles sounded the Last Post over the cenotaphs of Western Europe, the transporter bound for that distant slaughterhouse crossed over the border into Flanders.